SHADOW CATCHER

JAMES R. HANNIBAL

BERKLEY BOOKS, NEW YORK

THE BERKLEY PUBLISHING GROUP
Published by the Penguin Group
Penguin Group (USA) LLC
375 Hudson Street, New York, New York 10014

USA • Canada • UK • Ireland • Australia • New Zealand • India • South Africa • China

penguin.com

A Penguin Random House Company

SHADOW CATCHER

A Berkley Book / published by arrangement with the author

For information, address: The Berkley Publishing Group,
a division of Penguin Group (USA) LLC,
375 Hudson Street, New York, New York 10014.

ISBN: 978-0-425-26688-5

PUBLISHING HISTORY
Berkley trade paperback edition / October 2013
Berkley premium edition / December 2014

PRINTED IN THE UNITED STATES OF AMERICA

10 9 8 7 6 5 4 3 2 1

Cover design by Rich Hasselberger.
Cover photograph of plane by Joel Sartore / National Geographic / Getty.
Text design by Laura K. Corless.

Shadow Catcher is dedicated to John T. Downey and Richard G. Fecteau, CIA paramilitary officers who spent two decades illegally incarcerated in Communist China. The strength of character and mental fortitude of these men outshine any hero that I could write.

ACKNOWLEDGMENTS

An army of selfless heroes carried this work from idea to publication. Cynthia, my wife, is the greatest hero of all. She is my inspiration and my unwavering encourager. This beautiful, amazing woman counseled me through fits and frustration and she patiently read a hundred drafts of the same story, still remembering to laugh at every joke. Next and much more imposing is my best friend, John Carroll, who listens, critiques, sacrifices, makes fantastic book trailers, and never gloats when he outshoots me at the range. Surrounding the three of us, and comprising the beating heart of this army of heroes, is my family from both sides of the aisle. I am blessed to have more support and love to bolster my military service and my personal endeavors than any man I know.

At the head of the army, leading the charge, are the generals—my agent, Harvey Klinger, and my editor, Natalee Rosenstein. Next to them stand their lieutenants, Rachel Ridout and Robin Barletta. I am eternally grateful to Harvey and Natalee and their teams at the Harvey Klinger Agency and the Berkley Publishing Group for giving me the opportunity to do what I love most.

What follows is a list of other heroes as colorful in their character and backgrounds as the cast of *The Dirty Dozen*. Some I will name only by tactical callsign for security reasons. I am grateful to my units, past and present, for providing inspiration and support. I am especially grateful to London for canceling his vacation to cover me so that I could bring this project to New York, and to Smack for his day-to-day encouragement. My thanks to Baron 1, Fester, Sideshow, and the Millers for taking the time to read and critique—in particular Sideshow, whose contributions carried significant weight in this book, and Baron 1, whose years of experience and expertise brought to life Nick's PTSD. My thanks to Tawnya for her copyediting and her critiques. She spared Harvey and Natalee from untold horrors of grammar and spelling. Thanks to Mindy Weng for her help with Chinese culture and translation, as well as Joker, the best intelligence analyst alive. And thanks to Mason Moyer, who picked out the Springfield Armory XDm, Ethan Quinn's favorite weapon and now mine as well.

Finally, I give thanks to God for all of these blessings. He is my Rock, my Deliverer, and the greatest Author of all time.

PROLOGUE

South China Sea
January 1, 1988

David Novak held his gloved hand high against the cockpit glass, his three fingers counting down to a tightly balled fist. The execute command. His wingman peeled away to the northeast. He made no other response. Radio silence was vital.

For a moment, Novak remained transfixed by the power and beauty of Jade Two's high-G turn. A cottony dome of vapor formed above the F-16 Fighting Falcon's wings as the afterburner cut a marbled blue arc across the ocean waves less than fifty feet below. He smiled. These Vipers, as he and his squadron mates liked to call the F-16s, were so much sexier than the ungainly Canberras he'd flown over Russia. After a deep breath, he turned his attention back to the mission. The Chinese coast was coming up fast and, with it, a tangled bramble of newly installed surface-to-air missiles.

The coastline gained definition, turning from blue haze into a dark green tree line. Then, as if suddenly accelerating on their own, the trees loomed large and flashed beneath him.

"Fight's on," said Novak under his breath.

He flipped a toggle switch on the panel just forward of his right knee. A moment later, a green light illuminated. That was it—green: good; red: bad; on or off. The simplistic controls for his Red Baron photoreconnaissance pod would not show him what the cameras saw, but as far as he knew, they were rolling. From this point on, he would gather thousands of electro-optical and infrared images, documenting the buildup of Chinese forces directly across the strait from Taiwan.

Off to his left, Novak spotted a distinctive ridgeline with a V-shaped gap: his first navigation point. He rolled his wings on edge and pulled hard, changing course by forty-five degrees in less than a second, enjoying the feel of five Gs pressing him into the ejection seat. He shot through the gap and then rolled the Viper over, pulling down the other side of the ridge in an inverted dive before leveling out at the bottom of a narrow river valley. In just a few miles, his cameras would capture detailed imagery of a possible surface-to-surface missile pad that the high-altitude birds had found three days before.

Suddenly, Novak's radio crackled to life. "Radar spike, radar spike! I'm shifting west from point two." His grip tightened on the side-mounted control stick. His wingman had just tripped the Chinese radar net. Even worse, he had broken radio silence, and that was tantamount to suicide.

Agency intelligence said that Fujian's air defense commander usually kept his radars in coast mode. A single spike was no big deal. Jade Two could have continued on course, and the next hill would have masked him from the radar's sweep. With any luck, the station's automatic filter would have chalked up the blip to an anomaly. But radio transmissions—even encrypted radio transmissions—could be tracked. Jade Two's call had energized the Chinese defense net. Multiple frequency scanners would triangulate the foreign signal and send their solution to the radar operator, prompting him to focus his sweep and refine the track. If the operator achieved a lock, Jade Two was as good as dead.

Within thirty seconds, the wingman broke radio silence again. This time panic filled his voice. "Missile in the air! I'm defending east. My position is eight miles southwest of . . ."

Silence. No trail of broken words, no lingering static. The transmission simply ended.

Novak did not hesitate. He quickly plotted a course to Jade Two's last-known position and turned to intercept. He hugged the ridgelines, seeking the protection of the ground clutter, knowing that every radar station in the province had just gone active to search for a second aircraft. On the way, he double-checked his camera control. The green light still shined back at him. At least he could get photos of the crash site, vital evidence that his wingman had either lived or died.

His target area came up fast. Novak popped up to four hundred feet to search for the burning wreckage. The

Viper's bubble canopy offered a panoramic view of the wide valley beneath him, but he found no evidence of a crash site, not even a column of smoke billowing up from the trees. He couldn't understand it. Then he saw something that made his heart skip a beat. Not the black smoke of a ruined fighter but the orange flash and fast-expanding white cloud of an SA-3 missile taking the air.

A flood of adrenaline supercharged Novak's synapses as a feminine voice chanted, "Missile lock! Missile lock!" in his ear. Time slowed to a crawl. He lit his afterburner and pulled hard into the oncoming threat, straining against the unnatural crush of nine Gs. He had precious little altitude to spare, but he used all of it to build his energy, diving for the valley floor as he maintained his high-G turn. Emerald trees whipped by within inches of his low wing. With deft movements of the control stick, he kept the oncoming missile centered at the top of his canopy, and in the slow progression of the temporal distortion, it grew to the diameter of a telephone poll.

Then it disappeared.

For a fraction of a second that seemed to last an eternity, Novak saw nothing but the blue sky and green trees. He gritted his teeth and pulled even harder, pushing the Viper and his own body to the limit. He knew what was coming. He had forced the missile to overshoot his aircraft, avoiding a direct hit, but that would not stop the weapon's proximity fuze from detonating the warhead.

The giant missile exploded somewhere above and behind him. The blast rocked his aircraft, setting off a disorienting array of flashing red and yellow caution lights. He felt as if the air had been stripped from under his wings. He struggled to maintain control, fighting for every ounce of lift to keep from crashing into the trees.

Then it was all over. The air became smooth again. The caution lights blinked out one by one.

Novak checked his wings. They looked perfect. By some miracle, he'd escaped the burning fragments that should have torn the Viper to shreds. He breathed, relaxing his death grip on the stick and easing out of his high-G turn.

Still shaking from his brush with death, Novak tapped his threat indicator. Even though he had dodged the missile, the alarm continued to chant its mantra in his ears, "Missile lock! Missile lock!" He silenced the voice and pulled into a gentle climb to continue his search for Jade Two. Instinctively, he looked back to see the cloud formed by the missile's explosion. He only had a split second to realize his mistake. Another fiery SA-3 filled his vision. The alarm had been trying to warn him of a second missile.

PART ONE

GHOSTS

CHAPTER 1

Kuwait
March 18, 2013

Alone Westerner weaved his way along the crowded sidewalk in front of the Souk Sharq in Kuwait City, suffering the uneasy glances and occasional loathing glares of the locals. They did not bother him; with his flaxen hair and fair skin, such looks were unavoidable. On another day, he might have indulged his audience by slowing to gaze up at the beautiful souk, playing the part of the wandering tourist, admiring the high towers and ornate arches that hearkened back to the glory days of the Persian Empire. But not today. There was no time.

For ten years, the objective had lain hidden, dormant. For ten years, the secret had remained sealed in its watery vault. Now that he was back, he felt like that seal had been broken, as if his mere presence in the Persian Gulf had started a race against an unknown enemy. And somehow he knew he was already behind.

Once inside the souk, Air Force major Nick Baron moved into the shadow of a pillar. Now free from the usual disdainful looks, he let his steel blue eyes slowly drift over the crowd, scanning the potpourri of faces for something much more dangerous: recognition. He found none. Finally satisfied that he was not being watched or followed, he turned his attention to finding his teammate. It did not take long.

Nick slowly shook his head and sighed.

Major Drake Merigold stood in the center of the Grand Corridor at the base of a beautiful two-story water clock, staring up at the Jules Vernian sculpture with his mouth slightly agape. He wore an orange and blue Hawaiian shirt that hung untucked over his khaki shorts. He could not have stood out more amid the drab garb of the locals if he had worn a fluffy red wig and big floppy shoes.

The two field operatives of the Triple Seven Chase squadron had arrived on separate flights, on separate carriers, under assumed names. Each had used a unique, indirect route to reach the souk, where they were supposed to quietly join up before heading out into the gulf to meet the rest of the team. The stakes of this mission demanded strict adherence to the principles of covert movement. But then how could Drake be expected to fully grasp the stakes? No one had told him the real reason they were here.

"Magnum PI called," said Nick, joining his comrade at the water clock. "He wants his shirt back."

Drake nodded, still looking up. "It's called hiding in plain sight, boss." He was nearly a head taller than Nick, with broad shoulders to match and chiseled Greek features. With his flawless dark hair and obnoxious shirt, he looked like a movie star about to go on a cruise rather than a military operative. He glanced around the wide corridor, pulling the loud shirt away from his body and fanning it to take advantage of the air-conditioning. "They did a good job rebuilding. The last time we were here, an Iraqi missile had just crashed through the ceiling. You'd never know that there was once a huge crater right where we're standing."

"They've had ten years to fix it," said Nick. "We've been away a long time."

For the first time since Nick had stepped out of the shadows, Drake looked him straight in the eyes. "So, why are we back?"

Nick dropped his eyes from Drake's to check his watch. "The others should be reaching the rendezvous point soon. It's time we got out there."

Drake frowned. "You're starting to act like the colonel."

"Just pick up your bag and let's go."

Nick shifted the strap of the duffel bag that hung over his shoulder and started walking toward the central rear archway, the exit to the marina. Like Drake, he wore civilian clothes to hide his military affiliation, although his choices were a little more understated. His dark gray button-down shirt hung loose on his shoulders, masking the solid build beneath. Both men carried civilian duffel bags with enough gear to get them through a few days on the water, just as Colonel Walker had directed.

Warm salty air rushed over him as Nick pushed open the glass double doors. He started down the stairs to the wooden boardwalk, where several docks extended out into the gulf. Each had room for twenty small craft and each was nearly full, a forest of masts and canvas. Other than the whip and snap of the sails in the gentle breeze, all seemed quiet. Nick felt the temptation to relax.

The doors to the Grand Corridor clicked closed behind him, wrenching his senses away from the pleasant atmosphere. He paused halfway down the stairs. Scanning farther down the docks, he spied a pair of locals in the common white *thaubs* and keffiyehs. He watched them for a few moments as they prepared to launch a blue and white runabout, probably for an evening pleasure cruise. They looked harmless.

At the end of the third dock, he found a black dinghy waiting at the prescribed slip. He held it fast and tossed in their bags while Drake jumped on board and prepped the motor.

Within minutes, Drake had the throttle fully open, accelerating out into the open waters of the Persian Gulf. Every so often, he steered into a wave, sending white spray over the bow and onto Nick.

"I know you're doing that on purpose," said Nick, wiping the oily gulf water from his face.

"Just trying to lighten the mood," replied Drake. "You gotta learn to relax, boss."

"I'll relax when the mission is complete and the team is safely back at Romeo Seven."

"You know that ain't true."

Nick refused to respond. He was in no mood for friendly ribbing, and he feared that in a few hours' time, Drake's usual jovial temper would sour as well. Before the day was over, Drake would accuse him of betrayal, and he would have every right to.

Twenty minutes later, another craft appeared on the horizon. Despite his fears, Nick managed a thin smile. The commander of the Triple Seven Chase was well known in the covert ops community as an acquisitions wizard. Colonel Richard T. Walker had just pulled another rabbit out of his pointy hat, and this time she was a big one.

Nick estimated the vessel to be at least 250 feet long with a 50-foot beam. She looked fresh from the dry dock, with unblemished white paint and a thick red stripe along the rails. She was well equipped too, with three golf-ball-style radomes amidships and a docking station jutting out from the rear beneath two heavy salvage cranes.

"*Illustro ex Caliga*," read Nick, squinting at the black lettering near the bow of the craft.

"It means 'Illustrious Sea Monkey,'" said Drake.

"I don't believe you."

"Good call." Drake scratched his chin in thought. "If I remember my Latin correctly, it means 'Illumination out of Darkness.'" He guided the dinghy to the aft station, cutting his speed to a crawl and then inching into position in an agonizingly slow attempt at docking.

"Well, that was ugly, Merigold," said a booming voice from above. An imposing figure leaned against the rail of the upper deck. With his gray crew cut and perpetual scowl, Colonel Walker carried the aura of a man in full

U.S. Army service dress, even when wearing a golf shirt and khakis.

"Hey, I fly airplanes, not boats," retorted Drake, slapping the tubular black hull of the dinghy. "I'm used to touching down on a solid surface at a hundred and fifty knots, not wallowing in to a moving target at five. You should be glad I didn't ram this thing into your little rental here."

Walker ignored Drake's attempt to bait him. "Hurry up, gentlemen," he said. "We have a lot of work to do before dark."

"And what work is that, sir?" asked Drake, hopping onto the ship's dock to secure the dinghy.

The colonel's usual scowl faded into a grim smile. "Preparing to raise a ghost from our past, Major Merigold," he said. "Preparing to raise a ghost from our past."

CHAPTER 2

The sun burned a dull orange hue into the hazy gulf horizon as the *Illustro* finally slowed to a drift. Leaning against the rail next to Drake, Nick could see nothing but green water in all directions, a seductive illusion of solitude. In truth, the Iranian coast lay less than fifty miles off the port bow, far too close for his comfort. A soft whirring drifted up from below. Down at the waterline, he saw a small section of seawater bubbling and frothing against the hull like a hot spring.

"What's that?" asked Drake, following his gaze.

"It's a subsurface thruster," said Nick. "The ship's dynamic positioning system will hold our coordinates within a couple of meters. It looks like we're over the objective."

"That's right." Walker emerged from the pilothouse. "But we don't want to hold this position any longer than we have to, so let's get started."

The three of them abandoned the warm glow of the Arabian sunset for the cold fluorescent light of the ship's main lab. White powder-coated cabinets and counters stretched the full length of the room, except for the forward wall, where the Triple Seven's lead engineer labored before a wide bank of black computers. Above him, a large LCD monitor displayed a steadily growing mosaic of tiny black and gray squares.

"Are we nearing completion?" asked Walker.

Dr. Scott Stone looked up from his keyboard and reseated the glasses that had drifted down his sharp nose. "The submersible is covering the final section now, sir. It will complete its run momentarily." With the last word, a tiny burp escaped his lips. The engineer grimaced and raised a hand to cover his mouth. His face turned green.

"How ya doin', Scott?" asked Drake, perching himself on a stool at the long central table.

Stone did not answer. Instead, he stood up from his workstation, stumbled out the portal, and leaned over the rail.

Drake grinned. "That good, huh?"

"Does he realize there's another deck below that rail?" asked Nick.

"I had Doc Heldner give him some meds," said Walker. "She even gave him some gingersnaps."

They heard Scott let out a heaving belch, followed by a series of sickening splats from the deck below.

"I think he just gave 'em back," said Drake.

Walker frowned at the pilot. He took a sip of black coffee from a foam cup, paused to savor the black liquid, and then turned and stretched a hand toward the large screen. "Gentlemen, this jumble of mass confusion is a photo-map. We dropped off an autonomous ROV yesterday and then moved off-site while Dr. Stone monitored its progress. It doesn't look like much now, but once Stone's program unscrambles the mess, we'll get a detailed look at our objective." He focused his scowl on Scott as the seasick engineer trudged back to his workstation. "At least that's what he tells me."

"The ROV is on its way back up," said Scott weakly, dabbing his face with a small white towel. He sank into his chair. "Let me run the resolution software. We should have an image in under a minute, sir."

Nick gazed expectantly at the screen. At first, the picture remained an incomprehensible collage of black and gray photos. Then the hundreds of individual boxes began to move. They shifted, rotated, and adjusted until finally they merged into a single, coherent image: a massive B-2 stealth bomber, the *Spirit of Kansas*, lying in the silt at the bottom of the Persian Gulf.

Nick glanced at Drake. Realization washed over his teammate like an angry flood. His eyes grew wide, his jaw tensed. "That's our jet," he exclaimed. "*My* jet."

Looking back at the crisp ROV image, Nick could clearly see the blown hatch where Drake had ejected from the aircraft ten years before. Memories of their first combat mission together came racing back.

HUMINT had predicted a meeting between Saddam Hussein and Tariq Irhaab, the leader of al-Qaeda in Iraq. The Triple Seven Chase, then just a test squadron, had the only reconnaissance asset that could get to the target, an experimental stealth jet called Dream Catcher. Just hours before the Shock and Awe campaign began, Drake had slipped through the enemy radar fence in the Spirit of Kansas, carrying Nick and Dream Catcher in the B-2's weapons bay, and Danny Sharp, one of the Dream Catcher's developers, in his copilot seat.

The mission was supposed to be a cakewalk.

It wasn't.

The bay doors jammed half open during deployment, ruining the bomber's stealth and sending Nick and the Dream Catcher tumbling toward the desert floor. Nick had no choice but to eject, right in the path of a platoon of Republican Guard. Drake could have left him. He should have, to save the B-2. Instead, he came back for his teammate, taking out the platoon's missile launcher so that a rescue chopper could get in close enough to grab him. Unfortunately, the launcher got off a shot before Drake's bomb took it down. The last time Nick saw the bomber, it was limping south toward the gulf, trailing smoke and fire.

Drake tore his eyes away from the monitor to glare at Walker. "Of course, that *can't* be my jet," he said, tilting his head. "While medevac took Nick, Danny, and me back to the States, you salvaged my jet and towed it out to deep water. You scattered it into a thousand pieces over the Arabian Basin." He gestured at Nick, his volume beginning to build. "Nick and I sat next to you while you testified before the oversight committee. We corroborated everything you told them!"

Nick winced. Drake still hadn't put it all together, that Nick had kept the truth from him almost as long as Walker had.

"Stand down, Major," Walker fired back. "What would you have me do, tell a pack of two-bit politicians that we left a stealth bomber at the bottom of the Persian Gulf?" He folded his arms and snorted. "They can't keep their mouths shut. The Iranians would have picked the wreck clean by now, two billion dollars' worth of stealth technology out in the open. We had to keep it need-to-know."

The colonel's scowl deepened as he took another sip of coffee. "The first salvage op went bad, very bad. We started to bring her up, but one of the main cables snapped, then the other one. Two divers were killed immediately. The third was pinned under the bomber. I went in to get him out, but there was nothing I could do. I lost the entire team." He cast a glance at Nick. "After that fiasco, Major Baron and I decided it was better to leave the bomber where it lay."

Drake turned to Nick in shock, suddenly grasping the full truth. "You knew about this the whole time?"

Nick opened his mouth to respond, but after a decade of knowing this day would come, he could not find the words to say.

"I brought Major Baron into the loop as soon as I returned to Washington," said Walker. "I needed a sounding board, and I wanted a member of the ops team to be prepared in case word got out about the asset. Baron is the team lead. He had the need-to-know. You didn't."

The revelation that even Nick had kept the secret from

him robbed Drake's anger of its fire. He shifted his gaze to the floor. "Did Danny know?"

"No," answered Nick quietly. And he would never know. Danny had died the previous September. This lie was only a small part of the guilt that Nick still harbored in the wake of his death.

"If it's been safe this long, then why recover it now?" asked Drake.

"An Italian marine science group is planning to map the gulf floor," said Nick. "We can't wait any longer." He hesitated. "I'm sorry we kept you in the dark."

"Get over it, both of you," said Walker coldly. "We need to get this done. I don't like digging up graves in the Iranian's backyard. We've kept that bomber quiet for a decade, but now that we're out here, I feel exposed."

Nick placed a hand on his teammate's shoulder and looked up at the ghostly image of the B-2. A chill swept over him. He thought of the horror that lay beneath: the crushed body of a forgotten patriot and two fully armed five-thousand-pound bombs.

CHAPTER 3

Where am I?

Nick stood on a dirt road in thick darkness. He could not remember how he got there. On either side of the road, he saw the high mud walls common to desert villages. They seemed to be closing in on him. He could not feel the ground beneath his feet. The sound of his own breathing echoed in his ears. Then he saw the mosque, its distinctive dome with the worn crescent carved into the west side. Suddenly he knew where he was. He knew what he had to do.

He had to save Danny.

Nick found his teammate less than fifty yards ahead, crouched next to a gap in the wall surrounding the mosque's small courtyard. Danny looked back at him. He stood up and waved as if they were meeting on a neighborhood street back home in Maryland, wearing that same ridiculous grin that he always wore.

"Get down, you idiot," Nick whispered into his communications implant. "Stay there. Wait until I get to you."

Danny did not respond. Instead, he disappeared through the gap in the wall like a ghost.

"Drake, I lost visual with Danny," said Nick, rushing forward. "What's going on in that courtyard? Where is the target?" He had to get to his friend, but no matter how hard he ran, the mosque stayed fifty yards ahead of him.

"You can see what I can," replied Drake, his voice mechanical, distant. "Check the image on your handheld. I've got nothing on the thermal."

Nick checked the faintly glowing monitor attached to his Falcon ROVER handheld. The receiver pulled real-time thermal video from an RQ-7 Shadow UAV flying overhead. He held the small screen up to his eyes, but he couldn't focus his vision. He couldn't make any sense of the hazy green image.

The target, Zaman Ramiz, had smuggled a nuclear weapon out of southern Russia. The Triple Seven had chased him from Azerbaijan, across northern Turkey and into Bazargan, just across the Iranian border. Drake had stayed behind to fly the Shadow. Nick and Danny had crossed the border in pursuit. Now the arms dealer's men were dead, and Ramiz was holed up in the small mosque.

The whole village seemed to shift around him. Suddenly Nick was at the wall. Where was Danny? What a stupid question. He knew where Danny was. He was in that courtyard, and that courtyard was a deathtrap. He looked down at the handheld again. He still couldn't see the video feed. He put the receiver away and cautiously leaned into the gap to get a look with his own eyes. A spray of bullets ricocheted off the wall beside his head, kicking brick fragments and dust into his face.

"He just shot at me," Nick shouted as he pulled back behind the wall. He tried to rub the debris from his eyes. "I need to know where that's coming from."

Drake gave no response.

Nick had to keep the pressure on. He burst into the courtyard with his MP7 tucked into his shoulder, searching for a target, searching for his teammate. There, just ahead. Danny was lying motionless beside a wide, square fountain. The ancient stones were wet with blood.

Another burst of gunfire rang out from the shadows of the mosque. Nick felt two bullets slam into his vest. He dove into a prone position behind the fountain, shouting at Danny. But Danny did not answer.

Nick felt an icy grip crushing his chest. Pain radiated through his torso. He couldn't breathe. He rolled over and tried to rip off his Kevlar vest, but there was no vest. He wore no protection over his cotton undershirt. The fabric felt warm and wet against his fingertips. He raised his hand to his eyes. It was covered in blood.

Footsteps. Ramiz stood over him, a blur at first and then slowly coming into focus. The arms dealer smiled down from behind the barrel of his Stechkin machine pistol.

He pulled the trigger.

"Okay, that's really annoying."

Nick fought to open his eyes. Drake's hand was on his arm, shaking him.

"Seriously, how does Katy get any sleep when you're home? You're thrashing around in your bunk and moaning like a creature from a low-grade zombie movie."

Nick blinked until his small berth on the *Illustro* came into focus. He wiped the sweat from his forehead. After taking a moment to gather his wits, he rolled onto his side and glowered across the tiny room at Drake. "I wasn't moaning," he said, trying to steady his voice. "And for the record, all zombie movies are low grade."

"Not true. Zombies are the new vampires."

"It'll never work." Nick threw off the sheet and swung his feet to the floor. "A brooding, metrosexual zombie is still just an ugly dead thing."

"That's undead, thank you very much," said Drake, yawning and rubbing his eyes.

Nick regarded his friend with a curious look. After the briefing with Walker, Drake hadn't said two words to anyone for the rest of the night, even during the dive planning. Now he had slipped into his old self like nothing happened.

"What?" asked Drake.

"Are we okay?"

Drake stood up and stretched. "Need-to-know is Walker's call, not yours. You followed orders. I would have done the same."

"Really? All's forgiven, just like that?"

"I overreacted. In the grand scheme, this team is more important than one man."

"Noble words," said Nick, nodding slowly. He raised an eyebrow. "Then what about the colonel? Is he forgiven too?"

"Ahem." Drake coughed and looked away. "So, uh, another nightmare." He plopped back down on the bunk, put his hands on his knees, and stared Nick in the eye. "Don't tell me, Danny again? It's been six months. You have to let him go."

"It was my job to protect him. I let him down. I let his wife and kids down."

"Danny made his own choice," said Drake, shaking his head. "He ignored your order to hold his position. You got Ramiz *and* the nuke. I don't think you let anyone down."

Nick looked down at his chest, half expecting to see the bruises where the arms dealer's bullets had slammed into his vest, but those wounds had healed months ago. He was lucky he hadn't taken a round in the head like Danny. The family had to have a closed-casket funeral. Nick fed them the official cover story, that Danny had been in a helicopter crash. He looked up at Drake. "If I go down like Danny, will you lie to Katy like I lied to his wife?"

Drake gave him a thin smile. "I think you already know the answer to that, boss."

Nick stood up and stretched. "So I do." He checked his watch and then grabbed two wet suits from the shelf above his bunk. He tossed one to Drake. "Get dressed, my friend. We've got work to do."

CHAPTER 4

General Zheng Ju-long surveyed the trees passing by the windows of his sedan. They were beautiful—deep green and full, not like those sparse twigs in the hills above Beijing. He sighed. He hated the idea of leaving his beloved Fujian Province for the bustling, smelly metropolis of Beijing, but soon he would have to. Such was the price of destiny.

"Park the car outside the fence, Han," Zheng told his driver.

"But, sir, you are the most senior general in all of Fujian. This is your facility. We can park at the front door if you like. There is no need to walk."

"That is the point, Han. I want to walk. I want to taste the pure air before we enter the factory."

Zheng closed his eyes. How would underlings like Han view him in the coming days? He was not abandoning

Fujian—far from it—but could they see that? In time, they would understand. In time, they would see him as the Great Unifier in the tradition of his ancestor Koxinga. He would make them whole again.

All of them.

Han turned down a gravel road, and the trees abruptly ended, followed shortly by a high-security fence topped with a double stack of concertina wire. He parked the sedan next to a small guard station and then opened the rear passenger's-side door, offering an arm to help Zheng lift his stout but aging frame out of the soft leather seat.

"Most honored General Zheng. We were not expecting you today," said the guard, jumping to attention as Zheng approached his shack.

"Yes, that is as I intended," replied Zheng. "And I would prefer to keep it that way. Please refrain from alerting the factory chief to my presence."

Zheng said nothing more, casually lifting a hand to his graying temple to return the guard's crisp salute. As he reached the main building, he glanced over his shoulder. He saw the guard hastily replacing the guardhouse phone in its cradle. Zheng smiled. He expected nothing less. The guard's loyalty to his immediate superior was commendable. That was as it should be. Of course, he would have to be punished for disobedience. That was as it should be as well.

Dr. Tāo Luo stood in front of his glass-encased office, feigning a conversation with his secretary. "General," he said, bowing and subtly waving for his secretary to do the same, "what a most unexpected and yet delightful surprise it is to see you here."

"I'm sure it is, Tāo. I am here to inspect your progress. Kindly show me to the production floor."

"If it would please the general," said Tāo, "we have a special unit set up in Laboratory Two for just such an occasion. It will be much quieter there than on the factory floor."

Zheng waved his hand. "As you wish." He smiled inwardly. Tāo could not have produced a display in such a short amount of time. The factory chief was prepared for a surprise visit, and if he had the time for extraneous activities like setting up displays, then work must be proceeding smoothly here. Excellent.

Tāo led the general down a long hallway. On one side, a floor-to-ceiling window looked out over the various production floors below. In each section, he could see one of the five massive state-of-the-art production units that he and Tāo had procured for the factory. Four of them were humming away, producing detailed structural components for his weapons, each piece precisely tooled to a matter of picometers. The fifth machine lay dormant, but that would soon be rectified.

"Here we are," said Tāo, opening a door and stepping aside to allow the general to pass through.

Zheng nodded at Han as he entered, indicating that the aide should stand outside and wait.

Laboratory Two remained as starkly clean and white as the last time Zheng had seen it, several weeks earlier. Now, however, there was a display table in the center of the room. Three technicians in white lab coats stood at attention as Zheng entered. He waved magnanimously, indicating that they should relax. Then he surveyed Tāo's masterpiece. At more than four meters, the missile took up the entire length of the table. The light brown color of its exposed composite structure stood out well in the white room, allowing the general to see every seamlessly fitted juncture.

"As you can see, General," began Tāo, "we are now producing the full range of components for each major section: propulsion, control, warhead, and guidance."

Zheng nodded, still inspecting the display. "I assume you have projected its range capabilities?"

"Three hundred fifty kilometers with the new solid fuel motor, covering more than enough distance from the Quanzhou launch site. Of course, once we have the precise composition and weight of the skin, that range may change a little."

"Yes," said Zheng, crossing his arms and placing a thick finger on his chin, "I see from the activity below that you have moved into mass production. What numbers have you achieved?"

"We already have one hundred missile bodies, complete with guidance packages and warheads," answered Tāo. "We will produce a hundred more in a matter of days. That should be more than enough firepower to overwhelm Taiwan's defenses."

Zheng dropped his arms. "*I* will determine how much firepower is enough," he said.

Tāo winced and bowed. "Of course, General. Once we have a production model for the skin, we can finish the first two hundred in less than seventy-two hours and then continue as you see fit." He spoke his next words cautiously. "However, I cannot give you an accurate production timeline until we receive the sample radar-absorbent materials."

Zheng returned to his inspection of the missile, but he cast a sidelong glance at Tāo. "Don't worry. I will have them for you soon."

Three quick knocks on the door interrupted their discussion. Zheng waved for Tāo to open the laboratory door. Han entered and bowed. "General Zheng, you have a telephone call from our embassy in Kuwait."

Zheng turned back to Tāo and his technicians. "My apologies, gentlemen. I must take this call, which may be good news for all of us. In the meantime, keep up the good work."

———

Zheng reclined in the backseat of his sedan, watching with satisfaction as Han took the disobedient guard by the lapel and struck him across the face. As he lifted his satellite phone to his ear, he motioned for his aide to continue the punishment. "Go ahead, Wūlóng," he said into the phone. "I am secure on this end."

"General Zheng, your operatives are in position." The caller spoke in perfectly even tones, his voice as smooth as ice. "The Americans are here as well. It appears as though your intelligence is accurate."

Zheng nodded. "Good, good. After so many years, I am glad that my source remains reliable. Still, it is when you are closest to the object of your desire that it often fades away. Tell my men to proceed with extreme caution. And Wūlóng"—Zheng reached out his window and waved to Han, who released the bloodied guard, letting him collapse onto the gravel—"tell them that I want no survivors."

CHAPTER 5

Thin metal shavings rained down through the water like gently falling snowflakes, glistening in the white beam of Nick's dive light. After less than a minute of drilling, he removed the bit from the small hole in the side of the bomb to let it cool. He could not afford to overheat the casing that surrounded the fuze. A mistake like that might end his mission with a premature bang.

Nick lay on his side with his back pressed against the partial barrier that separated the B-2's left bay from its right. The bomb, like its twin, rested on the closed bomb-bay doors of the left bay. Both weapons had dislodged from their rack during the last, failed salvage, arming the fuzes.

These armed bunker busters were the main reason that Nick and Walker left the wreck alone for so long. Any shift during another salvage attempt could set one off, killing the crew and scattering the wreckage across the relatively shallow floor of the Persian Gulf, a smorgasbord of stealth materials for the enemies of the United States. Nick had to neutralize the weapons so that the team could raise the bomber to towing depth and move it out to deeper waters for scuttling. But he had never defused a five-thousand-pound bomb before. He carefully pushed the drill bit back into the hole, took a deep breath, and gently squeezed the trigger. There was a first time for everything.

Despite the claustrophobic conditions, Nick wished that Drake could have joined him in the bay. He could use the company. But the partially open doors of the other bay, half crushed against the seafloor, left only a tiny gap. Nick could barely squeeze through, even after removing his rebreather, mask, and tanks. With his broad shoulders, Drake could not follow. He had passed Nick's gear through the gap and then moved off to set up the air bags that would lighten the bomber for the salvage cranes.

Nick removed the bit to let it cool again, repeating the process over and over until he reached the seven-centimeter mark, just deep enough to penetrate the fuze casing. As he removed the bit for the final time, he let out a long breath. Halfway there. Unfortunately, the most dangerous and difficult part was yet to come. It might even prove impossible.

After a few moments' rest, Nick cracked open a drab green case and withdrew a monitor and a set of thin, melded cables. One cable held a fiber-optic camera and light, the other, a pair of tiny hooked pincers. He carefully slid the cable through the small tunnel and into the fuze casing. As the fiber-optic light illuminated the interior of the device, Nick's heart sank. The fuze had seen better days.

Long ago, during either the crash or the first salvage attempt, the fuze casing's vacuum seal had cracked, exposing the metal inside to corrosive seawater. Instead of the gleaming steel mechanism that he had hoped for, he found a rusty, brown nightmare.

Nick used a laminated diagram to identify the safing lever—a short arm with a loop on the end. He would have to pull that lever outward to manually disarm the bomb. A little round window next to the lever showed the status of the fuze. He checked his diagram. A red flag in the window meant the bomb was armed; a green one meant safe. He could clearly see red behind the glass.

It took several tries to get the pincers through the loop. The rusty buildup had narrowed the gap to a little wider than the eye of a needle. When he finally got both hooks seated, Nick gently pulled on the cable. The lever didn't budge. He tried again, gradually increasing the pressure until he feared the arm might break, but it had rusted solid.

Nick sat back in frustration. If he gave up, the team would have to attempt the salvage with at least one live weapon in the bay, an immense risk. Their only other option would be to detonate both bombs in place and destroy the bomber. The cleanup would take weeks, during which any number of hostile agencies might discover the operation. Nick was not willing to accept either scenario. He had one more trick up his sleeve. A forceful jerk might free the lever. It might just as well break the arm or set off the bomb.

There was no point in waiting. He leaned back, clenched his teeth, and yanked on the cable. Something snapped. He cringed.

After a long moment, Nick opened one eye and then the other. His gamble had paid off. The safing lever had broken free of the rust. With another, gentle tug on the cable, it clicked into place. The flag changed from red to green.

Nick sighed. One down.

The next bomb took half as long to disarm. Its vacuum seal remained miraculously intact. With no rust, the safing lever gave in to Nick's command on the first pull. Both bombs should now be so stable that no amount of jostling or shifting could set them off. *Should* was the operative word. Nick wished that he had some wood to knock on.

After packing up his gear, he switched on the transmitter in his mask. "Come and get me, Drake. I need you to hold my rebreather and tanks so I can get out of this hole."

He heard no response, not even static.

Nick tapped on the base of his mask, hoping to jolt its transmitter/receiver to life. "Hello? Does anyone read me?"

Still nothing.

Nick had been so focused on his work that he hadn't noticed the sparse chatter between Walker and Drake fade away to nothing. Now he realized that the aftermarket radio in his mask was completely dead, probably a consequence of removing the mask at depth to squeeze into the bay.

He swam over to the gap and peered through. Drake was nowhere to be seen. If he wanted to get his teammate's attention, he would have to make some noise. But as he flipped his flashlight around to bang on the side of the bay, he caught a glint of steel from the seafloor. He panned the light back to the object. Just on the other side of the gap, its hilt sticking straight up out of the sediment, was Drake's knife.

CHAPTER 6

Nick fought back a wave of dread as he stared at the knife.

"Drake? Are you out there?" His efforts were futile. He still heard no response. Something was wrong. The knife had not fallen onto the seafloor by accident. Drake had obviously stuck it into the silt as a signal, a warning.

There were hostile players in the water.

Nick slowed his breathing to focus his thoughts. If he shed his bulky rebreather and tanks to swim through the gap, he'd be a sitting duck for any intruders, blind and weakened as he struggled to re-don his gear. But shedding that gear was the only way to get out. Otherwise he might as well make the bay his tomb. He checked his air gauges. Too low. He couldn't just wait it out. Besides, Drake might be in trouble.

As Nick wracked his brain for a solution, a little brown fish swam through the gap between the crushed doors and the seafloor, kicking up a cloud of silt. That inspired an idea.

Nick loosened his gear, preparing to shed it quickly, and then began to kick up as much sediment as possible and propel it through the gap. The cloud would mask his exit and deny a hostile diver a clean shot. It wasn't a great plan, but it was the only plan he had.

He stripped off the miniature tanks strapped to his thighs, unbuckled the fasteners on his vest, and positioned his body just in front of the hole. After three deep breaths, he pulled off the rebreather and mask and pushed through the gap. On the other side, he remained just above the silt, working feverishly to put the rebreather back on. He allowed his fins to skim the seafloor and kick up more silt to maintain his smokescreen. Then he sensed a dramatic change in the light. Someone had fixed a powerful beam on his position.

Nick darted and rolled in the water, presenting his back to the light, hoping that the hard rebreather might provide some protection. He ignored his straps and fasteners and focused on donning and clearing his mask. Just as he opened his eyes and looked up, a small harpoon penetrated the silt cloud above him. He jerked his head to the left. The projectile missed by barely an inch. Grasping a tank in each hand, he shot for the only cover he could find, the cave formed by the bomber's wing.

Under the shadow of the B-2, Nick whirled around to face his attacker, but he could see nothing through the dark, swirling cloud. He took advantage of the moment's respite by strapping on his gear, finishing with the holster that held his rocket pistol, the Triple Seven's answer to the standard harpoon gun. Designed and built in-house by Scott's team, the weapon amounted to a compact rocket-propelled grenade. Its small club-shaped rounds were far superior to harpoon bolts—faster, with a more stable trajectory and fragmentation warheads that widened the damage envelope considerably.

Nick surveyed his surroundings. The crumpled bomb-bay door blocked his path to the right. Behind him and to the left, the wing sloped into the seafloor. There would be no attack from the rear or the flanks, but there would be no escape either. The only way out of this bizarre cave was back the way he had come, back toward an attacker that he could not see. Nick wondered if he had just made a fatal mistake.

He drew the rocket pistol from his belt and seated a round, but without a target, the weapon was not much use. And even with the pistol's advantages, the chances of scoring a solid hit against a wary opponent were slim. Somehow he needed to regain the element of surprise.

The light reappeared, panning back and forth across the seafloor beneath the wing's trailing edge. In the white beam, he could see the silt settling. Now he understood his opponent's plan. The intruder was patient, unwilling to enter the cloud of sediment and sacrifice his advantage. He would wait for the dust to settle and the water to clear before pressing his attack.

After a short time, the light stopped panning and

locked onto the spot where Nick had entered the cave. The beam formed a ghostly cone in the drifting particles. Nick watched it shrink as the attacker descended. He held his pistol at the ready, knowing he would only get one shot.

The beam slimmed, and then the flashlight itself appeared. There was no time to wait for a full target. Nick aimed just below the descending light and pulled the trigger. The pistol jerked in his hand with an audible *thump*. A rush of bubbles trailed behind the projectile as it accelerated away. The beam flashed up to Nick's face. Through the dazzling white light, he could just make out the silhouette of his attacker and the shadow of a small harpoon gun aimed at his chest. He did not attempt to evade or spoil the attacker's aim. He knew it wouldn't matter. The man would never get the chance to fire.

The projectile found its target a millisecond later, snuffing out the intruder's light in a surreal explosion, a spherical mass of blue fire and bubbles. The shock wave rippled out from all sides, hitting Nick like a punch in the chest even though he was several meters away. He shined his flashlight on the hostile and grimaced at the macabre effect of the fragmentation grenade. The man no longer had a left shoulder. In its place, a stringy mass of flesh and tissue. Blood poured from his body, tinting the water around him red.

The hostile diver began to rise, already lifeless, and Nick guessed that some of the steel shards had penetrated his heart. He raced over and grabbed the body before it floated to the surface. He tried to get an idea of the man's nationality, but the projectile had caused too much damage to the mask and face. Whoever he was, he had a small frame and thin arms, with a gray and blue camouflage wet suit that bore no unit markings of any kind.

"You didn't see that one coming, did you?" Nick asked the corpse as he pulled it up under the wing, hoping the current there would not be strong enough to carry it away. He noted that the intruder carried a small underwater flame cutter on his belt; he had come well prepared.

Nick doused his flashlight and felt his way to the edge of the wing. With his pistol loaded and ready, he swam low and slow over the top of the wrecked bomber, searching for other intruders. A flash of light caught his eye. It had come from the open ejection hatch. He steeled himself for another confrontation, advancing with measured strokes, ready to shoot anything that emerged from that hole.

Searing pain shot through Nick's right arm, causing him to drop the rocket pistol. A harpoon bolt flew by, followed by a trail of his own blood. The carbon steel tip had ripped through his wet suit, leaving a bleeding gash in his triceps. Acting on instinct, Nick wheeled around and kicked hard to his right, defeating a second shot. But he had left his gun behind. He tried to zero in on the assailant's position, simultaneously flipping on his light and drawing his knife from the sheath on his leg.

The intruder materialized out of the murky gloom less than ten feet away. He already had a third round seated in his harpoon gun. He wore a similar wet suit to the other hostile and carried a canvas bag over his shoulder: Drake's tool bag.

Nick knew that he'd been caught. He kept his movements slow and deliberate, willing the man not to fire. Then he remembered the light in the cockpit and shot a glance over his left shoulder, wondering if another intruder might be closing in from behind. He didn't see anything. Putting his focus back on the primary threat, he crouched into a defensive stance with his fins spread front and back, ready to make a final thrust to dodge the next harpoon.

The attacker milked his advantage. He stretched out the harpoon gun, taking a moment to refine his aim. Then Nick heard a familiar *thump* resonate out of the shadows to his left.

With a single thrust of his arms, Nick pushed himself backward, shining his light in the attacker's face. The man took his actions as an attempt to escape and gave him a slow, menacing shake of the head, as if to say, "Ah, ah, ah . . . there's no escape now."

Nick just nodded in reply. "Say cheese, moron," he said into his mask.

With a bright blue flash, Drake's rocket detonated on the wing just in front of the attacker. The man reeled back, stunned by the shock wave. Blood streamed from wounds on his legs.

Nick did not let the reversal of fortune go to waste. He shot forward, kicking with everything he had and rotating the knife in his right hand to turn the point downward. The intruder came out of his daze just as Nick closed to within arm's reach. He tried to raise his harpoon, but Nick fended it off, knocking it from the man's grip with his left arm as he brought the knife down in a slashing motion with his right. He barely nicked the intruder's neck with the tip of the blade. But the neck was not his target.

The knife slid easily between the base of the mask and the hostile's main air line, trapping the hose between the blade and Nick's forearm. He pulled down and away, yanking the mask right off the man's face as the blade severed the hose. Blinded and unable to breathe, the intruder flailed, pawing at Nick like a frightened animal.

Nick left nothing to chance. He found the auxiliary regulator and severed that supply line as well. As he did, the intruder broke free from his grasp and kicked toward the surface. With a final effort, Nick launched upward from the wing and slashed at his opponent, but he only succeeded in cutting the strap of the canvas tool bag. It fell free.

The attacker sped upward, out of reach. Nick let him go. Pursuing him was too risky; a straight shot to the surface with no decompression stops could lead to a deadly case of the bends. At least he'd recovered Drake's tools.

Drake!

Nick spun around, rapidly shining his light back and forth to find his partner. He found him a few feet away from the cockpit hatch, hovering motionless just above the fuselage. He still held the rocket pistol loosely in his hand.

It had been Drake's light that caught Nick's eye from the ejection hatch. Somehow he managed to sneak out of the cockpit and fire off a shot, but now he looked as lifeless as the body that Nick had stuffed under the wing. Nick sheathed his knife and kicked over to his friend's side, grabbing his arm and shining his light across Drake's face. Drake blinked with glassy eyes and feebly raised the hand holding the gun to block the light.

Nick lowered his light and gently took the pistol away, holstering it in Drake's belt. Then he turned the light on himself, pointed at Drake, and gave the okay sign with a questioning look. Drake responded with a thin smile, but rather than returning the okay sign, he pointed to the left side of his head. That's when Nick noticed the thin stream of blood coming from Drake's scalp.

Both divers' gauges read dangerously low. Nick gave Drake the sign for "Wait here" and then quickly retrieved his pistol as well as the body of the first attacker. Dragging the corpse with him, he returned to his teammate and thrust a thumb up toward the surface. Drake gave an affirming nod.

During the ascent and the decompression stops, Drake gave Nick several disapproving looks. Apparently, their cadaverous companion unnerved him. Nick smiled. His longtime friend had always taken zombie movies a little too seriously. Drake also spoke a few times into his mask—still in communication with the surface—but Nick couldn't decipher what he said. He hoped that Drake had warned Walker about the hostile that escaped to the surface. Both men were injured and exhausted, and Nick didn't relish another fight.

CHAPTER 7

Nick surfaced just aft of the *Illustro*, happy to see the sun peaking over the horizon. "Welcome back to the land of the living," said Scott. "For a while there, we thought you were both dead."

"There's another hostile," said Nick, ignoring the engineer and looking to Walker. "I wounded him, but he surfaced out of my reach."

"Relax, Major," replied Walker, holding up a hand. "He was in no shape to fight when he got to the surface." The colonel wore a wet suit instead of his usual khakis and golf shirt. A rebreather and tanks lay on the dock, off to the side.

Nick looked his boss up and down and then gestured at the rebreather. "Really?" he asked.

Walker offered a rare smile. "I was almost finished suiting up when Merigold checked back in."

"I'm touched that you thought of rescuing us, sir," said Drake.

The colonel's scowl returned. "I thought you were dead, Merigold. I just didn't want the enemy to get away with a chunk of my bomber because of your screwup."

"I see," Nick said. "Well, we screwups are both still kicking. Although I can't say the same for my pal here." He dragged the body over to the platform, where Walker pulled it out of the water. Only a little blood spilled onto the dock; most of it had already poured out.

Scott took one look at the cadaver and clambered up the ladder, running to the other side of the dock before ejecting his breakfast into the gulf.

"He just can't win, can he," commented Nick, taking the colonel's outstretched hand and climbing onto the dock. "So, where's my other hostile?"

"Your other friend is in the infirmary," replied Walker.

"Has he said anything?"

"I'm sorry, let me rephrase. Your other friend is in the infirmary-slash-morgue. He's wrapped in a body bag. He was unconscious when we dragged him out of the water, and Doc Heldner couldn't save him. She thinks the combination of the shock wave from Drake's rocket and the rapid ascent completely decimated his lungs. He began drowning in his own blood long before he reached the surface."

"Don't worry about me, I'm fine," said Drake, lifting himself out of the water and trudging over to Nick.

"Sorry man." Nick patted him on the shoulder. "What happened to you?"

"I saw one of the intruders trying to cut a piece off the jet with a torch," Drake replied, turning around to let Nick help him remove his rebreather. "I called you, but you were off comms. I couldn't risk making a noise by banging on the bay, so I stuck my knife in the silt as a warning. When I tried to sneak up on the guy, his buddy must've bludgeoned me from behind. I guess they stuffed me in the cockpit and left me for dead." Drake set his gear down and then reached up and gingerly touched the left side of his head. "It looks like I woke up just in time."

"Yeah, thanks. That guy had me dead to rights until your shot stunned him."

Drake frowned at his teammate. "Did you really have to bring your first victim along for the ascent? There's nothing creepier than swimming with a zombie." He shuddered. "I kept waiting for him to reach out and grab me with his one arm."

"Speaking of the corpses," said Nick, glancing down at the masked body and then up at Walker, "I never got a look at their faces. Do you have any idea where these guys came from?"

"We don't have an exact fix," said Walker, his eyes drifting to the eastern horizon, "but they're definitely not local."

CHAPTER 8

Nick pushed the dinghy away from the *Illustro*'s dock as Drake fired up the motor. The intruders couldn't have gotten that far out into the gulf without a boat. Walker had activated the surface radar and gotten an intermittent contact, but the range and heading were sketchy at best.

As the sun climbed above the horizon, visibility did not improve; instead of dissipating, the early morning fog simply darkened into a brown haze. The team's cover had become their biggest threat. There was a high probability that more hostiles waited aboard the enemy craft, and they had the advantage. Waiting silently in their boat, they would hear the dinghy coming well before Nick and Drake could make visual contact.

"She's northwest of us," said Nick, consulting a handheld GPS, "almost on a straight line to the docks in Kuwait."

"Were they running?" Drake asked.

"No. Walker said the contact was stationary." Nick set down the GPS and then loaded an extended magazine into his MP7 submachine gun. He winced as he pulled the nylon strap over his shoulder. Doc Heldner had been a little heavy-handed when she stitched up his arm. She could be that way when she was angry.

After ten years, Dr. Patricia Heldner remained a mystery to Nick, patient and caring one minute, merciless with a needle the next. A striking redhead in her late forties, she could still turn heads on any city street, but she preferred to be thought of as the Triple Seven's team mom. And like any mother, she had her secrets. Only Walker knew her story. She and the colonel had worked together well before the Triple Seven Chase came to be. When pressed about her past, the doctor would deftly steer the conversation toward her early medical training or her short tours with aid missions in Africa and eastern Europe, leaving decade-wide gaps in her history.

Most of the team figured that she had worked for the CIA, as was often the case when a D.C. operative had holes in their background. Drake had an alternative theory. He proposed that she had worked for the CDC and had been placed in the Triple Seven Chase for safekeeping because she was the only living soul with the top-secret knowledge necessary to thwart the impending zombie apocalypse.

After examining Drake, Doc Heldner had determined that he had a concussion and insisted he be kept under observation for twenty-four hours. The rest of the team, including Drake, had tried to convince her that finding the hostiles' boat was more important. Eventually tactical necessity prevailed but not without consequences for Nick. The entire argument took place while the increasingly frustrated doctor ran a needle and thread back and forth through his arm.

"I think I see something," said Drake, extending the stock of his own MP7 and seating it in the crux of his shoulder. He peered through the scope. "Yeah, tally one small craft, about a hundred fifty yards ahead."

Nick cut the motor to idle to reduce their noise. "Any occupants?" he asked.

"Not that I can see. They could be lying down inside, but it's just a runabout, so that would be tough to pull off."

The intruder's boat gradually emerged from the haze, a blue and white runabout. Drake was right; there was no one inside. Then a sickening feeling washed over Nick.

"I've seen this boat before."

"Where?" asked Drake.

"The docks. Two Kuwaitis were getting it ready as we loaded up the dinghy."

"I guess they weren't really Kuwaitis."

Nick clenched his fist. He should have investigated. A sunny day on the docks, and those two had been working on a boat in full white robes and headdresses. How could he have been so stupid? They had worn the traditional Kuwaiti garb because it obscured their features. "I'll drive it back to the *Illustro*. You lead in the dinghy," he said.

"Sure, boss," Drake replied. "Just don't lose me in the haze."

Nick cautiously stepped from the dinghy into the run-about, his weapon still up and ready. It appeared that the intruders had brought only what they needed for the dive. There were some extra tanks, the white clothes, and little else.

While Drake turned the dinghy around, Nick pulled in the anchor and then moved forward to start the motor. As he leaned down to turn the key, he placed his hand on a beach towel lying on the front seat. Something hard was wrapped up inside. He held up the bundle and let it unravel, catching the object before it dropped onto the deck. "Well, that narrows it down," he said out loud.

An hour after sunset, Nick and Drake hit the water again. Doc Heldner continued to pout, but the rest of the team agreed there was no time to waste in completing the salvage. Both divers used scooters, dragging the umbilical hoses that they would use to inflate the air bags they had brought down on the previous dive.

They made their final approach to the wreck with their scooters silent and their lights out. Nick wanted to maintain the element of surprise in case more intruders had converged on the wreck. Before beginning the salvage, they searched the bomber's perimeter for signs of enemy activity. They found none.

With no more bombs to disarm and no more rude interruptions, the operation ran smoothly. In a short time, they had the first set of air bags fully inflated. These did not lift the bomber off the seafloor, but they dramatically reduced the aircraft's effective weight for the cranes. Nick nodded to Drake to begin the lifting calls.

"Ready cranes one and two," transmitted Drake. "Start with the lowest setting and lift together. Ready . . . Ready . . . Now."

The cables creaked and groaned, but the bomber did not budge.

"Give 'em some more gas. Slowly . . . All together . . ." said Drake.

The cables quivered as Scott increased the torque on the cranes. Finally, like a massive ray lifting itself out of the silt, the aircraft inched upward. Great swirls of murk billowed out from beneath. Suddenly, an alarming *clunk* sounded from the bomb bay. Nick winced, painfully aware that no bomb was ever truly disarmed.

"Hold!" ordered Drake. But the defunct weapons offered no more protests. Once the silt settled, he started barking orders again at a furious pace, trying to keep the bomber level as the cranes lifted it to the first mark. After several stressful minutes, he had it ten feet off the bottom.

While Drake retrieved another air bag, Nick panned the light of his handheld scooter across the seafloor beneath the bomber. A shiny object reflected the light, a diver's watch. He swam over and tried to pull it out of the silt. After a few tugs it came up. And with it came a skeletal arm.

CHAPTER 9

Despite the shock of discovering the body of Walker's lost diver, the rest of the salvage operation progressed smoothly. Less than an hour later, the team had the bomber at neutral buoyancy twenty feet below the surface—towing depth. They left no trace that the stealth bomber had ever been there.

A professional salvage operator might have frowned upon it, but Nick and Drake used the top of the aircraft as an elevator, piling all of their refuse and equipment on top of the jet, even the body. It felt wrong lifting human remains that way, but the urgency of covert operations rarely allowed for ceremony.

Colonel Walker wasted no time. With the bomber in towing position and the intruders' runabout lifted aboard, he immediately directed the *Illustro* toward the Strait of Hormuz.

"So this is the guy who got trapped under the bomber during the original salvage op," said Nick. The team had gathered in the *Illustro*'s small sick bay to examine the remains.

Walker lifted a foam cup and took a sip of coffee, staring out the sick bay's small portal. "Martin . . . His name was Mitchel Martin. He wasn't even supposed to be on the dive."

"How so?" asked Nick.

"I put the salvage team together quickly, using two SEALs that I had worked with in the past. I wasn't sure that would be enough, so I consulted our man at the CIA. He recommended we add one of their experts."

"This guy was a spook?" asked Drake.

"More like a contractor," Walker replied absent-mindedly.

Doc Heldner leaned over the bones and started to cut away what remained of the tattered wet suit. Drake contorted his face in disgust. "Something picked him clean, even inside his suit."

"That'd be the creepy-crawlies of the deep," explained Heldner, brushing a lock of red hair out of her face. "Crabs, hagfish, and who knows what else. He's been down there ten years; they probably cleaned all the flesh off his skeleton in a matter of weeks." She completed her gruesome task and then piled the skeleton's clothing and equipment into a small container, immediately turning to store it in one of the sick-bay lockers.

"Wait," said Nick, intercepting her before she reached the locker. "I need to take a look at something." One piece of the diver's equipment had sparked his interest. He carefully took the container from her and placed it on the counter. Underneath the wet suit, he found an underwater cutter. He picked it up and slowly turned it over in his hand. "If you had already begun to lift the bomber," he said to Walker, "then what was Martin still doing under there?"

The colonel shook his head. "I don't know why he went back under. He was in charge of the air bags, but he had already finished. All I know is that he swam under the bomber just as the first cable failed. It must have been horrifying; thousands of tons of aircraft crashing down on him and nowhere to go." He looked down at the bones. "I'm glad you found him. Now he can finally go home."

Several hours later, Nick stood silently in front of the steel door to Walker's stateroom, holding a towel-wrapped bundle in his hands. He did not knock immediately but waited, gathering his thoughts.

"Enter," commanded Walker when Nick finally pounded on the door. As Nick pushed through the hatch, Walker swiveled around on a chair bolted to the floor of his quarters. He looked haggard. "It's a long way to the strait, Baron. What do you need?"

"I missed the hostile team at the docks in Kuwait. They were right there in front of me and I missed them."

The colonel drained the last drop of coffee from his cup and then tossed it into a trash can beneath the desk. "Remind me to get one of those big half-thermos, half-mug things for the next trip."

"I need help."

"Okay, then get Merigold to remind me too."

"No, sir, I mean we need another team member."

Walker furrowed his brow. "You mean you want a replacement for Danny Sharp."

"Not exactly. Danny was never supposed to be a field operative. The truth is, we've been shorthanded for a long time. Danny just filled the gap. If we'd had another trained field man in Iran, maybe Danny could have stayed behind to help Drake with the Shadow. If there had been another professional with us on this mission, he might have caught what Drake and I missed at the marina, and he could have watched Drake's back while I defused the bombs." He glanced down at the fresh stitches in his arm. "Instead, the other team got the jump on us."

Walker nodded. Nick tried to read his stonewall face, but he couldn't tell if he was getting through. The colonel remained silent for so long that he wondered if he had missed his cue to leave. Then the old warhorse's face finally softened, if only a little. "You make a good point, Baron. Maybe you could use some help. I'll look into it." He leaned back in his chair. "You're getting a break anyway. When we get back, you and Drake get to play pilot again. I'm suspending operations until you complete the final test flight of the M-2 Wraith."

Walker looked down at the towel-wrapped object in Nick's hands. His scowl returned. "Was that all? Or did you want me to do your laundry too?"

"Uh, right," said Nick, not quite sure what to make of Walker's minimalist answer. He let it go and began to unwrap the bundle. "You might not want to suspend ops just yet. I want to put together one more little mission before we go home. I think we have a shot at finding out who sent our attackers."

"I don't think so," Walker corrected him. "You saw the bodies. There was no unit insignia, no identification of any kind. We know what region they're from, but it will take weeks of forensics to determine their specific ethnicity, and we may never know who really sent them."

"Not necessarily, sir. I recovered something interesting from the runabout." Nick moved closer and pulled back the towel, revealing an odd-looking submachine gun with a translucent cylindrical magazine mounted to the barrel. A helix of bullets gleamed in the yellow lamplight, visible through the polymer wall of the cylinder. "It's a Chang Feng submachine gun," he said with finality.

Walker nodded in mock appreciation. "I can see that, Baron," he said. "In fact, I think I saw one at the gun show in Charlottesville last year. So what?"

"So it tells us who these guys were."

"No, it doesn't. Like I said, you can get one of these at a gun show or even order one on the Internet. Our guys could be from New Jersey and still carry this weapon."

"No, sir, not *this* weapon." Nick pushed a lever on the back of the magazine and popped out a round. "The export variants are chambered for nine millimeter, compatible with the rest of the world." Nick held the bullet under the desk lamp for Walker to examine. "But this one is chambered for Chinese military-grade five-point-eight-millimeter rounds. You can't get this weapon anywhere on the open market, and only one group has ever carried it." He pushed the lever back into place with a heavy *click*. "The Special Forces branch of the People's Liberation Army."

Walker took the bullet from Nick and turned it over under the lamp. "All right, Baron. What sort of mission do you have in mind?"

CHAPTER 10

A thick layer of high clouds hid the Special Operations CV-22 Osprey from the eyes of the world below. They masked its noise as well. Even without the clouds, from twenty thousand feet, the roar of its massive tilt-rotor engines would seem little more than a whisper to someone on the ground. Inside the aircraft, however, it sounded like the constant rush of a freight train.

"I still don't think she's as loud as an AC-130," shouted Staff Sergeant Gunnar "Guns" Haugen, "particularly when the howitzer is going off!"

The young man seated across the cargo space from the blond, thick-necked sergeant shook his head. He cupped a gloved hand to his ear and shouted, "What?"

"I said, I don't think she's as loud as an AC-130!" Haugen repeated at the top of his lungs.

Senior Airman Ethan Quinn smiled mischievously. "I

can't hear you," he shouted back, "because it's way louder in here than in an AC-130!"

Haugen rolled his eyes and sat back on the webbed bench. Quinn surveyed his team: six men, most as young as him, seated on either side of the Osprey's cargo floor. They wore slate gray wingsuits and carried an assortment of exotic gear and weapons. In the dim light of the cabin, the whites of their eyes seemed all the brighter against their darkly camouflaged faces. And those faces looked grim, as if tonight would serve as the defining marker in the short history of their lives.

Quinn nodded. It would.

"Approaching the drop zone," shouted the Osprey's loadmaster, offering a thumbs-up.

Quinn returned the signal and stood up, steadying himself against a large, sled-shaped crate positioned between the seats. Without a command, he donned his helmet and clipped his oxygen mask into place. The others followed suit. The loadmaster darkened the cabin, and Quinn switched on the night-vision system integrated into his visor. He could see every detail of the cabin, illuminated in the near-infrared spectrum by the covert beacons on each team member's helmet. There was a rush of air, and his ears popped as the pressure equalized. The cargo ramp behind him began to lower.

Quinn held up a balled fist, and the team stood as one. Two men, the largest of the group, moved to the back and grabbed the handles on either side of the sled-crate. They turned to face the ramp, bending their knees and setting their feet like sprinters in the starting blocks.

Haugen reached around to the back of Quinn's helmet and pulled their heads together. Quinn could see the fire in the sergeant's eyes, illuminated in the faint green glow of his night-vision system. "You ready for this?" Haugen asked, using their radio intercom for the first time.

Quinn pushed the big man away, patted the sniper rifle strapped to his chest, and smiled beneath his oxygen mask. "Just follow my lead and try not to screw up."

With that, he turned and ran, vaulting into space just as the ramp reached its full open position. Then he was flying. Real flying. No matter how many jumps he made, no matter the task that awaited him on the ground, that exhilarating feeling of hurtling through the atmosphere never got old. Quinn focused the adrenaline rush into purposeful action. He tucked and rolled to reverse his heading, stabilized his glide, and then surveyed the scene below.

The clouds formed a solid floor, blocking Quinn's view of the forest. Pressing a button on the control strapped to his wrist, he called up his visor's navigation system. An orange heads-up display flashed into view. A digital altitude tape appeared on the right side, the numbers rolling up the screen from bottom to top. A small square near the center highlighted the location of the objective, with a slant-range readout counting down the distance left to fly.

"The objective is in range," Quinn transmitted. "Esti-mated time over target is as fragged. Open chutes at your briefed altitudes." Instead of a reply, Quinn felt a tug on his leg. He looked over his shoulder and saw Haugen taking up a position at his left heel while another team member floated in at his right. Behind them were two more, followed by the two big guys with the crate. The entire team formed an inverted teardrop, streaking through the night sky at over one hundred miles an hour.

Despite their high terminal velocity, Quinn had no sense of speed—particularly with his helmet protecting his face and ears from the wind. But that changed when he came within five hundred feet of the clouds. He had never encountered clouds on a HALO jump before. The artificial ground rush of streaking toward a solid deck added a completely new dimension to wingsuit flying. As he watched the puffy mass rushing up to meet him at breakneck speed, he understood the addiction that proximity jumpers describe after flying down mountainsides in Europe.

"Stay tight, they're not supposed to be too thick," he transmitted just as he punched face-first into the deck. Flashes and swirls of green filled his night-vision display as he rushed through the layers and dead spaces of the cloud block. Then the flashes began to merge until they disappeared altogether and all he could see was a translucent green shroud. It took him just a moment to process what had happened; his visor had iced over. He felt Haugen's iron grip tighten on his heel.

"We're going blind here, Lead," Haugen shouted into his comm receiver. "I'm going tumbleweed. I can't tell up from down!"

"Hold it together," Quinn snapped. "I'm turning my horizon on." Without a natural horizon to watch, he could tumble out of control in the clouds, taking his team with him. He moved an arm to press the switch, careful not to disrupt his flight path. The digital horizon flashed into view. Immediately he saw that it was a mistake to fly into the clouds without it. He had already drifted into a shallow bank, losing precious lift and glide range. He realized he should have commanded his team to activate their own horizons before joining the formation. Now it was too late. They could become unstable enough to crash into each other, with deadly consequences.

"We have to get out of these clouds," he muttered to himself. One thousand feet thick, eight seconds, that's all this deck was supposed to be. How long had they been in here? He should have started counting after entry, but he'd been distracted by the thrill of the cloud rush.

Quinn began to count. Five seconds ticked by, and still he could not see. Worse, if ice was forming on their visors, it was forming on the leading edges of their wingsuits and chute packs as well. The extra weight could cause them to come up short of the objective or, worse, prevent some of their chutes from opening. He had to get them lower soon, but increasing the team's descent rate would guarantee a shortened glide and long walk.

"C'mon, Lead, we gotta get out of this!" urged Haugen.

Just as Quinn drew his arms in and increased his dive, a chunk of ice flew off his visor, then another and another. He could see. Looking up, he saw that the clouds were more than two thousand feet above. They'd been out for a while; it had just taken some altitude for the ice to start breaking off. Dense foliage spread out below like a massive dimpled carpet. Underneath the orange square in his display, he could see the sparse lighting of the target airfield, still twelve thousand feet below.

"I have visual!" Quinn transmitted, and then caught himself and started again, lowering his tone in an attempt to calm his own nerves as well as the others'. "I have visual. I have the objective in sight. We're on course, and I'm recovering the glide path."

Quinn looked over his shoulder in time to see a chunk of ice break off his chute and smack Haugen right in the visor. The big sergeant sacrificed his position long enough to shake his fist before fighting his way back into formation.

As his altimeter counted through fifteen hundred feet, Quinn deployed his team. "Stand by. Three, two, one, execute." He pressed another switch, and the orange target box shifted from the center of the airfield to a hill on its near perimeter. He felt a heavy smack against the back of his helmet. Haugen waved as he floated past and then tucked into a high-speed dive. Looking back, he saw the others spreading out to their individual landing points, their infrared beacons gleaming like embers, drifting on the wind.

At three hundred feet, Quinn pulled his chute, flaring just in time to alight on the peak of his hill. As he turned to gather his silk, he looked down and saw the last two team members touch down in the clearing below, followed by the sled-crate under its giant cargo chute. He quickly stripped out of his wingsuit and removed the oxygen mask from his mission helmet, replacing it with a boom mic. "All positions check in."

"Two's ready," replied Haugen, and the rest followed in sequence. Below, Quinn watched the two big guys lift a pair of dirt bikes out of their crate. They would walk the vehicles to the perimeter, keeping the engines quiet until surprise was spent.

Finding a solid patch of ground, Quinn set up his bipod. He wished that he could have brought his beloved M-107 fifty-cal. He chuckled to himself. The big gun might have been considered overkill for this particular mission. The smaller TM-110 that he carried now had an ungainly top-mounted dispenser that made it impossible to use the scope while wearing his mission helmet. Also, the awkward rounds would hardly travel a quarter mile, forcing him to choose a perch closer to the target.

Quinn sighed and took one last look over the objective area with his night-vision system. Two men patrolled the ramp, two sat in a guard post at the gate, and two more guarded the small fleet of three light aircraft. That only left the tower crew. The layout felt too easy, as if Petrovsky really wanted them to succeed. Quinn shrugged. That wasn't entirely beyond the realm of possibility.

He scanned for sources of additional manpower. At the base of the tower, he found a single-story building with two small windows. They were dark, but there could be troops sleeping in there.

Quinn removed his helmet, flipped on the wireless, and seated a featherweight comm unit on his left ear. "Hey, Guns," he transmitted.

"Go ahead," whispered Haugen.

"Can you see the windows in the low building on the south side of the tower?"

"Ay-firm."

"Good. On 'Go,' put one round into each window just to make sure there are no extra players."

"No sweat, boss."

Quinn nodded to himself. "All right, team, here's your target brief. Six, take out the ramp patrol—I only saw two. Seven, take out the aircraft guards; there are two of those as well. Four and Five, secure the guard post at the entrance. I'll take care of the High-Value Individual in the tower. Two, you know your assignment. Three, save your rounds for cleanup." Quinn checked his watch. "I'm down to my soda-straw scope for night vision, so call out pop-ups in all areas as you see 'em. Execute at twenty-six past the hour."

Each team member responded in sequence, and then Quinn settled down into his scope. The focused illuminator offered a crisp black-and-white image of his target. Aside from Petrovsky and his thick, eighties mustache, only one other officer occupied the booth. How easy were they going to make this?

Quinn checked his watch. Thirty seconds to go time. He noted the integrated wind meter on his scope display and then cross-checked the position of the crosshairs. The whole mission depended on this shot for success, but the light winds meant he could push the envelope a little. He hesitated for a moment and then adjusted his aim from the heart to the head. Petrovsky's unnaturally large noggin made too tempting a target.

"Three . . . two . . . one . . ." Quinn gently squeezed the trigger. A fraction of a second later, Petrovsky went down, hard. In perfect sequence, Haugen's first heavy round sailed through the window of the low building, and the high-pitched whine of the dirt bikes screamed from either end of the field. Quinn shifted to Petrovsky's lieutenant. The younger man dove for cover, but Quinn skillfully added lead and put a round into his back. He took a moment to check for movement. Knowing that his adrenaline had quickened his perceptions, he counted it out in his head. One potato, two potato, three potato. Nothing. Both men were down. Satisfied, he sat up and donned his helmet. He flipped on his night vision just in time to see Seven put the final round into the final target. All of the guards were down. No one came out of the low building.

"Six and Seven, clear that building!"

Both men dismounted from their bikes. One of them yanked open the door to the structure and then the other crept in. A moment later, Seven raised a thumbs-up.

"All team members report!" ordered Quinn, his heart pumping.

"Two and Three complete. Good shots."

"Four and Five complete. The gate is secure."

"Six and Seven complete. The ramp is secure."

"And Lead is complete. The tower is secure," said Quinn. "Good job everyone. I think it's . . ."

Suddenly a new voice broke into Quinn's transmission. "Senior Airman Quinn, get your team to the exfil point and then report to me immediately." Petrovsky did not sound happy.

————

Captain Chad Petrovsky paced back and forth at one end of the sparse room inside the building below the tower. Quinn could tell he wanted to sit down, but he couldn't, because Haugen's second heavy paint grenade had covered the only chair in the room with red goo. Petrovsky himself still bore the yellow residue from Quinn's sniper round on the side of his head. An ugly lump had started to form just above his right ear.

"I suppose you think you're funny," said Petrovsky, his mustache bristling with anger.

Quinn tried to look as contrite as possible. "Negative, sir," he lied. "I thought my rounds would explode on the window. I could not tell from the scope image that you'd removed the panels."

"There are no panels!" Petrovsky exploded. "There never *were* any panels. This is a practice range. There is no glass here of any kind!" He beat his chest emphatically. "You were supposed to shoot me in the vest!" The captain paused to feel the bump on his head, wincing as his hand touched the tender spot. Then he gestured at a small cooler sitting on a table against the far wall. "And look what your teammate did to my dinner!" In a stroke of incredible fortune, Haugen's first heavy round had sailed through the unprotected window, penetrated the fabric side of the cooler, and exploded inside. Petrovsky gingerly lifted a paint-soaked ham sandwich. "We told you there were only eight targets in the safety brief: the High-Value Individual, the Secondary, and six security guards. What madness drove you to attack my sandwich?"

Quinn stifled a laugh. "I guess I overthought the test. I wanted to show you that I was covering all the bases"— he shrugged—"and I wanted to give Guns a chance to show off his skills. I had no idea that the room was . . . er . . . occupied."

Petrovsky clasped his hands together, lowered his eyes to the floor, and let out a long exhale. "All right, kid, you win," he said, raising his head and looking Quinn in the eye. I can't fail you for killing my sandwich. Both of your shots were spot-on, even if one of them almost killed me for real. The rest of the attack was textbook perfect. Go and tell your team that they passed."

Quinn cocked his head to one side. "*We* passed?"

"Yes, all of you. Your training is now complete. Graduation is at zero nine hundred on Thursday. And heaven help you if I see your face before then. Or ever after. Now get out of here."

CHAPTER 11

F irst there!" shouted Haugen, sloshing beer onto the table as he raised his glass.

"That others may live!" responded Quinn in unison with the others. He had stopped counting how many times they'd shouted the motto, and a few beers back he'd stopped wondering when the manager of the Hog's Breath Saloon would politely ask them to leave.

"Mission Qual is done, little PJ!" yelled Haugen, reaching across and slapping Quinn on the shoulder, sloshing more beer onto the table in the process.

"Stop spilling your beer, Guns," ordered Quinn. "That's alcohol abuse!" He watched the foamy golden liquid swirl around the bases of the empty beer bottles in front of him. There were only two, along with a pair of shot glasses. Only four drinks? He was buzzing way too much for only four drinks. Then he remembered that the hot waitress in the blue-jean miniskirt had been steadily removing bottles and glasses from the table, replacing them with full ones. There was no telling how much booze he'd had. He smoothed out his short brown hair. Where did that hot waitress go, anyway?

Quinn knew he'd had too much to drink. But hey, they were celebrating. You only completed the entire Special Tactics Pararescue syllabus once in your lifetime. More than two years of training: survival, parachuting, combat diving, paramedic certification, and a host of other schools, all culminating in tonight's airfield seizure exercise in the Florida Everglades. In two days, he would graduate from Mission Qual and receive the coveted maroon beret, the mark of a full-fledged Special Tactics pararescueman.

Haugen and the others would get berets as well, but theirs would be scarlet. They were combat controllers: special ops fighters with the skills to take down an enemy airfield and the expertise to build it back up into a functioning friendly base. In this Mission Qual class, Quinn was the only pararescueman, known in the Special Forces community as a PJ, but the two training pipelines merged at many points. He and Haugen had shared a lot of painful weeks together over the last two years.

"You're not keepin' up, PJ," said Haugen, pouring more beer into Quinn's half-full glass. He didn't seem to care that he was pouring Guinness and Quinn was drinking pilsner. "That was some shot you took at Petrovsky."

"He had it coming," said Quinn with a wicked grin. "He's treated me like a second-class citizen ever since we got to Mission Qual."

"He made you team lead for the final exam," offered one of the others.

"He thought he was setting me up to fail," replied Quinn. "I don't think he believes PJs should be part of this phase." He raised a finger and imitated a politician giving a campaign speech. "Captain Petrovsky is a Combat Control PJ segregationist!"

Haugen frowned. "You idiot. That segrim . . . that segee"—he polished off his beer—"that jerk could've washed you out for violating safety protocols. He's been looking for an excuse to get rid of you, and you almost gave it to him."

Quinn gulped down the rest of his mixed beer while the others whooped and cheered him on. "Yeah, well, he missed his chance." He ran his sleeve across his mouth. "One more day to sleep this off and then a wake-up and we're done! And there'll be no paper tests in between to spoil the mood!"

"Speaking of sleeping it off," said Haugen, "I think I'm done for the night."

Quinn stood up, knocking his stool over. "As tonight's lead, I declare one final team exercise: Operation Get Home Without Puking! Six, go and get us a taxi-van."

While the rest of the team paid their tabs and made their way to the door, Quinn and Haugen headed for the men's room. As Haugen put it, "Somebody's gonna lose bladder control in that van, and it's not gonna be me," but when they entered the restroom, Haugen headed for a stall instead of a urinal.

"Aw, man, Operation Get Home Without Puking is

already a bust!" said Quinn, laughing and slapping Haugen on the back as the big man emptied his stomach into the toilet. "Whew, you shouldn't have had those fire wings when we first got here. They smell worse now than they did when you were eating them."

When Haugen was finished, Quinn made a perfunctory effort to clean him up and then the two of them went to catch up with the team. Just as they stepped outside, they saw their teammates climbing into a yellow van twenty yards up the sidewalk. Quinn waved and jogged unsteadily in their direction, shouting, "Hey, wait up, team!" but the van door slid closed, and the driver pulled into traffic.

Quinn slowed to a stop, holding his hands out to stop the streetlights from swirling around. "They left us," he said.

Haugen wobbled up beside him, staring at the retreating van in disbelief. "Hey, they left us," he complained.

"That's what I said." Quinn opened his wallet and looked at the lonely ten-dollar bill that remained. "Shoot, I hate using credit for a cab."

"You don't have to," said Haugen. "My truck is right over here."

"We can't drive, you idiot. We're drunk."

"Wrong. You're drunk. Don't you remember? I just puked out everything I've had in the last two hours. I'm also bigger than you. It takes a lot more to get me drunk. I'm fine."

Quinn closed his eyes and tried to think. Haugen's logic seemed sound. He *had* vomited a whole lot of liquid.

He was a big guy too, and didn't basic science say that it took a lot more to get big guys drunk? Still, something hidden in the heavy fog of his alcohol-laden subconscious was calling to him; he just couldn't make out the words. "Okay, Two," he relented. "Let's head back to base."

Haugen cranked the engine and pulled into traffic. His movements were solid and confident as he accelerated toward Hurlburt Field. Quinn relaxed. The flash of the white lines on the road began to make him queasy, so he closed his eyes and laid his head back on the seat. "Wake me before we pull up to the guardhouse," he said.

Quinn woke to the sound of light jazz, then acid rock, then bluegrass.

"We need some tunes," said Haugen, pressing the radio buttons to flip through the stations.

Quinn laughed and began to lay his head back again, but headlights flashed in his peripheral vision. Haugen had swerved into oncoming traffic. "Look out!" shouted Quinn, reaching out and wrenching the wheel to the right.

A horn blared. Haugen finally looked up and saw the oncoming car. He doubled Quinn's correction, cranking the wheel farther to the right. The truck careened back across the right lane and hit the low guardrail at more than seventy miles per hour. It cartwheeled over the barrier and into a drainage ditch, bouncing off the rear bumper before crashing into the muddy water upside down.

Blinding pain shot through Quinn's face and chest as he fought to push the air bag away. Water poured into the cab. "You okay, Guns?" he asked, searching for his friend through the flashes of white and red obscuring his vision, but Haugen was not in his seat. Quinn felt like his head might explode. He was upside down, his face filling with blood. The water lapping at his forehead continued to rise. He had to get out. He had to find Haugen.

It took several painful seconds for Quinn to unhook his seat belt and free his legs from underneath the crumpled dashboard. He tried the door, but he couldn't move it. Then he saw that the front windshield had torn away on Haugen's side. He struggled through, holding his breath to squeeze beneath the submerged gap between the hood of the truck and the bottom of the ditch.

Finally out of the truck, Quinn stood up and tried to run forward, but he stumbled, slashing his face on a torn piece of fender as he fell back down into the water. He came back up with a guttural cry of frustration. Where was Haugen? Then he saw him, a few feet ahead of the truck, floating facedown in the muddy water. He tried to take another step and fell again. His equilibrium was shot. Haugen split into two men before his eyes and then merged back into one. The headlights on the road seemed to head right for him before jerking away at the last second.

"Guns!" he yelled. Haugen did not move. With extreme effort, Quinn trudged forward until he reached his friend. He rolled him over. Haugen was pale. His eyes were open but unfocused. Quinn dragged him to the edge of the ditch and pulled him up onto the grassy bank below the curb. "Guns, wake up!" he shouted again.

He laid his cheek close to his friend's mouth to feel for breath and watch for his chest to rise, but before he could finish the assessment, he had to wrench his face away to vomit into the water behind him. With that out of the way, he turned back to Haugen, certain that he wasn't breathing. He checked for a pulse. It was there, but it was weak. He tried to pull himself up to his knees to begin rescue breathing. More headlights flew past. The road and the bank swirled around him. He faltered, sliding down into the water he had just puked in.

Quinn tried to crawl back up to Haugen, but his limbs would not move. A siren sounded in the distance. He laid his head down on the bank, still submerged from the waist down in his own swirling vomit. The image of his unmoving friend began to fade. He passed out.

CHAPTER 12

"Two years, Airman Quinn," said Captain Petrovsky, glaring at the young operative.

Quinn stood rigidly at attention in Petrovsky's office at Hurlburt Field, Florida. The late-afternoon sun shone through half-open blinds, casting broad stripes across the lone maroon beret sitting on the captain's desk. The lump on the right side of Petrovsky's head had gone down significantly, leaving an ugly bruise and several small cuts from the fragments of the paint bullet. Quinn's hand quivered as he subdued the instinct to touch the cut on his own face. It itched. Fifteen stitches for a three-inch gash down his right cheek; that was definitely going to leave a scar.

"And now Haugen is dead."

That phrase snapped Quinn's attention back to Petrovsky, who stepped around the desk and handed him a single page of paper. "This is the record of your Article Fifteen Nonjudicial Punishment and the statement of your offenses," he said. "The JAG came in early this morning to help me prepare it, just for you. It says that you have the right to prepare and present a defense to me. Do you wish to invoke that right?"

Quinn stared down at the page. He didn't have the heart to read it. He shook his head in silence.

Petrovsky nodded. "I didn't think so. That paper will follow you the rest of your career. That way, every one of your future commanders will get to read the highlights of your adventure last night—how you left the Hog's Breath Saloon stumbling drunk, how you allowed your teammate to drive despite his extreme intoxication, and how you—a pararescueman—lay passed out in your own vomit while Staff Sergeant Haugen breathed his last."

Quinn maintained a stolid military expression, but inside he screamed at the final charge. A tear escaped his right eye, rolling down his cheek and mingling with the stitches, making them itch all the more.

"Oh, so now you care?" asked Petrovsky, his face turning red. "Well, it's too late. You should have started caring last night when Haugen put his keys in the ignition. You should have started caring when you were in that ditch, too busy puking to give him mouth to mouth." Petrovsky reached back and picked up the maroon beret. "This was supposed to be yours," he said, thrusting the beret in Quinn's face.

Quinn's heart dropped when he heard the words

supposed to be. His eyes grew wide, and he shifted his gaze to meet Petrovsky's angry stare.

"That's right," said Petrovsky. "In a single night, you proved that you have neither the mental fortitude nor even the basic common sense required of a Special Tactics team member." The captain took a breath and let his tone return to normal. He paced in front of the desk. "Because of your skills, I was willing to let the other stuff slide: the attitude, the incident on the sniper range"—he reached up and touched the bump on his head—"even the personal attack last night. I was willing to view it all as youthful exuberance and moxy, but now I see it as a pattern of behavior. You're headed down a road to self-destruction. I can't allow you to bring that kind of risk into this community."

Petrovsky stood directly in front of Quinn so that their noses were just millimeters apart. "You're done here, Airman Quinn," he said in a low but intense voice. "You will not graduate with this class or any other." He jerked the form out of Quinn's hand without backing up. "This paper says that I have the right to keep you here, to put you on work detail like a common criminal. But I don't want to. I just want you off this base." He paused to glare a moment longer into Quinn's eyes and then turned and tossed the beret into his trash can. "Now get out of my office and go pack your stuff."

Fifteen minutes later, Quinn burst into his dorm room, not bothering to shut the door behind him. He went straight to the bathroom and vomited into the pedestal sink. Then he looked up at the face in the mirror, the stitched gash, swollen and red, a disgusting drop of yellow bile still clinging to his chin. He yelled and reached back to punch through the glass but caught himself. Petrovsky's words echoed in his mind: "A pattern of behavior . . . a road to self-destruction."

Maybe Petrovsky wasn't the problem. Quinn asked himself why he would take the risks that he'd taken over the past few weeks. Why destroy two years of work with childish insubordination and foolish pranks? And how could he have let Haugen drive? The image of his friend dying on the bank was seared in his mind, but no matter how hard he tried, he could not bring Haugen into focus.

Quinn stepped back from the mirror, wiped the spittle from his chin, and stripped off his shirt. He was in great physical condition by any measure. Even the big guys in the squadron said that he was abnormally strong. He could run faster, jump higher, and carry more than any of his classmates. Yet, for all his strength, he could not overpower the alcohol in his blood when Haugen needed him most. Worse, he was a highly trained medical technician, a certified EMT. Yet, for all his knowledge, he couldn't even provide basic rescue breathing when his friend lay dying.

The smell of bile stung Quinn's nostrils, and he reached down to wash the vomit out of the sink. As he turned the knob, he caught sight of the tattoo on his upper arm. The Angel of Mercy held the world in her hands. Beneath her, a scroll read THAT OTHERS MAY LIVE. Quinn flew into a rage, his green eyes flashing as he screamed at the mirror. He grabbed a sponge and scrubbed at the tattoo. When that did nothing, he grabbed the Brillo pad that he used for his pots and scrubbed even harder. Flesh tore from his arm. He ignored the pain, scrubbing until he could not see the angel anymore. Then he dropped the bloody Brillo pad into the sink, fell to his knees, and wept.

CHAPTER 13

It took a couple of days for the *Illustro* to drag the bomber out into the Arabian Sea, but when the captain finally set the stabilizing thrusters, the ship was more than twelve thousand feet over the ocean floor.

"Now, Dr. Stone," commanded Walker.

Scott used a remote control to detonate the air-bag charges. The underwater explosions made hardly a sign, little more than a distant *thump* and a frothing eruption of bubbles. The shadow of the stealth bomber faded into the deep.

Finally, at a preset depth of two thousand feet, the main explosives detonated. At that depth, no debris from the bomber would find its way back to the surface. The Triple Seven Chase could not leave their skeletons in any recognizable form for deep-sea mappers to find.

Walker used the *Illustro*'s underwater sensors to

confirm that the charges did their job. He nodded with satisfaction as the sonar showed the aircraft separating into hundreds of individual pieces, raining down into the abyss. The last remnant of the squadron's first tactical mission made its final descent into Poseidon's care. After ten years, he could rest a little easier.

Doc Heldner watched the sonar screen over Walker's shoulder. "It's too bad," she said.

"What's too bad, Pat?" asked Walker.

"That Nick and Drake weren't here to see the fruits of all their labor."

———————

"Tell me again why we're letting Joe tag along for this one?" asked Drake. "He's too soft and pudgy for field work." He and Nick sat in a white Pajero SUV just outside the corporate terminal of the Kuwait International Airport. They watched through the chain-link fence as a short, slightly round man with receding salt-and-pepper hair stepped out of a Bell commuter helicopter. Both of his hands were full, with a carry-on bag in one and an aluminum briefcase in the other. He crouched beneath the chopper blades and loped toward the terminal building.

"We need that cell phone interceptor for the stakeout," Nick replied. "And you know how Joe is about field ops." He put the Pajero in gear and pulled up to the passenger pickup zone. "The colonel wants to use this little milk run to build up some goodwill credit."

Joe Tarpin clumsily shouldered his way through the

terminal door, nearly smashing the glass with his metal case. The aging CIA agent had been the Triple Seven's go-to man at Langley for more than a decade. Anytime Nick needed special equipment, satellite networking, or just someone to run interference with the deputy director, Tarpin took care of it. But his help came with a price. Like any agent who has been relegated to a desk, Tarpin longed to be back in the game. He constantly pestered Nick and Walker to let him join the team for their missions. Usually, the colonel appeased him by letting him in on need-to-know details, making him feel like a part of the op. This time, he had offered Tarpin a ride-along as well.

"The least he could do is hit the gym once in a while," muttered Drake as he rolled down the heavily tinted window and waved the CIA man over.

"Is that you, Drake?" whispered Tarpin, setting his bags down and leaning close to the window. He lifted his shirt to wipe his sweaty brow, exposing his plump, hairy midsection.

Drake blanched at the sight. "If you don't know that already, you've got to be the dumbest spook ever," he replied. He thrust a thumb toward the backseat. "Get in."

"Don't mind him," said Nick as Tarpin squeezed into the backseat. "He hasn't had his latte this morning."

A half hour later, Nick parked the Pajero a few cars down from the entrance to the Kuwait City Mortuary Facility. "And now we wait," he said, settling into his seat.

A CIA helicopter had flown out to the *Illustro* two days before. Along with their duffel bags, Nick and Drake loaded up the least damaged cadaver. Heldner had implanted a micro-transmitter beneath a lymph node in its groin, where a mortician would be unlikely to find it. The transmitter sent out two encrypted signals: a long-range GPS locator and a very short-range audio broadcast.

Under the cover of darkness, just beyond visual range from the Kuwaiti docks, Nick had pushed the body out of the chopper. A fisherman discovered it the next evening, and the Kuwaiti authorities had locked it in the morgue that night.

The Chinese Embassy opened at 8:00 A.M. That was an hour ago. The Kuwaiti mortician was not a busy man. With any luck, he had already called them.

"We should have stopped for coffee," said Drake after twenty minutes with no activity.

"No, because then you would have to pee just as our target leaves the building," countered Nick. "Don't you remember what happened in Vienna?"

Tarpin looked up from the cell phone interceptor he had pulled out of his aluminum case. "What happened in Vienna?"

"Nothing," Nick and Drake answered in unison.

"I mean, nothing important," said Nick.

"Yeah, what he said," added Drake.

Tarpin leaned back in his seat and raised his hands. "I'm just gonna leave that one alone." Then his eyes shifted past the two operatives. "Wait, who is that?"

Nick turned to see an Asian man in a gray business suit stepping off the curb opposite the morgue entrance. He looked from side to side several times as he crossed the street, a little too much for someone just exercising good traffic safety. Nick positioned a camera on the dashboard to get some video. On the high-definition monitor in his lap, he could see a scar above the newcomer's left eye. His features were hardened, and as he opened the door to the morgue, Nick could see a hint of a tattoo showing just above his collar. This wasn't your average embassy attaché.

"That's got to be our guy," said Nick. "Turn it up. We need to hear this."

Drake turned up the volume on the receiver. Amid the static, they could hear a few ambient sounds consistent with a morgue examination room: a few *clinks* and *clanks*, someone running a sink in the background, but nothing else broke the morbid silence for several minutes. Then, finally, they heard voices, steadily increasing in volume as the conversation moved closer to the transmitter.

"Yes, yes. He came in just last night," said a man with a Pakistani accent. Consistent with much of their professional labor, the Kuwaitis preferred to import their morticians. "A fisherman spotted him near Al-Bidea. I'm afraid there's not much left. Even the fingertips only gave partial prints, too much soft-tissue damage from prolonged exposure to seawater."

"I understand," replied the Asian man. "This is just a formality. I must look at the bodies and take a few photographs for the embassy medical staff. At this time, we have no reports of missing Chinese citizens here or anywhere else in the region."

"He's lying," said Nick. "If no one at the embassy was interested in these guys, they could have had the mortician fax over the photographs."

"Or they would have sent one of the medical staff instead of this stiff," added Drake, and then caught himself. "Sorry. No pun intended."

The mortician and the attaché milled around the body for a while with very little small talk, and then the conversation receded.

"Get ready, now the fun begins," said Nick.

"Are you just going to leave your hardware in there?" asked Tarpin.

"Our micro-transmitters are one of Scott's best innovations," replied Nick. "They have a short life span; just a few days. With their last bit of juice, the batteries will release a compound that dissolves the capsules. You would have to know what you're looking for to detect any trace of them. In a couple of weeks, even that wouldn't help."

Tarpin nodded, and then his eyes drifted over to the morgue entrance. He sat back in his seat. "Here he comes."

The Chinese attaché got into a black sedan, several vehicles ahead of them. Nick waited for his quarry to make a turn at the end of the street and then pulled out to follow.

"Stay close to him," said Tarpin. "We need to be within range for me to isolate his cell phone signal."

"If I get too close, he'll know we're onto him, and then we won't get anything," countered Nick.

Suddenly, the attaché crossed two lanes to the left and reversed direction.

"He's onto us," said Tarpin. He sank down in his seat as the sedan passed them on the other side of the road.

"No, he isn't," said Nick. "Sudden maneuvers are

standard procedure for a Chinese agent. This guy is definitely more than just an attaché." His grip tightened on the steering wheel.

"You might want to hold on, Joe," said Drake, reading his team lead's body language. "Here come the Gs."

Nick waited for a gap in the oncoming traffic and then punched the accelerator and turned the wheel. The six-cylinder engine responded immediately, and the Pajero leapt over the median and into the opposing lane.

"Whoa," said Tarpin, clutching his instruments. "Take it easy."

Nick ignored the CIA man and continued the hard U-turn, aligning the SUV with the new traffic flow. He saw the black sedan a few hundred yards ahead. The attaché made another quick lane change and then turned right onto a side street.

"Look out," said Drake. "He's changing direction again."

At the next side street, Nick saw an opportunity to intercept. It looked clear, except for one problem: the Arabic ONE WAY sign pointed in the wrong direction. He cranked the Pajero around the corner and floored the accelerator, hoping to reach the next cross street before another vehicle turned onto the road in front of him, nose to nose. His luck didn't hold. With just a few car lengths to go, a light blue two-ton utility truck pulled onto the road.

"Hang on!" shouted Nick. He jerked the small SUV up onto the curb, narrowly splitting the gap between two parked cars. Two white-clad Kuwaitis jumped out of the way as he took out the plastic table they'd been sitting at. Tea splashed onto the windshield.

"Sorry!" Drake called out the window.

Safely past the truck, Nick hopped the Pajero back onto the road and skidded to a stop at the end of the street. Then he calmly turned right, pulled into traffic, and began weaving his way forward. Five cars ahead, he spotted the black sedan. "See, we're back in business."

"Right," said Tarpin, relaxing his death grip on the seat in front of him. He leaned down and gingerly retrieved his equipment from the floor.

As Nick moved closer to their target, the attaché lifted a cell phone to his ear.

"You're on, Mr. CIA," said Drake.

Tarpin gave a handheld dish to Drake and indicated that he should point it at the sedan. Then he turned up the volume on his receiver. Instead of voices, they heard piercing digital noise.

"The signal is encrypted," said Tarpin. "Wait. I can get it." He pulled another small box out of the suitcase in the back and plugged it in to his receiver. After punching a few keys, the annoying squeals faded and voices came through.

"Nǐ de rén dōu sǐ le, jiāngjūn."

"Wǒ xiǎng zhè yīnggāi búshì nǐ zuòde."

"Oh, great, Chinese," said Drake. "We should have thought of that."

"We did," said Nick in a harsh whisper. "Shut up."

Tarpin closed his eyes and tilted his head toward the radio. "He's talking to someone at the embassy. They're not even talking about the body. He's telling a colleague when he will be back in the office."

The voices ceased. Ahead, Nick could see the attaché put his cell phone away. He watched Tarpin through the rear-view mirror. "I picked up a little Mandarin during an operation in Singapore," he said. "I thought I heard the word 'plan' in there. What sort of plan were they talking about?"

Tarpin nodded. "I'm impressed. You heard '*Wǔfàn yǒu shénme dǎsuàn.*' They were talking about their lunch plans. In fact, here come the lunch plans now." He pointed ahead at the Gulf Royal Chinese Restaurant. Just as he predicted, the sedan pulled into the parking lot.

"Seriously?" asked Drake. "It's not even ten yet. And you'd think the guy could branch out with his culinary palate."

"We'd still like the recording," said Nick. "Could you digitize it before we head back to the States?"

Tarpin shook his head. "I'm sorry. This device doesn't record. I can jot down a summary if you'd like."

"You're kidding," said Drake. "You're CIA; you guys record everything."

Tarpin just shrugged.

Nick parked the Pajero across from the restaurant and waited. The attaché exited a few minutes later and returned to his sedan with two plastic bags full of Chinese food. He made no more phone calls before he reached the Chinese Embassy, where none of their surveillance equipment would help them.

"I guess that's it," said Nick. "Aside from confirming that our boys were Chinese, this was a complete waste of time."

CHAPTER 14

Zheng's attractive young secretary offered an elegant, almost imperceptible bow. "Will you require anything else, General?"

"No. Thank you, Ling. That is all." Zheng waved her off, but he did not immediately return to his work. His keen eyes tracked Ling as she retreated from the grandiose office, her modest heels clicking sharply on the granite tiled floor. He assessed her. Not with the seedy gaze of lust, for he had no time for such base pursuits. No, he assessed her as he did every day, every time she entered his office. He analyzed her walk, her mode of dress, her hygiene. He searched for anything that might seem out of place. He searched for any indication that she might be a spy.

Ling was not privy to Zheng's more delicate and important projects. She was, after all, a woman. But women could be cunning, particularly when driven by powerful men, and all of Zheng's rivals were powerful. How long had she been with him? Four? No . . . at least five years now. Thus far, she had not failed him. There would be no mercy if she ever did.

Zheng sighed. For too long he had lived with one foot in the shadows, denying his true spirit to most of those around him. All of this espionage and intrigue was distasteful. One day, he would surround himself with men he could trust, countrymen who understood the meaning of destiny. Until then, he must constantly be on guard. To do any less would be to fail the very people from whom he hid his true self. They were his people, his province, his country.

Realizing that he'd been staring at a closed door for several moments, Zheng shook himself free of his thoughts and looked down at the papers on his desk. The vertical lines of text seemed to move about one another, black ink blended into ivory paper as the characters shifted and changed. He could not focus. The disquiet of his thoughts had put him out of the temperament for office work. He needed to relax. His spirit was above such fleshly pursuits as ogling young secretaries, but he did have one vice, and now he was in a mood to partake.

Zheng pressed the intercom button on his telephone. "Ling," he called.

"Yes, General?"

"Send for Han."

A half hour later, Han drove the sedan through the south gate of the Fuzhou military complex and turned toward the deep jade hills to the south of the city. At more than seven million and growing, the population of

Fuzhou would soon rival or surpass most of the large metropolitan cities in China. Yet many of its citizens still rode bicycles and used the bus system. The people of Fujian knew the value of their beautiful province. They would not allow the pollution so prevalent in other provinces to destroy China's Green Treasury. Zheng echoed their sentiments, but he would not deny himself the luxury of a long drive through one of Fujian's sweetest forests.

The irony of his vice was not lost on Zheng: gliding through the ancient forest, drinking in the sweetness of the air, in a vehicle that left a trail of choking black exhaust in its wake. But were not exceptions made for exceptional men? Were not the sacrifices of the masses made to provide some measure of relief for their greatest leaders? The thousands of his beloved countrymen who abstained from driving afforded him these small respites from his otherwise constant struggle. A struggle that would one day bring them the unity they so richly deserved.

"We are close, Han, very close."

"So, the mission was a success, General?"

"I have not heard, but I have no reason to suspect otherwise. Once my men return, we will have the last piece of the puzzle, and Tāo can finally complete his work."

Zheng fell silent once more. He cracked the window to take in the scents of pine, jasmine, and daffodils. He did not bother directing Han. His trusted servant would take him precisely where he wanted to go.

A few minutes later, Han pulled the sedan into a quiet clearing that overlooked the northern bank of the

Fangshan reservoir. There, bracketed by towering redwoods, stood a small tree known as *xi shu*, the Tree of Joy. Zheng stepped out of the car to stretch his legs and regarded his favorite tree. It was not particularly impressive. It stood at less than half the height of the redwoods, it did not release any sweet scent, and its drab color could not compare to the jade of the cypress or the deep green of the pines. Yet its common appearance masked an incredible quality. The Tree of Joy had been used for medicinal purposes for time immemorial. For thousands of years, this species had cured colds, skin disorders, liver disease, and many other ailments, and now there were rumors that it held a cure for cancer.

Unfortunately, the Tree of Joy had been farmed almost to extinction over the last two centuries. Humans had squandered this amazing resource on common colds and foot fungus. Now that man's understanding had finally caught up to the plant's true potential, there were so few left that pressing forward might eradicate them from the earth.

Zheng closed his eyes and breathed deep the rich air beneath this holy tree. He reached out a hand and gently ran his fingers along the grain of the reddish brown bark. He could feel the sense of isolation, the loneliness. Its greatest brothers had long since given their lives for insignificant goals. Now it stood alone, a divine presence, hidden amid a sea of lesser reflections, waiting for the day when it would give life to the world. "I understand," he said out loud.

The insistent ring of the satellite phone shattered

Zheng's thoughts. "Let it ring," he ordered Han, without opening his eyes. "I'm in no mood to take calls."

"General, the number is from our contact in Kuwait."

Muttering, Zheng walked over and grabbed the phone from Han's waiting hand. "I'm secure on this end. Give me good news, Wūlóng."

"Your men are dead, General," replied the smooth, cold voice.

Zheng pounded the hood of his car. He took the phone away from his ear and stopped himself just short of smashing it against the tree. "I assume," he said, struggling to control his voice, "that this was not your doing."

The question did not faze the caller in the slightest. "No, it was not. I believe that your men failed to account for all of the variables. Either that, or your source has turned."

Zheng considered the possibility for a moment and then let out a short sigh. "No, I don't believe that is possible. Hēi Yǐng is reliable, if not perpetually ineffective in this one mission."

"Perhaps the general will consider trusting such work to me in the future." For the first time, Zheng detected a change in Wūlóng's tone, the tiniest rise in the tenor of his icy voice, an anticipation of pleasure in the work he suggested.

"Yes, Wūlóng, I will," Zheng replied. "In fact, I have something for you here. I am going to Beijing. I will need you to meet me there at your earliest convenience, at the usual place."

"Of course, General."

PART TWO

DRAGONS

CHAPTER 15

Ethan Quinn hefted the camouflage backpack on his shoulder and looked forlornly at the Human Resources Training Center. He had just arrived and he already hated this place.

Randolph Air Force Base would become his home for the next four years. After HR training, he would disappear into the massive black hole that was the Air Force Personnel Center. Then he would get out of the military at his allotted time with zero career prospects. He chuckled. Petrovsky probably intended this irony. Thanks to the captain's beautifully crafted Article 15, the only Air Force job that Quinn could get was to find jobs for other airmen.

The brown sign on the curb said it all. Not the lettering—HUMAN RESOURCES TRAINING CENTER—but the neglected condition. It said so much more. Forgotten. Ignoble. Unimportant.

When he lifted his eyes from the depressing sign, Quinn noticed an Army colonel seated on the bench outside the training center's glass double doors. He stopped and saluted.

The colonel leaned over to set his foam cup down next to the bench and then stood and saluted back. "Try not to look so happy to be here," he said with a thin smile.

Quinn dropped his salute. Clearly, the officer wanted to engage him in conversation. Why couldn't this Army meathead just let him pass and get on with his misery? "I'm sorry to rush by, sir. I have to report in for training."

The colonel smiled. "Perhaps I misjudged, Mr. Quinn. A moment ago you didn't look like you were in any hurry to be a Human Resources specialist."

Quinn paused. The colonel had called him by name. For a fraction of a second, he thought there might be more to this meeting than chance. Then he realized that the meathead had just read his name tag; senior officers were adept at that. He smiled congenially. "No, sir. This wasn't my first career choice. I'm sorry. I really have to get in there."

Quinn tried to step around him, but the big man deftly stepped back into his path. Quinn lowered his head and bit his lip. On the first day of his personal purgatory, he was going to have to punch a colonel. He wondered how many years he would spend behind bars at Leavenworth. Looking up, he forced another smile. "Sir, I don't want to be late. The first sergeant is expecting me."

Colonel Richard Walker smiled and shook his head. "No, Ethan. He's not."

Quinn's eyes grew wide. His name tag didn't include his first name. A number of detailed questions rose in his mind, but "Sir?" was all that he managed to spit out.

"Let's have a seat," said Walker, indicating the bench he'd occupied a few moments before. "You are Senior Airman Ethan Quinn, are you not?"

"Affirmative, sir." Quinn's mind reeled, still trying to catch up to the situation.

Walker picked up his coffee. He took a sip and then looked Quinn in the eye. "I run a small Air Force unit that operates out of Joint Base Andrews near Washington, D.C."

"But you're Army," interrupted Quinn.

Walker held up a hand. "Yes, I know. Try to get past that. It'll be a lot easier for all of us. As I was saying, I run this small *Air Force* outfit. We conduct small unit special missions at the request of the Joint Chiefs or higher authorities."

"Higher authorities? You mean, like, the president?"

"Very good. Your file says you're sharp," said Walker, taking another drink of coffee to punctuate his sarcasm. He set the cup down beside the bench. "Our missions have grown in scope over the years, and my team lead has requested that I expand the field team. Getting down to the point, I'm offering you a job."

"Let me get this straight," said Quinn, leaning back against the arm of the bench. "You run a clandestine Special Forces unit that deploys on the orders of the Joint

Chiefs and the president of the United States, and you're trying to recruit me—the guy who got kicked out of Special Forces training?"

"No, I run the *best* clandestine unit this country has ever seen, and I'm offering you a job *because* you got kicked out of training."

"I don't follow."

"Wow, kid, maybe you do need that HR training. Didn't anyone ever tell you not to look so thick at a job interview?"

Blood rushed to Quinn's cheeks. He opened his mouth to say something insubordinate, but he suddenly felt pain radiating from the scar left by the accident with Haugen. He bit back his response.

"Look," Walker continued, "you're not the only man for the job, but you *are* readily available. You have all the Special Tactics skills that I need, all the pipeline badges that I require. There are lots of guys who fit that bill. The difference is those other guys are all spoken for."

Walker lifted a file out of a leather portfolio sitting next to him. He waved it in front of Quinn. "You, on the other hand, did not technically graduate. Thus, you don't meet anyone's quotas. You're a free agent. Are you starting to catch on, genius?"

Quinn nodded. He finally understood. Despite the obnoxious and abusive comments, this old grunt was offering him a job doing what he loved. But the glorious image of jumping out of V-22s again did not fill his mind; instead, he saw the grotesque vision of Haugen dying next to the road.

The last vestige of blood and anger drained from Quinn's expression. He dropped his gaze to the concrete. "I'm sorry, I don't think I'm your man."

"Excuse me?"

"I'm not right for the job, sir." Ethan stood up and raised his hand in salute. "I have to report in to the first sergeant."

Walker nodded. "I see." He picked up the leather portfolio and removed a small bundle wrapped in black cloth. "Either way, I think this is yours. Petrovsky had no right to withhold it from you. You earned it." He put the bundle in Quinn's left hand and returned the younger man's salute. Then he picked up his coffee and walked into the parking lot.

Quinn stared down at the black cloth in his hands. Without a conscious thought, he began to unwrap it, revealing a maroon beret with the pararescueman's badge pinned to the front. He smiled despite himself.

Then a cloth patch slipped out of the black wrapping and fell onto the ground. Quinn picked it up and turned it over to dust it off. The design on the triangular patch looked muted, stealthy. The colors were so dark that he had to hold it closer to his eyes to break them out from the black background. A bronze dagger with a deep green handle stood blade down toward the base of the triangle. On the blade, scarlet lettering proclaimed THIRD TIME LUCKY, and beneath the tip, emblazoned in the same color, the number 777 was written with thick, elegant script.

Quinn felt a surge of electricity pulse through his body, the sensation of a thousand pinpricks assaulting his skin all at once. He felt as if his nervous system had suddenly woken up after days of sleep. He looked up at the entrance to the training center. Suddenly, the double doors, the sign, the whole center, looked as two dimensional as a Hollywood cutout thrown up in his path, a poorly conceived April Fool's joke that was never funny in the first place. He turned around in time to see the colonel getting into a blue Air Force sedan. "Wait!" he shouted, pulling off his camouflage cap and putting on the beret. "I changed my mind!"

CHAPTER 16

Chen looked down at the tin plate of slop that he carried and immediately recoiled at the smell. He held it away from his body as if it were a glass vial full of infectious disease. Spoiled rice, covered with pungent brown gravy that had already begun to congeal; this meal was not even fit for the mangy dogs that haunted the forest beyond the fence. *"Hong Mo,"* he yelled, banging on the cell door with his nightstick. *"Yidong, Hong Mo!* Get back! Your breakfast is here."

Chen gave the door a final whack with his stick and then opened it just wide enough to toss the plate into the cell, spilling most of its contents onto the concrete floor. He shut the door quickly, listening for the satisfying sound of the foreign devil scrambling forward to scrape his daily meal from the floor. But he heard nothing.

"Hong Mo!" he shouted, banging on the door even

harder. "Wake up, you lazy American dog! Come and get your slop!" He waited again, but still there was no sound. Was the American finally dead? Unlikely. Hong Mo had been in the prison for years, and he'd never complained of anything worse than a common cold or a toothache.

Chen felt his pulse accelerating. He hesitated a moment more and then burst into the cell. In his haste, he slipped in the spilled gravy and fell flat on his back, knocking the air from his lungs. It took a few moments for him to recover from the fall and regain control of his limbs. When he finally struggled to his feet, he let fly a tirade of Chinese curses and turned toward the cot in the corner, raising his nightstick to vent his anger on the American. But the cot was empty. Hong Mo was gone.

Chen cursed again. Disgusting brown goo covered his uniform, and his back ached. How had the devil escaped? There was no way to open the door from inside the cell, no window to the outside. His mind reeled, replaying the last few moments. Then fear gripped him. He remembered a flash of gray as he fell. Was it the prison wall or the prisoner himself?

He knew he should sound the alarm, but the commandant would surely ask what had happened to his uniform. The punishment for being so easily fooled would be severe. He kept a spare uniform in his locker. He could change quickly. Hong Mo would not get far.

Several minutes later, Chen stood in the cell with the commandant, unconsciously running a hand along the back of his new shirt, as if he might still find the telltale slop stuck to its fabric. The prison's small contingent of guards searched the hallways and the yard for any sign of the lost prisoner.

The older man, a colonel, eyed the smeared brown goo on the floor. "Tell me again how it happened," he prompted.

"I . . . I do not know," stammered Chen. "He made no sound when I brought his morning meal. I thought he might be dead, so I entered the cell to investigate. I found it empty, just as it is now."

"I see." The commandant nodded. He gave a final look around the cell and then walked out into the hallway. Chen followed close behind.

"Sir, you must call the Fujian Provincial Command. The prisoner may already be in the forest. We need more manpower for a search of this magnitude."

The colonel stopped short and slowly turned to face the young guard. "I must do nothing of the kind," he said. "I will not bear the embarrassment of losing such a weakened ghost of a man. This is an internal prison matter, and we will keep it that way. Is that clear?"

The commandant's response left Chen mystified. Surely a man of his station understood the political ramifications if Hong Mo escaped the country? Chen became angry. This fat, lazy has-been would sacrifice the honor of the whole country to save his own? He squared his shoulders. "But Colonel," he began.

The commandant held up a finger, stopping Chen before he could continue. "Is that *clear*, Chen?" he asked again.

This time Chen heard distinct malice behind the question. His shoulders sagged, and he bowed. "Yes, sir."

The commandant lowered his hand. "Good," he said. "This is for everyone's protection, you know. If the American's escape becomes a public affair, someone will have to be held accountable. *Someone* will have to take the blame . . . and the punishment." He paused and looked Chen up and down. "By the way, Guard Chen, I must compliment you on the pristine state of your uniform, particularly so late in the day. Although your shoes could use some polish."

Chen looked down. There were splashes of brown muck across the top of his shoes, some of it already crusted and dry. Both men had just inspected the empty cell, but the colonel only had a slight smear of gravy on the sole of one boot. Chen bowed again, more fervently this time. "My men are very resourceful, most respected Commandant. We will find Hong Mo on our own."

CHAPTER 17

Sergeant Will McBride sat alone in a small, darkened room. His only light came from the faint glow of the two LCD monitors at his workstation. On one of the screens, a series of black-and-white images flipped by at the precise rate of one per second, but they showed nothing of consequence, just dense forest and the occasional road. On the other, a tiny picture of an RQ-4B Global Hawk inched along the Chinese coast heading southeast, toward the Taiwan Strait.

The Global Hawk's two-man crew controlled the aircraft from a ground station in California while McBride monitored the mission from an intelligence center in Maryland. The young, freckled sergeant stretched and adjusted his headset. He could hear the idle conversation between the pilot and the sensor operator, which meant they had their radio set on VOX. The discussion centered on the potential for good surfing weather during the upcoming weekend.

How nice for them.

McBride keyed his microphone. "Pegasus, this is Intel. Request update."

"You can see everything we can, Intel," replied the pilot, annoyed at the interruption. "Nothing to report."

"Copy," answered McBride. "Just trying to stay awake."

With Seventh Fleet's Task Force 77 steaming toward Pearl for reconstitution, the Global Hawks had been flying extra sorties, keeping an eye on Chinese military operations across the strait. But the Chinese weren't doing much, and staying alert through long hours of staring at featureless pictures had become a real challenge.

McBride settled back in his chair and glanced over at the endless parade of forest. The Global Hawk's synthetic aperture radar could scan through multiple layers of clouds and still create incredibly fine digital images. For McBride, the result was this slide show of black-and-white trees. He sighed. They were unbelievably detailed trees, but they were still trees.

Just as McBride's eyelids began to fall, the forest cleared. The trees broke before a large fenced complex where low rectangular buildings stood at the center of a large open yard. McBride blinked hard and tried to focus. Through the slow progression of images, he could see the yard filling with troops.

"Pegasus, this is Intel. Please hold scan on these grids," said McBride.

"Uh, yeah, Intel, we were just looking at that. Looks like a little exercise or something."

McBride turned to his other monitor and opened his mission briefing. "Possibly," he said, scanning the document, "but we don't show any current exercises in our intelligence for this sector."

"Typical Intel," said the pilot, his voice distant and tinny. "If it's not on their calendar, it must not be happening."

McBride closed his eyes and bit his tongue. "Be advised that you're on VOX. I can still hear you."

"Oh, right. Sorry." There was a digital click on the line, and the stifled laughter in the background abruptly went silent. "Okay, Intel," the pilot continued, "What is this compound?"

"Stand by, Pegasus." McBride ran a program to correlate the exact coordinates of the imagery with recent intelligence files. Three documents popped open on his screen. The second one had a small photo in the top-right corner that matched the buildings in the imagery.

"Pegasus, you are looking at Detention Center Twenty-six of the Fujian Ministry of Justice. Our intelligence says that this facility is hardly used, just a small troop of guards with no current prisoners."

The pilot yawned. "Yep, it's an exercise. They must be trying to keep the guards sharp. Look, we've got a lot of ground to cover. If we hold the scan here much longer, we'll have to reprogram the bird to compensate. We need to move on. Now."

McBride stared hard at the advancing imagery. Several

of the men in the pictures now appeared to have weapons drawn. Others were leaving the yard and fanning out into the forest. This looked like more than an exercise. "Hold here for another two minutes, Pegasus. I want my supervisor to have a look." He picked up the hard-line receiver and began to dial the duty officer, but before he finished the compound disappeared and thick forest again filled the screen.

"Negative, Intel," said the pilot. "It's just an exercise. We're moving on."

McBride hesitated, his finger hovering over the telephone keypad. Finally, he placed the receiver back in its cradle. "Copy that, Pegasus. Moving on."

CHAPTER 18

General Zheng tapped the map lying on the defense minister's desk. "Thus, if we attack now," he said, "while the U.S. Seventh Fleet is out of position, we can overwhelm Taiwan in one strike." He took a conclusive step back and smiled. "Once we occupy the island, the Americans will do nothing. Their politicians will not allow it."

Zheng had spent the morning in the minister's austere Beijing office, detailing his plan to wipe out Taiwan's Patriot air defenses with short-range stealth missiles, allowing the PLA to overrun the island before the United States could react. Defense Minister Liang had listened attentively, patiently watching as Zheng maneuvered maps and charts about his wide ebony desk. Now he sat in silence, his chin resting on his hands, studying the maps. Surely he could see the undeniable wisdom of the plan.

Finally, Liang leaned back in his brown leather chair. He gave a short sigh of frustration. "How long have I nurtured you as my protégé?" he asked. "How many years have you observed my actions and decisions, listened to my counsel?"

The smile fell from Zheng's lips.

"And now you bring me this outlandish plan," continued Liang. He spread his hands over the maps. "This is utter madness."

For a moment Zheng could not speak. He knew that Liang might have reservations, but to call his plan madness? He had underestimated how weak the minister had become, a most unfortunate turn of events.

The defense minister slowly shook his head. "You still have not accepted our need for the Americans as an ally. The United States is the springboard from which China now leaps into an age of unprecedented prosperity. It is unwise to spurn such a lucrative partnership."

Zheng's disappointment turned to simmering anger at the mention of America as an ally, but when he heard the word *partnership*, he exploded. "Partnership?" he spat out the word. "We own the Americans! They depend on our loans, our exports. Without us, their economy would crumble." He tried to control his temper. He breathed deeply so that he could explain the realities of the situation to this ignorant old man. "Allowing the Americans to keep us from Taiwan is like allowing an impudent servant to keep his master from his own house. It defies logic." He leaned forward and slapped a heavy hand down on the maps. "With this plan, we can occupy Taiwan without American interference. Once we are established, politics will take over. A victory is inevitable."

"An impudent servant?" Liang responded in a cool, pedagogic tone. "You talk more like a Qing warlord than a practical communist soldier." He put his elbows on the desk, resting them on the scattered pieces of Zheng's plan, as if they were not even there. "Let's set aside our disagreement about the political ramifications for a moment. Even then, your whole operation depends on stealth technology that we do not have."

"We have ten operational DF-21 anti-ship missiles," argued Zheng, "as well as the J-20 stealth plane."

"Pure fiction. Propaganda, and you know it," countered Liang. "Do you think me an old fool? Or are you beginning to believe your own lies?" His eyes narrowed. "You are the one who brought that con man to my predecessor back in 2003. He was no more the father of American stealth than I am."

Zheng struggled to keep his features flat. Inside, he winced at the mention of Noshir Gowadia. The American traitor had come to him with a convincing résumé as a lead Northrop Grumman engineer, and Zheng staked his career on pushing the intelligence forward. The previous defense minister, General Chi, authorized billions to develop stealth technology based on Gowadia's designs. None of it worked, not even their new stealth jet. The children who made plastic F-22s for sale to American toy stores could have achieved a similar result. If not for Gowadia's fraud, Zheng might have followed Chi as defense minister. Instead, he had to spend the last eight years sucking up to Liang.

"None of our attempts to acquire American stealth have achieved success," said Liang, folding his arms. "Even the scraps sold to us by the Iranians and the Pakistanis proved worthless."

Zheng clenched his teeth and forced another smile. "I have abandoned my attempts to recruit American engineers or purchase black-market materials," he said, trying to regain control of the debate. "Instead, I have operations under way to acquire the materials directly. I expect favorable results in a matter of days from—"

"You mean your little Arabian diving expedition?" interrupted Liang.

Zheng's forced calm cracked, his nostrils flared.

"Yes, I know about your failed attempt to recover a piece of a downed B-2," said the defense minister. "Do not think for an instant that I achieved this position without my own resources."

Zheng nodded. "Yes, yes. My agents underestimated their American opponents. However, I have already set in motion a new operation that promises success. The missiles are ready. We will have the materials in a matter of days. We could strike within a week, well inside the window of opportunity."

"You do not understand," said Liang, suddenly pounding the desk with his fist. "There will be no strike, no attack on Taiwan!" He stopped and calmed himself, regarding Zheng with an expression of pity. "Not long ago, I recommended you to the Politburo as my replacement. I had such high hopes for you. But now that my retirement is upon me, I find that our philosophies diverge. Your ideas are too rash, too radical. I fear that as defense minister, you would be a political stumbling block rather than a stepping-stone for the people."

Liang stood up from his chair and clasped his hands in front of him. "General Zheng," he said, "it is with deep regret that I must inform you of my decision to recommend General Ho as my replacement instead of you. I will notify the Politburo of this change during our session tomorrow."

Zheng's eyes lit up with fire. He opened his mouth to respond, but Liang held up a warning hand. "You may leave now, Zheng. That is all."

―――――――

Zheng's anger faded into noble sadness as the ministry compound receded in the rearview mirror. Liang's betrayal had infuriated him, but in his heart he always knew this moment would come. Had he not been patient? Had he not done his upmost to prevent this confrontation? He had tried to build an ally instead of an enemy, but Liang had finally forced his hand.

With a heavy heart, Zheng placed a hand on his driver's shoulder. "Han, we must take a slight detour on the way to the air terminal. You know the way."

CHAPTER 19

"Five hundred eighteen . . . five hundred nineteen." David Novak rasped out a number each time his bare right foot crunched into the matted subtropical undergrowth. He knew the guards could be right behind, but he could not move any faster through the thick vegetation. Then his counting faltered. He tripped and fell down a short hill, tumbling into twisted, wet scrub. He lay still. The cacophony of the rain forest assaulted his senses. Flashes of blinding light burst through the canopy above. Moisture from the underbrush soaked his ragged prison uniform. Thorns from the vines tore his flesh. And the birds . . . The birds never ceased their shrill squawking. Yet beneath their incessant chatter, he felt sure that he heard the sound of Chinese soldiers yelling.

Novak could not focus his thoughts. For all the time he'd spent dreaming of escape, he now longed for the quiet solitude of his cell, his home for the last ten years of a twenty-five-year incarceration.

He picked himself up and stumbled forward through the tangled green. "Five hundred twenty-one . . . five hundred twenty-two." Fighting the unrelenting racket in his mind, he prayed to God that he had not miscounted. "Five and a half kilometers south, find the road, then two kilometers due west," he mumbled. With any luck, the cache was still there, still hidden.

Somewhere in his distant youth, the U.S. Air Force Survival, Evasion, Resistance, and Escape school had taught Novak that he had a thirty-inch stride in rough terrain. That translated to a distance of just over one and a half meters each time his right foot hit the ground. When his count reached 660, he knew that he'd traveled about one kilometer, one klick. With that knowledge, he could get to the general vicinity of his objective. After that, he'd have to depend on memory to find the entrance.

Ten years ago, Novak's transfer to Detention Center Twenty-six had been sloppy. The Chinese dumped him into the back of a partially covered troop carrier with just one guard. Then they drove him halfway across Fujian without even bagging his head to restrict his vision. It was the best day of his long stay in China. He caught a glimpse of his wingman, learning for the first time that he was still alive. On top of that, there were no beatings; there was fresh air and green trees; and best of all, he had a full view of the roads and signs leading up to his new home.

With the change in prison came a change in policy.

Hong Mo, as his captors liked to call him, would be allowed a few books to pass the time. The commandant personally delivered a stack of reading material for the American Devil's "reeducation": the writings of Chairman Mao, a collection of speeches by Deng Xiaoping, a Chinese–English dictionary—the content didn't really matter. Novak savored the musty smell of the pages, the feel of the bindings in his hands.

Then he found a map in a book about the forests of Fujian. Suddenly he knew exactly where he was.

Eventually one of the guards noticed the torn page in the middle of the book. The commandant himself administered the beating and found the map stuffed into Novak's pillow. He took away all of the books, as well as the pillow, but he could not purge Novak's memory. The American had what he needed. Using simple navigation and a few modern landmarks, he knew he could make it to the cache.

"Six hundred fifty-nine . . . six hundred sixty." Novak paused at the top of a short ridge. Only half a klick to go before he reached the road. The birds continued their noisy discourse. Their ridiculous screeching echoed in his brain. Flashes of emerald light blasted his swollen eyes. Novak forced himself to concentrate, straining to focus his blurred vision. He thought he could see the trees thinning in the distance. It must be the road. He had traveled five kilometers, according to his pace count. In a half klick, he should reach a wide paved road, and then he could turn west toward his objective.

He set off again. He tried to continue his count, but

concentrating on the numbers made his head pound. The road was down there. He saw it. Couldn't he let go of the count for a while? He continued trudging through the undergrowth in silence, willing his body to move forward on autopilot, but with no pace count to focus on, his mind began to lose its hold on reality. A familiar, faraway voice called to him from beneath the noises of the forest. "Relax, we're almost there."

"Yes," Novak mumbled, "almost there. Relax."

Slowly the flashes of light diminished and the trees darkened. The wide, moist leaves brushing against his hands took on the feel of stiff, brittle branches. His bare feet felt the stiff interior of combat boots instead of the painful press of matted vines. The sound of the birds disappeared entirely. In the quiet, the faraway voice became clear and close, right at his side.

"*Zrelaksować*, David. Relax. We're almost there."

Novak looked to his right. His blurred vision seemed to clear. The jade light of the sweltering subtropical forest became the dark hunter green of a cold pine wood at midnight. A smiling camouflaged face gathered into sharp relief.

"Jozef!" exclaimed Novak. "What are you doing here?"

Novak's best friend seemed aghast at the question. "What? You want to leave me behind?" he asked, the slightest hint of a Slavic accent tainting his speech. He smiled, his white teeth shining like beacons against the muted green and brown of his face paint. "Oh, I get it. You finally figured out how to get Anja all to yourself. Well, it won't be that easy, my friend."

Novak fought through his confusion. He searched his memory until he recognized the scene. Pine trees reaching fifty feet in the air, their trunks bare for the first thirty, springy turf covered in brushwood, conical bushes that resembled miniature Christmas trees, the faint scent of butterscotch suspended in the still, cold air. This was a forest on the northwestern edge of the Soviet Union, and judging from the youthful grin on Starek's face, this was 1986.

A thought in the back of Novak's mind screamed for attention, but the idea was so deeply buried that it seemed hardly a whisper. Then Starek's coaxing voice drowned it out completely. "Where've you been? You've been silent for the last hour."

"Keeping the pace count, I guess," replied Novak in an unsteady voice.

"I told you to let that go," admonished Starek. "I know these woods as well as I know the town I grew up in. Remember? I dodged the Russians here for more than a week last time."

Novak nodded, still looking around. He felt the survival vest on his chest, running his fingers over the bulge of the tightly wound extraction line. He started to gain some clarity. "The Canberra."

"Don't worry," said Starek, laughing and slapping his shoulder. "They'll give us another one." He patted a bulky satchel clipped to the webbing of his harness. "I've got the camera right here. If the Ruskies ever find that wreck, they'll find nothing but charred aluminum."

Novak forced a smile. He remembered now. He knew exactly where he was, and when. They were lucky to be alive. They'd flown a photoreconnaissance mission out of the Agency's forward base in northern Poland, the fourteenth mission of Operation Remote Icon.

Six RB-57F Canberras ran low-altitude recon missions as deep into Red territory as Moscow. The aircraft had been hidden in Poland since the late sixties. Back then, they flew at their design altitude, above eighty thousand feet. But the Reds' advanced surface-to-air missile network had forced them out of business. For the next twenty years, the Canberras stayed in mothballs, guarded by the Polish resistance. With the expansions in Soviet intelligence and the advancement of their radar technology, no one at the CIA was crazy enough to try reviving an air operation based behind the Iron Curtain. But the eighties brought with them the most ostentatious DCI in Agency history. He conceived a plan to fly the high-altitude birds at a few hundred feet, well below the radar.

The plan worked, mostly. Unfortunately, the pilots had to climb higher once in a while to get a better photo.

Novak and Starek always planned their missions to minimize the chance of a radar lock, but this time a Russian station was pointing at the right place at the right time. Their Canberra got caught on radar.

The missile took out the left engine and most of their hydraulics. They'd been able to limp away but not far enough. They ejected one hundred klicks from the Belarusian border—on the Russian side. Now the Canberra smoldered in a narrow valley, and six hundred klicks of enemy territory stood between them and the dubious safety of their secret HQ in Poland.

Novak reached up and felt the freshly crusted blood where the parachute strap had grazed his neck. Maybe the twenty-five-year Chinese ordeal was just a dream. Maybe he was in shock from the ejection. What did he care about the Chinese anyway? He was a Russian specialist.

"We just have to make it to the extraction point," Starek interrupted him again, his voice chipper. "I can't wait to use the cable again. It's foolproof. The chopper drops the line, we clip on, and *woosh!*" He waved his arms. "We're birdmen!"

Starek had already tested the UH-1 Huey's extraction cable once. He went down during a scout mission in a one-man light aircraft. Novak remembered his worst fears coming true as he listened to his friend's last radio call at HQ. Starek made a mayday call, and then the radio went dead. He was down behind enemy lines for more than a week before they heard from him again. Novak flew the chopper for the rescue mission, and Starek became the first Remote Icon operative to pull what the Agency called a Peter Pan, flying over enemy territory, suspended from a line beneath a rescue chopper.

"It doesn't seem that simple to me," argued Novak. "It also sounds painful," he added with a smile, letting go of his thoughts and succumbing to his friend's engaging banter.

"Nonsense," replied Starek. "In fact, the pickup is less jarring than the opening shock of a parachute. You took a worse beating a few hours ago."

Novak chuckled. "I'll believe it when I feel it."

"I don't care if it breaks my pelvis." Starek pulled his flight jacket close around his neck. "I'll just be happy to get out of this cold, depressing forest. As soon as we get home, I'm going to light a fire in the barracks' hearth. Hang the Agency's curfew."

"Yes. Home," Novak repeated. Not so much home as . . . her.

Remote Icon ran on Polish blood. A few Americans held administrative positions, including Wright, the supervisor in charge, but too many Americans living and working behind the Iron Curtain would draw unwanted attention to an operation that was already outrageously dangerous. The Agency left most of the grunt work to Polish nationals. In fact, Starek and Novak were the only Americans out of eight pilots flying for the operation. They'd been chosen for the assignment because of their Slavic backgrounds. Novak was born in the Midwest, the only child of Polish immigrants. Starek's parents were Czechoslovakian defectors.

Three days after Novak and Starek arrived at the base, Wright brought in a gaggle of Polish girls to process the film from the recon runs. One of the new recruits caught Novak's eye. Tall and slender, with strawberry-blond hair that fell in front of her round-rimmed glasses, Anja struck Novak as the archetype of an earthbound angel. He fell in love.

So did Starek.

For the last few months, the American pilots' competition for Anja's affections had grown from a friendly game into a friendship-testing rivalry. But lately Novak had gained the upper hand. The night before they left on this mission, he'd even tasted the cool, wet sweetness of her lips. Now he struggled to decide how best to break the news to Starek, afraid that he might lose his closest friend.

Casual conversation fell away as Novak and Starek concentrated on reaching their objective. Occasionally, Starek would pause, pull a wrinkled fabric map from his vest, and orient it with his compass. Each time he nodded his head knowingly. "Right where I thought we were," he'd say. "We're almost there."

Just as Novak began to question the sanity of Starek's oft-repeated claim, the tall pines abruptly stopped. The pilots stood on the edge of a small lake. Still and smooth as a garden pool, the dark water held the moonless sky in perfect reflection. Novak felt that if he leapt forward into the water he might fall endlessly downward toward the tiny stars below.

"I told you we were almost there," said Starek, grinning again. He dug a piece of the soft turf away with his knife and lit an evasion fire cube, a block of white chemical that burned with almost no visible flame. He warmed his hands and looked out across the water. "Like I said before, it won't hurt as much as the opening shock we got from the parachutes."

"I'm not as concerned about the jolt as I am about those," said Novak, pointing at the tall trees on the opposite side of the lake.

"Oh, we'll clear them," said Starek. He grinned impishly. "Assuming the chopper pilot is paying attention."

A half hour later, they heard the distinct pound of a

helicopter beating the air into submission. Starek stood up, stomping out the fire cube and replacing the piece of turf to hide its telltale mark. "Here he comes. Let the cable hit the ground before you grab it, or the static from the rotor blades will shock you like a lightning bolt."

As the chopper came into view over the trees across the lake, Novak removed the two-man line from his kit. He unraveled the twenty-foot cord and hooked one end to his harness with a locking D-ring. Then he tossed the other end to his friend.

"You know, she told me about last night," said Starek.

Beneath the noise of the UH-1, Novak could not gauge Starek's tone. Was that forgiveness or malice?

He saw the line drop from the chopper and splash into the lake. Then the pilot skillfully brought it to the shore-line. Novak ran over and grabbed it, pulling hand over hand until the end came out of the water. Just as he latched the hook to his harness, his radio beeped.

"Alpha One, ready," said a distant voice.

Novak fumbled with the radio hanging from his vest and then held the handset to his lips. "Alpha Two, ready."

The chopper started to rise, rapidly taking up the slack in the cable. The rotor noise became louder as the pilot fought for altitude. Novak looked at his friend.

Starek teased, waving the D-ring on his end of the cord as if he were not going to hook up. As Novak's feet left the ground, Starek beamed at him with his shining white smile. *You win*, he mouthed. Then he clicked the D-ring into place.

Novak felt a tremendous jerk as Starek was caught up

into the air with him. He looked below, but he could not see his friend, only the infinite starry depth of the lake. He looked up. The chopper had disappeared as well. He felt suspended in space.

The engine noise became deafening. As Novak reached up to cover his ears, the sound changed from the steady thump of rotor blades to the deep whine of a heavy truck. Suddenly a horn blared and the cold and darkness gave way to heat and blinding light. He fell. His knees hit rough, unyielding pavement, and pain shocked his body. Instinctively, he rolled. A huge tractor-trailer flew by, just missing him as he fell down an embankment into thorny wet vines.

Novak looked down at his soaked prison uniform. The grime covering his knees mixed with fresh blood. A few feet up the embankment, another vehicle drove past. His body stewed in the unmistakable wet heat of the Fujian rain forest. He lifted a hand and felt the old scar on his neck, left by a stray parachute strap during his ejection over Russia twenty-seven years ago. He let out a guttural scream.

Novak struggled to his feet amid the twisted scrub, panting and defeated. After a while he looked up at the sun, trying to determine north from south. His vision blurred. The birds resumed their incessant screeching. Finally, he turned to a heading that he could only hope was west. Pain wracked his brain. He forced himself to concentrate. Slowly, he stepped forward. "One . . ."

CHAPTER 20

Try as he might, Nick could not focus on his assailant. He fought wildly, but his movements felt slow and languid in the water. The hostile did not suffer from the same restriction. He moved so fast that he seemed a blur, a ghost that Nick could not touch. Nick lost his bearings; he could not distinguish up from down. In the murky water, he could see neither the surface above nor the silt-covered floor below. Something grabbed his left arm from behind, but the attacker remained in front of him. Was there another? He couldn't turn around. He was paralyzed, frozen. The hostile drew in close. He wore a mirrored full-length diving mask. For a moment, the face staring back at Nick was his own, but then his reflection twisted into someone else: Danny Sharp.

Suddenly the assailant brandished a blade. With an agonizing effort, Nick freed his left arm, but the man shoved the knife into his shoulder before he could stop the attack. Pain shocked his body. Nick grabbed the assailant's forearm and wrenched it away, pulling the knife out of his shoulder. The image of Danny in the mirrored mask let out a horrible scream.

"Ow! Let go!" yelled Katy Baron. "Wake up and let go, you big idiot!"

Danny's face dissolved, replaced by Nick's wife, Katy. Her hazel eyes were filled with anguish. He lay in his own bed, at their home near Chapel Point, Maryland. The comforter and sheets lay piled about him, soaked with sweat. Pain still throbbed in his shoulder. Shaking, he quickly released his death grip on Katy's arm. She retreated to the other side of the bed. Tears trickled down her beautiful face.

"What's wrong with you?" Katy asked through her tears. "You could have broken my arm."

Nick untangled himself from the sheets and assessed his shoulder. Recalling the nightmare, he realized that his arm had been caught up in the sheets and that he'd strained it during his thrashing. At least it wasn't dislocated this time. "Are you okay?" he asked, rubbing and rotating his shoulder.

"No, I'm not okay. You almost broke my arm."

Nick hung his head. "I'm sorry, sweetheart. I was having a nightmare."

"You say that as if you didn't have one almost every night. They're getting worse, Nick. Look at you. You almost dislocated your own shoulder in your sleep. Do you realize how messed up that is?"

"Baby, I think you're overreacting."

"Overreacting?" She held up her forearm for her husband to see. Red marks had formed in the shape of Nick's fingertips. They would surely become bruises. "I have more like these. My doctor is starting to ask questions. How do I explain this? Some husbands only beat their wives when they're drunk. Mine only beats me when he's asleep." She started to cry again. "There was a time when I couldn't sleep while you were away because I didn't feel safe. Now I can't sleep when you're home for the same reason."

Nick walked around the bed and tried to comfort his wife, but she backed away from him and shook her head. "Just give me a minute, okay?"

He sat down in frustration as she went into the bathroom to splash water on her face. He watched her lean into the mirror to fuss over her puffy eyes. She had no reason to; she was gorgeous, even when she'd been crying. Her long brown hair fell to one side of her beautiful neck. She wore a silk nightgown that barely came down to the middle of her slender thighs, taut because she was pushed up on her cute little toes. He wished that he hadn't just ruined the mood. The baby was still sleeping.

"You were gone an extra couple of days," she said, clearly trying to change the subject, like she always did after an episode like this one.

"Yeah. You know how military airlift can be, especially in and out of that region."

"Uh-huh," she said. "That seems to happen a lot lately."

Nick winced. She was avoiding one fight by starting another. He had told Katy that he'd been working in the bomber planning cell at Bagram Airfield, Afghanistan, the Triple Seven's standing cover story for field operations. "Like I said, babe, that region is a pain to get in and out of. The guys who are doing the fighting take priority."

Katy returned from the bathroom. Instead of sitting down next to Nick, she crawled onto the bed, leaning her back against an oversized pillow and pulling the comforter up to her waist. "Speaking of the guys doing the fighting," she said, "I was telling Jennifer about your nightmare problem, and she said that it sounded like PTSD. Of course, I told her that didn't make sense, because you're a planner. You're not doing any fighting." Her last phrase hung in the air between them, more of an accusation than a statement.

Katy's eyes drifted down over his body. Sitting there in his underwear, Nick suddenly felt exposed. She wasn't assessing his muscular form in any sensual way; she was examining the scars on his legs and torso, including the fresh stitches in his right arm.

"I see you have a new one," she said, pointing at the wound as if it were a collar with lipstick on it. "You got home so late last night that I didn't notice it. What happened this time?"

"I've told you about Bagram before," said Nick, using the story he'd rehearsed during the long flight home. "It's always under construction. I tried to take a shortcut to the base exchange and tripped over some scraps. I cut my arm on a piece of metal."

Katy cocked her head to one side. "You know, it's weird. You can stand on that rickety stool in the kitchen to change a lightbulb and then hop down like a cat. You can stand in our rowboat on the river without toppling us over. You can even do those creepy tricks with your knives, flipping them all around your hands like a Vegas magician." She gave him a sarcastic shrug. "But every time you leave the house, you become as clumsy as a teenager whose legs have outgrown his brain."

"That's not true," countered Nick, standing up. He turned slightly, pulling up the left leg of his boxer briefs to reveal two round scars. "Remember? These were from a roadside bomb north of Kabul. Clumsiness had nothing to do with it. I wasn't even driving." In truth, the wounds in his upper thigh were souvenirs from a gun battle with drug dealers in South America. At least, *he* considered the wounds to be in his upper thigh. Drake liked to say that he got shot in the butt.

Nick's attempt at humor had the opposite effect. Katy threw up her hands. "That's right, a roadside bomb. Thanks for reminding me. So when is Drake going to call and tell me that you've been in a helicopter crash like Danny?"

A cry came from the room across the hallway. Katy closed her eyes and let out a sigh. "He's up." She shoved Nick away and stood up, grabbing a robe that was slung over the rail of their treadmill. "We'll finish this later. I'm going to go and get him so that he can at least get a glimpse of his father before you disappear again." She paused at the bedroom door and rubbed her arm. "Try not to damage him. He's even more fragile than I am." Then she walked out of the room.

CHAPTER 21

Nick roared up Route 301 at twenty over the limit, losing himself in the steady resonance of his Mustang's 440 horsepower, supercharged engine. He tensed his forearms against the long curve entering St. Charles. He could feel every groove in the pavement, every tiny slip as the rear end tried to shift to the outside. His lovingly restored '67 Shelby GT350 was loud, hot, and a handful in the turns, but Nick liked her that way. Engineers with thick, horn-rimmed glasses designed her back when men were men and muscle cars actually required muscle to drive. Not like today's comfort-built sports "coupés," made for a generation of wannabe tough guys with personal trainers and an overdeveloped sense of entitlement.

Beneath the deep vibrato of the forty-year-old V8, Nick let his subconscious wander, drifting about in a tangled forest of memories. Somewhere in that dark confusion was the answer. There had to be a connection. The Triple Seven's first mission went horribly wrong. This mission had skirted the edge of failure. The fact that they both revolved around the same doomed stealth bomber could not be a coincidence.

Bad luck plagued their first mission from the beginning. Dream Catcher's testing wasn't complete, but the White House sent them in anyway. The results were devastating: one experimental aircraft destroyed, one multibillion-dollar stealth bomber lying on the bottom of the Persian Gulf, and Saddam Hussein still at large, fueling the insurgent effort for another nine months.

Ten years.

Ten years of making up for that first, botched mission. Ten years of training and fighting, of turning the Triple Seven Chase from a quiet embarrassment into the most effective clandestine unit in the DoD. Now it had all come full circle, and both he and Drake were almost killed. Again.

Nick felt sure that there was something more sinister than Murphy's Law at play here, but no one else could see it. Even Walker, with his legendary paranoia, had dismissed the notion immediately.

The sight of red and blue lights ahead brought Nick's attention back to the road. One of Prince George's County's finest had a little red Miata pinned down on the shoulder. Nick eased off the accelerator and moved over, waving to the officer. The cop stared at the Shelby as he drove by, wearing the expression of a fisherman who'd just pulled a two-pound perch out of the lake, only to watch the fifteen-pound bass swim away.

Nick parked the Mustang near a large hangar facility on the north side of the Joint Base Andrews Golf Course and entered the low adjoining office building. He threaded his way through narrow corridors, silent except for the sound of his heels echoing off the cheap tile floor. At the end of one particularly claustrophobic hallway, he stopped in front of a black door. A dim fluorescent light flickered lazily overhead. A small red and white sign on the door read:

R7

Cleared Personnel Only

Lethal Force Is Authorized

Nick swiped his access card and punched in his code. The door popped open with a hiss. He stepped into a small, circular chamber, and the door closed behind him. Then the wall rotated 180 degrees, and the chamber started descending. Five stories beneath the airfield, the elevator door opened into the main command center of Romeo Seven.

Given just one word to describe the home of the Triple Seven Chase, Nick would have chosen *excessive*. No one knew how Walker got the funding to reopen and renovate a defunct presidential bunker, and no one ever asked, but their little covert unit had the benefit of a two-story-tall command center with floor-to-ceiling screens and a platoon of fully stocked workstations, most of which were empty. They also had several large offices, a lab for Scott, bunk rooms, a well-stocked galley, a gym, and their very own freshwater supply. The taxpayers spared no expense.

"Baron!" Colonel Walker came barreling across the floor, his voice unnecessarily loud in the quiet room. He nimbly weaved his way through a line of crescent-shaped workstations, followed by a young man carrying a clipboard. The kid wore the same uniform that Nick and Walker wore, khakis and a black golf shirt, but Nick had never seen him before.

"Merry Christmas, Baron," said Walker, his ever-present scowl almost joyful in its most congenial mode. "Santa brought you a brand-new toy."

Nick surveyed the new recruit. He looked young, too young to be the professional he'd asked for. "Sir, there are so many things wrong with what you just said that I don't know where to begin."

Walker waved off the comment. "This is Ethan Quinn, your newest field man. He's a Special Tactics pararescueman, fresh from the pipeline."

"What's on the clipboard, junior?" asked Nick, shaking the kid's outstretched hand. He could see from the taut smile on Quinn's face that he did not like being called junior, or likened to a new toy for that matter. His eyes carried the usual cockiness of a greenhorn operator, but there was something else, something that Nick couldn't put his finger on.

Quinn glanced down at the stack of papers that threatened to overwhelm his clipboard. "Major Merigold gave me all of the forms for processing into the Triple Seven."

"*Major Merigold* gave you the forms?"

"Yes, sir. He said I needed to get them done now if I want to be part of the test mission tonight."

Nick nodded, biting his tongue to keep from laughing. Drake loved to prank newcomers to Romeo Seven, usually computer clerks and intelligence technicians, by slipping a pile of arbitrary forms into their first-day paperwork. Most recruits figured out the joke when they reached the application for pet insurance, but two of the computer nerds had actually completed the entire application for membership in the Justice League of America. "Um . . . right. Of course," said Nick. "You'd better get to it then."

Quinn dutiful wandered off to find a desk, and Nick leaned in closer to Walker. "Sir, if you have a few minutes, I'd like to revisit our conversation about security." Despite his low tone, Nick's words seemed to reverberate off the twenty-four-foot-high walls. As if by the cue of a conductor's wand, the handful of clerks and technicians ceased chatting and clicking all at once. Every ear in the place turned discreetly in his direction.

The colonel's scowl shifted from congenial to a look of deep frustration, bordering on real anger. To add insult to his rebuke, he ignored Nick's attempt to mask the topic. "I told you before," he said in a low, threatening tone, "there is no leak. We can't charter a huge research vessel and drive it into the Persian Gulf without tripping a few radars. Your little escapade in Kuwait City turned up nothing. The attackers were low-level opportunists. They tried, you took them out, end of story, case closed."

"But . . ."

"I said case closed," repeated Walker, louder and with undeniable finality. He turned and headed for the stairs to his glass-walled office, perched at the rear of the giant command center. "Get back to work. All of you."

Romeo Seven's tiny floor staff suddenly found renewed interest in their computer screens. Still, as Nick retreated to his office through the briar patch of desks and computers, he could feel the weight of ten sets of eyes intentionally not looking at him.

Nick sat down at his computer and called up the objectives for the final Wraith test mission. He tried to focus on the flight, to visualize the maneuvers, but he couldn't clear the thoughts of a leak from his mind.

"Knock, knock." Drake appeared at Nick's office door, carrying a brown file in his hands. "You trying to give the old man a heart attack?"

Nick swiveled away from his computer and looked up at his teammate. "I think we might have a serious security problem."

"You mean you think we have a mole," observed Drake. He set the file down on a shelf and then flopped down on Nick's couch, kicking his heels up onto the arm. "You can't be serious."

"I think someone has been trying to get their hands on a stealth aircraft."

"Everybody is trying to get their hands on a stealth aircraft."

Nick leaned back in his chair and put his hands behind his head, stretching his legs out in front of him and crossing his ankles. "Yeah, but what if the problems we had ten years ago weren't just Murphy's Law in overdrive? What if we actually had a mole? Our return to Iraq might have awakened a sleeper within our own network." He tilted his head back and searched the ceiling tiles for an answer. "I've been trying to remember everyone who was on our crew back then. You know, to match up the lists and find out how many people from the old days were involved in this mission."

"It's got to be a short list," offered Drake. "You, me, and Heldner, for starters. And what about Walker?"

"Very funny. Why would he hide the bomber for ten years and then bring in an enemy team when we were there to stop them?"

"Maybe he was trying to have you killed," said Drake with a grin. "He doesn't like you that much."

"But you were almost killed too."

Drake shrugged. "He doesn't like me at all."

Nick laughed, but then another name popped into his mind from the Dream Catcher mission. "What about your girlfriend?" he asked. "Amanda was there too, running Dream Catcher's propulsion team. And she works for us now." Then he shook his head, dismissing the idea. "But Amanda didn't know about this op."

"Right. Good point. Amanda didn't know," said Drake, sitting up and swinging his feet to the floor.

Nick caught an uneasy twist in his friend's tone. He raised an eyebrow. "You didn't tell your girlfriend that you were heading out to the Persian Gulf, did you?"

Drake became defensive. "Whoa, back off, Nancy

Drew. Even if I did tell her, she's our number one technology consultant. She's got plenty of clearance. And, anyway, Amanda is about to join the squadron permanently to lead the Wraith support team." His cheeks flushed. "She loves this squadron. She's no traitor."

Nick held up his hands. "All right, take it easy. It was a dumb question."

Drake nodded. "Yes, yes it was. And you're forgiven . . . again." He picked up the file and thrust it toward Nick. "Here."

"What's this?"

"It's the background on our new recruit. I thought you might find it interesting."

Nick accepted the file. "The kid said something about being part of the test tonight," he said, studying the picture clipped to the front of the folder. "Do you know anything about that?"

"He's going to be our test dummy for the new Skyhook system."

Nick looked up abruptly, giving his friend a wary look. "Does he understand the risks?"

Drake stood and raised his hands in the air, as if absolving himself of responsibility. "The colonel approved it," he said, turning to leave. He paused in the doorway and looked back. "Don't work too long, boss. You need to go home and get some rest before tonight's mission. You're not Superman, you know."

Nick nodded and waved Drake away with a few flicks of his hand. Then he laid the folder on his desk and studied the picture of Quinn again, trying to grasp what he saw earlier in those green eyes. "Okay, kid," he said, "what's your story?"

He opened the file to the first page. The bold print at the top of the paper read RECORD OF PUNISHMENT FOR OFFENSES UNDER THE UNIFORM CODE OF MILITARY JUSTICE.

Nick dropped his forehead into his hand. "You've got to be kidding me."

CHAPTER 22

Defense Minister Liang heard the sharp click of narrow heels marching across the worn tile floor of his office. He looked up expectantly and smiled to see Mei, his secretary, approaching. Then he noticed the young PLA guard at the door looking in his direction. The smile flattened into his usual, expressionless military veneer. "Yes, Mei?"

"Here are both generals' files," replied Mei, bowing slightly as she placed two manila folders on the minister's desk.

Liang let his eyes drift down from her long elegant neck to her narrow waistline and back up to her lightly rouged lips. Mei's eyes flashed up to meet his, and a brief smile crossed her small mouth. Then she cast them down again. "Will that be all, Minister Liang?" she asked.

Mei's question alerted Liang that he had paused a bit

too long. "Er . . . yes. That will be all, Mei," he responded awkwardly. "It is late. You may go if you wish."

Mei bowed again, catching Liang's eyes once more. "Yes, Minister. Thank you."

Liang glanced at the guard, but the young man only seemed interested in Mei, mesmerized by her leisurely retreat from the office. How could he blame him?

He turned his attention to the files on his desk, opening the first to take one last look at the service history of General Zheng Ju-long. What a distinguished and remarkable career. What a shame.

He slowly closed the folder. Despite his affection for the man, Liang could not justify maintaining his recommendation for Zheng as the next minister of defense. He had grown too ambitious, too reckless. Liang could not risk passing his legacy to a man who could easily lead China into the biggest political disaster of his generation, or worse.

He opened the other file. General Ho Geming had also served with distinction. His record boasted numerous accolades, as well as postgraduate degrees in electrical and aerodynamic engineering. Ho had given ardent support to the failed J-20 stealth aircraft program, but so had many. And his enthusiasm in the endeavor proved his loyalty. At the bottom of the file, Liang found the memo Mei had prepared for the Politburo, expressing Liang's endorsement of General Ho as his successor. He lifted a pen, paused a moment longer, and then signed his name.

On the way out of his office, Liang patted the guard on the shoulder. "You are a good guard, a good soldier," he said in a fatherly voice. "I am sure that you have many ambitions beyond standing watch over an old man. I appreciate your service, but you may go home now." He had no desire for state security to follow him through his evening activities.

Liang's driver waited for him by the elevators in the Defense Ministry's marble lobby. He crushed out his cigarette in the white sand of an ashtray. "Ready to go, boss?" His voice echoed in the wide, empty reception area.

"Chu," said Liang as they walked into the parking garage. "Thank you for your patience. Perhaps you could humor me once again?"

The young man bowed. A smile tugged at the corners of his mouth. He could not contain his anticipation. "Would you like me to accompany you, Minister Liang?"

Liang smiled. "No, Chu. I prefer the solace that my long drive provides. You may go for the evening. Meet me here first thing in the morning."

Chu did not wait for the minister to change his mind. "Thank you, boss," he said, bowing again. Then he hastily retreated to his bicycle, clearly excited to have a free evening with his friends.

Liang watched his driver pedal away and then unlocked his sedan. He genuinely enjoyed driving his own vehicle, despite the Politburo's insistence to the contrary. In reality, however, the innocent quirk provided the perfect cover for his true objective: Mei.

Liang's loneliness had engulfed him after the death of his wife, Lin. Forty-three years of marriage, of constant companionship, had left him unable to deal with the emptiness of life's winter. Mei filled the void. He could not imagine that she really loved him, but her pretense made life bearable.

The Politburo frowned on the slightest image of indecency, no matter how innocent. The Party expected him to play the stately widower. They would never approve of his relationship with Mei. So be it. With his considerable resources, this small impropriety, this small comfort, was easy to hide.

Liang knew from the look they'd shared earlier that Mei would be waiting at the hotel. He had a long-standing and well-funded agreement with the proprietor. The room belonged to him; he had no need to check in or out. Long ago, he had presented Mei with her own key so that she could arrive separately.

As he turned the sedan toward the north side of town, Liang popped open the glove box. Customarily, he made a call on his unregistered cell to let Mei know that he was on his way. He found the illegal phone to be a necessary evil; he certainly could not count on the privacy of the state-issued phone in his briefcase.

After fishing around for a few moments, he leaned over and glanced into the compartment. A horn blared. He jerked the wheel and swerved back toward his own lane. Bright headlights flashed across his vision. After straightening the wheel and reseating his spectacles, Liang glanced quickly around the car. The cell was not there. He gave up the search. Wrecking a car that he should not be driving, while searching for a phone he should not have, on his way to meet a woman he should not be seeing, might prove difficult to explain. He smiled at his own foolishness and let it go.

No clerk sat behind the hotel registry desk. No customers lounged on the gaudy red and gold fabric furniture in the lobby. Liang hurried through anyway. A night clerk might appear and recognize him, and young clerks were prone to gossip.

On the sixth floor, he quickly pressed himself into the room. "Mei," he called as he quietly closed the door. He heard the muted sound of running water. The bathroom light was on. "Mei," he called again, a little louder this time. Mei still did not respond. As he crossed the room, Liang noticed a wheelchair in the corner. He barely had time to wonder what it was doing there before a stabbing pain shot through his lower back.

Liang saw no one, but a smooth, icy voice whispered in his ear, "It is best not to fight it." He felt the life leaving his limbs. He could not move. Strong arms dragged him to the corner and lowered him into the wheelchair. Then a man with a scar above his left eye stepped into view. "Please relax. The drug has already taken hold. I am told that fighting its effects only causes pain."

"Mei," said Liang weakly, his ability to speak slipping away.

"Mei is not here." The man held up Liang's unregistered cell phone with a gloved hand and waved it for the minister to see. "Clearly, there are no secrets, Defense Minister Liang." He did not smirk. Despite the circumstances, he seemed to regard the minister with deep respect. "I removed this from your car earlier in the day.

A short while ago, I sent a text to your beloved Mei, expressing your desire to rest at home this evening. I offered an apology and the promise of a future rendez-vous. It will comfort you to know that Mei is unharmed and will remain so as long as she does not unexpectedly appear. I trust that she will not."

Why? Liang tried to form the words on his lips but only received pain for his effort. His head drooped awkwardly to one side. His vision began to fail.

"My apologies," said the scarred man. "The drug affects nearly all of your muscles, including the ciliary muscles that focus your eyes. They are the last to fail, but they will fail completely."

The last thing that Liang saw was a blurred vision of his briefcase, held open by the mysterious attacker.

"I greatly appreciate your bringing these files out of the ministry for me. Retrieving them from within the secure confines of your office might have proved impossible."

Why? The question still lingered in Liang's mind, but soon it too drifted out of focus. Then there was nothing but darkness and the ever-slowing pound of his heartbeat.

———

Wūlóng casually but smartly pushed the wheelchair through the empty hotel lobby. He had affixed a pillowed support to the backrest for the defense minister's head. He had also placed a surgical mask over the minister's face and a blanket over his body up to the neck.

Liang had parked in a dark corner of the garage, and Wūlóng thanked him for the courtesy of the relative concealment as he struggled to get the minister's body into the trunk. Before he closed the lid, he risked a quick check of the carotid artery. He found a weak but satisfactory pulse.

A half hour later, Wūlóng slowed to a stop a few meters short of a sharp bend in the road, not far from the defense minister's home in the hills west of Beijing. He had scouted the site earlier in the day. The guardrail appeared weak, the cliff face sheer. The sparse vegetation promised little impediment to the sedan's momentum. The long drop to the rocks below would ensure trauma sufficient to satisfy the state's coroner.

"Your moment has come, Minister Liang," said Wūlóng as he opened the trunk. Liang's eyes were open. His pupils shifted toward the assassin. Wūlóng's scarred brow creased at the unexpected movement. "I see the drug is beginning to wear off. We have little time." He set up the chair and then pulled Liang from the trunk. As he wheeled the minister to the driver's-side door, Liang's slumped head lifted a fraction of an inch. "Yes. Time is definitely short."

Wūlóng slipped a small capsule into the gas tank. The tiny charge would serve as a fuse upon impact, a method of ensuring the correct result. With sedans like this one, he could never count on an explosion, no matter how forceful the crash. Then he lifted Liang into the driver's seat. With great care, he positioned the minister's limp arms so that his wrists rested on the spokes of the steering wheel. "You must hold this steady for me," he said.

As Wūlóng turned the key to crank the engine, Liang let out a low but insistent groan. The assassin examined his eyes. They looked surprisingly alert. "I must say, Minister, that you are showing an impressive recovery from the drug. Most people would not find their voice for at least another hour. You should be very proud."

He cast a final glance around the sedan's interior. Then he placed Liang's foot on the accelerator and jumped back. The engine revved. As the spinning tires gained purchase, the car lurched forward toward the cliff and the driver's-side door slammed shut.

Wūlóng immediately turned away and started walking, not bothering to look back when the fireball erupted from below the cliff. He needed to get out of the area quickly. Besides, he had to catch a flight to America.

CHAPTER 23

Nick pulled his Mustang into the circular driveway of his home near Chapel Point. He turned the engine off and opened the door, but he did not get out of the car. A tiny breath of cool air drifted around the house, a taste of the refreshing breeze blowing over the Port Tobacco River, just fifty feet from his back porch. He needed that breeze, if only he could get through the house and onto the porch without a fight. He just needed a couple of hours to relax and rest before tonight's mission.

He leaned back in his seat and surveyed the beautiful stone facade of his country-style house, but its high-peaked roof and three-car garage only reminded him that the mortgage was eating him alive. Thinking they needed a big place to raise a family, he and Katy had bitten off way more than they could chew. Now they were trapped.

In this economy, there was no way to unload a house this size, and any time he brought it up, the discussion ended in another fight. He found it easier to just suck it up and pay the monthly bill.

As Nick's eyes drifted across the front door, he noticed that it stood open a few inches. That was odd. Katy always kept that door locked, even when she was home. He checked the garage. He could just see her Honda Civic through the window. There were no other vehicles in the driveway.

A hundred scenarios flashed through Nick's mind. A Chinese assassin, a drug cartel hit man . . . If the Triple Seven Chase had a leak, the list of killers that might show up at his doorstep would be long and terrifying.

Leaving the Mustang open, he crept silently onto the porch, pausing at the door to remove the double-edged knife from the holster at his ankle. He flipped it around to conceal the blade against his forearm. Then he pushed the door open and stepped into the house.

The wide foyer seemed empty. No movement in the study, no one darting across the landing beyond the vaulted entry. Only one thing caught his attention as out of place: an unopened package sat on the credenza at the base of the stairs. Nick tuned his senses. Just above the hum of the air-conditioning, he heard the quiet rush of running water coming from the master suite. He relaxed. Katy must have opened the door to receive a delivery and then forgotten to lock it. With the exhaustion of the new baby, she seemed to miss little details like that more and more.

Just as Nick turned to go and lock up the Mustang, he

heard a cabinet door close. His head snapped toward the sound. It had come from the kitchen. If Katy was up there, taking a bath, then she certainly wasn't down here making a sandwich. He brought his knife to the ready.

The house had an open kitchen, denying him any real cover if he approached from the living room. Instead, Nick turned and crept through the dining room. He coiled his body, crouching low, placing each step with purpose. His feet never crossed as he moved, keeping his center of gravity grounded, ready for an unseen attack. He picked up a crystal tumbler from the dining-room table as he passed and then made his way into the butler's pantry, the short entryway to the kitchen.

Silverware rattled as a drawer opened and closed. The intruder was still in there. Kneeling in the shadow of the pantry, Nick held the octagonal tumbler out from the corner, using it as a mirror. In the distorted reflection, he could see the intruder's hand and the glint of a blade.

Nick burst into the kitchen, extending his knife in a forward thrust. His target yelped in terror. Her knife clattered to the floor. Nick slammed his hand against the island to stop his momentum, just in time to prevent his blade from plunging into the flawless skin at the base of his wife's elegant neck.

Katy clutched the fold of the bath towel she was wrapped in with one hand and grabbed the counter behind her with the other. All of the color had drained from her face. She gasped for air as if she had been punched in the chest.

With wide eyes, Nick looked from his boot knife to

his wife and back again, trying to grasp what had just happened. He had jumped past every level of reason and deduction, straight to deadly action, and almost killed the woman he loved. What was happening to him? Was he really that paranoid?

With one deft movement, he tucked the blade into its sheath and then pushed his palms out toward Katy, as if that would stop the fury he could see building behind her horrified eyes. "Don't freak out, baby," he protested. "Please don't freak out."

"What is wrong with you, Nick?" she demanded as soon as she was able to speak.

"I thought you were upstairs. I heard a noise in the kitchen and I assumed the worst." He glanced down at the knife on the floor. "I saw a weapon."

Katy knelt down and picked up the pewter-handled carving knife. She waved it at Nick. "You saw a *utensil*!"

For the first time, Nick noticed the half-carved ham sitting on the island, along with a plate and a loaf of bread.

"Your son has not given me a moment's rest all day," said Katy, shaking the knife at Nick, forcing him to back away. "I finally got him to lie down, and I thought I could get a snack and a bath and feel like a normal human being again. Clearly, that was too much to hope for!"

An insistent wail erupted from upstairs.

"And now he's awake." She jammed the carving knife down into the ham, put her hands on her hips, and glared at Nick. "Well?"

Nick was at a loss. "Well what?"

"Well, go and get him," she said, gesturing toward the

stairs. "I'm going to take my bath and eat my sandwich. And don't you come knocking, because I don't think I can bear the sight of you for a while."

———

"Nick and Katy are the happiest, most well-adjusted couple we know." Amanda Navistrova took the seat that Drake held for her, tugging her khaki skirt around her tan thighs. "You just caught Nick on a bad day."

Drake took his own seat at the table and rested his arm on the white linen to take Amanda's waiting hand. She looked stunning. No, she had looked stunning when he picked her up from Northrop Grumman's D.C. headquarters, even with her hair pulled back and her blue eyes hidden behind glasses. Now that she'd had a chance to "freshen up," letting her blond curls fall down around her shoulders and replacing her glasses with contacts, she looked absolutely gorgeous. She could have been a runway model. Of course, there weren't too many runway models who could have been aerodynamic propulsion engineers with two degrees from MIT.

Drake ordered their drinks from the waiter and then turned his attention back to his date. "You haven't seen them together in a few weeks." He leaned forward. "Talk about your Shock and Awe. Between the strain of the baby and Nick's refusal to acknowledge his PTSD, I don't think they're going to make it."

"Nick does not have PTSD," argued Amanda. "He just has nightmares."

Drake shook his head as he buttered a piece of bread.

He took a bite and then shook the half-eaten piece at Amanda. "You should have seen him trying to sleep on this last mission," he said between chews. "Have I told you about his zombie voice?"

Amanda grimaced. She gently took Drake's hand and guided the bread down to his plate. "Keep your voice down. He doesn't know that you told me you were going to Kuwait, does he?"

Drake swallowed his bread. "Of course not. Besides, you didn't know why I was going. I didn't even know."

Amanda looked down at her hands.

"You figured it out?" asked Drake.

She scrunched up her nose. "I had an inkling. I never felt like Walker was giving us the full story about the salvage. But I always figured Nick was in the dark with the rest of us."

"It's not that he doesn't trust you," said Drake, lowering his voice to a whisper. "He loves you like a little sister. It's just that he's become even crazier about need-to-know than Walker is."

Amanda nodded knowingly. "I don't blame him, but enough about Nick and Katy. Let's focus on us now. We only have a few hours before we both have to get to the hangar. I have a few more tweaks to make to the Wraith before tonight's test."

———

Nick sat on his porch, holding his son in his arms and gently rocking back and forth. He ran his fingers along the silky strands of Luke's golden hair and looked out across the darkening water. He could not shake Katy's horrified expression from his mind. This morning he had bruised her during his nightmare, and tonight he had almost shoved a knife through her chest. The nightmares, the lack of sleep, the anger that he always felt boiling beneath the surface—what was he becoming?

Katy stepped through the open back door. "Easy boy," she said, "I'm unarmed. I left my spatula in the kitchen."

Nick continued to stare out over the water in silence, even though he could feel her effort to show him forgiveness.

She knelt next to him and kissed her baby on the head. Then she kissed Nick on the cheek. "I'm going to bed," she said. "Can you handle him?"

Nick closed his eyes and sighed. He should have seen this one coming. "I thought I told you. I have to go back to work tonight." He knew the words sounded harsh and accusing. He knew he should recant and reach out to her. But he didn't.

Katy stood up, her sweetened demeanor fallen away. "Of course you do. What was I thinking?" She pulled Luke out of his arms and wheeled around to head back into the house.

The sight of her walking away again filled him with rage. "I'm trying," he called after her, anger tainting his voice.

Katy kept walking. "Try harder," she said, and slammed the door.

CHAPTER 24

ighthouse, Wraith is leaving flight level two five zero, starting the descent for the Skyhook test." Nick sat in the mission commander's seat on the right side of the M-2's cockpit, with Drake in the copilot's seat to his left. A panoramic view of the Maryland coast spread out before them, displayed on a continuous 180-degree wrapping screen. The aircraft had no windshield, no windows at all. Instead, sensors embedded in the aircraft's skin fed the enhanced infrared display, showing them the world outside in crisp black and white. They could see every detail of the coast, every wisp of cloud in the sky despite the darkness of the night.

Nick programmed the autopilot for a long, spiraling descent through the restricted airspace. It would take more than twenty minutes for the Wraith to descend from twenty-five thousand feet to its new altitude, just five hundred feet above the Atlantic waves. He took the opportunity for a rest, removing his flight helmet and running his fingers through his sweaty hair. After a long pull from his water bottle, Nick turned in his ejection seat to face his copilot, his forehead creased with concern. "Are you ready for this one?"

Drake set his own helmet down on his knee. "Of course I am. Why? Are you worried?"

So far, the test flight had gone smoothly, just like the previous four test flights, all flown during the month before the Persian Gulf mission. The Wraith had arrived at Romeo Seven's hangar facility in late January. A casual observer, or even an aircraft buff, might have mistaken her for a B-2 stealth bomber, but she was something entirely new. The M-2 was bigger, with more deeply swept wings for supersonic flight. She also had new engines, stolen from the F-22 program and modified by Amanda's propulsion team.

This single M-2 was the only bird spawned from a doomed program called the LRS, the Long Range Striker. Originally the B-2's replacement, the LRS fell victim to budget cuts and a shifting political climate. Scott and Amanda were both lead design consultants on the project. When it lost funding midstream, Walker saw a tremendous opportunity. Black money finished the job, custom built to Triple Seven specs.

Tonight's test flight had gone like clockwork, with the Wraith's array of tactical systems functioning perfectly. But Nick had a bad feeling about using a live target for the Skyhook test, especially a live target that he didn't trust.

"Relax, boss," said Drake, one corner of his mouth twisting up into a grin, "just because the last guy to get yanked off the ground by a Skyhook cable was . . ."

Nick held up his hand. "Don't say it. I've already got a bad vibe about this test. You don't need to jinx it more."

Both pilots put their helmets back on and clipped their oxygen masks into place. Nick turned and pressed a series of squares on a large touch-screen monitor that angled up out of the console to his right. "Lighthouse, this descent is going to take a while," he said into the radio. "I'm going to send you our flight data so that you can get something useful out of it. I'm starting the telemetry feed now."

"Lighthouse copies, we are receiving your feed," replied Scott from Romeo Seven. "If you don't mind, give us some basic maneuvers on your way down for better data."

"I've got this one," said Drake, taking the controls. "This spiral descent is taking too long anyway. I think I'll take the express elevator instead." The Wraith lurched to the right as Drake rolled her up on a knife's edge, slicing through the horizon into a deep dive. The digital altitude readout became a green blur as the huge jet accelerated toward the water.

Nick leaned back in his ejection seat and stretched. "Do you really have to do stuff like this?" He watched the altitude readout blaze past ten thousand feet on its way to zero. "You're such a child."

"I'm showing massive spikes in the auto-stabilizer

inputs," said Scott. He sounded terrified. "It looks like you're plummeting toward the ocean."

"I think you've made your point, Drake," said Nick.

Drake righted the aircraft and pulled back hard on the side-stick control. The engines' vectored thrust system tilted the exhaust nozzles upward to help him power out of the dive. The surface of the Atlantic flashed by the screen, every peak and valley of the small waves standing out in sharp detail.

Nick grunted under the strain of seven Gs. He couldn't help feeling a little pride. No other aircraft this big could handle that kind of maneuvering, not even a B-1. He let out a long breath as Drake settled at five hundred feet. "Don't worry, Lighthouse," he transmitted. "Your numbers were correct. That was just Drake's version of basic maneuvering."

"And he wonders why I don't like him," replied Scott.

"All right, gentlemen, it's time to get serious," said Nick. "Let's not forget the gravity of what we are about to accomplish." He closed his eyes and said a quick prayer. The whole team agreed that the Wraith needed a Skyhook capability for covert exfiltration, and that meant conducting a human test, but consensus didn't make it any less dangerous.

This test would mark the first human trial of a Fulton Skyhook Surface-to-Air Recovery system in more than thirty years. The Department of Defense had officially banned live recoveries for good reason. The last man to get yanked off the ground by a fixed-wing aircraft had been thrown a quarter mile through the air and slammed into the ground at over a hundred miles an hour. It took the coroner's team a week to recover all the pieces. Only the CIA had maintained the option after that, and even they dropped it ten years later for lack of use. No one wanted to try it.

"Wraith, this is Dagger, radio check," came Quinn's voice through the radio.

"Dagger, Wraith has you loud and clear. Are you on coords?"

"Affirmative, I'm at the location you gave me," said Quinn.

Nick selected a waypoint labeled DAGGER from the touch screen on his console. Immediately, a green square appeared on the forward screen, fixed over Quinn's coordinates between the Wraith and the coastline. Another, larger square appeared at the base of the display, showing magnified video of Quinn's position, captured by one of the forward cameras. In the lower-right corner of the square, a small boat gently rocked back and forth in the black waves.

"There's our boy," said Drake.

Nick tapped the boat with his finger, and the video began tracking it, keeping it at the center of the square. "Dagger, pop a thermal marker for confirmation," he said.

A bright white spot flared in the video, nearly blotting out the boat before the computer auto-tuned the image. Nick put his thumb and forefinger inside the box and spread them apart, zooming in until he could see Quinn slowly waving the signal marker back and forth.

The pararescueman stood at the back of a runabout. While everyone else had taken the early evening off, Quinn had navigated the boat around Cape Charles, out into the open water beneath the maneuvering area.

"He looks cold," said Drake. "I guess it was kind of harsh for us to send him out there on his first day."

Nick pointed to the front of the boat where a young woman sat behind the wheel, huddled up under a blanket. "Nah, Molly went with him to drive the boat home."

"Molly the new tech with the big brown eyes?"

"That's the one," said Nick.

Drake grinned. "I guess he's okay then." He steered the aircraft to point directly at Quinn's position and then leveled the wings. "I'm stable and on target," he said. "We're ready to deploy Skyhook."

Nick entered the commands, and two more video squares appeared at the bottom of the main screen. One showed a V-shaped cable-catcher extending forward from a well beneath the nose. The other showed the claw, a long cylinder split down the middle, extending from the forward edge of the bomb bay.

Airborne personnel recovery systems had always been simple in concept but dangerously complicated in execution. Getting the target off the ground was easy: fly an airplane into a cable held aloft by a balloon, capture that cable in a V-shaped catch, and voilà, your target is airborne. Thanks to the vector physics involved, the target would experience little more than a mild jerk and slowly rise to a trailing position.

The deadlier problems arose while trying to reel the

target into the aircraft. There were just too many variables. Sometimes the cable got caught in the wing vortices and spun wildly in circles. Other times it tracked low and off center, trapping the target in the aircraft's engine wash. During the last human trial, it just snapped. C-130 crews solved these problems by hanging off the end of the cargo ramp and chasing the cable around with long J-hooks. Predictably, that didn't always work.

Scott had come up with a more technologically elegant solution to the cable problem. His claw had sensors that could detect the difference in motion between the cable and the surface background; in effect, it could "see" the line. Then its short robotic arm would adjust to the cable's motion and snatch it out of the air. A winch inside the claw would reel the target into the bomb bay and then retract, placing him directly in front of the ladder to the flight deck.

The system had worked perfectly on the last two tests with dummies. As Walker noted during the pre-mission briefing, there was no reason it shouldn't work just as well with Quinn.

"Dagger, deploy your balloon," said Nick, praying that Walker was right. On the screen, he watched Quinn unravel a line onto the floor of the boat and then pull a rip cord out of a small square packet. A miniature blimp rapidly inflated and shot skyward. The thermal panel on the balloon shined brightly on the infrared display, making it an easy target.

"Slow to one hundred and forty knots. Hit the line fifty feet below the balloon," said Nick.

"Roj," Drake replied, "just like last time."

The line came up fast despite their slow speed, but Drake hit it exactly where he needed to. The catch snapped closed, severing the line above the vise and sending the balloon sailing away behind them.

Nick checked the video squares. Quinn had disappeared from the boat, and he could see Molly waving her thermal marker in a circle, the okay sign. But the other video feeds didn't look right. The system still hadn't captured Quinn's line. The claw wasn't moving.

A red light began flashing on Nick's control console. "The system is frozen. We're dragging him toward the coast. Start climbing now!"

"Should I turn back toward the boat?" asked Drake

"Negative. You'll put him into the engine wash."

As the Wraith climbed through two thousand feet, Nick keyed the radio. "Dagger, cut away, cut away, cut away!" He waited for a response, but the radio remained silent. The kid might not even be able to hear him over the roar of the engines and the slipstream. "Dagger, this is Wraith. Cut away, cut away, cut away!"

Scott's Skyhook package came equipped with an emergency system—a lightweight parachute packed into a small pocket on the back of the vest. By Scott's design, Quinn could pull a single rip cord that would sever the line and deploy the chute. He wouldn't win any prizes at an air show, but the little chute would get him to the ground alive. Unfortunately, that emergency system had never been tested. Worse, if Nick released the cable before Quinn cut away, it could wrap around his neck or body during free fall, breaking his spine when he deployed the parachute or preventing him from deploying it at all.

They had a procedure in place. Quinn was supposed to count out thirty seconds. If the system hadn't started reeling him in by that time, he was to cut away on his own. It had easily been two minutes. By now, Quinn should have responded on the radio, confirming that he had separated and that his chute had deployed. He should be descending gently into the water. But the radio remained silent. Chances were that he was unconscious back there, getting bounced around by the jet wash or whirled in circles by the wing vortices.

The Maryland coast was approaching fast. If the kid was still attached, releasing the cable might kill him, even if he was conscious. But if Nick waited any longer, he would drop both Quinn and the cable into downtown Ocean City.

His finger hovered over the button.

Dear God, let the kid survive.

"I'm releasing the line in three, two, one . . . now." He opened the catch, letting the cable fall free. "Turn back toward the boat," he ordered Drake. "One way or the other, Quinn is well clear now."

Nick and Drake waited in silence for another full minute, neither willing to accept the gruesome reality. Then the radio crackled to life.

"Woohoo! What a ride! Oh man, you guys have got to try that!"

Nick let out a relieved sigh. "Dagger, say your status."

"I'm under canopy. My parachute deployed beautifully

after you released me. I'm activating my GPS beacon. I should hit the water in about thirty seconds. Tell Molly to come pick me up."

"Released me?" Nick repeated, raising an eyebrow at Drake. He keyed the radio again. "Dagger, did you hear my command to cut away?"

"Affirmative, Wraith," Quinn replied, "but when am I gonna get another chance to bodysurf the air behind a stealth plane? I cut the cable after you dropped me and the fun was over. The line fell away clean."

Nick dropped his oxygen mask and frowned at Drake. "I'm going to kill him."

CHAPTER 25

Nick waited until Drake lifted the large dark chocolate mocha to his lips. "I saw what you ordered," he said. "I told you that New Year's resolution couldn't last."

Drake coughed and sputtered. "Don't tell Amanda," he pleaded, wiping a drop of sugary coffee from his chin. "She'll never let me live it down."

The two sat on tall stools at a small table in Charla's, the base coffee shop. Next to them, backlit by the mid-morning sun, a window painting of a life-sized Spanish friar smiled, as if the steaming cup of coffee in his hand were a blessing from heaven. Nick squinted in the sunlight and yawned.

"Still not sleeping?" asked Drake.

A waitress appeared with Nick's order. "Here's your extra-tall Redeye," she said, handing him the supersized mix of espresso and black coffee.

"I retract the question," said Drake flatly. "How long has it been? Five weeks? Six?"

Nick took a long hit from his Redeye and firmly set it down on the table. "Don't worry about me. You forget. I went to the Air Force Academy. I didn't sleep for four straight years."

"You should have gone to a real college." Drake gave him a sly grin. "I didn't sleep at Notre Dame either, but for entirely different reasons."

Nick stared out the window. In the distance, he saw a young man pounding up the pavement in a black jogging suit and stocking cap. "Uh-oh, speaking of irresponsible behavior."

Drake turned in his seat to follow Nick's gaze. After a moment's pause, he said, "Hey, isn't that—"

"The new kid," finished Nick. "It's Quinn."

"You know," said Drake reflectively, "he runs a lot like you."

"You mean faster than you."

"No, I mean with a look on his face that says he's trying to punish the road for something. Or maybe trying to punish himself."

———

Quinn's breath came in easy, measured rhythm despite his quick pace. Two years in the Special Tactics pipeline had brought his cardio up to an Olympic level. He could have stepped up the pace even more, but he wasn't out here to set any records. He was out here to sweat, and think.

Last night's mission had revived him. He felt alive for the first time since his final test at Mission Qual. Of course, it didn't hurt that the colonel had sent that cute tech Molly with him, but mostly it was the thrill of being out there, doing something different, something dangerous.

Maybe that's why he ignored the order to cut away. Even when the Skyhook system failed, even knowing the history, he didn't feel the risk of death. He just felt alive, and he wanted that feeling to last as long as possible.

Then Walker and Baron had freaked out. The major acted like he had just crashed the Wraith or something. It took him hours to get back to the base, but when he walked into Romeo Seven, the colonel and Baron were still in Walker's office, surely discussing his fate. They didn't tell him what they'd decided. He didn't even know if he still had a job.

Quinn stepped up his pace, leaving the sidewalk to cross the short grass field next to the airman dorms. His room was on the fourth floor, but he wasn't planning on using the stairs. Not in the normal sense anyway.

He approached the external stairwell from the side, stutter-stepped across the gravel border, and then leapt up to grab the first landing. Using the strength of his arms alone, he launched himself upward, grabbed the powder-coated aluminum handrail, and pulled his feet up to the concrete edge of the landing. Then, without pausing to rest, he leapt up and grabbed the next landing and launched himself up to the next rail. He repeated the process with rhythmic cadence until he clambered over the final rail on the fourth level.

As Quinn pulled off his sweat-soaked shirt and tossed it on his bed, he noticed the message light blinking on his phone. He turned on the speaker and then hit the lit button. Walker's stern voice filled the room. The message was short.

"Quinn, report to my office immediately."

———————

Renovations to the Romeo Seven bunker had included a new office for Walker. The contractors installed the glass-enclosed room twelve feet above the floor in the southwest corner of the command center, giving the colonel a bird's-eye view of the entire operation. The team called it the Ivory Tower.

Nick and Drake waited at the base of the wrought-iron stairs like kids waiting outside the principal's office. Nick had received a text that interrupted their coffee, demanding that they report to Romeo Seven at once.

"Is this about last night?" asked Drake.

Nick shrugged. "What else could it be? Walker and I discussed the kid at length after his stunt with the Sky-hook system. The colonel is still holding out hope that we can fix him." He frowned. "I'm not so optimistic. The colonel is letting me put Quinn on desk probation: paper pushing only, no field ops until he proves that he can follow orders. He was going to let me administer the browbeating as well, but maybe he changed his mind. He does enjoy that sort of thing. It's the closest thing he has to a hobby."

Walker emerged from his office just as Quinn stepped off the elevator. He walked a few steps down the stairs before pointing at Quinn and then the two majors. "You three, get in here."

Nick and Drake waited for Quinn to join them before going up. "Just remember, kid," said Drake, "this is going to hurt him more than it hurts you." The corners of his mouth curled up into a smirk. "Oh, wait. Maybe not."

A moment later, Walker poked his head out of his door again. "Hurry up. I don't have all day."

Drake slapped Quinn on the back. "At least he's in a good mood."

The three of them piled into Walker's office. "Shut the door," he commanded. The colonel stood in front of his desk, his usual scowl burning a hole in the floor, a foam cup of coffee in his right hand.

Nick stepped forward. "Sir, about the Skyhook test—"

"That's not what this is about," Walker interrupted. He looked up, and Nick could see that he wore his business scowl as opposed to his angry one. "We have a more pressing issue to deal with."

Walker stepped to the side. For the first time, Nick saw that there was another person in the room. A young, red-haired sergeant sat at the colonel's desk, his nose buried in a laptop computer. Nick's eyes widened. "Will?"

Will McBride looked up from his work and waved. "Major Baron, Major Merigold," he said simply.

"It's been more than a year since we've seen you," said

Drake. "What brings you to our secret underground lair this time?"

McBride wasted no time with pleasantries. "A mystery. One that we are already behind in solving because I very stupidly chose to ignore it until I got a tip from the CIA."

"McBride works for a Global Hawk high-altitude reconnaissance unit now," said Walker. "Go ahead and show them what you've got, Sergeant." He nodded at Nick. "Baron, get the walls."

Nick slapped a wide black button that was set into a steel panel just inside the door. The smart-glass walls immediately became opaque, changing to a dull pearl. Then McBride punched a few keys on the laptop, and a media player appeared on the wall that ran along the command-center side of the office. The video frame showed a black-and-white image of uniformed men in a fenced-in compound.

"This is Detention Center Twenty-six in Fujian Province, China," said McBride. "These are successive stills taken by a Global Hawk's synthetic aperture radar." He pressed Play and the images progressed, showing the men running in various directions about the compound. Some were moving into the woods and drawing weapons. Suddenly the pictures shifted into the trees and the progression froze. "That was everything I got before the Hawk continued its scan," said McBride. "The crew refused to sacrifice their mission coverage to stay on this target. I didn't argue."

"That's not much," said Drake. "What are we supposed to make of it?"

McBride held up a finger. "Good point." He turned back to the laptop and opened another folder. "The next day, I received an audio file from the CIA relating to our mission. That's not an uncommon occurrence. Langley processes radio frequency intercepts that they receive from the Global Hawk. It has to be done after the mission because the receiver captures so many frequencies simultaneously. It sounds like garbage until their computers filter through it."

An audio file sprang open in the media player. Waveform lines jittered and danced to the sound of Chinese voices and twangy music drowning in a sea of static. Then another voice joined the confusion, a western voice. Nick strained to understand, but he couldn't make out the words.

McBride stopped the playback. "That's what it sounds like before the filtering," he said. "But after you isolate the target waveform and filter out the rest, it sounds like this." He opened another file and hit Play.

Without the noise, the western voice came through, rasping and weak, but clear and unmistakably American: "Red Dragon, this is Jade Zero One. I am alive. I repeat, this is Jade Zero One. I am alive and requesting immediate evac."

CHAPTER 26

Nick folded his arms and lifted one hand to rub the roughly shaven stubble on his chin. "So you're postulating that a U.S. citizen has just escaped from a defunct prison camp in southern China?"

"Not just me," said Walker, setting his coffee down on the desk. "The Joint Chiefs too. But the chairman isn't ready to bring in the State Department. With the current administration's weak Asia policy and Task Force 77 out of the strait, our political footing in China is delicate. A formal inquiry could be disastrous. Instead, the chairman has asked the Triple Seven Chase to look into it. Discreetly."

"The trouble is," interjected McBride, "that none of the services has lost anyone recently in China."

"What about those P-3 guys back in '01?" asked Quinn.

"They all came home," said Nick. "Will, have you talked to Langley?"

"That's part of the mystery." McBride gestured to the digital media player, still open on Walker's smart-glass wall. "That file came to me from a generic address in their audio analysis section. I called over there to compare notes, but no one could tell me who sent it. When I asked if they were missing any operatives in China, I got stonewalled. Later, I received a formal e-mail from the China division chief that said they could neither confirm nor deny."

"That means they don't know," said Nick.

"I thought that meant that they were lying," said Quinn.

"No, if they actually give you an answer, that means they're lying," said Drake.

"Enough," interrupted Walker. "Please don't say things like that when you go over there. Our two operations have such a tenuous relationship."

Nick shook his head. "Don't worry, sir. We don't even know if the spooks are involved. We have no intention of going over to Langley."

"On the contrary. You're going over there right now. This thing has CIA written all over it. I've already made arrangements with Joe Tarpin." Walker patted McBride on the back. "I've muscled the sergeant away from his unit. While you're gone, he can oversee our intelligence team and dig from here."

"I guess that's settled then," said Nick, turning to Drake. "We'd better get moving."

"Ahem." Walker coughed and nodded toward Quinn. "Baron," he said, his scowl sharpening, "don't forget about the new kid."

———

Nick gathered Drake, Quinn, and McBride in his office. "We'll take the Mustang," he said, handing his keys to Drake. "I'll meet you up there in a few minutes."

As Drake stepped out the door, Quinn got up from the couch and started to follow.

Nick blocked his path. "Who said anything about you coming along?"

"Colonel Walker did," argued Quinn. "He just told you not to forget me."

"No, he told me not to forget *about* you. And believe me, I haven't." He searched Quinn's face, still trying to figure out what made him tick, wondering what sort of crossed wiring drove him to blow off something as critical as a cutaway command. The last thing he needed was another operative who couldn't follow orders. His eyes settled on Quinn's, matching the kid's angry glare. "Until I say otherwise, you're on desk probation. Go find Molly and ask her to show you how to run a Defense Intelligence Agency search for 'Red Dragon.' The pile will build fast. When it does, your job is to start reading and filtering out the slag. It isn't peeling potatoes, but it's close."

The young operative glowered back in protest for a few more seconds. Then, without so much as a "Yes, sir," he stood and walked out of the room.

McBride gave a low whistle. "Wow. That was awkward. How dysfunctional is that kid, right?"

Nick sighed. "Until Walker sees reason, I'm stuck with him." He motioned for McBride to sit down at his computer. "I need your help with something, something that isn't really part of this Red Dragon thing."

"But the colonel wanted me to watch over your analysts."

Nick shook his head. "They can handle themselves. I need you to work on something else." He opened a desk drawer and pulled out a red thumb drive. "I need you to process the video on this drive. The password is Warthog one seven."

"What's in the video?"

"A fish who nibbled at some bait we left at the Kuwait City morgue. Someone knew about our last op, and I need to know who they are and how they got their information." Nick held up the drive. "This guy is our only lead." He started to hand it to McBride but then pulled it back. "Oh, and I'd like you to keep this under Walker's radar."

The young sergeant took the drive out of Nick's hand and shoved it into the computer tower. "Running an op behind the colonel's back, huh? Now who's the dysfunctional one?"

———

Crossing the infamous seal just inside the CIA's front door always struck a wary chord in Nick's gut. The enigmatic star and eagle crest seemed to radiate its own energy, like an etching in the stone floor of an ancient temple. It was hallowed ground, or perhaps something quite the opposite.

"My two favorite teammates," said Joe Tarpin, waving from the security desk. "What a pleasure."

Nick shook Tarpin's hand. "I take it that Colonel Walker apprised you of our situation?"

"He did. In fact, I did a little digging this morning, and I've already made some progress."

Nick and Drake followed Tarpin through security, flashing their Defense Intelligence Agency badges. The Triple Seven Chase had no parent agency, but badges were needed to open doors wherever you went in Washington, D.C., and DIA badges could open the most. Walker had the necessary contacts.

Just past the X-ray machine, Tarpin turned and started climbing a flight of stairs.

"I'm surprised we're going up," said Drake. "I expected to find the records for top-secret CIA projects in the basement."

"We're not as arcane as that," replied Tarpin, glancing over his shoulder as he climbed the steps. "As part of our efforts to pretend respectability, we maintain our archives in the same place as any venerable old institution." He rounded a corner at the top of the stairs and stopped in front of a pair of frosted glass doors. A polished nickel plate set into the wall read LIBRARY.

"I guess there's no better place to do research," said Nick.

Tarpin led them through the main collection room,

past infinite rows of bookshelves, to a simple wooden door in the rear wall. Despite its humble appearance, the CIA man had to place his finger against a pad and then enter a lengthy numeric code in order to gain entrance.

"After the colonel's phone call, I spoke to our department heads, trying to find out if we really had lost one of our agents in China." Tarpin closed the door and sat down at a computer terminal. "They all denied knowledge of such an event."

"That doesn't really mean anything," said Drake.

Tarpin smiled. "You're absolutely right, but this time I believe them." The prompt on the computer screen showed that Tarpin had already been working there. After he entered his password, the standard Windows screen appeared, displaying a line of active programs across the toolbar.

"Faced with the usual interdepartmental stonewall treatment, I had to get creative. Walker gave me two terms: Jade Zero One and Red Dragon." He opened one of the active windows and typed "Red Dragon" into the search box. An hourglass began rotating on the screen. "The most obvious place to start was a search for any operation named Red Dragon." The computer beeped, and Tarpin rotated the flat screen so that Drake and Nick could see it better. The red text below the search prompt read, "No archived operations match your request."

"So Red Dragon never existed," said Nick.

"Not according to our archives."

"Again, that doesn't mean anything," said Drake.

"Hey, I'm on your side. But this is the gold mine, the

conspiracy theorist's mother lode." Tarpin gestured at the computer screen. "The records from every black operation in Agency history are on this network. If Red Dragon isn't listed here, then either it never existed or someone with clout equal to the deputy director must have buried it."

Drake started to argue, but Tarpin held up a finger to stop him. "There is some good news, though." He minimized the first window and opened another. This one displayed a scanned image of an old document, printed on a dot-matrix printer. "The other term Dick gave me was Jade Zero One. That *has* to be a callsign, probably aerial. It dawned on me that the Agency never recycles a flight callsign once it's been compromised, which means they have to keep track of all of them, especially the burned ones. Look."

Nick leaned in closer to inspect the old document. The header read AERIAL CALLSIGNS, ASIAN THEATER OF OPERATIONS: 1985–1990.

Tarpin placed his finger on the screen halfway down the page. The callsign he indicated was, in fact, Jade, but Nick had trouble seeing it because a red stamp covered up the line. The block text read, "COMPROMISED, JAN 1988."

Tarpin nodded as Nick straightened up. "Obviously, something bad happened to an aircraft using the Jade callsign."

"Great," said Drake, "but that still doesn't tell us much.

Tarpin shrugged. "At least it's a start. I've been at this all morning. I can't tell you how many pages of callsigns

I had to root through to find this one. I didn't have a reference date to start with."

"No," said Nick, "but we have one now." He tapped the image of the red stamp. "January 1988."

"But I showed you, we don't have any record of Operation Red Dragon. The date won't change our result," argued Tarpin.

"Yeah, but our job isn't really to find the operation, is it? We're looking for a person, one who was probably lost during a flight and presumed dead." Nick started heading for the door. "We're done here. Log off and follow me."

Nick walked briskly out of the library and turned down the staircase, headed for the lobby where they'd entered.

"Slow down," puffed Tarpin, well behind Nick and Drake as they jogged down the steps. "I'm not as fit as I was when I was your age, running ops all over the globe."

At the base of the stairs, Nick turned into a wide alcove and stopped. The CIA kept the world's darkest secrets locked away deep within the bowels of its compound, and yet the answer he needed might be waiting right here, a few feet from the visitors' desk.

One hundred two black stars adorned an austere wall of pearl white marble. Below the stars, a small shelf jutted out, holding a steel case covered by an inch of bulletproof glass. A thin book lay inside, open to its only two pages.

"Of course," said Tarpin, breathing heavily as he came up beside Nick, "the Book of Honor."

Nick nodded. "The list of agents who died in heroic action or under hostile attack."

Drake strode up to the wall and bent over the case.

"The name we want would be from either 1987 or 1988. And 1987 has only one name, Richard Krobock."

Tarpin shook his head. "Krobock isn't our man. Everyone here knows that story. He died in El Salvador in a guerilla attack. What about '88?"

Drake sighed. "Another dead end. There's one star, but no name."

"That's our guy," said Nick. "It makes sense. There wouldn't be a name, not if the circumstances surrounding the death are still classified."

"Great. So why did you bring us here?"

"For confirmation," Nick replied. He turned to Tarpin. "Now we need to see the *real* book."

Tarpin raised both hands in protest. "I don't know what you're talking about." But Nick held his ground. He just stared at the CIA man, waiting, until finally Tarpin's shoulders dropped. "Fine," he said with exasperation. He turned back to the stairwell, but this time he started down. "Follow me."

Nick and Drake followed Tarpin down several flights of stairs. "Now we're talking," said Drake, rubbing his hands together as they reached the bare concrete of the basement level.

"Keep your voice down," cautioned Tarpin. He led them down a dark hallway and stopped in front of a heavy vault door. "You guys don't have clearance," he complained. "I could lose my job for this. I could lose my pension."

Nick pursed his lips. "An American patriot might be hiding somewhere in southern China, waiting for rescue.

We are already more than thirty-six hours behind. Every moment we waste is another chance for the Chinese to capture him again. You know Walker can get us the clearance. Take care of the paperwork later."

"If the Triple Seven Chase mounts a rescue, I want in," said Tarpin.

"Just open the door."

Tarpin finally nodded and entered his code. Weak fluorescent lights flickered on as he swung the door open, bathing the small room in pale green light. "This is the real memorial," he said as he led them inside.

One hundred two stars made of dark green stone were set into the marble wall at the back of the room. A short jade pillar stood beneath them, supporting a closed book, as thick as a family Bible, encased in a glass box.

"Can you open that box?" asked Nick.

"Not without a preservation specialist," Tarpin replied. "But we don't have to open it." He stepped over to the right-hand wall and typed a code into a keyboard that stood out at waist level. The light green wall lit up like a computer screen. Several rows of folders appeared, each one labeled with a month and a year.

"This is the digitized version of the actual Book of Honor," explained Tarpin, stepping aside. "These files contain images of the pages. They also contain other documents relating to the deceased."

Tarpin moved aside, allowing Nick to access the keyboard. Nick opened the folder labeled JANUARY 1988. Inside, there was only one file. He read the name out loud, "David Novak."

"This is it," said Drake.

"Good," replied Tarpin. He checked his watch. "Listen, I have to get to a meeting. Can I trust you two to log me out and close the vault door?"

Nick nodded. "We can do that. I'll put a good word in for you with Walker. You really came through for us."

As Tarpin slipped out, Nick opened the file. Handwritten lines filled the page from the book:

David Novak died on New Year's Day 1988 while flying a low-level reconnaissance mission over southern China. Progressive Blackbird imagery taken in concert with Novak's mission showed a surface-to-air missile launch followed by burning wreckage, presumed to be Novak's F-16. Flying as Jade 01, Novak broke from his planned mission for unknown reasons. Communications intercepts from a P-3 Orion also indicate that he broke radio silence. This combination may have allowed Chinese air defenses to gain a fix on his position and confirm their radar track, leading to the shoot-down. Novak served with distinction as part of Operation Distant Sage, flying photoreconnaissance missions over China, as well as Operation Remote Icon, flying over Russia. He made the ultimate sacrifice in service to his country. He will not be forgotten.

"Well, now we have a name and an operation," said Drake, "but we still don't know what Red Dragon is."

Nick scrolled down until he found a document labeled DISTANT SAGE POSTACTION REPORT. He opened the file and ran a search for "Red Dragon." The cursor immediately jumped to the middle of the document. He waved at Drake and pointed at the screen. "Bingo."

The report listed Red Dragon as an authentication code, a phrase used by covert operatives when forced to use an open frequency. "So Novak survived the crash," said Drake.

"It sure looks that way. Even if the Chinese recovered his body from the wreckage, they wouldn't have gotten that code. According to this, McBride's Jade Zero One is the real deal." Nick continued to search through the documents as Drake wandered over to look at the book beneath the glass.

"Uh-oh. There's more," said Nick presently, looking over at Drake with a furrowed brow.

"That look always means trouble," said Drake. "What did you find?"

"Both Remote Icon and Distant Sage were shut down because of possible leaks. The subsequent investigations were inconclusive."

"Two moles?"

Nick shook his head. "My guess is one, working both ops." He turned back to the report and quickly scanned to the bottom of the page. "And, according to this, he was never found."

CHAPTER 27

Novak sat huddled on a cot, leaning against the rough stone at the back of a small cave. A short line of supply crates lay along the eastern wall, one of them broken open, its contents strewn about the rocky floor. He wondered if the thirty-year-old MRE that he'd devoured might kill him. It didn't matter. The ancient chicken à la king tasted divine.

He glanced at the radio set on the cave's rusty table. Nothing. He made his radio call at the bottom of every hour, based on the radio's clock, hoping that the Agency was somehow still listening.

That the radio and its digital clock still functioned was no surprise. Long ago, the CIA had placed a small collection of nuclear-powered equipment—telescopes, radios, cameras, and so forth—in remote locations around the world. This one found its way into southern China in the late sixties. As long as the lead case remained intact, the radio operator suffered no threat of radiation. At least, that's what the Agency claimed. The fifty years that the radio sat in this natural safe house put hardly a dent in the half-life of its plutonium battery.

A group of agents working a long-term ground mission discovered the cave in 1967. Less than ten meters deep, with a low, narrow crawl space for an entrance, it seemed the perfect location for a weapons cache and safe house. Later missions restocked it with supplies and the atomic radio. They called it the Palace.

Distant Sage reopened the Palace for business in 1987. Downed pilots from Distant Sage were supposed to make their way to the cave, radio for help, and expect a high-risk Fulton Skyhook pickup. To Novak's knowledge, the Chinese had never discovered the cache.

He kept his eyes on the entrance, methodically cleaning a Colt .45 pistol that he had found in the supplies. He shivered. Despite the warm temperature of the summer rain forest outside, his body felt cold. He finished cleaning the weapon, loaded a clip, and set it down on the cot. Then he grabbed a musty blanket from the open crate and wrapped himself. He found the rough feel of the old sheep's wool comforting. His eyes began to close.

Something rustled through the undergrowth outside. Novak picked up the Colt and forced his eyes open. He pointed the pistol at the low entrance, but the sound did not return. Still, he kept the weapon up and leveled, trying to fight his exhaustion; to sleep now could mean missing a signal from the rescue crew or getting caught by the Chinese.

Steadily his grip on the gun loosened, his eyelids began to droop. Finally, the Colt fell from his hand.

Novak woke with a start, wildly looking left and right, but his vision was still blurry. Something burned dull yellow to his left. He rubbed his eyes. A fire materialized. Not an uncontrolled fire, but a low, soft fire, glowing in a stone hearth. A gentle hand caressed his chin.

"It's all right, darling. You were dreaming."

Novak allowed the soft touch and sweet voice to soothe him.

Anja.

"You drifted off again," she said, reaching across him to pull the wool blanket tightly around them both. "I know it's not safe to wake someone who is sleeping so deeply, but it's late. If you don't get back to the barracks, Mr. Wright will send you back to America."

They huddled together on a cushioned love seat in Anja's small apartment. Novak studied her beautiful face in the dim firelight, the pout of her lips, the subtle flecks of gold in her hazel eyes. Now that she held his gaze, he did not need to look away to know where he was.

Except for the toilet, Anja's entire apartment was just one room. It was dark. She always kept it that way when he visited. She said it made the fire more romantic, but Novak knew that she wanted to mask the small, dilapidated room, as if he might judge her for her poverty.

"I can't leave yet," said Novak, taking her hand in both

of his. "I came tonight to tell you something, something important."

A tiny tremor passed through Anja's body. Novak felt it in her slender fingers. "I'm listening," she said nervously.

"Including my crash," Novak began, "we've lost four aircraft in three months to Russian missiles. Two of the flight crews did not return. That's four men presumed dead."

Anja withdrew her hand. Her expectant expression changed to cautious curiosity, and not a little disappointment. "I know that," she said flatly. "You did not need to come to my apartment to remind me of our losses."

Novak sensed her frustration. He nodded. "Yes, I know, but there's more. The Company believes that these shoot-downs are not just bad luck or bad intelligence. They suspect that one of the Polish nationals is a Russian agent, but they don't know who."

"A mole?" Anja pushed herself out of the chair, straightened her jeans, and walked over to the hearth. Her waist-length silk blouse stretched up to reveal the alabaster skin at the small of her back as she leaned forward, resting a hand on the mantel. She tapped an index finger irritably on a brightly colored box that she kept there. "One of the Polish Pawns has turned on the Agency," she said, still facing the wall. "And the supervisor in charge sent you here to find out if I'm protecting them?" She looked back at him. A glint of red firelight betrayed a tear on her cheek. "You came here tonight to ask me if I'm a traitor?"

Novak leapt up, letting the wool blanket fall into the chair. "No!" he exclaimed. He reached for her, but she recoiled and turned away again. His arms dropped to his sides. "Wright doesn't know that I'm here. He doesn't believe in any of this, but the Agency can't afford a mole hunt to prove him wrong. Our situation is tenuous at best.

"If we spook the double agent, they might bring a brigade of SB down on the base," he explained, referring to the Służba Bezpieczeństwa, the Polish secret police, the same group that had taken Anja's parents away when she was just a child. "A mole hunt is out. The Agency is throwing in the towel. We're pulling out in less than a week."

"We're shutting down?" Anja stared down into the dying fire.

Novak sighed. "Only the Americans are supposed to know. The Company doesn't want to tip off the mole. Since we don't know who to trust, all of the Polish nationals will be left behind, abandoned."

Anja buried her head in her arms, leaning them on the mantel. Her delicate shoulders trembled. "You're leaving me," she sobbed.

Novak risked a touch, placing his hands on her silky arms. "I don't want to leave you, but the Agency will only evacuate American *citizens*." When he emphasized the word, he felt Anja's body tense. Finally, she was beginning to understand. "If you became a citizen, you could come with me." She turned, falling into his arms. Her sobs became gentle shudders as she pressed her cheek against his chest.

Novak slowly dropped to one knee, letting his fingers slide from her shoulders to her hands before bringing them together for a gentle kiss. He looked up and found her angelic eyes once more filled with hope. "Anja Zajac, will you marry me?"

Anja beamed. She grasped his hands tightly and pulled Novak to his feet. Before he fully had his balance, she jumped into his arms, wrapping her legs around him. Novak stumbled backward and fell into the love seat, but Anja took no notice. She kissed him passionately. He released her long enough to wrap the wool blanket around them both, and then he leaned back in the chair, savoring the excitement of her kiss, the warmth of her embrace. As he shifted his weight, his shoulder knocked a picture off the end table. He let it fall.

The sound of the Colt .45 clattering against the rock floor startled Novak to consciousness. His head jerked up from his chest. Sweat soaked his tattered prison uniform beneath the heavy wool blanket. After a few moments, he shook off the blanket and leaned down to pick up the .45. He held it flat in his hand for a long while, caressing the edge of the trigger guard with one finger. Then he slowly walked over to the radio table, set down the gun, and picked up the microphone.

"Red Dragon, this is Jade Zero One. I am alive. I repeat, this is Jade Zero One. I am alive and requesting immediate evac."

CHAPTER 28

Nick and Drake picked up their cell phones from security as they left the CIA headquarters building. A blue box on Nick's screen informed him that he'd missed a call from McBride. He pressed the box to dial him back.

"I'm secure. What've you got for me?" he said as soon as McBride picked up.

"I found your guy," answered McBride. "His name is Feng Wei, but that's just an alias. You're right to be suspicious. He's not part of the regular staff at the Chinese Embassy in Kuwait."

"That figures." Nick stopped at the edge of the sidewalk out in front of the CIA building.

Drake mouthed, *What?* but Nick motioned for his friend to be patient.

"Where does he usually work?"

"Everywhere. He's a courier. I have pictures of him in the diplomatic districts of a half-dozen major cities," said McBride. "He spends most of his time in London, but that's not where he went when he left Kuwait."

The line went silent for a moment. Nick remembered that McBride liked to add a dramatic pause when he had a juicy bit of intelligence. "Come on, Will. Spill it."

"You see, once I had a name and multiple pictures from our database, I was able to run a search for current intelligence from other agencies," McBride explained with enthusiasm. "That got me a hit from the Brits that had him boarding a flight to Beijing."

"So he's in Beijing."

"No," said McBride, a little annoyed at being interrupted. "You don't understand. The Brits *think* he's in Beijing, but he's not." McBride paused again.

Nick pinched the bridge of his nose to stave off the impending headache. "Where did he go?"

"So then I played a hunch. I used this algorithm that Scott developed and ran it on the public cameras in . . ."

"Will!"

"He's here."

"As in, he's here in Washington, D.C.?"

"Yeah. I've got a ninety-two percent match for Feng Wei on a guy getting into a black sedan at Dulles just a few hours ago. I tracked the car to the Chinese Embassy. As far as I can tell, he hasn't left since."

"Good work," said Nick. "Keep an eye on it. He's got to leave that embassy sometime. When he does, I want to know where he goes. And now that you have a face and a name, there's something else that I want you to do. I have a hunch of my own."

A few moments later, Nick hung up the phone and started walking toward the car.

"What's up?" asked Drake, jogging to catch up.

"Our suspect from Kuwait just turned up in D.C. Other than that, all Will got was a name: Feng Wei. I wish we knew more about this guy."

Drake grabbed Nick's elbow and stopped him. "I think I can help with that."

Back inside the CIA headquarters building, Nick and Drake stood waiting at the reception desk. "I thought you didn't like spooks," whispered Nick.

"This one is different," Drake replied mysteriously. "Terri is one of the CIA's top analysts for China." He tilted his chin toward the security checkpoint. "Here she comes, now."

Nick turned to see a stunning brunette gracefully descending the stairs beyond the metal detectors, one hand lightly caressing the rail. She paused at the bottom step and waved at Drake.

"I should have known," said Nick.

"Shut up. Our relationship is entirely professional."

"Yeah, right."

"Terri," said Drake, waving back as she walked over, "this is Nick, the guy I'm always telling you about."

Terri smiled genuinely and squeezed Nick's hand. "Terri Belfacci," she said in a melodious voice. "I'm so glad to finally meet Drake's sidekick. I hear you two have survived quite a few scrapes together."

Nick elbowed Drake in the ribs as Terri led them back through security. "Sidekick?"

Drake coughed and lengthened his stride to catch up to Terri. "We need to find out about a Chinese courier named Feng Wei."

Terri halted abruptly, her power heels clicking sharply together on the granite floor. "How have you two come across the Black Dragon?"

"The what?" asked Drake.

"Feng Wei is an alias," said Terri, folding her arms. "He also goes by Wūlóng, the Black Dragon. His real name is still unknown."

"He's a suspect in a little investigation we're conducting," explained Nick. "What else can you tell us about him?"

"I can tell you that we have good intel that he recently returned to Beijing. I can also tell you that you need to coordinate with us if you're crossing paths with this guy. He's dangerous."

"I think we can handle a courier," said Drake.

Terri shook her head. "The Black Dragon is a legendary Chinese symbol. Its meaning is hard to translate into English, but it combines the ideas of power and death. Wūlóng is no ordinary embassy grunt. He's a former PLA Special Forces operative, and like the symbolic dragon, wherever he goes, death follows."

Terri relaxed her stern expression and leaned closer to Drake, flirtatiously brushing a hand down his arm. "You know, you could have asked me about Wūlóng over a secure line. You didn't have to come all the way over here. Unless, of course, you just wanted to see me."

Drake blushed. "Well, we, uh . . ." he stuttered.

She put her fingers to her dark red lips in mock surprise. "Oops. I just embarrassed the great Drake Merigold, the most eligible bachelor in DC's covert society." She squeezed his hand sweetly, but he did not reciprocate.

Terri caught her breath and dropped his hand. "You're off the market," she said accusingly. "You're seeing that grease monkey again, aren't you?"

"Amanda is a propulsion engineer," said Drake quietly.

"That's a politically correct term for someone who works on engines; ergo, grease monkey." Her voice turned cold. "Hmph, that's weird. She didn't mention you at all when I saw her this morning."

"Wait," said Nick. "You saw Amanda Navistrova here? Today? What was she doing at the CIA?"

Terri's cheeks flushed. "I don't know. I just bumped into her in the cafeteria." She frowned at Drake. "Amanda and I don't talk much." After a moment of awkward silence, her smile returned, a little more forced this time. She put her hand on Drake's arm again. "You're not totally hooked. Otherwise you wouldn't have made an excuse to come over and see me."

"Actually," interjected Nick, "Wūlóng is more of a side interest. We really came here to look into one of your lost agents. A Book of Honor inductee named David Novak.

Joe Tarpin helped us out, but he had to leave us to get to a meeting."

Terri wrinkled her nose. "Left you in the lurch, huh. That sounds like Joe. So what did you think of the physical archive?"

"You mean the book?" asked Nick.

"No, no, no," she said, waving her hands. "I mean the personal-effects archive. You can't study an agent in the Book of Honor without getting into their archive box." She looked from one to the other. "I gather from your blank expressions that you don't know what I'm talking about."

"We didn't know to ask for it," said Drake.

"Well, Joe should have told you." Terri put her hands on her hips and huffed. "You men have no ability to communicate. If you want to dig up the dirt, you've got to call a woman. You two boys go back to your clubhouse," she said, turning and walking back toward the stairs. "I'll resurrect your missing agent's effects and have them sent to you. And Drake"—she paused on the first step and turned, holding her hand up to her ear like a phone and shaking it—"call me."

————

Wūlóng spotted the midnight blue Mustang as it passed his position off Dolly Madison Boulevard. They were headed south, just as Hēi Yǐng had predicted. "Tsk, tsk." He clicked his tongue against the roof of his mouth. How sad that these Americans cared so little for their craft.

He found it astoundingly easy to enter this country. And once inside, he could travel virtually anywhere unchallenged, acquire almost any equipment that he needed. The American spies had to know of their country's vulnerabilities, yet they drove straight from one intelligence site to the other, using none of the standard evasion techniques. Such carelessness showed a lack of discipline, a lack of respect.

Wūlóng maintained his distance, even though his targets gave no indication of wariness. He could drive up beside the unprotected car and finish them right here if he chose. But then, as General Zheng had taught him, timing was everything.

As the Mustang joined the 395 to cross over the Potomac, Wūlóng's cell phone rang.

"Do you have them?"

Wūlóng gripped the steering wheel a little tighter at the sound of the caller's deep, unnatural voice. These Americans and their gadgets could be amusing, but at a certain point, it just became an annoyance. "You are still using a distortion device," he said, keeping his own voice as smooth and even as always. "It seems that you still do not trust me, Hēi Yǐng."

"I mean no offense," Hēi Yǐng replied. "It is just that, in our business, to share information is to lose control of it. You and I know that very well."

"Of course." Several cars ahead, Wūlóng watched the Mustang turn on to Suitland Parkway, headed for Andrews. "The targets are approaching their base. I will not be able to follow. At which gate should I position myself to pick them up again?"

"Do not trouble yourself," Hēi Yǐng replied. "I have the primary target's home address."

"Tsk, tsk." Wūlóng clicked his tongue again as he hung up the phone. Such utter carelessness. Such disrespect.

CHAPTER 29

W hat do we know, gentlemen?" asked Walker, reclining in his big leather desk chair.

Nick nodded to McBride, who manned a laptop sitting on the edge of the colonel's desk. A picture of a young man seated in front of an American flag opened on the smart-glass wall. "This is our objective, David Novak," Nick began. "According to the Book of Honor, Novak perished on New Year's Day 1988." The picture shrank into the corner, replaced by an old map of the Taiwan Strait. "He was flying a low-level reconnaissance mission here, over Fujian Province in China, as part of a Taiwan-based CIA operation called Distant Sage."

"The record says that Novak was shot down by a surface-to-air missile," added Drake. "It also says that photographs, taken at the same time by an ultra-high-altitude SR-71 Blackbird, showed no evidence of a parachute.

However, it's possible that the Blackbird photos did not catch the parachute or that Novak somehow survived the crash."

Walker sat forward in his chair and regarded the photo of Novak with a contemplative scowl. "But if he *was* killed," he said presently, "then it would mean that the Chinese are spoofing us. They might be trying to lure us into a political trap, an artificial version of the Hainan incident, when their fighter collided with our P-3, forcing an aircraft full of classified equipment to land at Lingshui. That accident netted the Chinese plenty of political and intelligence capital. It's just their style to contrive a way to make it happen again."

"We considered that," said Nick. "But then there's this." The Distant Sage report appeared on the wall. A highlighted section of text expanded and filled the digital space. "The voice in the intercept used the phrase 'Red Dragon.' According to this, it's an authentication code, to be used if a pilot was forced to call for help over an open frequency. That way, the Agency could be sure the radio call wasn't a Chinese trick. The thing is: if an authentication code is ever used, it has to be scrapped." Nick leaned forward and placed his fingertips on Walker's desk. "No Distant Sage operative ever had to use Red Dragon. Technically, it's still a valid code."

"Yes, but if Novak survived the crash," argued Walker, "the Chinese could have tortured the phrase out of him and then killed him."

Nick straightened up and opened his hands. "You're right. It's a risk. But no matter how you look at it, there's a chance that an American agent is still alive in southern China, and he's calling for help. We can't begin to imagine what Novak has been through for his country. We have to attempt a rescue."

"Let's say I let you go after him," said Walker. "How do you know where to start?"

Drake stepped in front of the wall. Behind him, a satellite map of Fujian Province opened up. "McBride's intercept was only the first of many. Molly's intelligence team dug into the Global Hawk data for the last two days. Novak is repeating his call every hour." Several lines appeared on the map, running from different points along the Fujian coast. They all intersected in a small area, deep in the rain forest. "Using directional data from the Global Hawk intercepts, we've been able to narrow the source down to an area of less than five hundred square meters."

"That's still too big for the kind of snatch-and-grab that we're talking about," said Walker.

"Joe helped us with that one," said Nick, gesturing toward the CIA man, who leaned against the back wall. "In fact, his discovery is what makes this rescue possible."

"I got lucky," said Tarpin. He offered a modest smile, but he clearly relished his moment in the limelight. He strolled to the center of the room. "While I was gathering the digital files for Nick, I found a reference to a Distant Sage safe house in China called the Palace. I also found a set of coordinates. You'll never guess where they fell."

A red dot appeared on the map near the center of the area formed by the radio intercepts.

Nick tapped the red dot with his finger. "The audio

intercepts and the intelligence both indicate that Novak is waiting for us right here. But the Chinese could intercept those radio calls too. That means we're in a race, and we're way behind. If we're going to rescue this man, we've got to launch a mission tonight."

The colonel gazed down at his desk and slowly rubbed his hands together. After a few moments he looked up, his fingers steepled, his eyes drifting across the faces of his team. "All right, gentlemen," he said finally. "It's time for Mr. Novak to come home."

CHAPTER 30

Wūlóng ran his flat-bottomed skiff in among the trees on the eastern shore of the Port Tobacco River, less than fifty meters south of the target's home. The skiff's shallow draft allowed him to run it right up to the shore, so that the water only came up to the shins of his waders as he dragged it under the cover of some low-hanging branches.

He pulled two small aluminum cases out of the boat and then removed the waders before heading farther into the trees. Wūlóng smiled to himself. Opulence had a price. The American could not have chosen a more accessible dwelling. The water allowed Wūlóng stealthy access and a quick route of escape. The tall windows at the front and rear gave him a better view of the interior than he could have possibly hoped for. Best of all, a thick grove of trees surrounded the house on all sides except for the shore, covering his approach from almost every angle. His smile broadened. It would also mute the screaming.

Finding a well-concealed vantage point, Wūlóng set his cases down and popped the latches. The cell phone jammer alone took up one entire case. The powerful transmitter would block calls coming in and out of an area with a two-hundred-meter diameter, enough to cover this house as well as those on either side. The other case contained everything else that he needed: wire cutters, a suppressed pistol, a few other simple tools. The best jobs were the simplest, nothing complex like creating an accident or a heart attack.

Wūlóng checked his watch and then dialed his cell phone. After one ring, the line clicked. There was a short pause, presumably as Hēi Yǐng activated the voice distortion device.

"Go ahead."

"I am in position," Wūlóng reported. "When can I expect the target? I would not want to begin too early."

"Of course. His routine usually brings him home a little after dark. If I were you, I would start around sunset. Things are progressing nicely for me as well, events that may enable us to achieve an even greater victory. Contact me when it is done, and I will pass your success on to General Zheng."

A light turned on in the house as Wūlóng hung up the phone. He lifted his binoculars. He could see the woman moving into the central room, carrying the child. They were alone.

Excellent.

———

"While we wait for the colonel to call the big boys, you can show us what you've done with our other project," said Nick, herding Drake and McBride into his office. Tarpin had taken his leave and headed back to Langley, and Nick had given Quinn back to Molly for more intelligence potato peeling.

McBride obediently sat down at the computer and opened a grainy picture of Nick's Chinese suspect. The photo was taken from above at an awkward angle. He appeared to be unaware of the camera. "Meet Feng Wei, aka Wūlóng," he said. "I blew this up from a traffic cam near the Chinese Embassy. I tried to clean it up, but there's only so much you can do."

"Is he still at the embassy?" asked Drake.

"As far as I can tell, but that's no guarantee. There are gaps in our camera coverage." McBride swiveled around in his chair, forcing the two pilots to back up. "However, I *did* find something in that other search you asked for," he said quietly.

Nick leaned forward. "Anything interesting?"

McBride just grinned at the officers, enjoying their anticipation.

"Spill it, Sergeant. We're short on time," said Nick impatiently.

"Fine, fine," muttered McBride, swiveling back around. But he still did not open any new files. "You know, once you learn something, you can no longer enjoy the exquisite agony of *yearning* to know."

"Will!" said both Nick and Drake simultaneously.

The analyst threw both hands up in the air and then brought one finger dramatically down to the keyboard. With a single click, he opened a new photograph. Wūlóng loitered next to a light post on a nondescript street corner, talking to a Caucasian man.

"This picture is from late March of 2003, ten years ago, during the time frame that you asked me to search. You'll never guess where it was taken."

"Kuwait," said Nick quietly.

"How did you know?"

"Lucky guess."

McBride nodded. "You're absolutely right. Wūlóng just happened to be in Kuwait right after Major Merigold dropped the B-2 into the drink. This picture was taken just before Colonel Walker's team made the first salvage attempt."

Nick looked over at Drake. "Still think my theory about a mole is crazy?"

Amanda Navistrova strode into the office. "Hey, I was thinking maybe this time I could go with you and—" She stopped short when she saw the computer screen. Nick detected something in her eyes. Recognition? Fear? She recovered too quickly. Her expression shifted into a surprised smile. "Will!" she exclaimed. "I *thought* I heard Colonel Walker mention your name."

McBride stood up and offered his hand, but Amanda brushed it aside and gave him a hug.

"Hey, were you over at Spookville this morning?" asked Drake.

Amanda released McBride and nodded. "Scott has me branching out from engine work into SATCOM nets for the Wraith. We're using one of Langley's frequency sets. I had to do some coordination. Why?"

"Just curious. One of their analysts mentioned seeing you in the cafeteria," answered Drake, choosing his words carefully.

"One of their analysts, huh?" Amanda put her arms around Drake and pressed her body up against his. She looked up into his eyes, sniffed, and then pushed him away. "Terri Belfacci," she said, spitting out the words.

"Whoa, how did you know that?"

"Her perfume. She marks men like a cat marks its territory."

"I needed Terri to help us with an investigation," interjected Nick, coming to Drake's rescue. He pointed to the picture on the computer screen and narrowed his eyes just a touch. "We're looking into that individual. Do you happen to recognize him?"

"He's a Chinese assassin," offered Drake.

"Then he's definitely not part of my crowd," said Amanda. "I'm used to nerds and mechanics. The only violence they show is when they break their calculator or smack an engine with a wrench." Her smile returned. "And speaking of nerds. Scott and I have something to show you. Come with me."

CHAPTER 31

We need to get cracking on our mission plan," said Nick as the group stepped onto the elevator. "We don't have time for games." He didn't like surprises, and Amanda had refused to tell him why she'd interrupted his meeting with McBride or why she was taking them up to Romeo Seven's hangar.

"Don't worry," replied Amanda, ignoring his tone. "Scott thinks you'll want to take a look at this before you plan the rescue, and Colonel Walker agrees."

The group fell silent for a moment. Then Nick turned to McBride. "I need you to keep digging into that picture from ten years ago. Find out who . . ."

"This way, boys," said Amanda, cutting him off as the elevator came to a stop. She ushered them out into the dimly lit hangar. The M-2 Wraith filled up half of the massive structure. With its contoured form and curved beak, the great black aircraft looked like a sleeping dragon, guarding its treasure in a darkened cave.

"I hate to break it to you," said Drake, "but we've already seen this one."

"No. I don't think you have," replied Walker, emerging from the shadow beneath the Wraith's wing, followed closely by Quinn and Molly. The colonel pulled a remote control from his pocket and pointed toward the fenced hole in the floor, the shaft for the vehicle elevator from Scott's lab.

The dark pit lit up with yellow light. A loud buzzer sounded, and red lights flashed. Then the huge chains that lifted the elevator clattered to life, turning on their spindles. A smooth black shape emerged from below, like an otherworldly creature, breathing in cadence with the rotation of the red lights. Finally, the lift jerked to a stop, and the hangar fell silent again.

"This is better than Christmas," Drake exclaimed, breaking the reverent atmosphere.

Scott stepped out from behind the new aircraft. "And here I am without my reindeer."

"You finished the infiltration craft," said Nick in astonishment.

The group walked over to the lift, and Nick began to circle the little jet. The composite aircraft sat low on tricycle landing gear, so low that the apex of its frame barely came to the top of Nick's head. The whole thing was only slightly larger than a Humvee.

Nick lightly ran his fingers along the smooth black surface. Much like the Wraith, this craft seemed to be one uniform piece. There were no discernible wings. Instead, the fuselage thinned progressively from the center outward, terminating in a razor's edge. From above, it resembled a diamond, except that the forward point had been lengthened to form a nose, and the rear point had been cut off, replaced with a saw-toothed exhaust. Its profile sloped quickly up and then tapered gradually away like a teardrop. "I thought she wasn't going to be ready for another month," said Nick.

Scott shrugged. "If engineers didn't pad their estimates, how would we appear to work miracles?"

"Would someone mind catching me up on what's going on?" asked Quinn.

Scott smiled at the young airman. "This is Shadow Catcher, Major Baron's concept and my design. We took advantage of the Wraith's large bomb bay and built a deployable craft that can accommodate three men. As you can see"—he pointed to the squat landing gear—"Shadow Catcher does not have to return to the bay like a drone. She can land inside enemy territory. And not just on standard runways; she can use unimproved surfaces like dirt roads or grass fields."

"Sweet, an off-road airplane," said Drake.

Scott paused to regard him with a disdainful look. "Hilarious. As I was saying, Shadow Catcher can land behind enemy lines to deploy a team. Once the mission is complete, she will return to the Wraith." He turned his attention back to the group. "Her docking capability is greatly improved over past designs. A formidable array of embedded sensors and powerful autopilot processors allow Shadow Catcher to dock autonomously."

"I'd still prefer to do it by hand," said Nick.

"And I'd prefer that you didn't," replied Scott.

Quinn whistled. "Very nice. So, what've you got under the hood?"

"That's my department," said Amanda. "Based on our work with the M-2, we reverse-engineered an F-22 engine to be smaller and lighter. We lost some thrust in the process, but that's okay, considering Shadow Catcher's small size and light weight." Amanda crouched next to the rear of the jet. "Lights, if you please, Scott."

The hangar lights above the elevator went out, replaced with black lights mounted low on the four corners of the lift. A faint purple glow settled on the group.

"Your teeth are glowing," Drake whispered to Scott.

"Oh, grow up," replied the engineer.

Shadow Catcher's surface was no longer a uniform black. Faceted shapes—wide diamonds and flat hexagons—glowed brightly in the new light, spread out across the aircraft's exterior like puzzle pieces waiting to be matched.

"Now you can see the various sensors and access panels set into the aircraft structure," said Amanda. "We use an extra chemical in their paint that highlights them under a black light."

Scott pressed a few keys on a laptop sitting on a computer cart. A hiss could be heard from inside the small aircraft, and then two large panels popped open. Thick white vapor drifted out of each hole and rolled along the floor, glowing like spirits under the black lights.

"These are the lower exhaust ports," said Amanda. "The pilot can reroute most of the engine thrust here when needed."

"So she has vertical takeoff and landing capability," said Nick.

"Not quite," corrected Amanda. "I said we could reroute *most* of the thrust, but some of it is lost in heat against the curvature of the ducts. We haven't cracked that nut entirely. For the moment, Shadow Catcher has a very short takeoff capability. She only requires a small amount of lift in addition to the lower thrust, about fifty knots' worth. In a stiff wind, she could probably hover."

"What about a gun?" asked Quinn.

Scott threw up his hands. "I can't win."

"Seriously, kid," said Walker.

"It's a fair question," argued Quinn.

Scott returned the lights to normal. "No, she does not have a gun."

"And for good reason," added Walker. "Shadow Catcher is designed for infiltration and rescue missions. That's what makes her perfect for this job." He motioned to Scott, who pressed another sequence of keys on his laptop.

Shadow Catcher hissed again, and a long section dropped out of the structure beneath the right wing. It was covered in gray padding.

"Our team can strap a wounded man to this pneumatic stretcher and then quickly lift him into the ship," said Walker.

"It's all great, but we haven't tested her," said Nick. Memories of the Iraq mission fired in his mind. When the White House sent them in, Dream Catcher had only made one test flight. Shadow Catcher hadn't made any at all.

"Shadow Catcher's unique capabilities make her the perfect choice for this mission," argued Walker. "And you said it yourself, we don't have any more time to waste. I know how you feel about this sort of thing, Baron, but with the Skyhook system out of commission, I don't see any other choice."

"I like it," said Drake. "No risky HALO jump, no lengthy border run, and no Skyhook. In and out—stealthy, quick, and clean."

"I still don't get it. How does Shadow Catcher play into your CONOPS?" asked Quinn, referring to Walker's concept of operations, his plan for recovering Novak.

Nick kept his eyes on Walker as he replied to the young airman. "If I'm reading the colonel right," he said cautiously, "he wants me to land our newest stealth plane in China."

CHAPTER 32

Wūlóng watched Baron's woman walk out onto the back deck with a small bag of supplies slung over her shoulder, cradling her son in her arms. She appeared to be taking the child down to the dock or the shoreline. He watched with interest for a moment. Then he lowered the binoculars and raised his weapon.

A scope was not necessary, as she would pass within a few meters of his position in the trees. He lined up the tritium sites on her forehead, just above the left eye. Though Western women were not normally to his taste, Wūlóng found this one beautiful, and beautiful women made more interesting targets—the alteration that tragedy wrought upon their features was always more dramatic. As she passed his position, he shifted his aim to the child.

Wūlóng pressed his lips together. He hated to begin

out here. Even with the trees to mute the cries. The home's interior offered much better cover. The sun had just begun to set. He had time.

As the woman sat down by the shore of the river, he lowered his weapon. He bent down and flipped on the cell phone jammer. Then he silently crept through the trees, heading for the front of the house.

———

Nick glanced down at his cell phone and frowned. For the third time, Katy's line went straight to voice mail. Maybe she had turned her phone off to put the baby down. Maybe she was just still mad. He hung up and set the phone down in the Mustang's cup holder.

The rescue CONOPS was complete. Takeoff was set for the dark hours of the early morning. He hated to delay the rescue, but if the team launched any earlier, they would arrive over Fujian in daylight. In general, daylight infiltration into a sovereign nation was a bad idea. With nothing left but the waiting, Nick had headed home, hoping to reconcile with Katy before he had to leave again.

As he stepped onto the porch, Nick noticed that his front door was cracked slightly open again. He sighed. "Are you trying to bait me into another attack?" he called, walking into the house and closing the door.

Something whizzed past his head and thudded into the wall. Instinctively, Nick sprinted for the cover of the study. Fragments of plaster and tile pelted his arms and legs as a fusillade of bullets tracked down the wall and across the floor at his heels. He dove through the half-open French doors, rolling into the room and landing with a crash against his desk.

Katy.

Nick wanted to scream out her name, tell her to grab Luke and run. But he knew that calling to her could just as easily bring her into the line of fire. He tried to dial her on his cell phone. He had no signal. That was why he couldn't reach her before. The attacker was using a jammer.

Nick fought to suppress all the reactionary instincts of a husband and father. He had to slow down and think, become the same violent professional that his wife seemed to despise. Adrenaline pumped through his veins. A situation breakdown started rolling through his mind. How many bullets? Where had they come from? He knew the answer to the first question. His subconscious had recorded the unsteady rhythm of the impacts. Twelve distinct percussive sounds: eight shots and four ricochets, fired from a silenced pistol. Determining where they came from was another trick entirely.

Where was Katy?

Crouched in the corner of his office, Nick listened intently for movement, for Katy, the attacker, anything.

Nothing.

Four of the bullets had bounced off the tile and immediately thumped into the wall. Those ricochets meant the bullets had been fired at a low angle. The shooter was on the ground floor. Based on obstacles and walls, that left the sitting room or the kitchen. Nick used a toe to nudge open the closed side of the French doors. Instantly one of the glass panels shattered, and a bullet lodged itself into the far corner of his mahogany desk. That answered the second question. Wherever he'd started from, the shooter was now in the kitchen.

Nick lifted the cuff of his pants, reaching for his knife, but it wasn't there. He'd packed it with his mission gear in Romeo Seven's locker room. He needed a weapon. Crawling behind the desk, he reached up and groped around in the center drawer. Stapler, coins, *scissors*. Using a dime, he separated the two pieces, transforming the mundane tool into a pair of ring-handled daggers. He hefted them in his hands. They were a little too light, but they would have to do.

The longer he waited, the more advantage he gave to the shooter; Nick had to move. He stood, pressing himself against the bookshelf set into the study's back wall. Then he took two long steps and leapt headfirst across the foyer, twisting in midair. He saw a muted flash. Burning pain shot through his side. He launched one of his makeshift daggers. Just before he landed in the dining room, he saw the projectile sink into the hostile's left shoulder. He recognized the face. Wūlóng.

Nick forced himself to continue forward. Ignoring the pain in his midsection and the wet feel of blood trickling down to his waistband, he made for the dining-room entry to the kitchen, hoping to outflank the Chinese assailant. He ducked into the butler's pantry, crouching in the same spot from which he'd sprung into the kitchen the night before. For a brief moment, he wondered if this were some bizarre waking nightmare, if he were about to unconsciously finish what he started when he attacked Katy the evening before.

He pushed the thought out of his mind and listened. Silence. Wŭlóng was cautious. Stalking him. The last few minutes had shown the assassin that Nick was no easy kill. Now he carefully advanced, but from which direction? Then Nick heard the faintest scrape of coarse fabric against granite. It could just as easily have been a trick of the mind as a real noise, but he committed. He rose and spun out of his hiding place, holding the scissor handle like an ice pick, thrusting the blade in a wide arc.

Wŭlóng's eyes widened with pain and rage as Nick forced the makeshift knife between the bones in his forearm. He did not scream, though. He did not even grunt, even though the blade burst out the other side of his arm.

The strike knocked the gun from Wŭlóng's hand, sending it clattering across the kitchen floor and under the stove. Nick pulled back his homemade dagger, slicing tendons as he removed it from Wŭlóng's wrist. Only then did he notice that his first weapon was no longer embedded in the attacker's shoulder. He raised his right arm in defense, just in time to deflect a slashing blow aimed at his face. He felt the sickening slice as Wŭlóng carved a deep gash into his forearm. Then the back door opened. Nick risked a glance.

Dear God, no.

"Nick?" Katy stood just inside the back door wearing a look of horror. Luke slept peacefully, nestled in her arms.

"Run!" he shouted.

Wūlóng took advantage of his distraction. He landed a right cross that sent Nick reeling back. When he regained his balance, Nick saw Katy bolting through the back door with the assassin in close pursuit. He tore after them.

"Stop, or she dies," said the assassin.

Nick halted just outside the door. Wūlóng stood on the deck, just ten feet away. He had Katy by the hair, the point of the bloody scissors blade pressed against her throat.

"If she screams, I will kill her. If you move, I will kill her," said Wūlóng, his voice like ice.

Nick began to circle right, trying to put the assassin off balance.

"I said stop." Wūlóng pressed the blade harder into Katy's throat to emphasize his command. A drop of blood formed at the tip and rolled down the blade.

Nick froze. "She has nothing to do with you," he said. "She doesn't know who you are or why you are here. Let her go."

Wūlóng grinned, his expression full of malice. "Put down your weapon now, Major Baron."

Nick hesitated, but Wūlóng yanked Katy's head back by her hair. She let out a terrified yelp. Luke woke up and began to cry. Nick leaned forward and stuck his half of the scissors straight down into the wooden rail of the deck. Then he took a step back and slowly raised his hands. "Let her go. You came to kill me, not them."

Wūlóng smiled. "To borrow a cliché from your American movies, if I had come here to kill you, then you would already be dead. Tsk, tsk." He shook his head slowly. "You came home a little early this evening. You interrupted my process. Most unfortunate." He wiped his damaged arm on Katy's face, smearing his blood across her cheek. Katy recoiled, but he quickly grabbed her hair and jerked her back.

"This is not about killing. It is about control," continued Wūlóng. "I only need one of these in order to maintain that control. The other one will serve as a demonstration of my resolve." He glanced down at the wailing baby, his expression grim, decisive.

"If you do as you are told," said the assassin, lowering the blade toward Luke, "perhaps you will both live to have another son."

The world slowed, as if every movement were made against the heavy resistance of black tar. The killer's hand seemed to move only a fraction of an inch per second. Nick's eyes did not leave Katy's as he lunged forward. Her face contorted in pure maternal rage. She tightened her grip on her screaming child with her right arm. With her left, she pushed Wūlóng's scissors away. At the same time, her left heel came crashing down against his instep. Nick planted his left foot and snatched the scissors blade from the deck rail, slashing upward at the assassin's neck. Katy screamed as a shower of blood splattered the deck chair behind her.

Wūlóng went limp and collapsed. Katy fled to the other side of the deck and crumpled into a ball, sobbing and pressing Luke to her chest.

Nick dropped the bloody scissors to the deck and lifted

the assassin by the collar. Blood poured over his hands. "Who sent you?" he demanded.

Wūlóng only gurgled in response. Then the life faded from his staring eyes, and his head fell back.

Nick rushed over to Katy. He helped her to her feet and held her tightly. "Are you all right?"

Katy did not answer. She continued to cry, her cheek still pressed against her wailing son. The left side of her face and neck was covered in blood.

Nick led his wife over to a chair and sat her down. "I need to get you some warm washcloths to clean you up," he said, starting for the door.

Katy grabbed his arm and pulled him back. "Don't leave me," she pleaded.

Nick knelt down beside the chair. He kissed her forehead and caressed his son. "I won't, sweetheart. I won't." But the moment the promise left his lips, he knew that he could not keep it.

CHAPTER 33

"You're leaving again, aren't you?" asked Katy. She and Nick sat at the dining-room table. She still held Luke in her arms; Nick had not been able to convince her to let him go. At least the baby had fallen asleep again, exhausted from his crying. The assassin's pistol lay in the middle of the table, a trash bag full of bloody rags on the kitchen floor.

Walker was on his way with a team from Romeo Seven. Nick had only just called him. The phone lines were dead, and he had to peel himself away from Katy's grasp and treat her wounds before committing to a search for the cell phone jammer. It took him several minutes to find it, a small suitcase tucked into the trees outside. He discovered a skiff as well, but there was nothing inside but a pair of waders.

Their wounds were minor, considering the attack. Nick had already begun to treat Katy when he remembered that he had been shot, but when he lifted his shirt, he only found a blood-caked abrasion. Apparently the bullet had just grazed him. The deep gash in his arm was much more pressing and would probably require stitches. With Katy's help, he cleaned it thoroughly and then wrapped it with gauze. They also cleaned the puncture wound in her neck. Once they had wiped away all of the blood—both hers and Wūlóng's—they found only a minor cut.

"This isn't over," said Nick, diverting his eyes from Katy's pleading gaze.

"It is for you," she countered, grabbing his chin and turning his head back until their eyes met again. "You're just an adviser, right?"

Nick pulled away from her and sighed. Why couldn't she just be happy to be alive? Why did she have to interrogate him, make him lie to her? "I have to protect you," he said forcefully. "And to do that, I have to find out what's going on. You don't understand."

Katy looked down at Luke. "You're right. I don't."

Walker arrived with Drake and a small crew to clean up the mess. While Doc Heldner tended to Katy, the colonel pulled Nick into the study. "We've already contacted the Chinese Embassy," he said with his usual scowl. "They claim that they will launch a full investigation, which is dignitary speak for 'sweep it under the rug.'" His eyes narrowed. "McBride tells me this is your guy from the morgue stakeout. What did I tell you about digging into your leak theory?"

"It paid off, didn't it?" asked Nick. "How else do you explain his presence in Kuwait ten years ago?"

"The sergeant says this guy gets around," said the colonel, waving Nick's argument away. "A lot of foreign intelligence operatives found their way to Kuwait during the first few days of Iraqi Freedom. That place was brimming with the latest American military tech. As for his presence here, I'm thinking this is revenge for taking out his divers."

Nick shook his head. "No, Wūlóng said that he wasn't here to kill me."

"He just said that to keep you off balance. Would you expect the truth?"

Despite the colonel's frustration at being kept in the dark about Wūlóng, Nick convinced him to let the rescue attempt continue. But to make it happen, the team would have to stick to the original launch schedule. There would be no extra rest. Nick would have to report back to the base just after one o'clock in the morning, only a few hours away.

When the crew finally left, Nick lay down in his bed next to Katy. The full moon cast its light through their sheer curtains, sending dull white beams across the sheets. He stared at the ceiling, unable to shut down his mind. How did it all connect? What role did Wūlóng play in the failure a decade before? How could he possibly be tied to Novak? Nick could not find the answers, nor could he find sleep. Finally, he rose and began to dress. "Are you awake?" he whispered.

Katy just shifted in the bed, rolling over to put her back to him. Nick walked around to her side of the bed. Her eyes were closed, the comforter clutched tightly to her chest. He bent down to kiss her cheek and tasted the wet saltiness of tears. Her eyes opened, moist and glistening in the moonlight.

"I love you," he said.

She looked away in silence.

PART THREE

SHADOWS

CHAPTER 34

So much had changed in ten years.

Too much.

Sports cars could tell their drivers where to go. Cell phones could do almost anything. Even aircraft had become as smart as their pilots. Technology had killed simplicity.

Ten years ago, Nick would have arrived at a dark hangar with just his flight bag and a thermos full of black coffee. As he sipped the bitter black liquid from a plastic lid, he would get to know his steed, rekindle the fire between them before the dawn patrol. He would inspect the smooth curvature of her lines, the caged fury of her weapons, until he came to understand her, and she him. So the moment he lit the burners, she would become a part of him, an extension of his own body.

Not anymore.

Sleek painted aluminum and countersunk rivets had been replaced with molded composites and cured putties; pressure gauges and mechanically linked engines replaced with microprocessors and digital throttles. Aircraft had ceased to be the living chargers of twentieth-century knights and had become the cold, networked tool kits of twenty-first-century battle managers—emphasis on managers—and it took a small army to get them into the air.

When Nick arrived, the brightly lit hangar was already buzzing with activity. Scott and his crew fussed over computer carts, linked to the Wraith by bundles of cables. Technicians dutifully laid out an array of high-tech combat equipment on three tables under her wing. Drake, Walker, and Doc Heldner stood beneath the Wraith's bay, checking out Shadow Catcher and the docking system that held her in place.

Nick took a sip from his thermos lid and pinched his lips at the bitter taste. At least the coffee hadn't changed.

Without a word to the others, he walked over to the tables and began fitting and checking his gear, starting with an integrated tactical vest and harness.

Quinn appeared from beneath the Wraith and strode up to the table next to him. Nick eyed the pararescueman suspiciously. The kid wore a tactical combat uniform just like Nick's, Kevlar-impregnated fatigues covered in a seven-color camouflage called MultiCam. But Quinn was supposed to be grounded. "I'm sorry," said Nick. "Are you under the impression that you're going somewhere?"

"He *is* going," said Walker. Nick looked at the colonel in time to see him cast a concerned glance at Heldner. "After last night's attack, we've made a slight change to the plan. I've lifted Quinn's probation."

"And when were you going to tell your team lead about it?" asked Nick.

"I'm telling you now," replied Walker, his tone leaving no more room for argument.

Quinn had kept quiet, busying himself with his tactical harness, but he struggled, unable to adjust the fit.

Nick sighed. He roughly turned the young operative, adjusting the shoulder straps for him. "If I'd have known you were coming, I'd have called your mom to come in and dress you." When he finished, he turned Quinn back around. "Did you see how I did that, or do I need to do the legs for you too?"

"Yeah, yeah, I've got it," replied Quinn, pushing him away.

"Are we interrupting something?" McBride looked concerned as he stepped off the elevator with Amanda. The two of them carried a black reinforced crate the size of a large cooler over to Drake's table and set it down. "A courier brought this over from the CIA after you all left yesterday afternoon. It's addressed to Major Merigold."

Drake tore open a small manila envelope taped to the top of the crate and pulled out the note inside. "Drake," he read aloud. "Here are some artifacts to help you in your investigation. Let me know if I can do anything else for you, anything at all. Lo—" He suddenly stopped reading. "Ahem. Sincerely, Terri."

"What does she mean by 'anything at all'?" asked Amanda.

"These must be Novak's personal effects," said Nick. "There could be something useful in here."

Walker shook his head and motioned for two of the techs to move the box to the back of the hangar. "There's no time. We already have the information we need. McBride can go through it after you launch."

Nick watched the techs set the box against the hangar wall and then noticed that Quinn had walked over to Scott, who began to trade the M9 Beretta holster on his harness for a different one. "What is this?" he asked, gesturing at the two of them.

"I'll be carrying my personal weapon," said Quinn, "a forty-five-caliber Springfield XDm." He held up a brawny black pistol with a contoured polymer grip and a laser/infrared spotlight combo fixed to the lower rail. "It requires a custom holster."

Though Nick had never demanded that a subordinate call him "sir," somehow it bugged him that the kid didn't use it now. "We carry M9s as our sidearms," he said in a commanding tone, shoving his own weapon into its holster. "I didn't approve a change."

"I did," interjected Walker. "Quinn is most comfortable with the XDm. If you want him to be quick and accurate, let him use it."

Nick felt anger boiling up inside again. Walker had usurped his authority over this mission three times in the space of a few short minutes. He fumed as he returned to prepping his harness, hooking a custom knife sheath to each leg strap, each with five small stilettos canted forward at a thirty-degree angle.

"Speaking of nonstandard weapons," said Quinn, "what do you call those?"

"Contingency options," replied Nick.

Quinn gave him a smirk. "When I was younger, the slow kid at the end of my block had throwing knives."

Scott finished fixing Quinn's holster. He looked from Quinn to Nick and back again. "You should stop talking now," he whispered, and then quickly backed away.

Quinn continued, undaunted. "He also played with dragon games and throwing stars."

Nick scowled down at the table. He'd had all that he could take from this insubordinate greenhorn. His left hand flashed out from the knife holster. The stiletto made a soft *thock* as it stuck deep into Quinn's vest, buried to the hilt in one of the removable pockets. The camouflage fabric began to darken with moisture.

"Enough! Both of you!" said Walker.

"Honestly, Major Baron," said Scott, marching over and pulling the knife out of the stunned pararescueman's vest. He removed the interchangeable pocket and dumped out two punctured water pouches and a perforated bag of ration bars.

"The kid was clearly begging for a demonstration," said Nick with a wicked smile. He retrieved the knife, wiped it down with a cloth, and resheathed it.

"I think now is as good a time as any, Patricia," said Walker with a nod to the doctor.

Heldner took Nick's arm and tried to gently lead him toward an office at the other end of the hangar.

Halfway there, Nick pulled his arm away and checked his watch. "Time is short, Doc. What's going on?"

The doctor took a short breath and then looked him in the eye. "After the incident with Wūlóng, your fitness to lead this mission has been called into question," she said in a low voice. "Colonel Walker has asked me to make a spot assessment. If I decide that you're unfit, he's going to cancel the rescue."

CHAPTER 35

Nick felt his control slipping away. How could the colonel question his fitness to lead a Triple Seven op? He'd been leading this team for a decade. "What is this all about?" he asked.

Heldner pulled him into the office, closed the door, and motioned for him to sit down on a small couch. Then she turned a rolling chair backward and sat down, straddling the seat. She leaned her forearms on the backrest. "How are you sleeping lately?"

"I don't understand."

"It's a simple question," said Heldner with a shrug. "Both Colonel Walker and Drake have expressed concerns to me that you haven't slept solidly in weeks."

"I'm dealing with it."

"Really?" The doctor raised her eyebrows. "Because it looks to me like you're coming unhinged. In the last couple of days, you argued publicly with your superior, ran an investigation that countermanded his orders, and just now you threw a knife at the newest member of our team."

Nick laughed. "That was classic. Did you see Quinn's face when I . . ." His voice trailed off under Heldner's crushing glare. She was not amused.

She leaned forward and glowered at him. "Then there are the bruises on your wife's arm. I noticed them last night. They are too old to have come from Wūlóng's attack."

Nick's eyes widened at the accusation. "Whoa, is that what this is about? That happened during a nightmare. I thought I was fighting off an attacker."

Heldner straightened up and put her hands on her knees. "Finally, we get to it. Nightmares, inability to sleep, uncontrolled anger." She pointed her finger at his chest. "You need to acknowledge that you are suffering from PTSD."

The doctor's words made Nick's blood run cold. He knew the consequences of such a diagnosis. Walker would have to pull him from field operations completely, relegate him to a desk job, bury him in the bowels of the Pentagon.

"I do not have PTSD," he countered, his tone desperate.

The doctor held out her hands. "Don't worry, Nick. I'm not planning on making this an official diagnosis." She lowered her voice. "And I *will* tell Dick that you're good to go. I believe in this mission as much as you do.

But you need to understand what's happening to you, so you can turn this thing around."

Her statement did little to reassure him. "Everybody has nightmares," he argued.

"Yes, but yours have a consistent cause. Fear. Real fear that occurs during your missions."

"I don't experience fear in the field anymore."

Heldner shook her head. "Not true. You've just become so accustomed to it that you hardly notice it. Your fight-or-flight responses have become automatic. You push the fear aside and move on without a conscious thought."

"Then what's the problem?"

The doctor put on a pair of spectacles and motioned him to lean forward. "Something has changed," she said, taking Nick's chin in her hand. She tilted his head one way and then the other, as if examining a patient with a cold. "Something happened that has heightened your fears." She emphatically patted his cheek and pushed him back. "And I think you already know what it is."

Nick let out a long breath. "Danny."

Heldner nodded.

"So now I'm subconsciously afraid of dying?"

The doctor shrugged. "Maybe, but I don't think that's quite it. We lost Danny months ago, but you've only been showing symptoms for a few weeks. There has to have been a more recent trigger that compounded the trauma, something else that you're afraid of." She removed her spectacles and slid them into the pocket of her lab coat. "Whatever the source, the fear is too intense for your subconscious to let it go after your normal process. You're not truly dealing with it in the moment, leaving it to fester below the surface. That's what's causing your nightmares."

Nick started to stand up. "My brain is taking care of it in my sleep. Problem solved."

"Wrong." Heldner reached up and shoved him back down onto the couch. "Nightmares are not satisfying to your unconscious mind. They have no real conclusion. They also keep you from getting real sleep"—she poked him in the arm—"and you need real sleep if you're going to function as a healthy, happy human being, one who doesn't throw knives at his co-workers." She reached into her lab coat and handed Nick a pill bottle. "Take one of these during the flight over. It will force your brain to circumvent the bad dreams so you can get some real sleep. But that's just a Band-Aid placed over an ax wound. To really heal, you have to determine the source of the nightmares."

Nick frowned. "And how am I supposed to do that?"

"The next time the mission gets intense, don't shove the fear aside. Allow it in, accept it."

"And then what?"

Heldner's expression darkened. Nick detected more than the usual motherly concern in her eyes. "And then you'll know what truly terrifies you."

———

When the doctor and Nick returned to the group, she gave Walker a discreet thumbs-up.

"Okay, Pat," said Walker. "Then it's time to do your pre-mission magic."

Heldner nodded and hefted a large steel case onto one of the tables.

"Why do we need the doc?" asked Quinn. "Are we getting a physical?"

Heldner winked. "Come over here and find out."

Nick smiled despite his mood. Doc Heldner had quickly returned to her usual sarcastic manner. She loved to make her boys uncomfortable.

A tech set up two folding chairs next to the table. Nick sat down in one and looked over at the hesitant pararescueman. "Hurry up, kid," he said. "We've wasted enough time. We've got to get this show on the road before the sun comes up."

Heldner popped open her case and removed a syringe with a very thick needle. She held it up to Nick. "Turn your head, Baron. But if you cough, I'll make you regret it."

Nick winced as Heldner inserted the needle into the pocket of skin behind his ear. He pictured the small electronics capsule sliding into place. A cold gel followed, surrounding the capsule beneath the skin. He knew that it made no visible lump at all, but it felt like the doctor had just implanted a frozen tennis ball at the top of his jaw. He looked up at her and raised an eyebrow.

She waved a small black box over the injection site and checked its digital readout. She nodded to Nick. "It's stable."

"Wait, what's stable?" asked Quinn, looking squeamish.

"Among other things, it's a comm device," said Nick. He looked off in the distance and said, "Connect: code two six seven one."

The implant responded with a feminine voice that only Nick could hear. "Stand by . . . Connection complete."

Nick waved to Scott. "Comm check. How do you hear?"

"Loud and clear," replied Scott, speaking into a small microphone. "How about me?"

"Same," replied Nick. "SATCOM is up. Cease transmission."

"Ending transmission," the digital voice replied.

Heldner removed another black box from the case and opened it up. A second capsule lay in a small copper receptor. The digital screen next to the receptor read READY. "The biggest weakness of these capsules is power," she said to Quinn. "Keeping a constant open connection would drain the battery, so you'll have to request that it connect to the satellite when you want to talk to us. That requires a pin code." She held the box in front of his face. "It keys to your voice and your code. Say any four numbers that you will find easy to remember, but don't give me your debit card pin. I am not an honest woman."

Nick left Quinn to set up his comm implant and learn about its grim secondary function while he tended to a few last-minute details. At the base of the Wraith's ladder, he found Drake arguing with Amanda and Joe Tarpin.

"What's going on here?" asked Nick.

Drake put his hands on his hips and nodded toward the two of them. "We have two interlopers who want to go for a ride. One has been attempting to coerce me with her feminine wiles. The other . . ." He looked at Joe with a queasy expression. "Well . . . the other is Joe."

"You're both out of your minds," said Nick.

"You owe me," said Joe. "And don't forget, I speak Chinese. The Wraith can intercept ground comms, and I can translate for you."

Amanda stepped between Joe and Drake. "I'm a member of this squadron now. Don't you think it's a good idea for me to get a little operational experience?"

Drake opened his mouth to respond, but she put a finger to his lips. "Consider your answer very carefully," she said in a dark and sultry tone.

"It's not his call," said Nick. "And I have no intention of letting you come along, either of you." Tarpin began to protest again, but Nick held up his hand. "I need you both here, helping Will McBride investigate Wūlóng and dig into Novak's past. Once we take off, we'll have more than ten hours before we deploy Shadow Catcher into Chinese airspace. That's ten hours for you to get me information that I can use on the ground."

Walker and Quinn joined them at the base of the ladder. Quinn looked ashen, but he was suited up and ready to go. "What's all this?" asked the colonel, looking sideways at Amanda and Tarpin.

"Nothing," said Nick. "They're just seeing us off."

"Good," said Walker, turning his wrist to look at his watch, "because it is now zero three hundred. Gentlemen, it's go time."

CHAPTER 36

The dark foliage of Zheng's favorite forest park drifted lazily past the car's open window. He breathed deeply. One final drive with Han.

In just a few days, he would report to Beijing to take up his new post as defense minister, and he would bring with him China's greatest triumph since the foundation of the Politburo. These were his last days in Fujian. He wanted to soak in the pleasure of its green hills and fresh scents before committing himself to the dirty, crowded streets of the capital. Sadly, circumstances had denied him the pleasure of a smooth transition. As he approached his greatest triumph, he was beleaguered by incompetence.

And betrayal.

Zheng checked his watch. "It is time to return to the base, Han," he said, offering a thin smile to his driver.

Liang's revelation that he knew about the Persian Gulf

operation had been a heavy blow, for it meant that Zheng had a spy in his own circle of trusted servants and operatives. Wūlóng could not have been the traitor, and that left only a few alternatives.

Zheng gave two of his Special Forces operatives the task of checking out the divers that were killed in Kuwait: their apartments, bank accounts, the usual fare. As an extra precaution, he had them check out Ling and Han as well. He had never shared any truly sensitive information with Ling, but one could never be too careful.

The result of his investigation cut him deeply. His men found papers in Han's flat that tied him to Liang. His most trusted servant had been reporting to Liang behind his back. It appeared that Han had tried to serve two masters, playing one against the other, waiting to see who would come out on top.

The traitor could have warned the doomed defense minister about Wūlóng, but he did not. Perhaps Han had finally chosen a champion. Still, the fact that he chose correctly did not excuse the betrayal.

"We need to stop at the maintenance garage," said Zheng as Han pulled past the base guardhouse. "The motor pool would like to do some routine work on this car. They will give us a replacement for the day."

Han cast a furtive glance in the mirror. "Gen . . . eh . . . Defense Minister," he said hesitantly, "there is no need to interrupt your busy schedule. I can drop you at your office immediately and then take care of the vehicle myself."

Zheng smiled and gave him a benevolent wave. "No, Han. I am in no hurry to return to the office. Please pull into the garage." He could see the suspicion in Han's eyes, the moisture developing at the top of his brow. It did not matter. He would not dare disobey.

Han pulled into the garage, and the electric door closed behind them. Two men in dirty blue coveralls appeared with dust masks covering their faces. Han did not move from his seat.

"Come. Help me out of the car, please," said Zheng. "I need the strength of your arm."

The two men stood well away from the car. Nevertheless, Han kept his eyes on them as he climbed out and walked around to Zheng's door. As he opened it and bent down to offer the minister an arm, he positioned himself to keep the men in sight. Zheng could see the fear in his eyes. Good.

Shock filled Han's face as the minister locked his arm in an iron grip. He pulled back, but Zheng used his resistance as leverage, nimbly pulling himself to his feet. Once he had his footing, he spun Han around, pulling a garrote wire from his watch and looping it around the traitor's neck.

Han tried to strike at Zheng, his arms flailing behind him, but his efforts only tightened the loop. Soon his body went limp.

Zheng held the wire taut for another fifteen seconds. Then the two Special Forces soldiers in maintenance uniforms came over and helped him lower the body to the ground. As he straightened up, one of them handed him a cloth to clean the wire. There was a lot of blood. Han's struggle had caused the garrote to slice deeply into his flesh, cutting into the windpipe and perhaps an artery.

Zheng regarded the bloody cloth and shook his head. He hated this sort of thing, but occasionally a leader needed to get his hands dirty to show his subordinates his capabilities and the price of disloyalty.

The secure satellite phone that Han carried for Zheng started ringing. One of the operatives reached into the dead man's pocket to get it. "It is Hēi Yǐng," he said, handing the phone to Zheng.

Zheng flipped open the phone. "The line is secure. Go ahead, my friend." He flicked his hand at his men, gesturing for them to take the body away.

"Wūlóng is dead," said Hēi Yǐng.

Zheng's grip on the phone tightened. It seemed that Hēi Yǐng had become a constant source of bad news.

"From what I have been able to piece together," continued the American, "Baron came home earlier than expected. He is a skilled opponent. Wūlóng was outmatched."

Zheng closed his eyes. "That is most unfortunate," he said. "And what of your efforts to gain the information I requested?"

"Baron is too cautious."

The minister let out a heavy sigh. Traitors and incompetents—would these trials never end? He rubbed his forehead with the palm of his hand. "Then our operation now depends entirely on my men."

"You underestimate me," Hēi Yǐng chided. "I still have options open, options that will guarantee your victory."

CHAPTER 37

William McBride backed out of the Romeo Seven elevator, helping Joe Tarpin carry the crate of Novak's effects into the command center. As the two of them deposited their load next to a workstation, he spied Amanda standing at the center of the room. "There you are," he said, straightening up and stretching his back. "You disappeared before the takeoff. You're not still mad because Drake didn't take you along, are you?"

Amanda did not reply. She stared up at the main screen. A triangular symbol moved across the map, showing the Wraith's progress, already making its way out of D.C. airspace.

McBride turned his attention back to the crate and saw that Tarpin had already started rummaging through its contents. He looked concerned. "Something wrong, Joe?" asked McBride.

Tarpin looked up, startled. "Hmph? Oh, I was just taking inventory. There's supposed to be a journal in here, but I don't see it. Has anyone else opened this crate?"

"I saw Nick crack it open before the takeoff. Maybe he took it with him on the plane."

Tarpin frowned. "He shouldn't have done that, not without checking with me first."

McBride slapped the side of the crate to get Amanda's attention. "Come on, quit brooding and get over here. There has to be something in here that will help our team."

Amanda reluctantly joined the two men. She slumped into a chair at the workstation and stared down into the box with an unenthusiastic sigh. "It's been twenty-five years. You'd think if anything in there were useful, someone would have found it by now."

"Maybe no one was looking," countered McBride. But after a glance at the contents, he feared she might be right. Despite its weight, the crate held disappointingly few artifacts: just an aged yellow file, a thin photo album, and a pilot's flight log. McBride gingerly pulled the ancient rubber band off the file.

The first document was the initial incident report for Novak's shoot-down, signed by a man named Jozef Starek. The report confirmed what the team had already learned from the digital Book of Honor file. Novak flew a solo mission over China, broke from his planned route, broke radio silence, and then was shot down. Further into the file, McBride found transcripts of the P-3 radio intercepts that backed up the report, as well as glossy black-and-white photographs taken from an SR-71 Blackbird at the time of the shoot-down.

He handed the file to Tarpin. Then he picked up the flight log and thumbed through the pages to the last entry. It was dated 21 December 1987. Novak had not logged his final mission on New Year's Day. That was not unexpected. Pilots normally logged their flights after landing, an opportunity that Novak missed, having been interrupted halfway through the flight by a surface-to-air missile. But then McBride noticed something else. All of Novak's previous flights over China were flown with a wingman in another F-16, every single one. "Doesn't it seem unusual that Novak flew solo on his last mission," he mused, "especially after he flew all of his other missions with a wingman?"

"Just because something is unusual," said Tarpin, "doesn't make it criminal."

"Good point." McBride stared down at the half-empty page for a moment longer. Then he suddenly looked up, snapping the book closed with a loud *slap*. He reached over and snatched the incident report from the file in Tarpin's hands, quickly scanning the pages a second time. When he finished, he waved the report at the other two. "But that *does* make it something that should be addressed in the incident report, and I don't see it here."

"Maybe," said Amanda, wrinkling her nose. She seemed unimpressed.

Tarpin shook his head. "I'm with her. Your logic is pretty thin."

"Wow, tough crowd." McBride put the papers back in

the file and then laid the Blackbird photographs down on the table, side by side. "Twenty-five years," he muttered, slowly bending closer to the photos until his freckled nose practically touched the glossy paper. After a few moments, he stood up and glanced around the command center. "I need a magnifying glass."

"What for?"

"There's a distortion on this photo." He started rifling through the workstation drawers.

Tarpin picked up the photo and squinted at it. "That's a smudge," he said. "Probably the smudge where you just touched it with your nose."

"Millions of dollars in tech, but we don't have a simple magnifying glass?" McBride continued rummaging through desks and cabinets. "I didn't touch it with my nose."

"Maybe there was a smear of something on the camera lens," offered Amanda, finally beginning to take interest.

McBride stopped ransacking the command center and gave her an incredulous look. "That photo was taken from eighty thousand feet. If there was a smear on the lens, it would have covered several acres."

He tapped a blond technician on the shoulder. "Magnifying glass?" She looked up from her screen and frowned at him, pointing to an earpiece to indicate that she was listening to something.

"I'll take that as a no. Wait a sec." He grabbed the photo out of Tarpin's hand and placed it on a scanner.

"You can't do that!" exclaimed Tarpin. "You don't have the authority to copy the Agency's materials."

McBride looked back at him and grinned. "Then it's a good thing you're here to supervise," he said. He sat down at a workstation, and a few moments later he had the photo displayed on one of its monitors. He expanded a small section and then rolled his chair back so the others could see. "Look, there's a clear distortion here. Doctoring photographs used to be a much more refined science. Twenty-five years ago, there was no iPhoto, not even Photoshop. It took a real professional to fix photographic evidence." He circled the distortion with his finger. "Whoever did this was no professional. It's a simple masking job. That photo is a duplicate of the original, with this section intentionally blurred into the forest background."

Amanda removed the photo from the scanner and held it up to her eyes. "It may be a hack job, but it could have fooled me. And the perpetrator got away with it for two and a half decades."

"This is getting us nowhere," argued Tarpin. "Let's assume you're right and the photo was masked—that still doesn't tell us who masked it."

McBride considered the CIA man's point for a moment and then raised a finger. "Maybe we shouldn't focus on the *who*," he said, rolling his chair over to a different computer at the station. "Maybe we should focus on the *what*." His fingers flew across the keyboard. Windows flashed up and down on the monitor. Then he abruptly slowed, loudly tapping the last two keys. He rolled his chair back again. "Edward Masters."

"Who?" asked Amanda.

"The pilot of the Blackbird that took these photos. He can tell us what's missing from that picture."

Disbelief covered Tarpin's face. "You've got to be kidding me," he said.

"Your agency lost control of the Blackbird program in the late sixties," replied McBride. "By the eighties, those assets belonged to the U.S. Air Force, and the U.S. Air Force keeps better records than any military service on the planet—even when it makes no sense to do so." He used the mouse to highlight a name on the screen. "Thus, I give you Edward Masters."

"That's great," said Tarpin, his tone flat. "How long ago did he pass away?"

McBride clicked open another window and highlighted more text. "He's alive and living the good life on Lake Anna." He pulled the address up on a map for them to see.

"That's only two hours south of here," said Amanda.

McBride checked his watch and then looked up at her. "Do you think he's awake?"

CHAPTER 38

The Wraith still had a long drive ahead before reaching Fujian. Nick left Drake at the controls and retired to the crew bunk for some rest. He placed a hand on his vest pocket and felt the pill bottle that Heldner had given him, but he wasn't ready to sleep. Too much had happened in the last few days.

As he sat down in his bunk, Nick struggled to fit the puzzle together. Chinese operatives attempt to steal stealth technology in Kuwait. The man who turns up to identify their bodies just happens to have been in Kuwait when the Triple Seven's first mission went horribly wrong. Then a missing CIA operative turns up in Fujian, an operative that may well have been sold out by a mole in the Distant Sage operation. And as soon as Nick's team develops a rescue plan, the same man from Kuwait shows up at his house and threatens his family.

Nick shut his eyes tight. The puzzle pieces seemed to move in circles. He wasn't even sure they all came from the same box. How could events split by twenty-five years be related? Maybe they weren't. Maybe he was just grasping for deeper meaning after the shock of seeing Katy and Luke threatened.

Maybe not.

He removed an old leather-bound book from the cargo pocket on his pant leg.

"What's that?"

Nick looked up to see Quinn peeking down from the crew bunk above him. "I thought you were resting," he said.

"Yeah, right," replied Quinn. "Like I could sleep on the way to my first real mission."

"You're not even supposed to be here. It's not a good idea to remind me how green you are," said Nick. He sat back in the bunk and brought the book up to read.

Quinn refused to take the hint. "You stole that from the CIA's archive crate," he said. "That's another agency's classified material."

"This material was entrusted to *my* team, and *I* deemed it essential to the accomplishment of *my* mission," countered Nick without lowering the book. "*Your* job here is to shut up and stay out of the way."

Quinn disappeared back into his bunk. "Whatever."

Nick ignored the young airman and turned his attention to Novak's book. Faded handwritten notes filled almost every page, along with several sketches. He read a few of the labels beneath the pictures: *RB-57 Canberra with Company Recon Mod, Photo Analysis Room—Pruszcz*

Gdanski, Red Baron Recce Pod. Novak was a skilled artist and apparently a technology buff. With all of the detail in the sketches, Nick began to wonder if Novak had an ulterior motive for keeping this journal. He flipped to the last few entries, all made at the CIA's forward operating location on Taiwan, and began to read.

September 26, 1987, FOL Sincheng, Taiwan

Jozef is finally warming up to me again. He's been so distant since Anja and I married that I felt like I'd lost a brother. The environment here is a great catalyst for reconciliation. Like in Poland, we are the only two American pilots. But there, our Slavic heritage gave us a bond with the others, at least a superficial one. Here we have nothing. The Taiwan nationals keep us at arm's length and treat us with suspicion, even the pilots. The ready room chatter is Chinese, filled with the laughter of inside jokes, and often it seems as if we are the butt of them. Jozef is learning Mandarin. He's doing quite well from what I can see. Maybe that will help.

October 24, 1987, FOL Sincheng, Taiwan

It's happening again. We lost three Taiwan nationals this month. One got hit by a missile just after crossing the mainland coastline. He limped back to the base, only to cartwheel down the runway in an unholy fireball. Two more disappeared last week. We sent them on a shore mission to check out a possible buildup on Nanhaixiang. They took a runabout out of Sincheng harbor eight days ago. We haven't heard from them since. Wright couldn't care less. As always, he seems constantly preoccupied with something else.

November 23, 1987, FOL Sincheng, Taiwan

Another national has disappeared, a photo analyst. She took a weekend leave to Taipei and never came back. She's been gone eleven days. Wright, our benevolent spook in charge, claims that she just got burned out and quit. He certainly isn't devoting enough resources to hunting her down.

It's not just the losses. Our reconnaissance runs are becoming less fruitful. Jozef says that it's because the Chinese have stepped up their camouflage, ever since they shot one of our F-16s. But these are huge military sites; they can't stay camouflaged all the time. I think someone is warning them. Maybe we can't trust the nationals no matter where we go. Maybe one of the Taiwan natives has turned, the same way that we think one of the Polish did. I know that I check my six more often when my wingman is a Taiwan national. Thank God for Jozef and Anja. They are the only people here that I can talk to, the only people I can trust.

December 12, 1987, FOL Sincheng, Taiwan

It seems that something goes wrong on every mission: broken reconnaissance pods, Chinese camouflage, bad navigation systems, engine malfunctions. Two days ago, we almost lost Jozef. His engine quit and he had to dead-stick his Viper back to the runway. We still haven't been able to determine what caused it. We haven't lost any personnel since the analyst, but I am still utterly convinced that there is a mole. I get the sense that the nationals agree that something is very wrong. They won't talk to me about it. They don't trust the Americans. Why should they? Maybe one of us is selling them out.

December 25, 1987, FOL Sincheng, Taiwan

Merry Christmas. I've come up with a plan to weed out the mole. I brought in Wright and the director of photo analysis to get approval, but none of the nationals will know about it. After my New Year's Day mission, I'll have a good idea where to find the mole.

Nick flipped the page. Blank. There were no more entries. He placed the journal on the bunk next to him and lay down. So Novak had started his own operation to smoke out the mole. Maybe he was getting too close, about to turn up the right stone. Then he disappeared, and the mole was never found. Nick closed his eyes and rubbed his temples. None of that connected Novak to the mole in the Triple Seven Chase, if there even was one. Nick blinked. Unless Novak's mole and the Triple Seven's mole were one and the same. He swallowed Heldner's pill and closed his eyes. He was chasing shadows.

Even after taking the pill, he could not quiet his mind. For several minutes, random phrases and fragmented visions paraded through his mind. Then, finally, the drug overpowered his thoughts, and he slept.

CHAPTER 39

Where was she?

McBride checked his watch. Almost 6:00 A.M. The sun was just peeking over the airfield's eastern runway, causing the tarmac to ripple like a glassy lake.

The archive crate had produced no other leads beyond the doctored photograph. Exhausted by the predawn launch, the group had split for some much-needed rest. Tarpin would have to stay in D.C. and check in at Langley, but Amanda had agreed to drive out to Lake Anna with McBride to find the Blackbird pilot. They were supposed to meet in the parking lot at a quarter to six.

"Just like a woman," he muttered, "never ready on ti—"

A spellbinding sight interrupted McBride's disparaging words. Amanda strode around the corner of the hangar like a model on a catwalk, her athletic form flattered by the morning play of light and shadow. McBride suddenly felt ill prepared, even dirty. He had merely showered and re-dressed in the same red polo and khakis. She wore a fresh skirt and blouse, with a matching blazer casually slung over her shoulder. He found it difficult to recall, but he could swear she'd even managed a change of shoes.

"Sorry I'm late," said Amanda brightly.

"How did you . . . Did I miss something?" stuttered McBride, looking from his wrinkled khakis to Amanda's pressed suit.

She looked at him quizzically and then suddenly caught his meaning. "Oh, you mean this?" she asked cavalierly, waving a hand from her shoulders to her hips with a flourish. "I keep a spare outfit in the car. Fortune favors the prepared, you know."

McBride opened the passenger's-side door of his car. "I take back everything I said in defense of Drake last night," he said, taking Amanda's hand to help her in. "He shouldn't have left you behind for this mission. He's a bum."

A little over two hours later, McBride parked the car in the gravel driveway of a chocolate brown two-story lake home. As he opened the car door for Amanda, a gray-haired man waved from the screened-in porch.

"Hello there," said the man in a rich bass voice. "You two must be McBride and Navistrova." He opened the screen door and beckoned them onto the porch. "Thanks for calling before you came over. Margaret hates surprise visitors."

"Colonel Edward Masters, I presume?" asked McBride, flashing his Department of Defense ID.

"Retired colonel," corrected Masters. He waved off

the ID and shook McBride's outstretched hand with an iron grip. "And you can call me Ned."

"Yes, sir," replied McBride. He never knew how to respond to informalities from officers, retired or not.

"On the phone you said this was a matter of national security," said Masters, smoothing the front of his flannel shirt. He motioned for them to sit at a glass table and then took his own seat. McBride expected the older man to lower himself slowly into the chair. Instead, he moved with the ease and strength of a man twenty years younger.

"Yes, sir," McBride began. "We wanted to ask you about some photos you took back in your Blackbird days."

Masters narrowed his eyes. "You can't be serious. I got all those photographs declassified through the proper channels. Did you folks really drive all the way down here to complain about the reunion website?"

McBride pulled the photos and old file from the CIA out of his briefcase. "No, sir, we're not here about photos you took *of* the plane. We're here to ask you about some photos you took *from* the plane."

A tall woman with neatly bobbed hair and denim capris interrupted the conversation. She gracefully weaved around the porch furniture and placed a tray of juices and pastries on the glass table. McBride instinctively retrieved the file to hide the classified photos.

Masters smiled. "Oh, don't worry about her. The Blackbird wives got scrutinized by the security folks as much as their husbands." He looked up at her and smiled, giving her hand a tender squeeze. "And it's a good thing they did. Too many secrets can play havoc on a marriage."

McBride abashedly replaced the file on the table. He stood up and offered his hand to the old pilot's wife. "Sergeant Will McBride," he said. "It's a pleasure to meet you, ma'am. You didn't have to go to any trouble."

The woman gently shook McBride's hand and then waved hers dismissively. "Oh, it's no trouble at all," she said. "It's not every day we get to entertain visitors." She patted Masters on the head. "Mostly it's just me and Ole Blue here."

Masters rolled his eyes. "Thank you, dear."

A telephone rang inside the house. "Oops, that's my cue," said Margaret. "Y'all holler if you need anything else." She retreated back into the house as gracefully as she had come out.

"We understand you worked in concert with Operation Distant Sage," prompted McBride, getting back to business.

"Haven't heard that name in a while," said Masters, leaning forward and resting his arms on the tabletop, "particularly not outside of a secure room." He nodded. "Yes, our squadron cooperated with the spooks to share intel."

"I've been wondering," said Amanda. "Why the overlap? If the CIA was running low-level photo flights over China, why send out the Blackbirds as well?"

Masters gave her a sly grin. "It's better if I show you. We'll do a little demonstration with your partner here." He leaned back and picked up a postcard from an end table behind him. "Just got a stack of these from the Smithsonian," he said, placing the card on the table with its photo side down. Then he pulled a document from the CIA file and rolled it into a tight cylinder. "Close one eye and look through this." He held the cylinder just above the table in front of McBride.

McBride smiled awkwardly and complied, bending forward to look through the paper.

"No peeking," said Masters, waving a hand in front of McBride's closed eye. Then he turned over the postcard and carefully slid it under the homemade scope. "What do you see?" he asked.

"I see an American flag blowing in the wind, with gray sky in the background."

"Mm-hmm," said Masters. "Now put away the paper and open your eyes."

McBride sat back and looked at the card. It was a color photo of a lunar landing. An astronaut stood between the American flag and a Moon rover.

"That flag isn't blowing in the wind," said Masters, his sly grin returning. "It's standing straight out because NASA put a telescoping rod behind it to give it a rippling look. And that gray background isn't a cloud. It's a lunar mountain.

"We call that the microscope effect. You need a close-up view to see important details, but if that's the only view you have, you miss the bigger picture. The Blackbirds provided that big picture, and then the CIA Vipers went in with the microscope."

McBride nodded. "Speaking of pictures, we need you to tell us what you can remember about some photos you took back in '88."

"I don't know if I can help you much there. You might want to talk to my backseater; he ran the cameras and the radar. Shoot, we didn't even see most of the pictures we took."

"I think you might remember these." McBride handed the photos to Masters. "It was New Year's Day."

Masters pulled a pair of reading glasses out of his pocket and seated them on his nose before scrutinizing the pictures. After almost a minute, he sat back and let out a low whistle. "I do remember this day," he said, looking hard at McBride. "This was the last flight operation for Distant Sage, the day that one of the Vipers got shot down."

"That's right," said McBride. "We're conducting an investigation to find out what really happened. We're not sure that we have all of the details right."

Masters bent over the photos and studied them again. When he looked up, his face had changed, the levity of an aging gentleman replaced by the gravity of a military commander. "I was the supervising officer who packaged the photos and sent them over to Distant Sage after the incident," he said, "and I can already tell you one detail that you've got wrong."

"What's that?" asked Amanda.

Masters removed his reading glasses and set them on the table. He shifted his gaze from McBride to Amanda with a deadly serious expression. "These aren't the original photos. The pictures that I sent over showed *two* F-16s."

CHAPTER 40

Nick woke up to find Drake shaking his shoulder.

"You're doing the zombie thing again. Quit it. You're freaking me out."

Nick blinked hard, trying to regain his orientation. He felt the aircraft bank roughly to one side and then level out again. "Whoa. Who's flying the plane?"

"I'm giving Quinn a flying lesson," Drake replied. "Come on up front. Lighthouse wants you on the radio."

Nick cranked his stiff neck to one side, making an audible pop. "I don't want you to teach the new kid to fly the plane," he said. "For the same reason a father doesn't let his son teach a stray dog new tricks."

"Because we're not going to keep him?"

"Exactly. Don't get too attached."

Nick followed Drake to the front of the aircraft and sat down at the copilot station. Next to him, Quinn held the side-stick control with a white-knuckle grip, staring at the horizon on the main screen with wide eyes. Nick snorted at the pararescueman's nervous flying and then keyed the radio microphone. "Lighthouse, go ahead for Wraith."

"This is Will McBride," the voice in the radio replied. "I've got some new information for you." He explained the doctored photographs and the missing F-16.

"Did you find out who was flying the other aircraft?"

"There's no record," replied McBride. "It could have been any one of the Taiwan nationals or the other American pilot."

"The second aircraft confirms there was a mole. Novak suspected as much. He was getting close to smoking out the traitor."

"I guess that means you're the thief who stole the journal from the crate."

At McBride's mention of the journal, Nick glanced over at Quinn, but the kid was too focused on flying the aircraft to listen to the radio conversation. He lowered his voice. "Why is everyone hounding me about that. My mission, my resource."

"Hey, it's no skin off my back. Tarpin made a fuss though."

"Tarpin will live," said Nick. He recounted what he had learned from the journal entries. "Only a few people knew about Novak's plan: the supervisor in charge, the director of photo analysis, maybe Novak's wife, and a pilot named Starek. One of those four people is our bad guy."

"It's not the photo analyst," said McBride confidently.

"How do you know that?"

"He's dead. It's right here in the digital file you got from Tarpin. He was our first suspect because the Blackbirds sent the incident photos directly to him. If anyone had the opportunity and the know-how to doctor up the evidence, it would be the head photography guy. Unfortunately, he died in an accident on the airfield while the operation was packing up to move out."

"What kind of accident?"

"He was crushed by a pallet loaded with heavy machinery."

Nick winced. "Ow. That's the kind of accident that leaves nothing to chance. Okay, keep on it. Also, keep digging into that photo of Wŭlóng from 2003. We need to know who that other guy is. Maybe we'll find a connection to the salvage op or to the Triple Seven Chase. Wraith out."

On the main screen, Nick could see the sprawling Chinese coast stretching away to the southwest. He tapped Quinn on the shoulder. "Your flying lesson is over, kid. It's time to suit up."

―――――

The rushing sound of wind and engines filled the flight deck as Nick popped open the crew hatch. He and Quinn wore their tactical harnesses, along with gray flight helmets and portable oxygen systems.

Drake also wore a helmet and mask. From the pilot station, he manipulated a display that read SHADOW CATCHER DIAGNOSTICS. He looked back and gave Nick a thumbs-up.

Despite the mask covering his friend's face, Nick could

see that he was concerned. Drake's eyes said it all. Nick and Quinn were about to take an untested aircraft into the heavily defended airspace of a sovereign country, a country that the United States at least pretended to be friends with. They were not supposed to be there. There would be no rescue if the mission suddenly went pear-shaped. Nick pulled down his mask long enough to give Drake a thin smile. Then he dropped down the ladder.

Shadow Catcher's top-mounted engine and intake system left no room for an upper entry hatch. Instead of climbing straight into the little aircraft's cockpit, Nick and Quinn had to descend all the way to the bomb-bay doors and then squeeze underneath Shadow Catcher's belly.

As he climbed down the ladder, Nick cast a glance at the two thermite bombs hanging above Shadow Catcher. If they could not get her airborne again after landing in China, Drake would use the five-thousand-pound weapons to wipe her from the face of the earth. Then Nick and Quinn would have to get Novak out on foot.

Nick could feel the pulsing slipstream through the thin composite sheeting as he moved across the bomb-bay door, crawling on all fours to distribute his weight. In his mind, he could see the cross section; mere inches of light-weight material separated him from an endless fall into cold darkness.

"You look nervous," shouted Quinn as Nick opened the entry hatch.

He turned and looked at his young partner. Despite the bravado, the kid's face was pale, his eyes wide. "So do you," he shouted back.

Once Shadow Catcher's hatch clamped shut, the rushing noise dimmed to a dull hum. Nick and Quinn lay prone in their crew stations, concave shelves on either side of the small cockpit. Green block letters on a wide screen in front of them proclaimed Shadow Catcher's status.

SIGNAL ESTABLISHED

SYSTEM READY

"Go ahead and activate the Bluetooth in your helmet," ordered Nick. He found a small slide switch near the ear guard of his helmet and moved it to the On position. Instantly, he heard the distinct static of an open line. "Drake, this is Nick. How do you hear?"

"Loud and clear. You guys are online through Shadow Catcher's transmitters. Let's spin this baby up."

Nick, Drake, and Quinn ran the small aircraft through a series of checks. When they had finished, Shadow Catcher's main screen showed an infrared display of the bomb-bay wall in front of the aircraft. A heads-up display was overlaid on the screen in front of Nick, similar to the Wraith's display. All of his engine indications read zero, but his airspeed, altitude, and attitude displays were active, fed by Shadow Catcher's GPS systems.

"Whoa, the Chinese radar net is hyperactive tonight," interjected Drake, his voice registering concern. "It's almost like they're looking for us."

"Relax," said Nick. "For all we know, they run the net hot every night at this hour. We can't start second-guessing everything we see."

Quinn looked over from his station and lowered his mask. "Aren't you worried about opening the doors when we deploy? Doesn't that hurt our stealth?"

"Not in the Wraith." Nick changed Shadow Catcher's screen to the belly cameras. The infrared picture displayed the closed bomb-bay doors below them. "One of Scott's engineers got an idea from a TV show about the Bermuda triangle," he said. "According to the show, aircraft and ships get lost in clouds of electric fog, put out by aliens." A gray mist began to roll over the doors, masking them from the cameras. Nick dropped his own mask and smiled. "Welcome to the mothership."

"What is that stuff?"

"Nanoparticle mist. Basically it's atomized radar-absorbent material. It will create a stealth barrier to cover the gap when the doors open. Then we simply drop through. Since the engine won't start until after we fall away, the fog won't damage the aircraft."

"We're approaching the drop zone," said Drake.

"Can't we call it a launch zone?" asked Quinn. "'Drop zone' makes me feel like this thing is going to fall into the ocean."

"Call it whatever you want, we're there. Initiate deployment on my mark in three, two, one . . . mark."

The words *AUTO DEPLOY* appeared on Shadow Catcher's screen. Nick heard the hydraulic pistons pulling back the telescoping doors. There was an exponential increase in wind noise. With a resounding *thunk*, the catch released, and Shadow Catcher dropped into open air.

Nick anticipated the free fall and braced his body

against the sides of his station, but he heard a painful "Oomph!" in his headset. He looked over and saw Quinn shaking his head as if he'd just been punched by a prize-fighter. The pararescueman had smacked his head against the roof of the cockpit. "It's a good thing we gave you a helmet, kid."

"Very funny. A warning would have been nice."

Shadow Catcher's autopilot stabilized the aircraft in a shallow dive while the auto-deployment sequence counted off on Nick's heads-up display.

FLIGHT CONTROLS: OPERATIONAL

ENGINE START: INITIATE

ENGINE: STABILIZED

AWAITING COMMAND . . .

He used the touch-screen controls to direct the aircraft toward its first waypoint, and Shadow Catcher obediently turned toward Fujian. Nick called up the radio frequency display. The image on the main screen changed into a chaotic melee of undulating spots and lines. Multicolored streaks and flashes clashed against a black background.

"Psychedelic," said Quinn.

"That's all of the electromagnetic energy coming from the Chinese coast," Nick explained. "Hold on." He refined the image to filter out all frequencies except for ground-to-air radars. Pulsating green and blue cones swept back and forth from numerous points along the Chinese shoreline. Some of them passed directly across the aircraft, tracking a bright vertical line across the screen. "Drake was right. It looks like they're running every radar on the Taiwan Strait tonight."

"Should I be scared?" asked Quinn.

"No. We're already inside most of their sweeps, but none of them have focused on our sector. We're good."

Quinn remained silent for a while and then rolled onto his side and stared at Nick. "How do you know if it's really working?" he asked.

"What?"

"You know, stealth, how do you know if it's working?"

Nick gave him a grim smile. "Faith."

"That's it?"

"Yep."

"That's not really the answer I was looking for."

"Sorry, kid. That's the reality of combat. This is our foxhole, and in foxholes, sometimes faith is all you've got."

Nick switched the display back to infrared. A small green square blinked over a patch of jungle several miles inland from the coast. He tapped it with his finger. "That's our landing zone. I'm going to start the approach." He pushed forward on the side-stick control, disengaging the autopilot and diving toward the LZ. It looked just as it had in their satellite imagery: a thin gravel road cutting diagonally across a long ridge that rose out of the rain forest, an access road for power lines that had long been out of service. Unfortunately, the ridge lay nestled between two taller ridges. In order to land uphill,

Nick would have to make his approach at a very steep angle, hugging the trees of the neighboring hillside.

"You're going to land there?" asked Quinn as Nick lined up the aircraft. On the infrared, the forgotten road looked like a hiking trail, and a short one at that.

Nick nodded toward the lights of Fuzhou, blazing white on the infrared horizon. "Would you rather I land at the airport?"

A thick blanket of trees whipped by the right wing as Nick banked into the valley between the ridges. He pushed Shadow Catcher down to the very treetops, where the dense foliage would trap the sound of his engine. The road slowly opened up before them, but the gap in the trees looked barely wide enough for Shadow Catcher to drop through. Then he spotted the huge fallen tree that marked the beginning of his improvised runway. He knew their landing area was supposed to be short, but now that he saw it, he wasn't sure they could make it, even with Shadow Catcher's short takeoff and landing capability.

Nick used a thumb switch on the throttle to open the lower exhaust panels, slowly transitioning the power from forward thrust to lift augmentation. He eased back on the side-stick control, lifting Shadow Catcher's nose into a flare. "One hundred feet," he said, reading the radar altitude display. "Fifty, thirty, ten . . ."

Suddenly, an unexpected gap appeared in the make-shift runway. A recent rainstorm had cut a wide chasm across the gravel road, right where he intended to touch down. With part of the engine's thrust vectored down,

Shadow Catcher was making more of a cushioned fall than a traditional landing, and Nick feared that hitting the edge of that cavity might rip his main gear off. He jerked back on the stick and reverted to forward thrust, hoping to propel the aircraft over the gap.

It worked. Shadow Catcher ballooned across the washed-out chasm but not without sacrifice. On the other side, the aircraft ran out of lift. She dropped like a stone.

Nick clenched his teeth as the gear slammed down onto the gravel. Then he realized that the worst was not over. His last-minute correction had made them land farther down the road than expected. The end of their landing zone was coming up fast.

Two T-handles, set into the panel in front of Nick, served as hydraulic brake controls. He pulled hard on both. The tires skidded on the gravel, and Shadow Catcher veered toward the trees on the right side.

"You're going to clip the wing!" shouted Quinn.

"No, I'm not." Nick released some of the pressure on the right brake in order to straighten the aircraft, but that sacrificed some of his stopping power.

Up ahead, the improvised runway ended in a switchback as the access road continued its steep climb up the ridge. Nothing but a short dirt embankment, only a few inches high, guarded the impossible curve. Beyond that, the terrain dropped off into darkness.

"Watch the end of the road!"

"*Shut . . . up,*" Nick grunted, fighting with the brake controls.

Finally, Shadow Catcher slowed, aided by the upward

incline of the road. Nick's arms burned. As the aircraft rolled up to the switchback, he pulled with everything he had against both brake handles. Just as the little embankment disappeared under the nose, she jolted to a stop. A tree branch lay against the front of the aircraft, every detail of its wide, heart-shaped leaves distinctly visible on the enhanced infrared display.

"Nice one," said Quinn flatly.

Nick ignored the pararescueman. He uncaged the wing camera controls and panned them to the rear. The infrared cut nicely through the dust that he had kicked up on his landing. The gravel road descended into the forest behind them, silent, empty. He prayed that it would stay that way. "Bounce up and down," he said to Quinn.

"What?"

"You heard me. Do it." Nick released the brakes and started bouncing heavily in his crew station.

Quinn reluctantly joined him. "This is a little weird."

Soon, Shadow Catcher started rolling backward. Nick stopped bouncing and held out a hand for Quinn to do the same. He watched the road behind them closely, twisting the side-stick control and lightly pulling individual brake handles to steer the aircraft. A few meters down the incline, he saw what he was looking for. He allowed the aircraft to pick up speed, and then pulled hard on the left brake while twisting the nose gear. Shadow Catcher swung into a small gap in the trees and stopped.

"Well," said Quinn, "your landings suck, but you sure can parallel park."

CHAPTER 41

Nick inspected Shadow Catcher as Quinn draped a MultiCam tarp over her frame. The aircraft's skin looked little worse for wear, apart from some splashes of tree sap. "She's looking pretty good," he said.

"Maybe not." Quinn had crawled underneath the nose to tie the front edge of the tarp to a stake. He motioned to Nick. "Take a look at the nose gear."

Thick fluid oozed down the strut, glistening bloodred under the tinted glow of Quinn's flashlight. Nick joined him on the ground and shined a white LED light on the gear, shielding the beam with his hand. Even under white light, the fluid still sparkled translucent red. He traced the drip back up the strut until he found a crack in the housing. "Hydraulic fluid. In a couple of hours, the front strut will be fully depressed."

"Will we be able to launch?"

Nick crawled out from under the nose and evaluated their takeoff path. The neglected gravel road looked rough, really rough. He grimaced. "It's going to be ugly, but she'll manage. She'll have to."

The two of them finished hiding Shadow Catcher and then moved into the dark forest. Two-thirds of the way up the ridge, Nick stopped and crouched down, signaling the pararescueman to do the same. He scanned the valley behind them through his multifunction tactical goggles, looking for any sign of Chinese forces or civilians. The clarity of the new wide-spectrum goggles still astounded him, a major step up from the fuzzy green of the old binocular-style night-vision sets. Instead of simple light amplification, the ultralight MTGs offered several zoom levels of panoramic multispectrum video, with less bulk than a pair of ski glasses. They also served as a heads-up display system, fed by a wireless control box clipped to Nick's harness. Turning his attention to the path ahead, he could see a digital readout of the range and bearing to their objective.

Quinn grabbed his arm. "We're behind schedule. Let's get moving," he said in a harsh whisper.

Nick bit his tongue. He was finding it harder and harder to let the pararescueman's lack of respect slide. A few hours of solid sleep had calmed his mood, but Quinn seemed to have a knack for getting under his skin. "Easy, tiger," he said. "The phrase 'slower is faster' was never more true than it is now. The last thing we need is to run smack into a Chinese patrol." He tapped his ear. "One more thing. We need a comms check."

Quinn raised his hands in defeat and leaned his back against a tree as Nick moved a few paces up the hill.

"How do you read?" whispered Nick, using the implant's short-range mode.

"Loud and clear," replied Quinn impatiently.

"Same. Stand by one." Nick used voice commands to activate the link with the Wraith. There were no Milstar birds directly over China. With the ground team's limited horizon, they had to relay through the aircraft to reach a satellite and talk to Romeo Seven. A distinctive beep told him when the line was ready. "Wraith, this is Shadow One on SATCOM."

"Wraith is up, loud and clear," said Drake. "Stand by for the relay."

A few seconds later, Walker joined the line. "Lighthouse is up," he said, his voice distorted over the encrypted satellite link. "You are twenty minutes behind schedule, Shadow. What's the holdup?"

"We had a little trouble with the LZ," replied Nick.

"He means he crashed into the road," said Quinn.

Nick pulled his goggles down to his neck and scowled at the pararescueman. He pulled a level hand across his throat to tell him to pipe down. "The touchdown zone had an unexpected rut," he explained. "I bounced the aircraft. She has a damaged nose gear strut, but I can get her in the air."

"Lighthouse copies. Proceed."

"Wilco." Nick severed the link and switched to a short-range signal again. Using the low-power mode would save the implant batteries. It would also give him the opportunity to have a much-needed private chat with his young teammate. "What is your problem?" he asked.

"You're my problem," replied Quinn, standing up from his crouched position and pointing at Nick. "You treat *me* like a liability, but you're the one who nearly killed us back there. Were you even going to tell the colonel that you crashed the plane?"

"That was not a crash, and the information I choose to relay is not your concern. I don't answer to you. Got it?"

"Yeah, whatever."

Nick's anger finally boiled over. He crossed the few meters between them with rapid steps and pinned Quinn to the tree with his forearm against his neck. "Maybe you don't understand," he hissed. "We are not equals here. This is my operation and my responsibility. I don't ever have to explain myself to you." He ripped off Quinn's goggles so that he could stare him in the eye. "I don't want you here, and I don't need you here. If I think for an instant that your stupidity is jeopardizing this mission, I will put a bullet between your eyes and leave you for the Chinese. Am I clear, Senior Airman Quinn?"

Quinn stared back in silence. Shock and anger filled his eyes.

Nick pulsed his arms, bouncing Quinn against the tree. *"Am . . . I . . . clear?"*

"Yes, sir," replied Quinn reluctantly.

The kid's tone was conciliatory, but Nick could still hear anger behind it. He didn't have the time to wait for a better response. He backed up and tossed the goggles at Quinn's chest. "Fine. Let's move out."

CHAPTER 42

Zheng's missile factory was so much more than a simple production facility. Just as he had designed. With an integrated airfield, a state-of-the-art communications suite, and several other specialized resources, the compound made a perfect staging area for operations that required more secrecy and privacy than Fujian's military bases could provide.

He arrived at the compound dressed in battle fatigues and escorted by two of his commandos. A business suit and a pair of executive assistants would have been more fitting to his new position as defense minister, but tonight's mission began the combat stage of an odyssey two decades in the making, and he intended to act as a combat general until that stage was complete. He would not take on the trappings of a minister until he stood ready to present the Politburo with the gift of a unified China.

Zheng walked out onto the tarmac behind the main building and surveyed the small group of soldiers setting up his temporary headquarters. He found the commander of his Special Forces unit supervising a crew as they unfolded a temporary fiberglass pavilion from the back of its flatbed transport.

"Colonel Sung," he called, raising his voice over the rumble of the flatbed's engine. "What is your report?" He stopped short of the operation, unwilling to approach the truck while the choking exhaust still poured from its stack.

The gaunt colonel left his troops and crossed behind the truck to meet Zheng, dodging one of the hydraulic arms as it unfolded the pavilion. "Minister, the regulars are still positioned as you requested," he said with a curt bow. "Ten men surround the cave, remaining hidden and keeping watch over the prisoner, while two conduct regular sweeps of a five-hundred-meter perimeter. Four more are watching Detention Center Twenty-six, in case the Americans go there." He gestured toward a hangar at the other end of the flight line. "Our specialized troops are bedded down in that hangar, awaiting activation."

Zheng nodded. Colonel Sung appeared to be executing his orders efficiently. He had chosen him well. Zheng had given him a platoon of regulars to augment his commandos. They maintained a constant watch over the prisoner, a long and exhausting mission. Once they identified the

Americans' approach, their orders were to notify Sung and then delay the intruders until his elite forces arrived to close the trap. Keeping the commandos in reserve would keep them fresh and ready for a fight with the American covert ops team.

"And what of the prison troops?" asked Zheng.

Sung's lips stretched into a grim smile. "Thanks to the body you provided, they will not get in the way. As ordered, the prison's commandant identified the remains as Novak's and then had them destroyed. No one else saw anything but a closed body bag. The guards are convinced that the prisoner is dead. Their search is over."

The men finished setting up the pavilion and brought chairs for the minister and the colonel. The driver shut down the flatbed's engine. The offensive smell of diesel began to dissipate. "I will wake our attack force shortly," said Zheng, leading Sung under the pavilion. He eased himself down into a chair and nodded for the colonel to do the same. "I have good intelligence that the Americans are already on the ground."

Sung's eyes widened in surprise. "I was not aware of this. The Air Defense Net has reported no intrusions."

"And that is good news," said Zheng. "It means that the fools have brought us their best stealth aircraft. If it can penetrate our defenses, then we can surely use the same technology to render our missiles undetectable. Our dominion over Taiwan is assured."

"If the Americans are already here, would it not be wise to bring in additional forces? We could flood the forest with regulars."

"No, my friend," said Zheng in a fatherly tone. "These fish cannot be caught by casting a wide net. They would get spooked and make their escape before it collapsed upon them." He did not say that he also feared a larger force would draw the attention of the Politburo. The moderates might shut him down before he could capture his prize. He gazed out at the forest beyond the runway. "No, we must catch these fish with the hook in their mouths. And we will, Sung. The bait is set. They are about to bite."

CHAPTER 43

Less than six hundred meters," said Nick, reading the heads-up display in his goggles. The GPS symbols told him that he was still on track, but he could hardly see anything through the dense vegetation. The lower bushes and vines had grown steadily thicker, filling the spaces between the heavy, broadleaf trees and the thinner pines.

"That checks. More than half a klick to go," said Quinn tersely. He moved on a parallel path with his team lead, several meters behind and to the left. "Of course, if you weren't so slow, we would be there by now," he added, muttering under his breath.

Nick's jaw tensed. "Hey, chucklehead," he said, continuing to pick his way forward. "The great thing about these comm implants is that no matter how quietly you whisper, I can still hear you."

"Oh. Right."

"Just shut up and stay close. The visibility is getting worse."

The two had covered nearly half the distance from Shadow Catcher to the Palace, the CIA's old hideout. They had crested the ridge and then dropped down the other side, crossing a stream and a small road without incident. Now they worked their way through rippling jungle terrain, up miniature ridges and down into small bowls and valleys where the scrub slowed them down considerably. Nick wished that this had all started in the summer. In July, they could have stomped through the underbrush with bells around their necks and still not been heard over the racket of the rain forest bugs. Now, in the early spring, only a few crickets chirped, and every snapped twig made him cringe inside.

After another hundred meters, Nick stopped, just short of a small meadow. The circular gap in the trees was no larger than the width of a small hangar, but that was more open space than he wanted to cross. He signaled Quinn to join him.

"What'd I do now?" asked Quinn.

Nick bit back a rebuke and nodded toward the clearing. "We need to get around this meadow, rather than go through it. It's too much exposure. I just wanted to show you the reason that we're deviating from the GPS track." He moved off to the right, allowing Quinn to fall back to the short wedge formation again.

Nick's deviation did not last long. He quickly ran into thickly tangled brush. Soon it became impassable. After a few minutes, he returned to his starting point and tried the other direction, but dense vegetation stopped him again less than a quarter of the way around. "It looks like the forest isn't cooperating. We're going to have to skirt the inside perimeter of the meadow."

"What happened to too much exposure?" asked Quinn.

"We're short on time. Besides, the noise of forcing our way through the brambles will cause just as much risk." He pointed at the clearing. "This is the lesser of two evils."

Just as Nick stepped forward into the open, he heard a faint rustling in the brush. He crouched and motioned for Quinn to do the same. Night sounds always seemed louder than they actually were. They were harder to locate too. Had he heard Quinn moving behind him? Maybe it was just a rabbit in the undergrowth. Whatever the source, the rustle quickly disappeared amid the faint noises of the nocturnal rain forest.

After listening for nearly a full minute, Nick cautiously rose up and signaled Quinn to move forward, staying close to the tree line. Then, as they reached a point halfway around the meadow's perimeter, he heard another sound, far more alarming than a rustle. A sharp voice barked, "Halt!"

CHAPTER 44

Novak strained his mind to filter the fog. He was with Anja again, in their small apartment in Sincheng. Her homemade Christmas decorations hung from the walls and over the door. Several open gifts still lay under the tree.

He knew he was dreaming. Over the past few days, he'd come to realize that the dreams were part of his body's defense mechanism, a way of forcing him to rest. But these were more than dreams; they were vivid memories. Somehow, in order to heal, his mind had to escape its present suffering by regressing to the past. At least, that's what he told himself. Maybe he was just going crazy. Maybe this was what people with dementia experienced inside their heads. He didn't care. Despite the knowledge that there were real threats in the real world, Novak released his mind into fantasy.

He watched Anja happily putter around the kitchen, preparing one of the sweet-smelling hors d'oeuvres that she loved to fix for him. In marriage, she had shown him more ways to love than he could ever have imagined. Her devotion carried so far beyond the physical. From Washington, D.C., to Taiwan, no matter where they lived, Anja made a home for them. Her efforts allowed him to feel normal, even while living a life that was far from it.

In Poland, Anja's whole life revolved around the photo analysis shop at Remote Icon. It was her contribution to the resistance, something she owed to the memory of her parents. Now, with the Służba Bezpieczeństwa thousands of miles behind her, photo analysis had become just a job. Each night, when they returned to the apartment, Anja did not slump into a chair, exhausted from the day. Rather, she brightened, throwing herself into the passion of creating and fueling something amazing. Them.

As the dream solidified, Novak became aware of another presence. He discovered his friend Jozef seated beside him at the table, his eyes fixed in a thousand-mile stare. In this dreamlike state, Novak found it difficult to determine whether Starek was really lost in thought or was gazing at Anja. "I wish I could read your mind, my friend," he said out loud.

Starek stirred and blinked at Novak. He looked at a loss for a moment and then settled into a concerned expression. "I was just thinking that it might be wise for you to reconsider this little sting operation of yours," he said.

"Why? Don't you want to find the mole?"

Starek sighed and shook his head. "There *is* no mole.

Every operation has its problems. It is Murphy's Law, right?"

"Is that what all the nationals are saying?"

"You know, you would do well to learn a little Mandarin yourself. It is good for our relations with them. Instead, you're going to alienate them by running a mission without their knowledge. They are smart people. They will realize your purpose."

"That is a possibility I am willing to accept," said Novak with finality.

Starek ignored the response. "What do you hope to accomplish? If we have a smooth mission that uncovers some Chinese secrets, do you really believe that will prove that the nationals are behind our failures?"

Novak frowned thoughtfully, staring past Starek to the picture of Washington, D.C., on the wall behind him. "I'm sorry," he said regretfully.

"Sorry for what?"

Novak looked his friend in the eye again. "I have not told you everything about our mission. I fully expect that it will go smoothly, and I do not believe that such a mission guarantees there is a mole among our nationals." He paused as Anja brought a platter of blueberry pierogi to the table. He looked up at her. She gave him a comforting smile and nodded. Novak took a long breath and continued. "The whole thing is a trap for the supervisor in charge."

Starek set down the dumpling he had just stabbed with his fork. "Explain."

"I have suspected Wright for a while. We have the same troubles here that we had in Poland, and he is the most obvious link. There is a chance that it might be the director of photo analysis, but I can't be certain. Whoever it is, the mole is almost certain to do whatever he can to give us a smooth mission. That will implicate the nationals and divert attention away from him. To that end, he will have to communicate with his Chinese contacts."

"So?" said Starek with a skeptical look.

"Let me finish. The mole can't use a messenger because that would take too long, and all the phone lines are monitored. That only leaves the radio. And thanks to the big mountain in the middle of the island, only one kind of radio is going to reach the mainland."

"HF," said Starek quietly.

"Exactly. Wright, or whoever the mole is, has to be running the set out of his room or his office—those are the safest places to keep it—but I can't get into either to check." Novak paused and took a bite of pierogi.

"So?" prompted Starek again.

"So I sort of requisitioned two SIGINT payloads from our pod shop. I modified them to record directional hits from an HF signal and placed them several hundred meters apart. They have enough juice to run for a few days. With any luck, we already have a few hits."

"The crossing directional intercepts from the two pods will pinpoint the source of the radio signals," said Starek.

"Exactly. X marks the spot."

"Haven't you checked it? You might already have enough hits."

"No, I don't want the mole to get suspicious. If he catches me heading out to the payloads, the game is up.

I must be patient. I'll go after the mission. Then we're almost guaranteed to have the evidence we need."

"Where did you hide them?" asked Starek.

Novak smiled and slowly shook his finger back and forth. "You'll have to wait. When we get back, we can go out and look together." Novak checked his watch. "Speaking of going out . . ."

Starek jumped up from the table. "Biyu!" he said, smacking his head with the palm of his hand.

Novak laughed. Starek had forgotten about his late date with his new girlfriend.

Starek bowed slightly to Anja. "Pardon my hasty departure. The pierogi was lovely, better than my mother could make, but don't ever tell her I said that."

Anja smiled warmly. "Go. We wouldn't want to come between you and your girl."

"No," called Starek over his shoulder as he opened the apartment door. "Friends should never do that."

The sound of the door slamming shut shocked Novak back to reality. He stood up from the cot he'd been sitting on. Had the noise just been a part of the memory, or was it a manifestation of a sound in the real world? He crept up to the cave entrance and listened.

Nothing.

In the dim glow from the radio's control head, Novak surveyed the state of his hideout. Several crates lay open, their contents scattered. Empty ration packs were strewn about the cave. He'd been eating the MREs for days and felt stronger for it. He chuckled to think that the unnatural twenty-five-year-old food served his body better than the filth served to him by the Chinese guards. How much more healthy would he feel if he could just have some of Anja's pierogi?

Anja.

Was she waiting for him? Was she even still alive? Novak looked at the nuclear-powered radio. He had come to hate it. Night and day he stared at it, waiting for a return message, but no reply came. How much longer could he wait here? The food rations could last for months, but he would run out of clean water within a week.

He really did feel stronger. Taiwan was no short trip across the strait, but it was possible—if he could only get to the coast. He bent down and tried to peer through the tunnel's camouflage into the night outside. What he wouldn't give for a set of night-vision goggles. He knew that the Chinese would have them. Day or night, it didn't matter: leaving the Palace was suicide.

Novak glanced around the cave again. So was staying there.

Quickly making up his mind, he sat down and put on a set of boots and camouflage fatigues from the Palace supplies. Then he strapped on a Skyhook survival vest and filled its pockets with dry socks, a few K-rations, and every water pack he could find.

After crawling through the low entrance and replacing its leafy camouflage, he turned to face the rain forest. A night bird screeched. The sound sent pain through his head. He forced himself to breathe. Using a compass tied to his vest, he found a heading southeast and took a step forward. "One . . ."

CHAPTER 45

A Chinese soldier emerged from the forest to Nick's right, on the other side of the small meadow. He moved toward them with purpose, his pistol out and leveled. He wore the mottled camouflage of the People's Liberation Army Ground Force, the Chinese regular army.

"Keep calm, and follow my lead," Nick whispered. He did not raise his hands or ready his MP7; instead, he turned nonchalantly to face the intruder. The soldier had an older-generation night-vision system mounted to his infantry helmet. Between his voice, the little he could see of his face, and the way the soldier carried himself, Nick assessed him to be very young, probably the equivalent of a private or a private first class. He walked to the center of the clearing to meet the young man, keeping his head still but actively scanning, searching the periphery for more soldiers. There were none.

"Halt!" the young man repeated.

Nick quickened his pace toward the intruder. *"Shuōchū nǐ de xìngmíng hé dānwèi!"* he said with authority, commanding the soldier to state his name and unit. He prayed he'd gotten the pronunciation correct. He had learned the phrase during a previous operation, but that was years ago. He intended to take advantage of an idiosyncrasy of Chinese culture. Young Chinese soldiers were not just obedient; they were submissive.

His plan also banked on the soldier's poor night-vision system. With an older model of Chinese goggles, the soldier wouldn't be able to distinguish Caucasian features from Asian, particularly with much of Nick's face covered. The older system could not break out the pattern of the American camouflage either. With any luck, this guy might think Nick was from one of China's myriad specialized units. *"Shuōchū nǐ de xìngmíng hé dānwèi!"* he said again, more forcefully.

The soldier slowed and lowered his weapon a few degrees, but he kept coming, rattling off a long string of Mandarin.

Nick had no idea what the man was saying. He took another gamble. *"Wǒmen shì tèzhǒng bùduì,"* he said, claiming that he was Chinese Special Forces. At least, he hoped that was what he said. He tried to feign indignation, but he found that difficult to do while maintaining an accent in a language he did not speak. With those last words, he had exhausted his reserve of Chinese military phrases.

The soldier replied with another string of Mandarin, this time in a defensive, subordinate tone. The ruse was working. He stopped and lowered his pistol until it pointed at the ground. In another second, Nick would be within striking distance.

Suddenly, he heard Quinn's voice in his comm device. "I've got him."

Nick did not get the chance to argue. He saw the Chinese soldier jerk his head to the left and raise his pistol. At the same time, he heard three heavy spits. The soldier fell at his feet, gurgling and spitting blood. He grabbed desperately at the radio clipped to his shoulder, repeating the same phrase over and over—*"Tāmen zài zhèlǐ"*—but he never reached the transmitter.

There was no time to ask questions. Nick grabbed the soldier by his battle vest and dragged him into the trees on the other side of the meadow. By the time he laid him down and tore off the awkward helmet and goggles, the young soldier was dead. He stared sightlessly up at the dark forest canopy.

"What were you thinking?" asked Nick as Quinn jogged up beside him.

"I was thinking of saving your crazy hide!" retorted Quinn, his gun still leveled at the dead man. "What was your plan, to dupe him with pig Latin in a bad Chinese accent?"

"You can holster your weapon, hero. He's dead."

"Good."

"Not good," Nick countered. "We could have gotten information out of him. We didn't have to kill him."

"Of course we had to kill him. The only response to unexpected contact during a black operation is to kill; otherwise, you risk discovery." Quinn rattled off the sentence as if he were reading from a textbook.

"Real-world ops aren't so black and white," said Nick. "This guy wasn't a real threat to us. He wasn't a terrorist, and he wasn't involved in some genocidal battle. He was a kid just like you, following orders during peacetime." He closed the young man's eyes and stood up. "He was probably ordered to search the forest for the escaped prisoner."

"If he was searching for one escapee in prison rags, then why didn't he seem more surprised to see two armed Americans in full combat gear?" asked Quinn.

Nick made no response. He hadn't thought of that. He lifted his goggles and rubbed his eyes. The rest he got on the Wraith could not make up for weeks of poor sleep, and he knew it. He was beginning to feel the mind-numbing effects of exhaustion. Maybe the kid was right. "I don't know, Quinn," he replied honestly. "I don't know."

CHAPTER 46

A message indicating that the Palace lay just ahead of him flashed in Nick's goggles, a welcome sight. Hiding the body of the Chinese soldier had put them further behind schedule. In addition, Nick had slowed the pace considerably, moving forward in sweeps to search for other patrols, but there were no more contacts. Now, with the Palace in sight, his frustration and exhaustion started to ebb away. In a few more minutes, they could reclaim Novak for the United States and then spirit him back to Shadow Catcher for a predawn launch back to the Wraith.

Nick scanned the area slowly, unwilling to leave the last stretch to chance. He would rather take an extra minute or two now than be caught by hostile forces just a few feet from the objective. Their path looked clear. He slowly rose from his crouched position and motioned Quinn to follow. They crept forward with their MP7s at the ready, scanning their respective fields of fire. Finally, the two of them stood on either side of the low cave entrance, masked by a tangle of fresh tree branches.

"Someone has definitely been here recently," said Nick, carefully lifting one of the branches free and feeling its leaves. They were pliable, not dry and brittle as they should have been if the cave had not been used for many years. "These leaves are still green. This cover was placed within the last couple of days."

Quinn kept scanning the surrounding forest. "Yeah, well, let's hope he's in there."

Nick quietly removed the branches, unslung his MP7, and ducked inside. He crawled through the low entrance with his weapon in front of him, ready to fire. For all he knew, there might be a platoon of Chinese waiting on the inside.

"Hello?" said Nick, springing to his feet inside the cave. There was no answer. He removed an infrared flashlight from his vest and shined it around the enclosure, further illuminating the scene for his goggles. He saw no prisoner, no body, and no other rooms, only a small cave littered with ration packs and old supplies.

Nick set his MP7 down on a crate and helped Quinn to his feet. "He's gone."

"He can't be." Quinn jerked his arm away and drew his XDm pistol, scanning the cave with the infrared light mounted on its rail. "Where else would he be?"

"My guess is that he got tired of waiting," replied Nick.

He walked deeper into the cave to get a better look. After examining several of the spent rations that lay on the floor, he found a good sign. Smears of tomato sauce still covered the torn polypropylene coated foil of one of the packets. He removed a glove and picked it up, running his index finger through the sauce and rubbing it against his thumb. "The sauce in this MRE hasn't dried out yet." He held his fingers to his nose and smelled the sharp scent of garlic and basil. "Yeah, it's still fresh, if you can ever say that about an MRE. My guess is that he hasn't been gone more than a few hours, if that. We need to get out there and find him. But first I've got to check in."

Nick activated his comm implant's connection to Drake. "Wraith, this is Shadow One."

An intermittent voice replied, masked by heavy static. Nick could not make out the words.

"Wraith, I need you to boost your signal. We're in a cave."

After a few moments, Drake's voice came through. "Shadow One, this is Wraith. How do you hear me now?"

Nick breathed a sigh of relief. At least the comms were holding up. Once they failed, everything usually went to pot very quickly. "Loud and clear, Wraith. It's good to hear your voice."

A moment later, McBride joined Drake on the comm line. "Shadow One, this is Lighthouse."

"Got you loud and clear too, Lighthouse. Where's the Old Man?" he asked, wondering why Walker hadn't come up on the line.

"He's taking a coffee break, but I can tell you that he's not happy. You've been on the ground for an hour and a half. You are way behind schedule. What's the holdup?"

Nick gave both of them a brief summary of the mission since leaving Shadow Catcher. He focused on the encounter with the lone Chinese soldier.

"It's odd that you only encountered one," interjected McBride. "PLA patrols usually go out in groups of five."

"We thought the same thing," replied Nick, "but we didn't find any others. Not a soul. There's something else that I need you to look into for me. After Quinn took him down, the soldier went for his radio. He kept repeating the same phrase: *Tā men zài zhèlǐ.*"

"Stand by, Shadow One."

Nick waited while McBride looked up his question on Romeo Seven's network. It only took a few moments.

"Are you sure he said *tā men* and not *tā zài zhèlǐ*?" asked the intelligence analyst.

"Affirmative, Lighthouse. He said it several times. I got a good sampling."

There was a long pause. Nick could almost hear the wheels turning in McBride's head. "What did you find?" he asked cautiously.

"It means, 'They are here,'" said McBride slowly. "Shadow, do you want to abort?"

Nick remained silent for several moments.

"I don't understand," said Quinn. "What's going on?"

Nick moved deeper into the cave, sounding out his thoughts as he walked. "The soldier said, 'They are here,'" not 'He is here' or 'I found him.' He wasn't looking for a single escaped prisoner. He was looking for *us*. That was why he spoke English when he told us to stop." He turned and faced the entrance, half expecting Chinese soldiers to begin pouring through. "This whole thing is a trap."

"I don't like this, Shadow," said Drake. "I only have enough fuel to loiter for a few more hours. We don't have tanker support for the return trip, and launching an alert tanker out of Guam would raise too many questions. You don't know where this guy is or if he's even real. You need to get out of there."

"Wait. This doesn't make sense." Nick scanned the cave again. The open crates, the disheveled cot, the freshly opened rations—all of it added up to a refugee hiding out. And where were the enemy soldiers? If this was a trap, they would have already moved in and captured them both. Instead, he and Quinn found one random soldier roaming the woods and took him down without a fight.

Nick took in a short breath. He suddenly understood. They weren't competing against the entire Chinese military; they were competing against just one unit, one that didn't seem to want the rest to know what it was doing. "No, Lighthouse," he said finally. "We're going to stay. Novak is real. He's down here somewhere, and we need to know what these people are up to. Trap or no trap, we're not leaving."

"Belay that!" said Quinn. "We need to get back to Shadow Catcher and . . ."

The kid kept going, but Nick talked over him. "Shut him up, Drake," he ordered. A short tone sounded on the line as Drake severed Quinn's signal from the comms. Nick could still hear his rant, but at least the kid's voice no longer rang in his ear.

"Some team management issues?" asked Drake.

"I'll handle him," replied Nick. "And one more thing, Lighthouse."

"Go ahead," said McBride.

"I don't like the direction this is going. Wūlóng spoke of control before he threatened Luke. Maybe he really wasn't there to kill me. If this whole thing is a trap, then maybe his job was to hold my family hostage and get me to hand Shadow Catcher or Wraith over to the Chinese during the mission. There might be other operatives in D.C. I need you to pick up Katy and Luke and bring them in to Romeo Seven."

"The colonel won't like it. That's a lot of paperwork."

"I don't care if he fires me for it. Too many things aren't adding up. Whoever is behind all this has already shown that they know where I live. I'm not willing to leave my wife and kid exposed out there."

"Lighthouse copies. I'll take care of it."

"Thanks," said Nick. "Shadow out."

The hair on the back of Nick's neck suddenly stood up. He slowly turned and found that he was staring down the long suppressor of Quinn's XDm pistol. Nick raised his hands. "You are so fired."

"Call him back," said Quinn angrily. "Call him back and tell him that we are headed for Shadow Catcher right now. Tell him to get ready to pick us up. We'll be airborne in an hour."

Nick wished he could see Quinn's eyes behind the goggles. He heard no fear in the kid's voice, only anger. The pararescueman seemed to believe that he was doing the right thing. "Back down, Quinn. I'm not calling anyone," he said with icy calm.

Quinn kept the pistol perfectly steady. "Yes, you are. We're not going to stay here and walk directly into a Chinese trap. If we do that, we're going to hand them Shadow Catcher and all of its stealth. Call him back." He pressed the suppressor into Nick's forehead. "Do it."

The press of the gun into his skin was more than Nick was willing to take from the rookie. He rapidly brought his raised hands together under the pistol, shoving the weapon up and right while jerking his head down and left. He heard a spit as the XDm discharged a round. The bullet ricocheted off the cave wall and slammed into the radio control head, sending up a shower of sparks. Nick spun, intending to trap the kid's shoulder under his biceps and slam his face into the wall. But Quinn recovered too quickly. With stunning agility, the pararescueman muscled out of the hold and ran up the wall, flipping backward over his head.

The move shocked Nick, but it did little to undermine his advantage. During the fancy escape, Quinn had to let go of his weapon, which Nick now held by the barrel. The pararescueman landed swinging and caught Nick in the jaw with a powerful left hook, but he had to thrust out his right hand to keep his balance, exposing his temple.

Nick shook off the hit and swung the pistol at the kid's head. Quinn let out a surprised grunt and then crumpled to the floor.

Nick ejected the XDm's clip, cleared the round from the chamber, and tossed the weapon onto Quinn's chest. He massaged his throbbing jaw and spat a spoonful of blood at the unconscious pararescueman. "Flip over that, junior."

CHAPTER 47

The metallic clacks of ammunition belts cranking into loaders echoed in Zheng's small hangar. Two teams of commandos prepared Norinco fast attack vehicles for battle, mounting 12.5-millimeter machine guns to their small cargo beds.

Zheng stood at a table between the off-road vehicles, pouring over a map of Fujian Province with one of his men. He drew a finger along the map from a dirt road to Novak's cave. "You can make your approach from here, to the north," he said. "Then split to flank them on either side."

Suddenly, Sung burst into the hangar. He strode briskly up to the table and gave a short bow, pausing only for a short second to catch his breath. "Minister, the prisoner is on the move. He has left the cave and is heading south toward the coast."

The news did not faze Zheng at all. "That is no surprise," he said calmly. He had expected that Novak would become impatient if the Americans waited too long. "How many men did you send to follow?"

Sung grimaced. "That is the problem. My foolish lieutenant took all of his men to follow the prisoner, all but the two making sweeps of the forest around the cave. I ordered him to send a man back, but the cave has been unguarded for some time."

Zheng tensed. He should have expected a mistake like this from the regulars. His prison doctor had installed a tracking implant in Novak some time ago. There was no need to follow him. But now the Americans could reach the cave without his knowledge. He quickly turned to the commando standing next to him. "Take four men from your team and head to the cave. Make your approach quietly. If the Americans have already arrived, notify me immediately." Then he started for the hangar door, motioning for Sung to follow. "How long until Novak reaches the coast?"

"At his present pace, he could reach Hanjiang in less than three hours. He is armed now. I expect that he will try to hijack a boat and then make a bid for Taiwan. Do you want me to have the men pick him up?"

Zheng shook his head. "No, not yet."

"We must recapture him before he reaches a populated area," advised Sung. "Otherwise, this operation may become very public."

"I said no," said Zheng impatiently. He stopped just outside the hangar and clasped his hands behind his back.

"We will leave him in the open until the Americans make their move."

Sung bowed. "Then let us hope that they do it soon."

Looking east, Zheng could see a magenta glow already forming on the tree-lined horizon, washing upward into dark, faded blue. "They will, Colonel. They have no choice."

CHAPTER 48

Quinn awoke to a tickling sensation, the feel of a thousand tiny legs scrambling across his upper lip. In his confused state, he found the sensation more intriguing than terrifying, but then the owner of those legs tried to crawl up into his right nostril.

He sat up with an involuntary yelp, slapping the millipede away from his face. His right temple throbbed. A ginger touch revealed a good-sized lump. *Baron.* His team lead had actually left him for dead out in the jungle, just like he promised. At least that psycho hadn't put a bullet between his eyes.

Instinctively, Quinn reached for his weapon. He found it right where it should be, holstered on his harness, a full clip loaded. He found his MP7 lying by his side as well. It occurred to him that Nick had shown either a lot of faith or a lot of stupidity in leaving him with two loaded weapons.

After a much-needed pull of water from his CamelBak, Quinn cautiously stood up to survey his surroundings. To his naked eye, the rich vegetation seemed a slightly lighter shade of green than before. How long had he been out? He saw a pale gray patch of sky peeking through a break in the tree canopy above, the light of the breaking dawn. Still, only sparse scraps of dim light reached the forest floor, so he was still shrouded in darkness.

Quinn lifted the MTGs that hung from his neck. Part of the right temple support hung loosely by a bundle of wires. The stem had broken in two when Nick clubbed him with his own gun. He seated the goggles awkwardly on his face, tightened the strap, and powered them up. They still worked.

Aided by the illumination of enhanced infrared, Quinn could see that Baron had not dragged him far from the Palace. The GPS in his heads-up display showed the cave less than twenty meters away. Using the wireless control to zoom in on the green triangle, he could even make out the entrance. He took another swig of water and started to push his way back to the cave. Then he abruptly stopped. There was a line of text flashing in the corner of his display.

MESSAGE WAITING

Insult to injury. That arrogant jerk had actually sent him a message through his MTG control. He pushed the command button to display the message. Lines of green text began to scroll up his screen:

I'M GOING AFTER THE OBJECTIVE.

GET BACK TO SHADOW CATCHER.

IF I'M NOT BACK IN TWO HOURS, YOU WILL HAVE TO GET HER AIRBORNE ON YOUR OWN.

POINT HER DOWNHILL, GIVE HER A TWO-SECOND BURST OF FULL FORWARD THRUST. THEN VECTOR THE EXHAUST DOWN.

YOU NEED A MINIMUM OF FIFTY KNOTS.

ONCE YOU'RE UP, SWITCH ON THE AUTOPILOT AND SHE'LL DO THE REST.

GODSPEED.

P.S. WHEN WE GET HOME, YOU'RE FIRED.

Something flared in the goggles behind the text, a short heat bloom somewhere to his left. He deleted the message and focused on the area but couldn't make anything out amid the brush. Then it happened again: a circular bloom of heat expanded quickly and then contracted into nothing. Suddenly, Quinn remembered the pattern from his infrared training.

He crept forward, cautiously picking his steps. Soon he could make out an infantryman, dressed like the one he had killed, moving in the direction of the cave and carelessly smoking a cigarette. Apparently nobody had ever told this soldier that death sticks were a great way to get picked up on infrared. Was this guy the Chinese response to an American black ops insertion? Quinn felt a little insulted.

Instead of continuing past the Palace on his patrol, the soldier walked straight up to the entrance. He stamped out his cigarette and pocketed it, listened for a moment, and then moved the camouflage to the side of the entrance and crawled in. That clinched it. McBride's questionable translation could have meant several things, but if the Chinese knew about the Palace, this was definitely a trap. And Nick was still walking into it.

Quinn activated his comm implant. "Shadow One, this is Two, over." He heard nothing but faint static. "Shadow One, this is Shadow Two, come in." Nick did not respond. He must have moved out of range for the line-of-sight mode. Quinn switched his implant to SATCOM and tried to contact the Wraith for a relay.

Still nothing.

He remembered that Nick had ordered Drake to mute his signal during the argument. Maybe Drake had forgotten to put him back on the link.

A branch cracked somewhere to Quinn's right. He crouched low. Five more soldiers walked up to the Palace entrance. This group moved more deliberately than the first, actively scanning the area, weapons up and ready, sweeping distinct fields of fire. Quinn tried not to breathe. He still had several meters of cover, but if one of them looked in his direction with their NVGs, they might get lucky.

The newcomers looked better equipped than the smoker. For one thing, they carried Chang Feng submachine guns with helical magazines, decent firepower if you didn't mind the MADE IN CHINA stamp on the pistol grip. All that the smoker carried was a pistol. The newcomers' helmets and gear looked custom fit too, as opposed to standard issue.

The leader of the group noted the camouflage lying to one side of the cave. He leaned down to the entrance and called out in a low voice. A moment later, the infantryman came scrambling out, speaking rapidly. The largest of the newcomers roughly pulled him closer and put a hand to his lips. The leader waved and pointed, directing three of the soldiers to fan out and keep watch. Then he and the big guy lifted their NVGs and began a tense conference with their new friend.

There was a long exchange, during which the smoker's voice grew loud again. Finally, the leader snatched the radio microphone from the smoker's vest and thrust it in his face. The young man took the microphone and made a radio call. He waited a few moments, but there was no response. He called again. This time, in the intervening silence, he nervously withdrew a cigarette from his trouser pocket. The big one slapped it from his hand. Again, the smoker received no reply to his radio call. Quinn realized that he was trying to call the soldier that Quinn had killed.

While the big guy continued to abuse the smoker, the leader stepped away from his little group. He picked up the wayward cigarette and then moved in the direction of Quinn's hiding place.

Quinn's pulse quickened. He quietly raised the MP7, measuring the distance and angles to the other five soldiers. If the leader discovered him, he would have to take him down with one three-round burst so that he could quickly shift to the others. The big guy would get the next two bursts. Even while bullying the smoker, he stayed alert, his eyes roving, always keeping one hand on the Chang Feng's pistol grip. Then Quinn would have to change his position as he tried to take out the other three serious operators. He could save the smoker for last. That guy looked about as ready for a firefight as a meter maid.

With both hands on his weapon, the leader scanned back and forth over Quinn's head with his naked eyes. Then he froze his gaze in a direct line with Quinn. He started to look down.

Quinn slid his finger into his MP7's trigger guard. He couldn't raise the weapon all the way to his eye for proper aiming, but he didn't have to. At this range, he could shoot from the hip and still put three rounds in the center of the leader's forehead. He slowly depressed the trigger.

Just as he felt the MP7's action about to give, Quinn noticed the man's eyes. The leader wasn't looking straight at him. Instead, he was glancing down at his battle vest. With his left hand, the soldier let go of his weapon and pulled a cell phone from a vest pocket. Then he turned to face the cave. Quinn released the trigger. He could feel sweat gathering above his eyebrows where the padding of his MTGs met his forehead.

The leader dialed his phone and waited. After a few moments, he spoke, his voice carrying a very different tone from the one he had used with the infantryman. Clearly, he was reporting in to a superior. Quinn had never wished that he could speak a foreign language more than he did right now. If only he knew what this guy was saying.

After his report, the soldier hung up his phone and rallied his group. His commanding and demeaning tone returned as he spouted a series of orders. The six of them quickly disappeared into the forest.

What set them off like that?

Quinn tried to put it all together. The smoker had crawled out of the cave speaking excitedly, but nothing about the Palace should have upset him if he already knew that it was a hideout. Quinn and Nick hadn't been in there for long, and from the outside it appeared that Nick had left the cave just as they'd found it. Then Quinn remembered the radio. His bullet had shattered the control head. There was no way to hide that, and no easy explanation.

Between the broken radio and the missing soldier, the hunters now knew that their quarry was somewhere under the net, and the guy with the phone was Quinn's only link to whoever would spring the trap.

He took off after them.

CHAPTER 49

I might as well be searching for Bigfoot.

Nick knelt down in the underbrush for a breather. He had moved quickly southeast, his best guess as to Novak's track, searching for some sign of the long-missing pilot. With only circumstantial evidence that Novak even survived the shoot-down in '88, he felt like a crackpot, roaming the woods in search of a hairy mythical creature.

After a swig from his CamelBak, Nick cracked open the control box for his MTGs, revealing an LCD screen and a small keyboard. He activated the map function. Three-dimensional satellite imagery filled his goggle display and moved to center on his position. He noted that the population density increased exponentially in the direction of the coast. Villages popped up with growing regularity along major roads to the east and west. They would funnel Novak toward the coastal city of Hanjiang. Nick couldn't let him get that far.

He saw a strip of lighter green on the map. When he zoomed in, he found just what he needed. In another kilometer, there was a long farm valley that ran perpendicular to his course. A narrow strip of cultivated land spread for miles along a meandering river. That was where he would catch up with Novak.

Whatever evasion skills the old pilot had forgotten during his long incarceration, he would remember enough to avoid open areas unless absolutely necessary. Novak would have to stop and search up and down the tree line for a good place to cross the valley. Nick, however, had the benefit of current satellite imagery.

There.

A narrow orchard spanned nearly the entire width of the valley. Novak would likely see it from the tree line and make for its cover, but he would probably be a few hundred meters to one side or the other when he saw it. Nick could go straight there. With any luck, he would be waiting when Novak arrived, if he arrived at all.

Nick set off again, moving as quickly as he could without making an absolute racket in the scrub. He could not afford to move with more caution. There was no time. Every minute of daylight increased his chances of getting seen by locals or caught by the PLA.

As he trudged through the brush, Nick tried to raise Drake on his comm unit. "Wraith, this is Shadow One, come in."

Drake did not respond. Despite the climbing temperature, Nick felt a chill. The mission was going pear-shaped fast. Maybe he should have waited with Quinn until the idiot woke up. He could only hope that he had pounded some sense into the kid, that he was finally following orders and heading for Shadow Catcher. Without a link to the Wraith, he could not communicate with him to find out. Worse, he could not talk to Drake or Romeo Seven to keep them apprised of the situation.

Without comms, Nick had become completely isolated, the textbook sign of a mission on the verge of catastrophic failure, just like the mission in Iraq ten years before.

A bead of sweat rolled down his cheek. The temperature was rising. He lifted the MTGs to rub his eyes and found that the forest had lightened considerably. The trees seemed to be thinning as he moved toward the coast, and now the early-morning sun broke through the canopy, casting rays of jade light all around. He pulled the goggles off and stowed them in his harness. He knew that their fused multispectrum sensors could give him a technological advantage, even in broad daylight, but there was something about seeing things with his own eyes, some elusive sense that science had yet to reproduce.

Pain throbbed in Nick's jaw, pounding in cadence with the thump of his quickened gait. The kid had really landed a good one. He was lucky that the punch hadn't buckled his knees. Of course, Quinn was lucky that Nick hadn't shot him for mutiny. That kid had too much baggage.

Maybe Quinn was a product of this Entitlement Generation that all the Washington pundits were talking about. Maybe he just had trust issues. The source of his problem didn't really matter. He was going to jail as soon as they got home.

Nick tried the Wraith again.

Nothing but static.

A half hour later, the wet scrub underfoot melted into a soggy layer of rotting leaves, and the trees thinned to the point that Nick had to give his full attention to moving between them unseen. Visibility improved to easily thirty meters on either side. A PLA search patrol or even a stray villager might spot him if he traipsed rapidly through the forest as he had done earlier. He was almost to the tree line. He checked the GPS screen in his MTG control box. It showed the orchard less than fifty meters ahead.

Nick began scanning left and right, looking for any sign of Novak or his Chinese captors. Then he heard the rumble of a powerful motor. Creeping to the edge of the trees, he looked southwest down the valley and saw that a farmer had already driven his tractor out to an adjacent field. To the northeast, others were out on foot, moving along rows of plowed land, spraying it with chemicals from pumps mounted on their backs. The day's work had begun.

Nick's heart sank. He hadn't thought of the orchard as something that might need daily maintenance. How long would it be before workers came to spray these trees with pesticides? Novak might have the same thought and find a different route.

He pulled back into the trees. Who was he kidding? The guy had probably died twenty-five years ago. He was chasing a ghost and risking Shadow Catcher in a Chinese trap.

Then, out of the corner of his eye, he caught movement to his left. He raised his MP7 and tracked it along the tree line, his eyes just above the scope. Instead of one smooth scan, he searched in sectors, periodically steadying his gaze to make movement easier to spot.

Within a couple of seconds, Nick found him, a single individual skirting from tree to tree. His head wasn't turned toward Nick; instead, he watched the farmers. Nick peered through his scope. The newcomer wore a different uniform from the man they'd killed. He wore a tactical vest, and his tiger-striped camouflage did not match any of the Chinese variants that Nick knew of.

Then he caught a glimpse of the man's weapon. That gun was unmistakable. The monstrous, unwieldy barrel of an old Colt .45 M1911 jutted from the newcomer's hand like a caveman's club.

Hello, Bigfoot.

CHAPTER 50

They have no communications." Hēi Yǐng spoke in measured but fluent Chinese. "I severed the SAT-COM link at the Wraith, the hub of their network. The command center, the aircraft, the ground team—each of them is now isolated from the others."

The spy reclined in the driver's seat of a sedan, parked in the shadows behind the Romeo Seven hangar. The mission had stretched late into the day, much later than expected. Darkness had already begun to fall.

"Very good." Zheng's voice was mottled by the sat phone's heavy encryption. "And what did you learn before you cut them off?"

"They did not reveal the position of the landing craft, but their team did reach the cave. They plan to head south to locate the prisoner."

Zheng sighed into the phone. "I already knew as much.

You must do better than that. It is time to implement the final contingency that you proposed."

Hēi Yǐng hesitated. The spy had hoped that it would not come to this, but very little had gone to plan so far. "I am prepared. But I am taking a major risk of exposure. I expect to be compensated, twice the original figure."

"Yes, yes," said Zheng. "Just as we discussed. I will see to the money, but you will only be paid if you succeed where Wūlóng failed."

The sound of a door opening and closing drifted across the parking lot. Hēi Yǐng instinctively sank into the seat. "I must go. I will contact you when it is done."

———

McBride pounded the desk next to the computer. Nada. Nothing. It was like everyone associated with Distant Sage had either died or disappeared.

Maybe they had.

With a little help from Molly, he had turned Nick's office into his own intelligence center, adding two more high-power computers and a server to link all three CPUs. The added speed wasn't necessary for most of his work, but it was vital for the facial recognition search.

Earlier in the day, he had isolated the image of the Caucasian man from the 2003 picture of Wūlóng. Then he fired up Romeo Seven's facial recognition program and started a match search. It was a long shot. He and Molly had run several algorithms to clean up the image, but at the end of the day, it was still a grainy, ten-year-old picture. It might not be clear enough for a good match.

While waiting for the recognition software to run its search for Wūlóng's associate, McBride had dug into Major Baron's Distant Sage mole theory. For the last few hours, he had plowed into the CIA's data mine, looking for anything on Wright or Jozef Starek. But for all his digging, he came up empty-handed.

The two men were ghosts.

He abandoned his efforts and jiggled the mouse on the computer running the recognition software. The screen came alive. An endless stream of ID photos, mug shots, and candids flashed by, each image processed in microseconds as the program compared key facial features to McBride's target. The network of databases was huge. Even with the added speed, the search could take another ten hours or more, and it still might not find a single match.

McBride checked his watch. He had promised the major that he would go get his family, and he had already waited too long. As he stood up to leave, the computer running the photo match gave a loud beep. The cycling images froze on a candid picture from the CIA database. A sandy-haired man in a wet suit smiled through a bushy mustache. Incredibly, the system declared the man a seventy-one percent match to McBride's target, better than he had ever expected. The file listed a number of aliases. He immediately noted a pattern in the names: Adam Albee, Gregory Gartner, James Johannes. There were nine in all, and they were all alliterations. He chuckled. Spooks and their games.

Spooks. Maybe Joe Tarpin could find more information in the CIA's internal archives. McBride attached the file to an encrypted e-mail.

Joe,

This guy turned up in an old picture with our Chinese assassin. See if you can find him in your archives. I'm on my way to get Major Baron's family. I'll call you as soon as I get back to find out what you've turned up.

Will

He sent the file to the printer so that he could have a hard copy and then shut down his systems and headed out the door, only to slam into Molly as she raced down the hallway. She let out a startled "Ooh!" The stack of papers in her hands flew in every direction.

"Whoa, take it easy," said McBride, bending down to help her clean up the mess. "What's going on?"

Molly gave him a fleeting smile as she collected her papers into a disheveled heap. "I'm so sorry. We've lost communications with the Wraith and the ground team. The colonel is throwing a fit."

A torrent of unintelligible shouting erupted from the command center. McBride cringed. "I see what you mean. Amanda set that network up," he volunteered. "Maybe she can fix it."

"I know. I was headed to the back offices to look for her." Molly's brown eyes pleaded with him. "Do you know where she is?"

"You mean she's not in the command center?"

Molly shook her head. "She said she was going up top to get some fresh air, but she never came back. She's not answering her cell phone either." She stood up with her papers and looked around helplessly. "It's like she just vanished."

CHAPTER 51

Quinn found the Chinese soldiers easy to tail, even though the leader wouldn't let the infantryman smoke. As the morning light grew, the six of them removed and stowed their now useless NVGs, but Quinn's multispectrum goggles allowed him to track their heat signatures even in the daylight. The more they marched, the hotter they became and the easier they were to break out from the foliage. He tracked them from as great a distance as possible, so that he could move quickly enough to keep up without fear of the noise reaching their ears.

As the trees thinned, Quinn drifted farther and farther back, making room to scan for other signatures. A couple hours into the march, his scans paid off.

He had drifted well southwest of the soldiers to take advantage of some rising terrain, coming almost parallel with them as he climbed two-thirds of the way up a short ridgeline. Looking forward from his higher vantage point, he thought he saw his objective. A figure crouched in the trees on the edge of a cultivated valley. He couldn't be certain that it was Nick. The man definitely looked bigger than the Chinese soldiers he'd been following, and the battle gear outlined in the infrared looked a lot like his own. Then he moved, raising his weapon, and Quinn saw a holster of knives strapped around his leg.

Quinn resisted the urge to scoot down the hill and snag his rogue team lead. He held his position and watched. Nick seemed to be taking aim with his machine gun. Following his line of fire, Quinn saw that he was tracking another figure, moving along the tree line. Then he saw something else. There were more soldiers, farther back in the trees, following Nick's target. Nick lowered his weapon as the target moved closer to his position.

"What are you doing?" whispered Quinn, as if Nick could hear him through the implant. "Keep your weapon up." Then he noticed a difference between Nick's target and the other Chinese. The soldier's gear was all wrong. It didn't match any of the others. He moved differently too, quickly, furtively. He wasn't stalking. He was evading.

Novak. Nick was right.

Quinn looked to Nick and then back to the Chinese, realizing that his boss didn't see them. The soldiers moved in a wide arc, encircling the two Americans. The net was already falling.

The smoker and his new friends changed course to join the others, now moving more carefully, spreading out and crouching as they jogged from tree to tree. The leader took charge of the whole group. He signaled the others, pointing directly at Nick.

"Shadow One, this is Shadow Two, *come in*," pleaded Quinn, but he got no response. He had to alert Nick somehow. He looked down at the long suppressor affixed to the front of his MP7 and shrugged. "Why not?" he said under his breath. He quickly unscrewed the suppressor, dropped his MTGs to his neck, and took aim at the soldier closest to Nick. Then he changed his mind and shifted to the group's leader. "Sorry, buddy," he said, and then took the shot.

The sound of the 4.6-millimeter rounds exploding out of the chamber reverberated through the forest, echoing off the hill on the opposite side of the valley. It had the desired effect. Quinn watched as Nick immediately took cover and began searching the trees for targets. Novak dove to the ground as well and then rolled over and fired wildly into the forest behind him.

The Chinese soldiers spread out and ducked behind any cover they could find. Quinn could see confusion setting in. None of them knew where the first shot had come from. All they knew was that two of their number had been shot; Quinn had dropped his target and Novak had winged another one. No one looked up toward Quinn's hill. He took advantage and tried to pick the big soldier from before out of the crowd. He was easy to find.

The big guy had run over to help his leader. Finding the man dead, he grabbed the radio and started barking orders.

"I guess that makes you the new man in charge," said Quinn. "Not for long."

He squeezed off two bursts and the big soldier fell on top of his dead comrade. Suddenly mud splattered up into Quinn's face. He heard heavy thuds and cracking wood as bullets rained down around him. "Jig's up," he said out loud, diving for the cover of a rock formation jutting out from the hill.

The heavy rounds kept pelting his previous position. The shooter had not seen him move, so Quinn took the risk of rushing forward, finding new cover behind another boulder. He searched for the source of the gunfire. What he saw astonished him.

Weapons fire exploded all over the valley. Two off-road vehicles had stormed into the field next to the orchard. Quinn recognized the Norinco fast attack vehicles from his intel training; the instructors liked to call them dune buggies on steroids. The heavy fire came from a 12.5-millimeter machine gun mounted on the back of one of them. The thing had a scope on it, probably infrared, but the operator made little use of his optics. Instead, he leaned into his back support and snaked the weapon back and forth, spraying Quinn's hillside.

Novak appeared to be shot in the leg. Nick had run to his side and now dragged him toward the orchard with one hand while firing sidelong at the FAVs with the other. Quinn saw that the Chinese could have cut him down at any time, but the other vehicle's machine gun operator kept his weapon strangely silent.

Quinn took aim at the driver of one of the FAVs, but

the vehicle was too far out of range, even for his MP7. He wished that he had brought a sniper rifle on this trip. He turned his weapon toward the soldiers in the forest, taking down two more.

He stood up and ran toward Nick again, but soon he had to dive for cover behind a fallen tree. One of the FAVs found him and pelted his position with more heavy rounds. The fallen tree split and splintered, showering him with tiny pieces of wood.

Quinn saw the crest of the descending ridge just a few meters behind him. He abandoned his rapidly deteriorating cover and low-crawled over the top, putting solid ground between himself and the machine guns. After a quick recovery breath, he got up and ran in a crouch toward the valley, hoping that the FAVs would not see him pop out at the base of the ridgeline. He found a new vantage point behind another rock formation, seated a fresh clip in his weapon, and searched for another target.

The situation looked hopeless.

Nick had stopped his retreat in the middle of the field between the forest and the orchard. He crouched amid waves of tall grass, shielding Novak, alternating fire with his Beretta in one hand and Novak's Colt in the other. The MP7 hung at his side, empty. The FAVs circled him like wolves while the troops from the tree line slowly advanced. Several others now jogged toward Quinn's last position, their weapons up, searching.

Quinn had closed the range with the FAVs, but he couldn't get a clean shot at the gunners because of the armored mounts around the machine guns. Just as he shifted his aim to the closest driver, he saw the soldier in the passenger's side pull out a huge shotgun and point it at Nick. Before Quinn could react, the man fired. Sparks flew from the end of the barrel. Nick dropped like a stone and disappeared in the grass.

A single bullet ricocheted off the rock next to Quinn's hands. Then a hail of bullets followed. The soldiers had found him. Quinn ignored them. "Get up, Nick," he said under his breath.

Chips of flying rock stung his cheeks and bounced off his vest. Still, Quinn would not take his eyes off the spot where his team lead had fallen. "Get up!" he screamed.

A gunner in one of the FAVs jerked his weapon toward the sound and began obliterating the rock. Quinn had no choice but to run.

CHAPTER 52

Katy Baron laid her son, Luke, in his crib. He was finally asleep. She'd been rocking him for the last hour and a half, but every time she tried to lay him down, he would open his eyes and cry again. She cringed as she set his little body gently down on the mattress, knowing that a few hours' relief was probably too much to hope for. But Luke did not cry. He breathed the sweet, even breaths of a sleeping baby boy. Suddenly she didn't want to leave.

Despite all of the work it took to get him to go down, part of Katy wanted to stay and watch Luke sleep, just to soak in the sight of him. Another part of her wanted to race from the room and get a hot shower, and the rest of her felt tremendous guilt over the selfishness of the thought. After the previous night's attack, she felt an incredible urge to sit next to his crib and watch over him all night. She knew that was silly. Nick's boss had told her the attack was an isolated incident, the act of a nutcase working alone.

Katy laughed inwardly at her own indecision. *Get out of here, you idiot.*

Feeling the guilt that only mothers know, she backed quietly out of Luke's room and headed for the comfort of the shower. She never even made it to her bedroom door.

The sound of the door chime reverberated through the house like the deep peal of the bells of Notre Dame. Katy raced down the hallway, wondering who could possibly be at her doorstep at this hour and swearing that they would die a violent death if they woke Luke. As she rounded the corner into the foyer, she saw a hand reaching for the bell again. She sprinted for the door, slamming her hand against the narrow window next to it and waving at the intruder to prevent him from ringing again. In the darkness, she could not see the man's face. He wore a red polo shirt and slacks, not exactly the garb of a killer. Probably some salesman.

Katy promised herself that she would not open the door, no matter what this guy was selling. She flipped on the porch light and a face appeared in the window. She couldn't believe her eyes.

"Will?" she asked through the glass. "Will McBride?"

"Hi, Mrs. Baron. I'm sorry to show up on your doorstep so late."

Katy swung the door wide. "Will, you can call me Katy, just like I told you the last time I saw you—which was what, six months ago?"

"A year, ma'am," replied McBride.

"Nick's not home, Will. He's TDY. He'd be thrilled to see you, though. How long are you in town?"

McBride shifted side to side on each heel, creasing his freckled brow. "Mrs. Baron, I'm working with your husband on a special assignment right now. He asked that I come and collect you and Luke and bring you back to our office."

"You're not making sense, Will," said Katy, fighting to understand. "Nick is out of the country. Did you join his unit at Andrews? Does this have something to do with the attack last night?"

McBride nodded slowly. "Yes. Yes it does. And yes, I am working with Major Baron's unit." A car door slammed shut in the distance. He looked warily over his shoulder. "Please, ma'am, your husband feels that you are in danger. We need to get you back to the base."

Out in the driveway, Katy struggled to install Luke's car seat in McBride's Corolla while he lifted her duffel bag full of baby supplies into the trunk. "I didn't know babies needed anvils," he grunted.

"You can never be too prepared," said Katy. "If Luke has an accident in your little hideout, you'll thank me."

Just as McBride finally cranked the engine, his pocket gave an obnoxious chime, the sound of a doorbell.

Katy nervously glanced over her shoulder to check that Luke was still sleeping. Then she folded her arms and glared at McBride. "Really?"

"I'm sorry, it's my text alert." He struggled to get the phone out of his pocket before it chimed again. "We're going to have to make a short stop and pick up Amanda Navistrova," he said, staring down at the screen. "I've been trying to find her. She says she went home to freshen up and now her car won't start." He put the phone away and pulled down to the edge of the driveway, but then he stopped again, looking up and down the street.

"What is it?" asked Katy.

McBride let his head fall back against the headrest and lifted his hands from the steering wheel in frustration. "I don't know where she lives."

Katy guided McBride to Amanda's condominium in Oxon Hill, just to the west of the base. She lived in one of the older models, a narrow three-story that capped the end of a long block of fifteen attached units. Most of the residents appeared to be sleeping. Only a few lights still burned in the windows of the other units.

Katy frowned. The streetlamp closest to Amanda's place had shattered, leaving her end of the street in total darkness. "You'd think she would have left the porch light on," she said, squinting out the window.

"She must be ready to go," replied McBride. "She's in as big a hurry as I am. I'll be right back."

Katy got out and moved to the backseat, so that she could sit next to Luke and leave the front for Amanda. She closed the door as quietly as possible, buckled in, and then gazed down at her son, amazed that he still slept. She wanted so much to touch his face, to run her fingers down his soft cheek, but she didn't dare.

Suddenly, Katy heard a cry from outside the car. Constricted by her seat belt, she tried to lean across the backseat, angling her body around the baby to peer out the window. From the odd angle, she thought she saw McBride fall forward into Amanda's dark doorway. "What's going on?" she muttered to herself. Then she saw a shadowy figure hovering over McBride. She saw a long black object in his gloved hand. There were two dim flashes. McBride's body convulsed.

Katy let out an involuntary yelp. The dark figure backed into the shadows.

Luke began to cry. "It's okay, it's okay, baby. Mommy's sorry," said Katy breathlessly as she fought with her seat belt. She tried to keep her eyes on Amanda's doorway, but in her panic, she couldn't get the catch to release. Finally she looked down and found the button. The buckle sprang loose. When she looked up again, McBride was gone. Luke's crying became more insistent.

Katy stared at the empty doorway for just a fraction of a second. Then she started scrambling over the front seat. "Mommy has to drive the car now, sweetie," she said. She punched the lock as she settled into the driver's seat. A shadow passed over the steering wheel. She looked left and saw a gun swinging toward her. The window shattered.

Katy screamed.

CHAPTER 53

Colonel Walker lifted a fresh cup to his lips, glancing around the command center as he took a lengthy sip. Romeo Seven had become a ghost town. Navistrova had disappeared, and now McBride. Tarpin wasn't answering his phone either. Scott had left him several messages asking for help with the SATCOM problem, but all he received in return was a cryptic text indicating that the CIA man was tied up with another op at Langley.

The command center staff had withered down to just Scott and a couple of low-level techs. "Where is everyone?" asked Walker. But the few minions that remained just shrank down behind their workstations.

"I've got it!" Scott popped up from behind the SATCOM terminal like a gopher from a hole. Wires and cables fell down around him. "We still have a few second-generation birds working," he said. "They use elliptical tracks rather than the geostationary orbits used by our new Milstar satellites. One of them just rose over the ground team's horizon. It will be in view for several hours."

"What good will that do?" asked Walker.

The engineer moved two of his cables to new ports on the terminal and then started typing frequencies into the control heads. "I still can't talk to the Wraith," he said as he worked, "but I can crosslink from our SATCOM bird to the old one. Then I should be able to force open a link to the ground team's comm implants, one at a time."

Scott moved from the terminal to the adjacent workstation and started working the keyboard. The command center's big screen changed to a satellite map of Fujian Province. "The easiest part is getting their telemetry, their GPS data." A blue dot labeled *SHADOW TWO* appeared on the screen. Then, several seconds later, another one appeared, labeled *SHADOW ONE*.

"Tell me that's not the real data," said Walker. "Tell me you still have to make some adjustments." He didn't like what he saw. Several hundred meters separated the two dots, and Shadow One was moving farther away, fast.

"I'm sorry, sir," said Scott, dread creeping into his voice. "That's it. What you are seeing are their true positions."

Walker moved around the stations to join the engineer. "Get their comms up. Now!"

Scott's fingers pounded the keyboard, sending line after line of commands to the computer, but the comm link still showed no connection. "I can't get Quinn," he said. "Someone muted his implant. It will take me a while to get it working."

"Forget Quinn," ordered Walker. "Get me Baron."

The engineer repeated his procedure. This time, the link connected. "I've got it," he said. There was a lot of static, but they heard voices. Men were talking close enough to Nick for the comm implant to pick them up. They were speaking Mandarin.

"That's not good," said Walker.

Scott returned to his keyboard. "Stand by. I'll run the feed through a language filter." A digital voice began to translate:

"Where are we taking them?"

"The general said to bring them to the factory."

"You mean, the minister."

There was a chuckle. "It is so hard to keep up."

"The prisoner will be happy that we are not bringing him back to Detention Center Twenty-six."

Another laugh. "I don't think he is going to be happy about anything."

The two men stopped talking. Walker's eyes widened. "Baron was right," he exclaimed. "This whole thing was a trap."

"Is he dead?" asked Scott, the color draining from his face.

Walker stared at Nick's GPS track, rapidly moving away from Quinn. "Baron isn't the prize," he mused out loud. "This wasn't a trap for him. This was a trap for our stealth plane." He drained his coffee cup and then crushed it decisively. "He's still alive. He has to be. They don't want revenge for the Persian Gulf operation. They want to finish the job. They still need him so they can find Shadow Catcher."

The colonel quickly turned back to Scott. "Get working on Quinn's comms," he said. "We're going to need him." Then he signaled Molly. "Get me Dr. Heldner. If Baron is alive, we have to activate the Kharon Protocol."

CHAPTER 54

Nick thought he heard someone calling his name. He felt numb. He tried to open his eyes, but he couldn't tell if he succeeded. He saw only darkness, a void.

"Shadow One, respond. Can you hear me?"

Whose voice was that? Which direction was it coming from? It seemed as if the words came from inside his head.

"Come on, Baron. Respond."

The voice sounded urgent. He felt compelled to answer. He tried to answer. But he couldn't make his mouth form the words. He couldn't remember where he was or what he was doing. The memories were there, lined up like words on a page, but he couldn't read them. The letters were all jumbled up.

"Major Baron, answer me!"

This time Nick recognized the voice. The void before

his eyes turned gray, and the silhouette of a man formed. He forced his lips to form a single word. "Colonel?"

"He's alive. Clean up the channel, I'm getting too much static. Focus, Shadow One, they have you. You have to enable Kharon. Do you understand? You have to activate the Kharon Protocol."

Kharon. Shadow One. The words drifted around the page in his mind like flowers in a pool. He tried to grasp them, but each time he reached, his hand caused a ripple of letters that carried them away.

The silhouette became solid. As the fog in his vision thinned, Nick began to see color. The man wore a green uniform, but he seemed to be facing away. "Colonel, what are you doing? What's going on?"

"Shadow One, this is Lighthouse. Focus. You have been captured. You need to activate the Kharon Protocol. Respond."

Shadow . . . One . . . Suddenly, Nick caught hold of the words. Like the key to a cipher, they unscrambled all the others. The memories came flooding back. The mission. Novak!

As his mind cleared, so did his vision. He could see now that he lay in the back of an open vehicle. The man in front of him no longer faced away. He wasn't Colonel Walker. He was a Chinese soldier. There was a bloodied bandage on his arm.

Nick tried to sit up. Pain wracked his body. The wounded soldier gave him a vengeful grin. He said something in Mandarin, hefted an electric shock baton in his good hand, and then viciously shoved it up under Nick's chin.

He felt his flesh burn. Everything went black.

After what seemed like an instant, Nick opened his eyes. This time the fog cleared almost immediately. He saw green branches moving past him against a pale blue sky. His neck stung horribly beneath his chin, and his head throbbed. The jostle of the ride did not help.

He no longer lay in the back of a vehicle. Instead, a pair of men carried him on a litter. They marched quickly, with little regard for their patient, exchanging snippets of conversation, always in Mandarin. Nick tried to look around. He tilted his aching head at an agonizingly slow rate so as not to draw the attention of his human transports. He did not relish another shock with the baton.

The soldiers carried him through an opening in a tall chain-link fence, topped with two rolls of concertina wire. Nick wondered whether it was meant to keep intruders away or to keep prisoners inside. A wide gravel yard separated the gate from a three-story building. Beyond the crunch of the soldiers' footsteps and the whine of their conversation, Nick heard the low drone of heavy machinery. He cautiously righted his head again. Instead of open blue sky, he found the face of an angry Chinese soldier. The man spoke rapidly to the soldiers carrying the litter. They halted obediently. Nick noted with frustration the same bloody bandage on the soldier's arm. He brandished his miniature cattle prod. Nick winced.

After a few seconds without the burn and involuntary calisthenics of electric shock, Nick opened one eye. He saw an older man in a white shirt and white lab coat scolding the soldier. This new arrival lifted a syringe and squirted a bit of brown liquid through its needle. Nick felt a prick in his arm. The trees started spinning. The void returned.

"Wake up!"

Once again, Nick found it hard to focus his thoughts. Hadn't he just been through this?

"Wake up. We have to get out of here!"

Walker. The colonel had brought him back before.

"Can you hear me? Please get up!"

No, this voice was not Walker's. It was an American voice, but it was not the colonel's. Walker commanded him in clear, even tones. This voice begged him to get up in harsh whispers. Nick tried to answer, but as before, he found it difficult to force the words out of his mouth.

"You're mumbling. They drugged you. I need you to fight it. You've got to wake up before they come back."

This time, the void glowed white when Nick opened his eyes. Bright, almost blinding light spread across his vision. He tried to shield his eyes, but his arm wouldn't move. He turned his head in the direction of the voice. The light dimmed. Shapes began to form.

"That's right. Fight it."

Nick's head still throbbed. His body ached. He squinted and blinked until his vision cleared. A man lay next to him on a gurney, only a few feet away, wearing green and brown tiger-striped camouflage. He was belted down with heavy leather straps. "What is your name?"

"Novak. My name is David Novak. Please, we don't have time. You have to get up."

With effort, Nick moved his head around, tilting his chin and straining his neck. He was lying on a metal table in some sort of infirmary. There were short rails running along either side of him. He tried to move other parts of his body, but nothing worked. "I can't move my arms, David."

"That's just the drugs. The fact that you're awake means they're wearing off. Fight it."

Nick struggled against his paralysis. It felt as if a two-hundred-pound sandbag were lying on his chest. After a few seconds, he found that he could move his fingers. He gripped the rails and tried to pull himself to a sitting position.

"That's it. You've got it," urged Novak.

The steady throbbing in Nick's head became a relentless pound. He felt certain that some of his ribs were broken. Sharp pain stabbed at his chest as he pulled, but finally, he sat completely upright. The first thing he saw from his new vantage point was the IV line running into his arm, descending from a bag full of clear liquid that hung on a rolling stand. He had no way to tell whether the fluid was saline or something more. His captors had removed his armor, shirt, and pants, leaving only his black Kevlar-elastane boxers. A thin sheet covered him from his bare feet to his waist.

Nick tried to shift onto his side. That's when he noticed the cuffs and chains, securing his hands and feet to the rails. "My hands and feet are bound, David," he said quietly. "I can't move them more than a few inches."

Novak pounded the back of his head against the thin mattress of the gurney and thrashed against the belts. "I'm not going back in," he exclaimed. "I'll fight them until they kill me."

For the first time, Nick took a good look at the man he'd come to rescue. Novak should be about fifty, but this man looked well over sixty. He had coarse gray hair. His cheeks were taut, stretched so thin that Nick could see blue veins beneath his pale skin. His uniform lay over his gaunt frame like a blanket. The Chinese had cut away a section of his pants to treat his bullet wound, and his leg looked thin and frail. Nick had never seen the effects of extreme malnourishment up close before. Twenty-five years. An involuntary shiver shook his frame.

"Did you make those radio calls?" Nick spoke his next words slowly. *"Are you Jade Zero One?"*

Novak stopped struggling, exhausted. Tears formed at the corners of his eyes and slid down his crow's feet, gathering in tiny pools on the vinyl mattress. "Are you the one they sent to rescue me?" he asked, staring at the ceiling.

"I'm still working on it," Nick replied.

Novak snorted. Then a spark of hope flashed across his face. "What about Jozef? Did you get him out?"

Jozef. Nick searched his mind, fighting the cobwebs. "Do you mean Starek?"

"Yes, Jozef Starek. We were shot down on the same day. I know he survived. I saw him."

Nick stared hard at Novak, trying to determine how

much delusion had corrupted the poor man's memory. "You saw Jozef Starek in a Chinese prison? Are you certain?"

Novak turned his head and looked Nick in the eye. He spoke confidently. He seemed to be in right mind, mostly. "Ten years ago, they transferred me to a new facility. They forgot to bag my head. As they marched me out of the old prison, I saw him, surrounded by guards. He looked older, but it was definitely Jozef Starek."

Nick wondered if Walker was getting any of this. He hadn't heard anything on his comm unit since he woke up on the table. He wanted to check its function, to whisper a call to Lighthouse, but he dared not risk the exposure.

They were being watched.

CHAPTER 55

The room looked very much like an infirmary. There were cabinets with glass-paned doors filled with medicines and bandages. All the labels were in English. A long counter held a stainless-steel sink and a bottle of antibiotic hand cleaner. There was a rolling rack of electronic equipment in the corner, with a heart monitor and a blood pressure machine. Nick sat on a sterile metal table. Novak lay on a gurney. Someone had even neatly stacked their tactical vests and equipment on chairs in the corner—except for the guns, of course. Novak's leg wound had been treated. Nick's chest had been wrapped tightly with bandages. If not for the restraints, the two of them might be recovering in the clinic at Andrews.

This was the first stage of interrogation.

Treat the prisoners' wounds. Put them together in a nonthreatening environment. Then vacate the premises and watch them spill their guts to each other through an observation mirror or closed-circuit television. This was the easiest and most effective interrogation technique available. Nick had experienced it before, though not from this side of the glass. He couldn't risk trying to contact Lighthouse because he knew that Chinese cameras and microphones were picking up every word that he said.

"We don't know Starek's whereabouts," said Nick. "As far as we know, you are the only prisoner."

The hope fell from Novak's expression. "Then it is likely that he and I are both dead now." He became silent for a while, and Nick turned his attention to his restraints, trying to assess their strength without being too obvious. Both the cuffs and chains were made of good steel. He would not be able to break them. They were tight too. He couldn't wriggle his wrists free.

"How did you get here?" asked Novak after several minutes.

"HALO jump," Nick lied.

"We tried that in the eighties," replied Novak in a matter-of-fact tone, still staring at the ceiling. "Back then, we couldn't get the drop bird deep enough inside the Chinese radar fence for the jumpers to make the shoreline. How did you manage it?" He seemed to take a passing interest, just making conversation until it was his turn to die.

"Wingsuits," explained Nick. "They greatly extend our range."

The door to the mock infirmary suddenly opened. "Are you so cruel that you will even lie to the condemned?" asked a stocky Chinese man in general's fatigues. "Please, Major

Baron. You are his first American visitor in twenty-five years, and you are treating him like a hostile interrogator."

Nick assessed the newcomer. He entered the room with swagger, followed by a cordon of troops with their weapons raised. This was no mere interrogator. This guy was running the show.

Novak did not bother to look up at his captors, even when one of the soldiers stuck a needle in his arm. He did not resist. He just closed his eyes and went to sleep.

The same soldier moved over to Nick and began unlocking his restraints. The others brought their weapons up to their shoulders and tightened their fingers around the triggers, making it clear that any false moves would invite a storm of bullets. Then two more men entered the room. They wore white lab coats and pushed a heavy metal contraption that looked like an industrial-sized coatrack. One of them carried an aluminum briefcase.

The soldier roughly pulled Nick off the table, standing him up next to the unconscious Novak. After yanking the IV out of Nick's arm he marched him around the table and stopped him in front of the doctors and their strange coatrack. They unfolded heavy stabilizers and locked the brakes on the rack's wheels. Finally, it dawned on Nick what the contraption was for. "This is going to get uncomfortable," he said out loud.

The soldier put new cuffs on Nick's wrists and a set of shackles around his ankles. Then he jerked Nick's hands in the air and lifted the center chain of the cuffs over a U-shaped hook on the rack. Nick heard a whirring sound. The top of the rack telescoped, lifting him up by his wrists until his feet dangled a few inches above the ground. His shoulder blades pinched together, forcing his chin to his chest. He winced with pain.

Suddenly Nick heard an electronic shriek in his ear, followed by radio static. He tried to look around and see if anyone else had heard the sound, but none of those that he could see from his awkward position showed the slightest reaction to it.

"Shadow One, this is Lighthouse. Do you read?"

Nick smiled for the small victory. "What took you so long," he said out loud.

The Chinese general pointed at Novak. "I would have waited even longer, but it seemed pointless if you were just going to lie to him."

"We read you, Shadow One," said Walker. "We're with you now. Something shorted the implant out for a while, but now we've got you back." Walker paused and then came back on the line. "Shadow One, activate Kharon before it's too late." The command came slowly, but firmly.

The general waved his hand, and all of the soldiers left except for one. Nick recognized the remaining man by the bandage on his arm. "Looks like I have a fan," he said.

"This is Ma," said the general. "He is one of my elite Special Forces soldiers. You shot him three times, wounding his arm and leaving bruises on his chest despite his body armor. We think that you cracked one of his ribs."

"Must've got him with the Colt," said Nick.

"Ma is most interested in watching our interrogation

techniques. He has even asked for some . . . how would you Americans say it? Oh yes, hands-on training."

"Good, he needs the training. So far his technique is horrible," replied Nick. His head and neck still throbbed from Ma's previous attention.

"You should not make jokes with me, Major Baron. It is not proper. I am an important man here in China. You may call me Defense Minister Zheng."

Nick's shoulders began to ache from the strain. He tried to shift his weight, but with every movement, the steel cuffs cut into his wrists. "Okay, Defense Minister Zheng, I'm on vacation here in beautiful Fujian. Why have you detained me?"

Zheng sighed. "Please, Major Baron. Or should I call you Nick? As I said, I am an important man, and I have little time for games." He checked his watch—a gaudy gold number that seemed completely out of place with his fatigues. "I have a schedule to keep. I need you to tell me where your transport is, the stealth vehicle with which you violated my country's sovereignty. I also need to know where I might find your compatriot. What was his name?" One of the doctors handed Zheng a clipboard, and he made a show of flipping up a page and studying the one beneath it. "Ah, here it is. Quinn. Senior Airman Ethan Quinn."

Nick said nothing. He saw the doctor with the case lay it on the table and flip it open. A cold fog lifted up from the interior. The doctor removed a glass vial and then held up a syringe. He shoved the needle through the top, withdrawing a large amount of translucent red liquid.

"I'm already in plenty of pain," said Nick.

"Don't insult my intelligence," replied Zheng with a frown. "You and I both know that pain drugs are useless as interrogation tools; they are only used by amateurs and your Hollywood writers. The subject must feel that he has something to lose—his thumb to some bolt cutters perhaps. Or, in the case of your CIA's favorite technique, his life during waterboarding."

Zheng walked over to the doctor and gazed admiringly at the syringe. "Dr. Chao is an expert in narco-interrogation. He will give you just enough of his cocktail to lower your defenses." He brandished a scalpel, eliciting an evil grin from Ma. "But it will not defer the pain of my more *traditional* techniques."

"Shadow One, activate Kharon," said Walker, his voice calm but still commanding. "It's time, Nick."

The doctor pressed his needle into the crux of Nick's arm. He felt the icy cold drug entering his vein. He closed his eyes and tensed his muscles, bracing himself for the neurological onslaught of barbiturates and stimulants. "Nicholas J. Baron," he said, forcing the words out, "Major, U.S. Air Force, seven one three, two six, four zero two one."

"Now you are just being ridiculous," said Zheng, pushing his face close to Nick's. His breath smelled of rotting garlic. "The name, rank, and serial number technique went out of fashion years ago."

Nick coughed and opened his eyes. Zheng's unpleasant visage began to deform. The room seemed to tilt one way and then the other, as if he were on the deck of a ship, riding out a storm. He heard three sharp beeps in his ear. A digital voice said, "Activation code accepted. Kharon Protocol initiated. Local control is online. Lighthouse control is online." He gave Zheng a grim smile. Then he heard Walker's voice again.

"Good work, Shadow One. You have the lead now. We have your back."

CHAPTER 56

Quinn squeezed the last drop of water from a green ration pouch. He was sore, fatigued, and thirsty. He patted the pockets on his tactical harness; there were no more water pouches, and he had drained his CamelBak hours ago. This mission was never supposed to last this long.

The Chinese weren't moving subtly in small groups anymore. They were after him in force now, and he knew that he needed to keep hydrating if he wanted to stay ahead of them, both physically and mentally. He knelt down beside a small brook and stared apprehensively at the water. The stream was barely a trickle, descending through a narrow valley in the rain forest. He shuddered to think what sort of amoebas and microscopic worms it carried in its flow. He pulled a pill bottle from his vest and shook it, examining the two small capsules inside.

He hoped that whatever life forms this stream carried, they would be the sort that the bacteria in the pills liked to eat.

Doc Heldner had given him the capsules after she installed his implant. Called "Intestinal Fortitude" by Special Forces operators, each one contained more than a million helpful bacteria, bioengineered to consume any harmful organisms that untreated water could dish out. "Take two million of these and call me in the morning," the doctor had said.

Funny.

"Oh well, you gotta die of something," muttered Quinn. He swallowed the pills and then slipped an iodine tab into his CamelBak for good measure. If the dysentery got too bad, he could just run out in front of a Chinese machine gun.

As he reluctantly dipped the polyurethane bladder into the stream, a shrill squeak sounded in his ear. He jerked his head up, smacking it into a low-hanging branch. "Ow. I just can't win," he complained, rubbing his head. Then a burst of light static crackled in his ear. He realized the squeal had come from his communications implant.

Quinn sat down on the bank, gingerly touching the place behind his ear where Heldner had installed the device. He cringed at the idea that the unit might be malfunctioning. What if it accidentally went off?

"Shadow Two, come in." Walker's voice cut through the static like a searchlight through fog. "Shadow Two, respond."

"Lighthouse," Quinn replied, trying to contain his

elation at hearing a voice from home, "this is Shadow Two. I have you Lima Charlie."

"Loud and clear also, Shadow Two. What is your situation?"

"I am evading a large enemy force, trying to return to Shadow Catcher. The objective has been recaptured. Shadow One is down. I repeat, Shadow One is KIA."

"Negative, Shadow Two. Your team lead is alive."

A chill swept through Quinn's body, but he didn't dare to hope. "I saw him go down, Lighthouse. The shotgun they used was massive. It should have blown him apart."

"It was probably a blunt trauma round, a nonlethal. He's hurt and captured, but he's alive."

A dizzying mix of emotions assaulted Quinn's weary mind: anger against the Chinese, joy that Nick was alive, but most of all, he felt ashamed that his foolish rebellion had broken up their team.

"We are monitoring Shadow One on another channel," continued Walker. "They want Shadow Catcher. They are torturing him for its location, for yours as well."

"Has he said anything?" asked Quinn.

"Negative. He's holding for now. He already activated the Kharon Protocol on his comm device. If they get close, he can trigger the sequence . . . or we can."

Quinn drew a slow breath. "You mean, if you don't like where the conversation is leading, you can blow a big hole in the side of his head."

"It's what you both agreed to," replied Walker. "Shadow One did the right thing by activating the contingency." The colonel paused for a moment, leaving only cold static. "No one wants it to come to that," he said finally. "We want you to get him out."

Adrenaline surged, washing away Quinn's fatigue. "What's the plan?" he asked, dipping his CamelBak into the stream again.

"We need intelligence. We have Shadow One's location. They are holding him at an isolated facility less than a kilometer southeast of your position. Previous intel lists the compound as a factory, but it is surrounded by a tall fence, and it has a runway and an aircraft fueling station. We think it's a base of operations for a covert unit working directly for Zheng. We need you to get there and assess the potential for a rescue attempt. You need to move quickly. We haven't reestablished communications with the Wraith yet, but we know that it's getting low on fuel."

"I'm on it," replied Quinn, installing the full Camel-Bak in his tactical harness.

"Good, we can bounce a data burst through your comm unit into your MTG control. We'll send you Shadow One's coordinates. We think he is being held in the northwest corner of the building on the top floor, but our signal was corrupted earlier, so the spherical error is nearly one hundred feet."

"Right. So for all you know, he could be in a storm cellar out in the woods next to the compound," said Quinn as he typed a command into his MTG control box. "I'm ready for the data burst."

"We're sending it now. Good luck, Shadow Two. Lighthouse out."

CHAPTER 57

The kidnapper wore all black—black gloves, black pants, and a black hooded sweatshirt. He always kept his face in shadow, shining the blinding light attached to the base of his pistol in Katy's eyes. He spoke only in harsh whispers, ordering her to pull Luke out of the car and enter Amanda's house, threatening to shoot them both if she did not comply.

Inside, Katy saw no sign of McBride or Amanda, although it was hard to see anything at all. The condo was dark, lit only by the waving beam of the kidnapper's light. There was a stairwell to her right, just inside the door, but there were no lights coming from the top floor either. He ordered her to lay the baby on Amanda's small sofa and then bound her hands behind her with zip-tie handcuffs.

Luke wailed at the top of his lungs.

Katy sat down next to her son. "Hush, baby. Mommy's here. It's okay." She tried to force the edge out of her voice, to make her tone light and soothing, but she could barely keep her own crying in check. With her hands bound, she could not give him the mother's touch that he needed. "It's okay, sweetie. Mommy's here," she repeated.

"Keep your baby quiet, or I *will* shoot him," said the man in black, his whispered tone strangely even given the horror of his words. "I don't really need three hostages. I can get by with two." He leaned casually against the granite bar separating Amanda's tiny kitchen from her living room and then raised the weapon again, forcing Katy to avert her eyes from the powerful light.

"You're sick," said Katy through her tears. "There's a special place in hell for men like you."

The man checked his watch, as if bored by her accusation. "I don't believe in heaven or hell, sweetheart. Life is all about the cash. The rest doesn't really matter."

"Then you're in for a big surprise."

"Just shut the kid up."

Katy glanced down at her crying son and then back up at the kidnapper. She realized that she had a bargaining chip, but she had to be careful. "You're going to have to uncuff me so that I can hold him. It's the only way that I can calm him down."

The kidnapper hesitated for a moment, but Luke's cries became even more insistent. He let out a frustrated sigh. "If I even think that you're making a move, I'll put a bullet in his head. Got me, soccer mom?"

Katy nodded, fighting back the tears evoked by his terrible words.

Every cell in her body wanted to recoil as he approached with wire cutters to clip her restraints, but she dared not move for fear that he would make good on his threat. As he drew closer, she found that he was shorter than she first thought. Then, just before he turned her around to clip the cuffs, she got a look at his face—not the whole face, but a faint glimpse into the shadow beneath the hood. His cheeks and chin seemed soft, not sharp or scarred as she'd expected of a heartless thug.

Katy took her son into her arms, and the man retreated to the bar, pausing halfway to peek through the vertical blinds that covered the sliding patio door. Katy took the gesture as a sign of nervousness. Maybe he had heard something. Maybe one of the neighbors had gotten suspicious and called the police.

Between the kidnapper's willingness to uncuff her and his behavior at the back door, Katy wondered if his menace might be mostly talk. Surely he wasn't demented enough to make good on his threats to harm her baby, especially if he thought this might turn into a standoff with the police. Once she had calmed Luke down, she looked up, shielding her eyes from the flashlight. "This really isn't your cup of tea, is it?" she asked, forcing confidence into her voice.

The kidnapper stormed up to her and placed the barrel of his gun against her forehead. "You have no idea what I'm capable of, what I have done," he hissed. "I guess you need a reminder." He grabbed her by the hair and yanked her across the room to the entryway closet. Then he opened the door and shined his light inside.

Katy let out a terrified cry. Will McBride lay crumpled on the floor of the tiny enclosure, his shirt soaked through with blood. The LED flashlight cast his face in ghastly white. His mouth gaped open, and his empty eyes stared back at her. She turned away, trying desperately to control her tears.

"Do not forget what you saw," whispered the killer, shutting the closet door and shoving her back toward the couch. "I will end your life or your son's life without hesitation, so keep your mouth shut and do as you're told." He sat down on a stool at Amanda's bar.

Katy cowered on the couch with her baby. "What have you done with Amanda?" she asked, suppressing her sobs.

"She's fine. She's resting upstairs."

"I don't believe you."

The killer sighed. "I told you to shut up." He removed a phone from a holster on his hip, raising the pistol again as he flipped up a fat antenna and dialed. "Keep the kid quiet. This is an important call . . . for all of us."

CHAPTER 58

The rain started shortly after Quinn's conversation with Walker. It began with a few fat drops, falling lazily through the forest canopy and splashing on the low vegetation. Then it grew into a vicious downpour. How, he wondered, could the seamless blanket of green above him stop so much light yet do nothing to shield him from the rain? He chuckled. He shouldn't complain. Aside from a slight chill and the general feeling of being soggy, the deluge was a blessing.

This weather gave Quinn the advantage. The MTGs cut through moisture better than any other vision-enhancing device ever conceived. He was one man, moving under the guidance of heads-up GPS graphics and communicating with his headquarters through an internal comm device. The Chinese were moving in groups, unguided and searching with their naked eyes, trying to coordinate with one another using handheld radios or shouting over the noise of the pounding rain. Quinn could move faster now, with the sounds of scrub shifting and cracking under his boots completely masked by the storm. The Chinese had to slow down, listen harder, and group closer together. He looked up into the surreal stream of digitally enhanced raindrops falling from the canopy above. Right now, this storm was a gift from God.

Quinn's heads-up display showed the target compound less than thirty meters ahead. He stopped, found some cover, and pulled up a topographical map in his goggles. The terrain rose sharply to the south, with a ridgeline that pressed in toward a concave notch in the fenced perimeter. Quinn zoomed in and switched to satellite. He nodded. He had found his observation point.

"Lighthouse, this is Shadow Two, come in," said Quinn. He stood on a thick branch, two-thirds of the way up a tall oak. The elevated position brought a new threat. Though the forest hadn't been shielding him from the rain, it had been shielding him from the wind. Now the storm's gale threatened to blow him out of the tree. He dug his gloved fingers into the bark.

"We have you, Shadow Two. Go ahead."

"I'm on the north side of the compound. The perimeter fence is at least ten feet tall with a double stack of concertina wire. There are no guard towers, but there are patrols covering the north and south sectors and a guard shack at the entrance to the east." Quinn removed a small cloth from the pocket on his leg and wiped the outside of his goggles. "There are four buildings: the main structure, a hangar and fueling center at the south end of the tarmac, and another, lightweight structure in the northeast corner. Shadow One could be in any of them. Wait a second . . ." He had been watching three soldiers push a large cart from the main structure toward the northeast building. Halfway between the two buildings, the wind caught the tarp that covered it and blew it completely off. Quinn let go of the tree with one hand long enough to zoom in.

"Lighthouse, our boy is probably in the main structure. The northeast building appears to be a warehouse. They are moving something to it now. It looks like a missile."

"What kind of missile?" asked Walker.

Quinn wiped his goggles again. "Hard to say. Gauging the relative size against the soldiers, it looks to be about fifteen feet long and about as big around as two Chinese guys put together."

"Short-range surface-to-surface," mused Walker. "Does it have any markings? Flags, numbers, anything?"

The soldiers had re-covered the tarp and now struggled to secure it over the missile again. Quinn gripped the tree tightly and scratched the back of his neck with his free hand. "That's the weird thing," he said. "I can see the guts."

"Say again, Shadow Two."

"The guts," repeated Quinn. "It's not just that there are no markings. I can see some of the electronics in the guidance area, and I can see parts of the rocket motor. The missile doesn't have any skin at all."

There was a long pause. "Copy that, Shadow Two," Walker finally replied. "Now we need to focus on getting Baron out of there. Do you see any options?"

"The facility is well protected. I can't make a daylight run, even in this rain. There are too many of them. If we could land Shadow Catcher on that runway, I could coordinate a snatch-and-grab, but I need my pilot, and he's in there."

Then Quinn realized what he was saying, what Walker might do if he thought Nick could not be saved. "But I can do it tonight," he said, backpedaling. "I just need a little more time."

"Lighthouse copies," said Walker, his monotone showing no hint of his intentions. "Stand by and hold your position. We'll be in touch."

CHAPTER 59

The cut felt deep to Nick, but what did he know? With the cocktail of drugs in his system, he could be lying on a table, hallucinating the whole thing. It felt real. He could feel the blood trickling down his leg. "I'm going to need a bandage for that," he said out loud.

"I have opened your femoral artery," said Zheng in an informative tone. "You will slowly bleed to death without treatment. The longer you delay by refusing to give me the information I require, the more difficult it will be to save you."

Nick tried opening his eyes, but the room tilted and rolled and drifted in and out of focus. He closed them again, intentionally eliminating the only negative stimulus that he could control. He couldn't maintain his concentration on a single thought. He felt like his mind was in that uncontrollable state just prior to falling asleep. But sleep never came. There was too much pain.

"Hold on, Nick," a motherly voice coached in his ear. "You're doing great. We're going to get through this together."

He felt the blade slide down his arm, a long, shallow cut, the tactile equivalent of nails dragging down a chalkboard.

"There goes another artery. You are running out of time," said Zheng. "Where is your stealth plane? Where did you send your underling, Mr. Quinn?"

"He won't cut arteries, Nick," the woman continued. "The cuts are painful but inconsequential. He can't run the risk of killing you before he gets the information he needs. Hang on."

"You cannot shut me out, Major Baron. Your armor is gone. Without it, you cannot stop the blade from penetrating." To make his point, Zheng slowly sank his scalpel into Nick's forearm and then withdrew it. Nick grunted against the sickening pain. "That one didn't cut anything vital. It was just for fun."

Suddenly Zheng rattled off a hail of Mandarin.

"I don't understand your language, you commie halfwit," said Nick. He expected a painful retaliation, but the defense minister did not respond. After a few moments of silence, he opened his eyes and strained to lift his head and look around. He could not find Zheng's distorted frame amid the swirling confusion. Dr. Chao had disappeared as well. The two had left him alone with Ma.

"Whoa, don't leave me alone with this guy. He's crazy," slurred Nick. The Chinese soldier flashed a twisted grin and picked up the scalpel.

———

Colonel Walker closed the line with Quinn and looked over at Patricia Heldner. He had known her for longer than they both cared to admit. The motherly redhead had worked as a volunteer in war-torn countries. She had treated injuries from countless covert missions well before the existence of the Triple Seven Chase. She had faced exposed intestines and crushed limbs, and she had witnessed horrifying deaths. But she had never dealt with anything like this.

Heldner sat at the SATCOM terminal, holding a standing microphone with a white-knuckle grip, trying to make her voice sound rational and calm. Walker knew that she felt neither.

"Put the knife down, Ma." Walker could hear Nick's slur through the mild distortion of the satellite link. "It's not like you can understand a word I'm saying, so what's the—" He let out a short grunt of pain instead of finishing the sentence.

Heldner cringed. Walker touched her shoulder. "How is Baron doing?" he asked.

The doctor looked up from the comm station, brushing a fiery wave of hair out of her face. Beads of sweat lined her forehead. "He's holding up, but I don't know how much more he can take."

Over the open line, they heard the distinct crackle of a powerful electric instrument. Nick screamed.

Tears welled up in the doctor's eyes. Her slender shoulders trembled with rage. "I don't know how much more *I* can take." She took a quivering breath and returned to the microphone. "It's a ploy, Nick. I know it hurts, but it's just a ploy. Ma is the *wild card*. Remember the wild card from your counterinterrogation training? You know that Zheng won't kill you, but they want you to believe that Ma will."

Walker lifted her hand away from the microphone. "Is that true?" he asked.

"I think so," replied Heldner. "It's a known technique. Nick and this Chinese soldier appear to have a real history, but all of it could be theatrics to cause fear, to make him talk." She shrugged. "Or Ma could be a truly sadistic killer bent on revenge. That's the trouble with wild cards. By their very definition, you just don't know."

"I can't think straight," said Nick out loud.

Heldner keyed the microphone. "Take it easy, Nick. They drugged you. Based on our intelligence, the Chinese use a light mix of barbiturates, hallucinogens, and stimulants. They keep the mixture thin, especially on hallucinogens and barbiturates, to keep you from unintentionally creating false information. The effects aren't permanent. They're just trying to break down your mind's defenses. You have to fight to keep your focus. Stay with me, Nick. Help is on the way."

Walker straightened up to take a drink of coffee. He glanced over at the command center's main screen. Scott had switched it to a broad view of the Pacific. A symbol representing the Wraith orbited just outside of Chinese airspace. He frowned. Scott still had not established communications with Merigold. Then he noticed something else, or the absence of something. The Romeo Seven system showed all military traffic, even submarine positions, but the Taiwan Strait was conspicuously empty. He remembered that Seventh Fleet's Task Force 77 had left the Strait for their regular reconstitution at Pearl. The only thing standing between the Chinese and Taiwan was a small network of Patriot batteries.

Finally, he understood. The missiles without skin, the trap for Shadow Catcher, Zheng's comment about "a schedule"—it all added up. Zheng wasn't after Shadow Catcher just for the glory of stealing an American stealth plane. He had a timeline, and a higher purpose. He was going to invade Taiwan.

No matter the cost, Walker could not let that happen.

Over the comm link, they heard Nick scream again. Then he laughed. "That's good, Ma. You're really improving. *Lots* of pain. One small critique, though. You're supposed to ask me questions!"

"I see you two are getting along well." Zheng's voice could be heard on the link again.

Nick said nothing. He breathed heavily, his exhalations coming in hoarse grunts.

"I applaud your resistance, Major Baron," said Zheng. "Truly remarkable. I am sorry about the blood loss, though. At this stage, we may not be able to save your leg or even your left arm. However, if you volunteer something helpful now, we still might be able to save your life."

"You're going to be okay, Nick," countered Heldner. "They won't risk it. They need you. Think of Novak. They've kept him alive for twenty-five years now. The Chinese are a patient people."

Nick said nothing. He continued his labored breathing.

"Don't care about life and limb?" asked Zheng brightly. "Then I have something even better to motivate you. I'm certain that you have heard of the concept of *yīnyáng*, the interdependence of contrary natural forces, the ebb of one making room for the flow of the other. I believe that this applies to fortune as well."

Nick grunted, and Walker feared that Zheng had set to work with his scalpel again.

"My father used to warn me that one man's fortune opened the gate for another's misery," continued Zheng. "This hour has been most fortunate for me. You, on the other hand, look quite miserable. I am the *yīn* and you are the *yáng*."

"I'm so confused," complained Nick in a sarcastic slur.

"That's right, make jokes, Major Baron. In the meantime, a stroke of fortune has brought me a gift. An associate of mine has captured your family."

"What?" The colonel slammed his hand down on the communications desk, knocking his coffee onto the floor. He searched the room for a face he recognized. "Does anyone know anything about this?" he shouted in desperation, but he only received blank looks in reply.

"My associate lured your friend McBride into a detour," Zheng's mocking voice continued through the SATCOM. "He is dead. If you do not cooperate, your wife and son will die as well."

Walker shook his head. "That can't be true." He pointed at one of the techs. "You! I want a full accountability check of the Triple Seven Chase and all cleared associates, starting with McBride, and then Navistrova and Tarpin. I don't care if you have to call the NSA. I want firm locations on everybody." Then he shifted his finger to Molly. "And you! Get me Baron's wife on the phone. Now!" He grabbed the microphone from Heldner. "Shadow One, this is Lighthouse. Your family is safe at home," he lied. "McBride is out on an errand. We'll put him on as soon as he gets back."

Nick spoke quietly between breaths, his words barely coherent. "I . . . don't . . . believe you."

Walker released the microphone. "Is he talking to me or Zheng?"

Heldner shook her head. Her face had turned ashen. "He's beginning to blur the line between communicating with us and with his captors. There's no way to tell."

"I thought you might be skeptical," replied Zheng. "I'm going to put my satellite phone on speaker." Walker heard the muted static of an open phone line. Then he heard Katy Baron's unmistakable voice. "No, leave him alone!" she begged. An infant began to wail in the background. "Just tell us what you want. Why are you holding us here?" The phone line went silent again.

Molly looked up from her phone, her face white with fear. "There's no response at the Baron residence. It went to voice mail. She's not answering her cell either."

Walker felt Heldner's small hand gripping his arm. She was shaking. "Please don't," she said, her voice barely a whisper.

The colonel straightened his sagging shoulders and hardened his expression. "We don't have a choice. He won't risk his family, and he won't initiate Kharon on his own if he thinks he can escape and save them. The drugs are affecting his judgment. Major Baron is compromised. Start the sequence."

"No. He can still resist."

Walker pulled away from her grip. He slowly picked up his fallen coffee cup and placed it on the table. "Doctor, you always knew this was a possibility," he said. "Baron knew it too."

Heldner stood up, clenching her fists defiantly. "I *never* agreed with that program."

"You were the advising physician to the Congressional Oversight Committee. You signed off on the protocol."

She glared up at him and shook her head. "You didn't give me a choice. I'll swear to it during an inquiry." In desperation, she turned and reached for the other comm link. "Shadow Two, come in."

Quinn responded immediately. "Shadow Two is up. Do you have an update?"

Heldner's words came out in sobs. "Quinn, you have to go in now. Do you understand? Go in now!"

"I . . . I can't. There's too many of them. We have to wait until dark. If I move now, neither of us will make it out alive."

Walker pushed Heldner away from the communications station. She fell into a chair, her face blank, her mouth open in stunned silence. "Ignore that command, Shadow Two," he ordered. "Get back to Shadow Catcher. Get her airborne."

"What's happening with Nick?" asked Quinn.

"You have your orders." Walker closed the channel and then grabbed the other microphone. "Kharon, make ready to receive."

"Kharon ready," replied the digital voice. "Remote encryption: Lighthouse. Say password."

"Password: obolus," said Walker. The word felt heavy, resistant. He had to force it out of his tightening chest.

The digital voice showed no signs of remorse. "Obolus accepted," she said immediately. "Kharon sequence initiated. Detonation in thirty seconds."

Colonel Walker sat down. He dropped his head into his hands. "I'm sorry, Nick."

Nick gave no reply.

CHAPTER 60

Nick waited for the fear, but it never came. Maybe it was the barbiturates. Maybe it was the hallucinogens. He did not feel the approach of death. All he felt was loss. "Dear God, save Katy and Luke," he mumbled.

"Praying won't save your family," said Zheng, chuckling. "Only you can do that, by giving me what I want."

The implant counted down in Nick's ear. "Twenty . . ." He ignored Zheng and continued his prayer. "Protect them. Help them to forgive me for leaving them alone."

A look of understanding suddenly washed over Zheng's arrogant face. "That is a death prayer," he said, half to himself. He motioned the doctor closer. "My source told me that he has a comm implant. It is cut off from their network, but it must have a suicide device. Find it."

The bewildered Chao just shook his head and shrugged his shoulders. Zheng rolled his eyes and began shouting in Mandarin. He shoved a scalpel into the doctor's hand and pointed at Nick's head.

"Ten . . ." the cold, digital voice continued. More frantic Mandarin. Nick felt a stabbing pain behind his ear. Then he saw it. Chao held the bloody implant between his thumb and forefinger. Ma and Zheng moved in closer to see it. Hope sparked. Nick began to summon his strength. He took over the count in his head. Three . . . two . . .

With everything that he had left, Nick pulled up with his biceps, allowing the cuffs on his wrists to cut deeper into his flesh as he pulled against them. When he reached the apex of his pull, he pushed upward, unhooking his cuffs from the stand with a metallic ring.

Zheng turned at the sound. He gaped in surprise at the sight of Nick dropping out of the air, landing on the cold floor like a cat.

Nick had just a millisecond to flash a smile at Zheng. Then the implant exploded.

Dr. Chao died instantly, his hand and part of his head obliterated by the implant. Ma wheeled toward the medical counter, screaming. He held his face in his hands. Blood poured between his fingers. Zheng let out a string of Mandarin curses. His sleeve was on fire, along with the hair on that side of his head.

Unable to run because of the chains, Nick leapt forward. He targeted the vicious Chinese soldier first, coming down with a heavy elbow strike to the back of Ma's skull. The soldier's head slammed through the upper glass door of a standing cabinet. He staggered back and fell to his knees.

As he struggled to his feet again, Ma took his hands away from his face. It was a bloody mess of charred flesh, and Nick could see exposed bone and cartilage at the nose. One eye was destroyed, but the other was open, glaring in mindless rage. The soldier rushed forward. Nick clasped his hands together and swung them upward, catching Ma under his chin. Ma's head snapped up, and he reeled backward. The back of his head smacked against the jagged frame of the broken cabinet door. His body slumped to the ground. A shard of glass protruded from his neck at the top of his spine.

"Novak!" shouted Nick, but the prisoner did not respond. He still lay passed out on his gurney. Something tore into Nick's shoulder. He whipped around to find Zheng brandishing a scalpel. The defense minister had successfully extinguished his burning hair and clothes. Now he screamed rapidly in Mandarin, threatening Nick with his blade. Nick let disgust fill his expression. Ignoring the weapon, he hobbled toward Zheng, backing him up against the counter. Zheng lunged, but Nick knocked the scalpel away with a two-handed blow. He caught the shorter man by his lapels and swung him around, pulling his handcuffs up under the minister's chin from behind. He squeezed. Zheng's constant stream of Mandarin ceased in a pitiful rasp.

"Release him." Another Chinese officer entered the room, followed by a swarm of soldiers.

"And who are you?" asked Nick. He shook Zheng, tightening his hold around the minister's neck.

The officer's face remained placid. "You may call me Colonel Sung. Our people have located your stealth plane. A flatbed is on its way to retrieve it as we speak. All we need now is your friend, Quinn. You have run out of leverage. Now please release our defense minister."

"I'm gonna have to say no."

"I am sorry that you see it that way." Sung picked up Zheng's fallen sat phone and dialed.

The soldiers began to fan out, and Nick backed away, careful to step over the corpses behind him. His vision still swirled from the drugs in his system, but he managed to hold his balance and keep a firm grip on Zheng. Occasionally he relaxed his wrists, allowing the minister to take a rasping breath before he tightened his hold again.

"How is Baron's family?" asked Sung, speaking English into the phone. "I see. I am afraid Major Baron has been most uncooperative . . . Yes. It is time for us to make good on our threats. He must understand that we are serious."

"I'll kill him," threatened Nick. He bore down with his forearms, cinching the cuffs even tighter around Zheng's throat. The minister began to shake.

"Perhaps, but it is more likely that we will kill you first. In the meantime, our associate is moving to kill your wife. Do you want to lose your son as well?"

Nick fought against the drugs, trying to find the opening, the way out. Options lined up in his mind like doors in a dark hallway. He could see them open, but he couldn't see past the thresholds. He couldn't see where they would lead.

Sung's thin lips curled into a sneer. "Kill them," he said into the phone. "Kill them both."

Nick stretched out his hands, releasing his chokehold on Zheng. "No! Don't!"

"I am sorry, Major Baron. Your time is up." Sung hung up the phone.

Something hard and heavy smashed into the back of Nick's head. The lights in the room flashed blinding white. Then everything went black.

CHAPTER 61

Katy watched the kidnapper slowly fold up his phone and place it back in its holster. He looked up. She could not see the expression beneath the shadow of his hood, but the room seemed to turn cold. Instinctively, she squeezed her son to her chest, covering his face.

The killer stepped toward her. He raised the gun and pointed it at Luke.

"No!"

"Come on, soccer mom, did you really think this was going to end any other way?"

Katy turned, trying to shield Luke from the killer's gun.

"I'll shoot through you if I have to," he said.

"Please don't kill him!" she begged. Luke began to cry.

The killer sighed. "Have it your way."

Katy sobbed as she waited for the pain. Her body jerked at the deafening sound of the gunshot, but she felt nothing. Instead, she heard the killer cry out. The shadows in the room shifted and merged together as something dropped onto the wood floor with a heavy clunk. More shots rang out. Glass shattered. A terrible crash. Then the room went completely dark.

Katy quickly felt her way around the couch and crouched down. She pressed Luke's tiny face to her cheek, trying to soothe him. As her eyes adjusted to the light, she took in the bewildering scene.

The killer's gun lay on the floor, just beyond her reach, and the sliding door to Amanda's backyard had been shattered. Several of the vertical blinds had been knocked out. Broken glass covered the patio. Katy stared out into the darkness, utterly confused, thanking God that she and Luke were still alive. Then she caught movement in her peripheral vision. She turned. A dark figure stood at the base of Amanda's stairs. The killer was still in the room.

Still clutching her son with one arm, Katy scrambled for the weapon, but she only succeeded in kicking it away. It skittered across the floor, well out of reach. She stumbled and fell, twisting just in time to protect her son and landing hard on her back.

The shadow slowly extended both hands. Katy thought she could see the silhouette of a small pistol clutched between them. She tried to scream, but the fall had knocked the wind from her lungs.

Instead of pulling the trigger, the shadow flipped a switch on the wall. Katy squinted against the sudden light that filled the room. Then she gasped. "Amanda?"

"I think I winged him." Amanda Navistrova slowly

collapsed onto the stairs, one shoulder sliding down the wall as she sat down. She dropped her bound hands between her knees, loosely gripping a compact pistol. "Let's hear it for the Second Amendment," she said with slurred speech.

Katy struggled to her feet. For several minutes she did not speak. She simply pressed her son to her chest and gently bounced him until his cries diminished into soft whimpers. Then she hobbled over and sat down next to her friend, exhausted. "You've been drugged," she said in a matter-of-fact tone.

"Yep." Amanda's head bobbled in agreement. "The idiot must've underdosed me."

"We should get you to a hospital. We need to call the police."

This time Amanda shook her head wearily back and forth and then let it come to rest against the wall with an unsettling thud. "No police. No hospital. It's too dangerous. We need to get to the base." Her glassy eyes drifted over to the broken back door. "The killer is still out there."

CHAPTER 62

Nick's head felt like it had been split open. "Ugh," he moaned, sitting up. When he tried to lift a hand to feel the bump on the back of his head, he found that he was handcuffed to the table again. The room no longer tilted or spun. His mind and vision quickly cleared, and with that clarity came pain. His neck, his chest, his legs, every part of him burned or ached, but the pain of his physical maladies paled in comparison to the ripping torment he felt inside.

"What happened to my family?"

"They are dead, Mr. Baron." Zheng grinned, his twisted smirk made even more grotesque by the missing hair and the burns on the side of his face. His doctors had treated him with some sort of greasy salve, making the yellow blisters gleam under the harsh fluorescent lights.

"Did I not warn you that you would suffer? All you had to do was give me the information I wanted."

Nick screamed inside. He searched the room for objects that he could shove through Zheng's eye. "You found our jet," he said in an even tone. "You got what you wanted. They didn't have to die."

"Perhaps you've forgotten that you threatened to kill me," countered Zheng.

"I released my hold. Your lackey could have called off the killer."

Zheng sighed as if he were a teacher speaking to a particularly slow student. "I am not a vengeful man, Mr. Baron. But I cannot abide rampant disobedience." He gestured at his burns. "Look at my face. There must be consequences. You really left me no choice."

Nick's grief began to overwhelm him, but he could not let it shut him down, not if he was going to do any good with the few extra moments of life he'd been given. Instead, he took control of the grief, focused it, refined it into another emotion that came all too easily. Hate. He told himself that he had a new mission, to get justice for his family, for Will McBride. In his heart, he knew the truth. There was no mission anymore, only revenge.

The soldiers at the door parted and Sung strode into the room, walking straight to Zheng. He gave Nick a furtive glance, catching his eye for just a moment. Nick thought he saw a flash of fear. Maybe this one understood that, one way or another, Nick was going to kill him.

Sung spoke to Zheng in a low voice. Zheng nodded. "Good," he said in English. "We will all go out to meet them." He snapped his fingers at the soldiers, and four of them stepped forward, two going to Novak and two to Nick. When they pulled the straps off Novak, he just lay there on the gurney, his face a lifeless etching of despair. The soldiers jabbed him with the butts of their rifles and forced him to his feet, half supporting him, half pushing him toward the door.

Another soldier with two thick chevrons on each shoulder stretched out a key on a retractable lanyard and fumbled with Nick's left handcuff. He acted nervous, fearful of the American. He carried no rifle, but his holstered pistol was tantalizingly close. Nick considered his opportunity to strike. The soldier would have to uncuff both hands from the table before recuffing them together. As soon as he was free, he could take the gun and make a play for Sung and Zheng. He didn't have to survive; he just had to get off two clean shots, one for each of their heads.

The young man with the key moved to the other handcuff. Nick's arm twitched. The other soldiers in the room crowded closer, raising their weapons and separating him from Zheng.

"I know exactly what you are thinking, Mr. Baron," said Zheng. "Don't try it. Your efforts will be wasted."

Soon the soldier had cuffed Nick's two hands together and pulled him to his feet. The window had passed without an opportunity to strike. Justice would have to wait.

Zheng motioned to his men. "Bring his equipment. We may need it when his aircraft arrives."

While two of the soldiers scooped up the prisoners'

gear, the others pushed them out into a well-lit hallway. "You now belong to me, Mr. Baron," said Zheng. "Your family is dead. Your unit has surely abandoned you, certain that you dutifully activated your suicide device. Like Mr. Novak, you are now a ghost, the shadow of a warrior that once fought your country's hidden battles, nothing more."

Nick looked down at his body. His captors still hadn't given him back his clothes. The Chinese doctors had made a passing effort to dress his wounds. The damage seemed superficial. He could not see any excessive bleeding or severed muscle tissue. He glanced up at Novak, stumbling down the hallway ahead of him, roughly propelled by his Chinese escorts, emaciated, broken. Novak looked like the shadow that Zheng described. Nick vowed that he would not live long enough to become one himself.

After a turn down another hallway and a trip down a broad flight of stairs, the soldiers pushed Nick and Novak through a set of glass doors, out onto a wide tarmac. Steady rain fell from dark clouds. The heavy drops sent tiny explosions of spray up from the pavement. After the cold interior of the building, the warm afternoon air mixed with the cool splash of the rain felt good against Nick's bare skin. He felt his strength returning.

The tarmac was joined to a commercial-sized runway through a complex of paved taxiways, separated by green turf. Toward the middle of the wide paved area, a gaggle of soldiers stood around tables under a temporary pavilion. One end was still attached to a flatbed truck.

Zheng led the group toward the pavilion. "You should

feel honored," he said as Sung handed him an open umbrella. "Of all the many prisoners in China, you and Mr. Novak alone will enjoy my occasional visits, even after I take my place as defense minister, even after I become president. The two of you have made my vision possible, and I will not forget it."

When they reached the cover of the pavilion, Nick watched the soldier who carried his tactical harness set it down on the bed of the truck. He noticed that the young man had grabbed Novak's vest as well. "If we're destined for a life in prison, then why don't you just send us to our cells instead of dragging us around in the rain?"

Zheng shook out his umbrella and handed it back to Sung. "Ah, there are a couple of reasons. The first is arriving as we speak." He stretched out his hand and gestured to a gate at the northwest corner of the tarmac. Two soldiers pulled back the chain-link sections so that another flatbed rig could drive through. A dark green tarp covered the large object that it carried on its bed.

Shadow Catcher.

The truck pulled through the gate, turned toward the runway, and then parked, still more than a hundred feet away.

"I could hack into its structure like a barbarian," said Zheng, "but I would rather have you open it for me, give me a tour of its secrets, if you will."

"Good luck with that."

"We shall see. More important, though, I want to make sure that you understand the totality of your failure."

"I get it. You got my stealth jet. Let's get on with this."

Zheng wagged a thick finger at Nick. "Oh no, Mr. Baron, you do not fully understand." He held out an open palm, and Sung handed him a hardened tablet computer with a fat communications antenna attached to the side. Zheng rotated the antenna up and tapped the touch screen. He paused a moment, satisfied with what he saw, and then barked a few orders in Mandarin at three of the soldiers. They responded with sharp salutes and then jogged over to a white pickup and started driving toward the runway.

"You see, Mr. Baron, not only have I captured your small stealth transport, I have also managed to capture your new attack plane, the Wraith."

Nick's eyes narrowed. "You're out of your mind."

Zheng chuckled. "I captured your loved ones. Did you think that I would stop there? No, I captured your partner Major Merigold's woman as well." He waved the tablet computer in the air triumphantly. "I have severed your command center's communications with the plane. Only I can communicate with your pilot now. On my orders, he will descend through those clouds and land my prize on that runway. Or else I will kill his woman too." He moved closer to Nick, grinning up at him with mock enthusiasm. The choking stench of rotting garlic filled his nostrils. "Exciting, isn't it?"

Nick lurched forward. The soldiers on either side of him managed to grab his arms and jerk him back, but the movement surprised Zheng. He stumbled backward, almost falling on his rear. Sung grabbed his shoulders to steady him, but Zheng shook him off and marched back up to Nick. This time his eyes flared with malice. "You should know that my agent will kill her anyway, just like your family."

Nick strained against the men who held him. "Who?" he demanded. "Who is your agent?"

"Oh, I don't think I'll give you his present alias," said Zheng. "Let's call him by his nickname, Hēi Yǐng. He is a most valuable contact who was passed to me by my mentor." He turned toward Novak. "Out of all of us here, only Mr. Novak knew him by his real name, a name that has long been forgotten."

Life flashed into Novak's dead eyes. He raised his head. "What?" he asked in a barely audible voice.

"Ah, Hong Mo, you are not entirely dead after all," said Zheng. "Yes, my old friend. You are quite familiar with Hēi Yǐng, but you knew him as—"

"Starek," interrupted Nick. "Jozef Starek."

Zheng jerked his head toward Nick. His face showed genuine surprise, but his features quickly smoothed back into a gloating smile. "Very good, Mr. Baron, your intelligence team has clearly done its work. I will have to advise Hēi Yǐng that he has been most careless."

"Novak mentioned that he'd seen Starek in one of your prisons," said Nick darkly. "He couldn't have been there as a prisoner. He oversaw the investigation of Novak's incident and helped shut down operations in Taiwan. He was the mole."

"Jozef?" asked Novak slowly.

"Don't look so surprised," said Zheng. "Who else do

you think sabotaged your operations in Poland? Back then, he worked for the KGB. They handed Starek to my mentor when the CIA moved to Taiwan." He patted Novak on the arm. "Poor Mr. Novak. I do sympathize with your sorrow. When I first heard of you, I took great interest in you as an asset simply because you were such a tragic figure: your most trusted friend betrayed you"—Zheng stepped directly in front of Novak—"and you lost your love, Anja."

Novak squared his slumped shoulders. His voice grew stronger. "What did you do to her?"

"Me? Nothing, of course. I only came into this a little over a decade ago. In fact, she is alive and well. I only meant that the irony of your situation is truly delicious. After your untimely death, she married Starek."

Novak strained against the soldiers holding him. He let out a scream of rage.

As Zheng turned away with a grotesque, gleeful smile, Nick saw a change in Novak's emaciated form. He saw new energy. He saw a new will to live.

The tablet computer beeped. "Here he comes now, gentlemen," said Zheng, checking the screen. He rattled out a few sentences in Mandarin, and all eyes turned toward the north end of the runway.

At first Nick saw nothing through the rain. Then a dark shape appeared, cutting through the feathery swirls of vapor below the clouds. There was no sound, only the ominous sight of a huge black beast gliding down into the green valley.

"Wū lóng," said Sung in an awed voice, "the real Black Dragon, the messenger of death."

"No," replied Zheng, "for us, it is the Golden Dragon, the messenger of our prosperity."

Nick squinted at the black triangle. Something seemed amiss. Its angle looked too high for an aircraft on a glide path for landing. It was also coming in too hot. Then he saw a gray mist forming on its underbelly. A grim smile spread across his lips. "Minister Zheng, I think you should have listened to Colonel Sung."

CHAPTER 63

Panic broke out among Zheng's troops when the long black silhouette of a five-thousand-pound bomb dropped out of the Wraith's weapons bay. Some shouted in rapid Mandarin. Others ran for the cover of the factory. Zheng stood frozen in utter shock.

Nick stared as well, trying to gauge the bomb's speed and trajectory, trying to see where and when it was going to hit. He quickly guessed at a time to impact.

Seven . . .

Movement at the flatbed trailer holding Shadow Catcher caught his eye. A solitary individual rolled out from under the vehicle and popped up to one knee. Quinn.

The soldiers to Nick's left and right gaped up at the sky, their hold on him loosened by the sight of the unthinkable.

Six . . .

Adrenaline pumped through Nick's system, heightening his senses. He could hear the whisper of the bomb, every syllable shouted by the soldiers, the slap of their boots on the wet pavement. He sidestepped to his left, yanking his arm away from the man to his right. Then he grabbed the other soldier by the vest with both hands and threw him over his hip, slamming him to the ground. He turned toward Novak, knowing that the man behind him was reaching for his weapon, acting on faith that he would never get the chance to use it.

Five . . .

The commotion roused Zheng. He screamed orders at his men. Nick ignored him. He sprinted toward Novak. Water splashed up in a rooster tail behind him from the impacts of his bare feet.

Four . . .

Bewildered soldiers lifted their guns to stop the crazed American, but as each one reached for his trigger, he fell. Nick could hear the whistle of the bullets as they cut through the rain, the dull thud as each one struck its target with perfect precision.

Three . . .

The soldiers on either side of Novak released their grasp on his arms and lifted their rifles at the same time. One dropped from Quinn's bullet before the stock of his weapon ever made it to his shoulder. The other continued to take aim, and Nick realized that Quinn did not have a clean shot around the prisoner. He bore down. He had to reach the man before he could fire, but he knew that to be impossible. Then his eyes met Novak's.

Two . . .

Instead of the unfocused stare of a despondent prisoner, Nick found a look of recognition, determination. Novak clasped his bound hands together and brought them down hard on the rifle. Flame spouted from the barrel. The bullets flew wild, kicking up fountains of sparks and water from the pavement. Then Novak swung his hands up under the soldier's chin, knocking him off his feet.

One . . .

Without breaking stride, Nick lowered his shoulder and thrust his body upward, catching Novak in the gut and lifting him off his feet. Together, they tumbled over the side of the truck.

Zero . . .

The impact was deafening. Nick hit the pavement on top of Novak behind the shelter of the heavy tires, trying to cover him with his body. He closed his eyes and buried his head in his hands, but the orange-red glow of the flash still penetrated his vision. Intense heat washed over him. The thirty-ton truck groaned and shuddered. For a moment, he feared that it might tip over and crush them. Then, with the echo of the explosion still rolling across the valley, it was over.

As the echo died, Nick struggled up to a crouch. He looked down at his fist and unfolded his fingers. In his palm, he held the key that he'd ripped from the soldier's vest when he threw him over his hip. He quickly unlocked his handcuffs and then did the same for Novak.

"Oh, the ringing," complained Novak, blinking and shaking his head.

"It'll stop soon," said Nick. "Are you okay?"

Novak looked up at him with perfect clarity and gave a pained smile. "I'll live," he said.

"That you will, my friend," said Nick, smiling back. He placed a hand on Novak's chest. "Stay down."

Nick cautiously peered over the bed of the truck. The shower had intensified into a downpour, as if the explosion had ruptured the clouds overhead. Through the sheets of rain, he saw that the bomb had struck an auxiliary building on the far side of the factory, reducing it to a blazing pile of twisted, melting steel, sizzling and popping in the rain. The blast had also collapsed the northeast corner of the factory itself, exposing cracked ivory walls and overturned desks. The rubble burned despite the rain. "You gotta love thermite," said Nick under his breath.

The shock wave had fractured the fiberglass shelter, contorting it so that one leg jutted out to the side and the other threatened to buckle and bring it crashing down. None of the remaining soldiers had kept their feet. Some lay dead; others writhed on the ground in pain. Nick saw Sung, dragging an unconscious Zheng off the tarmac. He started after them, but then he heard Quinn shouting.

"Come on!"

He looked over his shoulder at the pararescueman, who had set about removing the tarp that covered Shadow Catcher. Quinn beckoned to him. "We've got to go!" he shouted.

Nick turned back toward the factory, squinting through the water pouring into his eyes. He caught a blurry vision of Sung pulling Zheng through the shattered frame of the glass doors. Then they disappeared.

"Can you move?" he asked Novak.

"Do I have a choice?"

As he bent over to help the CIA pilot, Nick noticed his tactical harness lying on the ground beneath the flat-bed. "Hold on." He grabbed the harness and thrust his arms through the shoulder straps. "All right, let's get out of here." He pulled Novak to his feet and wrapped an arm around his back.

Together they jogged toward Shadow Catcher. With every hobbling step, Novak winced with pain. Then he slipped on the wet pavement. Nick lost his grip, and the older man crumpled to the ground. "My leg," he said. "I think it's broken."

"I was afraid of that." Nick turned around and heaved Novak up again. "The gunshot to your leg did most of the damage. I probably finished it off when I tackled you." He crouched down and put his shoulder into Novak's midsection, careful to wrap his arm around the good leg as he stood up. He found the malnourished prisoner incredibly light. "Shoot. I should have done this to start with," he said.

"Let's go!" shouted Quinn. "Drake says there are more troops coming."

Nick lumbered toward Shadow Catcher with Novak over his shoulder, the torture wounds in his legs burning with every step. It seemed an eternity before he reached the truck, but finally he laid Novak down on the bed beneath the aircraft. Quinn had already managed to remove the tarp and two of the three nylon tie-downs that secured Shadow Catcher to the vehicle.

"I told you to guard the plane," said Nick.

"What does it look like I'm doing?" countered Quinn. He grimaced. "You look horrible."

Nick glanced down at his bare legs, underwear, and tactical gear. "Good point. I've had anxiety dreams like this."

"I meant your injuries," said Quinn, pointing at the dirty bandages hanging from Nick's body. "That's shoddy work. I'll fix you up later. Right now, we've got to move." He pointed at a gate in the chain-link fence on the opposite end of the tarmac. "Drake is tracking a column of vehicles headed for the south access point: two troop carriers, two FAVs, and a couple of fire trucks." He stepped back and gazed up at the aircraft. "How are we going to get our baby off this flatbed?"

"We can't," replied Nick, looking at the nose gear, "not without a crane. The nose will collapse if we try to jump her off with thrust. Then there'll be no way to get her going."

He walked up and down the truck, scanning Shadow Catcher, searching for an idea. Then he looked in the cab and saw the keys in the ignition. He checked the aircraft. Thankfully, the Chinese had placed her on the truck with her nose facing forward.

Nick waved a hand toward Novak. "Get him into the jet. Use the deployable stretcher."

"What are you going to do?"

"I don't have time to explain. Just trust me."

Quinn opened his mouth to argue but then stopped. "I can do that," he said with a nod, and then scrambled up onto the bed.

By the time Nick had cranked the engine and removed the final strap, Quinn had secured Novak onto the deployable stretcher and sent it up into the jet. The pararescueman crawled into the cockpit to check his handiwork and then stuck his head out. "Novak's all set," he shouted, offering a thumbs-up. "What's the plan?"

"We're going to use the truck as a catapult," replied Nick. "Shadow Catcher is a flying wing. With the vectored thrust helping, she only needs about fifty knots of airflow over the lifting body to get airborne. We can get that with the truck."

A fusillade of bullets struck the side of the truck, forcing Nick to duck behind the cab and Quinn to retreat back into Shadow Catcher. Three soldiers came running across the tarmac, firing their rifles. "Where did they come from?" asked Quinn. He leaned out of the hatch and returned fire.

"I think that's the crew that Zheng sent out to the runway," yelled Nick over the earsplitting crack of Quinn's XDm. "I guess they finally figured out that the plane wasn't going to land."

Quinn picked one of them off, but the others took cover behind equipment on the tarmac. They kept firing. He ducked back inside Shadow Catcher as bullets skipped across the truck bed. "Get in here! I'll drive the truck."

As the soldiers settled into their cover, their bursts of gunfire became more accurate. Nick gauged the distance from the cab to Shadow Catcher's hatch. Too far. If he and Quinn attempted to trade positions, at least one of them would wind up taking a bullet. "Too late," he yelled. "You have to get her airborne. Do it just like I told you in the text." More bullets hit the truck and glanced off Shadow Catcher's composite shell.

"I can't fly this thing. I'm not a pilot."

"You flew the Wraith. One lesson will have to be good enough. Now shut up and get her ready."

Quinn stopped arguing. He tossed Nick a radio from Shadow Catcher's supplies. "I'll be on channel three."

Nick jumped into the cab and ducked below the steering wheel as more bullets tracked up the hood and into the windshield. But the windshield didn't shatter. He cautiously sat up and glanced around the cab. All of the windows were made of Lexan. "Thank God for Chinese overkill," he said out loud. He shoved the clutch down with his bare foot, shifted into reverse, and accelerated backward until the rear fender slammed into the chain-link gate. Ahead of him, he saw the Chinese troops ditch their cover and advance. "Oops, you guys think I'm trying to get out," he said. He shifted into first. "You couldn't be more wrong."

CHAPTER 64

The truck lurched forward as Nick released the clutch. He pressed lightly on the gas at first, willing the tires to gain traction on the wet pavement. Then he shifted straight into third and pressed it to the floor. "You ready, Quinn?" he asked, keying the radio.

"No, but that's not going to stop you. I've got her idling. Are we gonna make our speed by the end of the tarmac?"

Nick checked the speedometer; they were passing thirty kilometers per hour. Some quick math told him that he'd have to get the gauge up above ninety-five to make fifty knots, and he wasn't exactly a genius with heavy equipment. He had no idea if he could make that speed before he ran out of pavement. "Sure. No problem," he said into the radio.

A new voice joined the conversation. "How's it going, Shadow One?"

"Drake!" exclaimed Nick. "It's good to hear your voice. Nice shot with that bomb. Although some might call it overkill."

"Ordered by Lighthouse," replied Drake. "He figured out that Zheng was making missiles for an attack on Taiwan."

Bullets continued to ricochet off the windshield. The Lexan covering cracked in a few places, but it held. Nick adjusted the wheel, angling toward the approaching soldiers. "It's pretty ugly down here, buddy."

"Well, it's about to get worse. In less than a minute, two full platoons of PLA are going to reach your position. I jammed all signals out of the compound, but there was no way to hide that explosion. I have another bomb. Do you want me to use it?"

"No, they're just responding to the blast. We don't know if they're part of Zheng's group."

"Then what's your plan?"

Nick checked his speed. Sixty-five kilometers per hour. Not good enough, and the truck was eating up real estate fast. "I'm still working on it." An instant later, he plowed between the bewildered Chinese soldiers. They tumbled out of the way to either side, but one of them came up firing. Suddenly, the truck started to shimmy. Nick struggled to hold it on a straight line. He fought back the urge to let up on the gas.

"What was that?" asked Quinn.

"I think they got a couple of our tires." Nick checked the speedometer. It read seventy and continued to climb. "The trailer has four on each axle. It can still make it. Go ahead and position the exhaust ports for vertical thrust."

As the truck passed the pavilion at the center of the tarmac, the speedometer topped eighty-five. The hangar loomed ahead. Nick suddenly realized that Shadow Catcher would be too close to clear the structure. He jerked the wheel left to adjust his trajectory, pushing closer to the grass between the tarmac and the runway. As he cranked it back to the right to hug the edge of the pavement, the flatbed lifted up on one side, threatening to tip over. It slammed back down and started rumbling again. The speedometer faltered in its climb. "Come on," he urged.

Finally, the gauge read ninety-five. "Punch it!" Nick shouted into the radio. Blue flame shot out from both exhaust ports. Shadow Catcher lifted on her struts and wobbled on the back of the truck, her tires barely in contact with the rusty bed. The fence was approaching fast. At exactly one hundred kilometers per hour, Nick slammed on the brakes. Shadow Catcher leapt into the air, just clearing the cab. For a terrifying moment she dipped down in front of Nick and skimmed along the tarmac, mere inches above the pavement. Then Quinn banked her away and she gradually lifted into the air over the field, leaving a trail of fire across the grass.

"Yeah!" shouted Quinn. "I'm up."

"The column is almost at the gate," warned Drake.

"I've got that covered," said Nick. His braking had cut the truck's speed in half, but it was still rolling. He shifted into gear and pushed the gas pedal back to the floor, accelerating toward the gate and the approaching troops. He could already see the FAV at the head of the column. Fire spouted from the machine gun mounted on its back end.

"Quinn, get up above the clouds," ordered Nick.

"What about you?"

Nick's eyes narrowed. If he slammed into that FAV he could silence their lead gun and block the road. "I'll buy you some time. There's nothing left for me back home. My family is dead."

The next words that came across the radio hit Nick like a city bus. "Negative!" shouted Drake. "Lighthouse has them! Katy and Luke are alive!"

Nick went numb. He couldn't feel the steering wheel in his hands. The icy hatred that he'd built up inside melted back into waves of emotion. Sorrow. Joy.

Terror.

For the first time in ten years, Nick stopped his subconscious from blocking the fear. In that instant, he let it through, he let it hit him full force. And in that instant, he realized that he was not afraid of dying. He never had been. Rather, he was afraid of leaving his family behind like Danny had, of leaving Katy alone, of leaving his newborn son fatherless.

Nick took hold of that fear. He owned it, made it his driving force. Filled with hatred for Zheng, he would have done anything to kill him. Now, finally accepting the fear that came with the love of his family, he would do anything to get home.

The gate and the FAV were less than twenty meters

ahead. The gunner lost sight of Shadow Catcher and turned his weapon toward the truck. Nick knew that the Lexan windshield would not hold up against the high-power rounds. Without another thought, he hooked the radio into his harness, unbuckled his seat belt, and cranked the steering wheel hard to the right.

The cab jerked sideways. The trailer fishtailed, skidding into the grass to his left. With an awful groan, the truck began to tip over. Then it crashed onto its side and continued sliding toward the gate. The driver's-side window caved in. Sparks flew up from the skidding armor, spraying into the cab, burning Nick's bare leg. He pushed open the passenger's-side door and climbed up onto the frame.

Bullets slammed into the cab and ricocheted off the hood as smaller weapons joined the machine gun. Nick wasted no time. He dove off the sliding truck and rolled out onto the pavement, banging his shoulder and hip in the awkward landing.

The truck crashed into the fence, its cab and trailer completely blocking the gate. As Nick struggled to his feet, he could hear shouting on the other side. That barrier wouldn't hold them for long. He wiped his forehead with his hand. The smell of diesel overwhelmed his nostrils. Looking down, he saw a glossy trail leading down the tarmac to the truck. The abuse of sliding on pavement had ruptured its fuel tank. That gave him an idea.

Quickly, Nick patted the pockets of his tactical harness until he found a miniature signal flare, the size of a fountain pen. Taking care to keep the business end well away from the diesel dripping down his body, he popped off the cover and pulled the tab. The chemical charge sparked into a blinding white flame.

He dropped the flare onto the trail of fuel and turned to run. From behind, he heard the distinctive *whoomp* of fire eagerly gobbling up hydrocarbons. He didn't dare look back. Instead, he ran until he could no longer stand it and then threw himself to the ground, covering his head with his hands.

The truck exploded in an angry roar, sending a blast of intense heat across Nick's back. In the next moment, he was up and running again. "Drake, I have my harness. Get Skyhook ready."

"I don't think that's a good idea, boss. Maybe you should have Quinn turn around and pick you up."

"Talk about your bad ideas," interjected Quinn. "I can't land this thing. And even if I could, the nose gear is trashed."

"Just do it, Drake," said Nick.

"That system doesn't work," argued Drake.

"We know it will pick me up. If it doesn't reel me in, you can drag me out to sea and drop me over international waters. I'll just pull the reserve parachute. Now get her ready. I'll deploy the balloon at the center of the tarmac. That should keep you well away from those machine guns on the other side of the fence." Nick looked over at the factory's shattered glass doors where he'd last seen Zheng. "Just before you grab me, release your bomb. I want that factory destroyed."

Bullets whizzed past Nick's ear. The two soldiers who previously shot at the truck ran toward him, firing short bursts from their rifles. He took cover behind a green aircraft utility cart. "You two are really starting to tick me off," he muttered, reaching for his Beretta. The holster was empty. He'd forgotten that his captors had removed it from his harness. The clang of bullets slamming into the metal cart stopped. The Chinese shouted to one another. He could hear them flanking his position. In a few seconds, they would have him.

Nick glanced down at his harness, looking for ideas. He smiled. Zheng's men had missed something. He still had his stilettos. He drew two of them, gripped them by the blades in each hand, and waited.

He made his move just as the soldiers came around either side of the utility cart. With colossal effort, he leapt up to the top of the four-foot-tall cart, launching himself upward again as soon as his right foot found purchase on the metal. By the time the soldiers opened up with their machine guns, he was already well above the level of their fire. He let the first blade fly before he reached the apex of his jump, twisting in midair to give it power. It found its mark, embedding in the soldier's skull at the temple.

The second attacker raised his weapon, adjusting to Nick's height, but Nick was ready for him. He let his natural momentum turn him halfway toward his target and then hurled the second knife with a powerful back-hand. This one missed the soldier's temple, but it stuck deep into his right eye, accomplishing its mission just the same.

Nick landed hard, rolling out over his shoulder, and came up running. "How long, Drake?"

"I've almost reached my final approach now. Deploy your balloon."

At the center of the tarmac, Nick unzipped the pouch that held Scott's miniature Skyhook balloon. He tossed the contents out ahead of him and pulled the rip cord. The balloon did not climb into the air as expected. Instead, it flopped onto the pavement and started spinning in a circle, letting out a shrill hiss like a slashed tire. Nick checked the pouch on his harness and found two bullet holes: one entry, one exit. The second soldier had gotten much closer than he thought.

"Forty seconds. I can't see the balloon yet," said Drake. Nick could see the massive form of the Wraith now, lining up to the west of the runway. He started searching the tarmac for other troops, wondering if it was clear enough to risk having Drake land the bomber on the runway to pick him up. But then his eyes fell on something better. Over by the wreckage of the pavilion, he saw Novak's old harness.

Maybe. Just maybe . . .

Nick sprinted over to the harness. It had the telltale bag hooked to the side. Novak's Skyhook system was much larger than his own, an eighties-era package with a heavy balloon and cable. It was more than twenty-five years old, but with a little luck, it might still work. He quickly pulled off his own harness and strapped on Novak's, tucking two of his stilettos into the webbing just for luck. After a short prayer, he clipped the D-ring to the center of his harness, set the balloon on the wet pavement, and pulled the rip cord. With a loud rush of helium, the miniature blimp expanded to full size and lifted into the air. The cable jerked at his chest as it pulled taut. The old D-ring held.

"I see it. I see your balloon," said Drake. "Hang on!"

Nick watched with cautious hope as the Wraith approached, praying that the old cable would not snap after capture and send him flying into the factory. The gray mist that masked the opening doors began to form beneath the bomb bay. Then the silhouette of Drake's second thermite bomb appeared.

Just as the forked receiver on the Wraith's nose grabbed the cable, Nick felt an iron grip take hold of his shoulder strap from behind. A thick hand reached across in front of him. He saw the silver sheen of a garrote wire sliding out of a gaudy gold watch.

Nick shoved his right arm up between the wire and his throat as the Wraith jerked him into the air. The attacker let out a surprised cry.

"Get a little more than you bargained for, Defense Minister?" grunted Nick as he struggled to keep the wire away from his arteries. The thin steel started cutting into his forearm.

"Now we will both die," said Zheng, "and you can join your family in hell."

Nick could see Drake's bomb trading levels with him, falling below as the Wraith pulled him upward. With his left hand, he let go of the wire and pulled a stiletto from his harness. He plunged it into Zheng's right hand. "My family is alive," he shouted over the rush of air. "And I'm going home!"

He twisted the knife, severing tendons and forcing Zheng to release the garrote. Instantly the psychopath fell away, entering a macabre free-fall race with Drake's bomb, a race to see who would reach the factory roof first.

The five-thousand-pound thermite weapon won.

Time froze. For a fraction of a second, Nick could see the hole where the weapon sank through the roof. He could see the individual drops of rain, like swollen tears, falling onto the forest canopy. He could see China's newest defense minister on his back, a hundred feet above the factory, his eyes wide with terror. Then, in a blinding ball of white fire, bounded by the glass sphere of the expanding shock wave, all of it was gone.

CHAPTER 65

The shock wave buffeted Nick into a nauseating tumble. He threw his arms and legs out into the spread-eagle pose and arched his back, trying to stabilize. The strain threatened to open every wound on his lacerated frame.

Finally, his body settled into a stable drag position. Without his goggles, he could barely see. The wind blasted his face at 150 knots, forcing him to squint and making his eyes water. Through the teary blur, he tried to assess their location. Drake was dragging him due east, out over the northern end of the Taiwan Strait. In less than three minutes, he would be over international waters. Then he could pull the cutaway line and parachute down to the dubious safety of the open ocean.

When Nick reached to his chest to check the rip cord,

a horrible sinking feeling gripped his stomach. He had made a terrible mistake. There was no rip cord.

He mentally kicked himself. The eighties-model Sky-hook harness had no reserve parachute. How could it? The pack would have been huge, not like the tiny compact chute in Scott's state-of-the-art design. He searched his mind for options. He could try to unhook, but even if he could overcome the tremendous force pulling on the D-ring, the fall into the water would surely kill him. Drake might think of docking the Shadow Catcher, letting him ride the top of the small aircraft into the bay, but the Shadow Catcher's engine intake would likely suck him in as soon as the cable went slack. His only other option was to pull himself in, hand over hand.

Suddenly, Nick felt a jerk on the line, then another, and then a pull that moved him a few feet closer. He wiped his eyes and squinted at the bay, trying to see what was going on. The gray mist had long since cleared, but he could still only see shadows. The line jerked again. He started moving steadily toward the aircraft. Somehow, Drake had made the system work.

The winch pulled Nick into the bay and retracted, leaving him dangling in front of the ladder to the main flight deck. He waited until the doors closed beneath him. Then, with a prayer of thanks, he unhooked his D-ring and started climbing. Drake stood above him, holding a long J-hook like a shepherd holding his staff.

"What magic hat did you pull that thing out of?" asked Nick as he climbed up the ladder.

Drake reached down and helped his friend up onto the flight deck. "Not me. Scott," he said. "After the failed test, he added it to the Wraith's equipment. He planned another sandbag test to isolate the problem, figuring one of us could snatch the cable old-school style, but then the mission got in the way." He hefted the J-hook and grinned. "Turns out, we got to test the system anyway. The problem is with the motion sensor. Once I yanked the cable into the winch, it worked like a champ."

"Scott will be so pleased to hear it."

Drake laughed. "He won't care that this baby saved your life as long as it helped us figure out what was wrong with his system."

Nick reached into the crew bunk and grabbed a spare flight suit. "Let's pick up Shadow Catcher and get back to Romeo Seven," he said. "Katy and Amanda are still in danger."

"No, they're not," argued Drake. "I told you, they're with the Triple Seven now."

Nick nodded. "So is the mole."

CHAPTER 66

Nick had always loved flying over Washington, D.C., at night. In the predawn hours, Capitol Hill shined like a white diamond amid the glimmering gold and bronze lights of the city. Now, as Drake lined the Wraith up with the runway at Andrews, America's capital looked more welcoming than ever.

There had been a lot to discuss during the long flight home. After Nick's last communication from the cave, Drake had been isolated for almost three hours. He tried every trick he could think of to regain his link with the ground team, but he could not make the SATCOM work. Then he received a strange text through the very same channel. Someone claiming to be the Chinese defense minister threatened to kill Amanda, Katy, and Luke unless he landed the Wraith at the factory.

In desperation, Drake had taken a huge gamble. Using

an open radio frequency—a frequency that he knew the Chinese might intercept—he contacted a U.S. Navy ground station in Taiwan and requested a phone patch to Washington. He pretended to be the pilot of an Air Force tanker on its way to Japan. His whole plan almost collapsed right after the Navy operator got Romeo Seven on the line. Molly answered the phone. Still trying to maintain his cover on the open frequency, Drake told her that he was a tanker pilot with "Task Force Zombie," hoping that she would get the hint. She hung up on him. On his next attempt though, he got Scott, and through a lengthy exchange of improvised code talking, the two of them got the Wraith reconnected to the original SATCOM bird. Then they linked Quinn to the same channel.

By that time, Amanda and Katy had made it to Romeo Seven. Drake was relieved to learn that they were okay, but he still had big problems. He thought his best friend was dead, and Zheng still had Novak and Shadow Catcher, so he played along with the Chinese psychopath, keeping him on the hook while Walker came up with a plan. In the end, though, the final rescue scheme didn't come from the colonel. It came from Quinn.

Convinced that Nick was dead, Walker wanted to cut their losses. He wanted to use the two bombs to destroy Shadow Catcher and the missiles, abandoning Novak and leaving Quinn to fend for himself. But Quinn had hidden inside Shadow Catcher when the Chinese captured the aircraft. When he saw Nick, everything changed. He convinced Walker that they could mount a rescue and destroy Zheng's stockpile of missiles, leaving one thermite bomb for Shadow

Catcher if it all fell apart. It hadn't gone as smoothly as Quinn predicted, but here they were, almost home.

Drake taxied the Wraith into a dark, empty hangar. Even with the illumination of the enhanced infrared display, Nick did not see a soul. That worried him. He should at least see a maintenance crew. Then the massive hangar doors began closing noisily behind them. Those doors did not operate automatically. Someone was in the hangar with them, someone who preferred to remain hidden.

Nick lowered the entry ladder and cautiously stepped down into the inky void. "Hello?"

A cheer rose up out of the darkness. With an electric *clang*, the lights flipped on and Romeo Seven's staff poured into the hangar from every door. Everyone was smiling. Nick smiled graciously in return and shook hands as young technicians and grizzled aircraft maintainers rushed up to welcome him home, but his eyes kept roving the crowd, searching for Katy.

Finally, a small group of techs parted. Katy rushed out from behind them and wrapped her arms around him. Tears streamed down her face. She kissed him passionately. Her embrace crushed his broken ribs, but he didn't care. He picked her up and swung her around.

"It appears we have a lot to talk about, Mr. Secret Agent," she whispered in his ear, giving it a shameless nibble despite being surrounded by strangers.

"It appears that we do." He set her down and looked deep into her hazel eyes. "I'm sorry. I was so afraid of leaving you and Luke alone that I've been pushing you away. I know that now."

Katy wiped her tears away with a joyful sniffle. "I'm sorry too. I've been so hard on you. I didn't know what you were going through." She wrapped her arms around him again and buried her head in his chest. "Things are going to be better now."

Nick found Walker coming out of the elevator with Heldner. Another man got off with them, but Nick could not see his face. He disappeared behind the colonel's over-sized frame. Nick waved to get Walker's attention. "Colonel Walker, I hereby withdraw my consent for participation in the Kharon Protocol," he said firmly.

The colonel scowled and cast a glance down at Dr. Heldner, who stopped, folded her arms, and scowled right back at him. "There seems to be a lot of that going around," he said. "I'll leave it open for discussion."

Behind him, Nick heard the pneumatic hiss of Shadow Catcher's stretcher being lowered. Novak lay still, passed out from morphine. A moment later, Quinn emerged from the little craft's lower entry hatch, fussing at a group of techs to be careful as they transferred his patient to a gurney. He had traded his combat gear for a simple black T-shirt and a medical pouch, although he still wore his XDm in a leg holster.

Over the last few hours, Nick had learned to see Quinn in a new light. The pararescueman had said little after Shadow Catcher recovered to the Wraith's bay. He had treated Nick's wounds with the care and skill of an emergency room doctor and then returned to the landing craft's cramped cockpit, spending the rest of the flight watching over Novak. Now, as Quinn hovered over his patient in his black T-shirt, Nick could see the Angel of Mercy tattoo that he had tried to scrub away after losing Haugen. The wound had left an ugly scar, but the angel still remained.

Nick kissed Katy lightly on the lips and then held up a finger. "I'll be right back." He left her side and strode over to Quinn, pulling him away as Heldner took charge of Novak's care. "We need to talk about what happened at the cave," he said quietly.

"I know," Quinn replied. "I'll pack up my stuff as soon as we're done here. I'll submit to whatever punishment Walker decides. There's no need for a trial."

Nick subtly shook his head. "That's not what I had in mind." He glanced over at Novak. "Without you, Novak and I would still be prisoners in China and Zheng would have Shadow Catcher. Thousands might have died in his invasion of Taiwan." He smiled. "I think that warrants a reprieve. If it's okay with you, I'm going to leave the whole cave incident out of my report."

Quinn's somber expression cracked into a grin. "So I still have a job with the Triple Seven Chase?"

"If you want it."

The pararescueman beamed. "Yes, sir."

"Hey, I could use a little help over here," called Heldner. Novak was stirring. The doctor began pushing his gurney to the other side of the Wraith, where an ambulance had backed up to the hangar's cargo entrance. Nick nodded his consent, and Quinn rushed over to take his place next to the doctor.

Drake and Amanda had joined Katy by the time Nick

returned. Amanda held Luke in her arms, smiling down at the baby and fawning over him. Drake looked very concerned, and Nick knew his expression had nothing to do with her ordeal the night before.

Before Nick could reach for his son, someone touched his arm. He turned to find Molly, the intelligence tech, looking up at him. Her big brown eyes were puffy and red. She handed him a piece of paper. "I found this on your printer," she sniffed. "Will—I mean, Sergeant McBride—must have discovered it before he . . . before he . . ." She turned abruptly and walked away.

"She's sweet," said Drake somberly. "For someone who had only just met him, she's taking Will's death pretty hard."

Amanda nodded, fighting back her own tears. "They've been working together closely for the last few days. I think she developed a crush on him." Then she looked down at the paper in Nick's hands and gasped. "I know that guy," she said, wiping her eyes. "He's the guy that the CIA sent to help us set up our command center back in 2003, the night before the Dream Catcher mission." She scrunched up her face. "I thought I recognized him in the old picture of Wūlóng. But I couldn't remember from where. The picture was so fuzzy I thought I was imagining things."

"I know him too," said Nick. "At least, I know one of his aliases." He held up the paper and pointed to the name. "Mitchel Martin."

"The guy we found under the B-2?" asked Drake.

Nick nodded. "The guy that Walker's CIA contact sent

to beef up the team." He stared Drake in the eye. "I'll give you one guess as to which CIA contact that was."

The two of them spoke the answer in unison. "Tarpin."

Walker glanced up from a discussion with two of the command center techs. "What about Joe?" he asked.

"We need to talk to him. ASAP," Nick replied.

"That won't be difficult. Scott has been calling him all night. He finally showed up. He arrived just as you did."

"He's here?" Nick scanned the hangar. There were too many people. Romeo Seven's small staff of techs, clerks, and aircraft maintainers seemed to have become a small army, noisily bustling around the hangar in their postmission duties. Then he spied movement in the shadow of the Wraith's huge landing gear. He squinted. A dark figure crossed behind the aircraft. As the man passed through a patch of light, Nick caught a glint of steel in his left hand.

"Tarpin!" called Nick, but the man disappeared behind the next set of landing gear.

Drake grabbed his arm. "The ambulance," he said. "Novak is the only one who can identify Tarpin as Starek." He pointed toward the cargo entrance at the other end of the hangar, where Quinn and Heldner were still treating their patient. "Tarpin is going to kill him."

The two of them raced toward the ambulance, dodging roving techs and equipment carts. Nick pulled ahead. He shouted for Quinn to look out, but his words seemed to disappear into the general echo of noise around him. Oblivious to his efforts, a group of maintainers moved across his path. He lost sight of Novak. Suddenly the deafening sound of gunfire tore through the hangar.

Someone screamed. As the maintainers hit the deck in front of him, Nick expected to see Quinn and Novak dead, shot by the mole. Instead, he saw Novak sitting up on the gurney with his arms extended, holding Quinn's XDm with both hands. A wisp of smoke rose from the barrel. "Why, Jozef?" he asked "Why?"

Tarpin stood a few feet away, his eyes wide with shock, his dark gray windbreaker slowly turning black with blood. He opened his mouth to speak, but no words escaped. As he collapsed to the floor, a steel cylinder fell from his hand and rolled across the polished concrete, bouncing to a stop against the wheel of the gurney.

EPILOGUE

"Nerium," said Dr. Heldner.

"I'm sorry?" said Nick.

The doctor pursed her lips together. "White oleander. One of the CIA's favorite poisons."

Three days had passed since the mission to China ended. Walker had been steeped in discussions with the State Department and the Congressional Oversight Committee. The colonel wanted to see justice. He wanted State to make a public indictment of the Chinese for Novak's imprisonment and Zheng's thwarted plans to invade Taiwan. State wanted to sweep everything under the rug. Nick didn't know why the colonel even bothered to fight with them. The politicians would do the wrong thing in the end. They always did.

Everyone had returned to the Romeo Seven hangar for a covert retirement ceremony, Novak's retirement. The pilot had started his career with the U.S. Air Force, and the CIA never resigned his commission. Thus, assuming regular promotions, Novak would be a colonel by now. After one of Walker's Pentagon contacts did the math, it turned out that the Department of Defense owed their newest colonel more than two and a half million dollars in retroactive pay and allowances. Colonel Novak elected to retire immediately. The speeches had been mercifully short. Now he leaned on his crutches in front of the Wraith, wearing dress blues and shaking hands with Romeo Seven's small crew.

Nick and Drake stood off to the side with Amanda and Katy. Nick held his son in his arms. He had hardly let him go for three straight days. Heldner had just joined them, carrying the lab results from the weapon that fell from Tarpin's hand. "Nerium is slow acting but very deadly," she continued. "Novak would have gone to sleep at the hospital and never woken up. The cylinder that Tarpin carried was a CO_2-powered injector with a micro-thin needle. Used correctly, the victim hardly feels a thing." She looked over at Katy. "There were two charges. I think the second one was for you."

A murmur went up from the group. All eyes turned toward the elevator. A slender woman with short strawberry-blond hair stepped into the hangar. Nick found her age difficult to determine. She walked with the grace of a woman in her late forties, but her angelic face did not look a day over thirty. A few paces into the hangar, she hesitated, unsure of herself.

"Who is that," whispered Katy.

"Anja," said Nick. "She has to be."

One of the techs took the woman's elbow and guided her toward the Wraith. The small crowd parted. When she saw Novak, she hesitated again. "He told me you were dead."

Novak smiled at her. There was no blame in his eyes, only love. She broke into tears and ran to him. They held each other for a long moment. Then she took a step back and looked him over. A short laugh escaped her lips. "You look terrible," she sniffed.

Novak reached up with a trembling hand and gently wiped a tear from her cheek. "You look exactly as I imagined."